TRAIL OF BROKEN WINGS

TRAIL OF BROKEN WINGS

SEJAL BADANI

LAKE UNION
PUBLISHING

Published by Lake Union Publishing, Seattle
www.apub.com

Amazon, the Amazon logo, and Lake Union Publishing are trademarks of Amazon.com, Inc., or its affiliates.

ISBN-13: 9781477822081
ISBN-10: 1477822089

Cover design by Mumtaz Mustafa

Library of Congress Control Number: 2014950441

Printed in the United States of America

To my family—
Without you, I would not be here.
For everything I am, thank you.
I love you.

SONYA

My mother's voice echoes in the background, her message blaring from my cell phone's speaker. With each word come memories, filtered through shards of broken glass. I want to, need to, shut the phone off, but my body refuses to move. Her voice gets louder as she calls to me, the desperation in her voice seeping through the fog that is clouding my mind.

With approximately seven billion people in the world, I wonder how one person's voice can have such an effect. I imagine I am stronger than I used to be, more resilient. That I am the master of my destiny and everyone is a pawn in my game—not the other way around. Because if I am the poker chip, then I have to wait to see how I'll be played. The unknown is the hardest. Which might explain why we try so hard to rule our worlds. It is the only hope we have to make sense of our lives.

Noises of the city waft through the open window. My apartment sits on the tenth floor, but the honk of the yellow cabs and the sounds of people moving on the streets below easily make their way up. Though winter has arrived, the only signs within the skyscraper walls of Manhattan are heavy jackets and the smell of salt mixed with remnants of snow on the streets. Otherwise, no one misses a step. A fortitude I have come to admire in the three months since my arrival.

I glance around, staring at the framed pictures that fill this temporary home. Every place I have been, memorialized forever on glossy paper. Through the prism of a camera lens, I have seen the beauty of the world. Monuments created by humans stand in competition with art sculpted by nature. Each image serves as a reminder that a light shines through so many people, and yet, no matter how far I run, I cannot seem to escape my shadow.

"Come home. Please. I need you. We need you. Your father, Brent, he . . ." My mother's—Ranee's—voice falters. A woman who rarely spoke during my childhood now says so much: "Sonya, he's in a coma. I don't know how long he has."

As if my father is here, in the sanctuary I have created, I feel his breath on me as my own comes in gasps. I clutch the counter behind me, pressing my fingers against the cool tile. Images of the past fill the room, each one stronger than the last. Shaking my head, I grip the tile harder, my muscles constricting with the effort. Finally, the pain breaks the noose of the past tightening around me and I can breathe again.

Closing my eyes, I try to imagine him lying in a hospital bed, dependent upon machines to keep him alive. It seems impossible to believe. Yet I am sure my mother is not playing a game. Over six years have passed since I left her on the doorstep, watching as I drove away. Not once since then has she asked me to come home. Or begged to see the daughter she bore and raised. Her anguish is not a ploy, but nonetheless I am helpless to ease her pain.

I stare at the evidence of my travels, each photograph proof of my desperate search for a place to call home. Now, the only home I have ever known beckons, demands my return. I am a grown woman, capable of making my own choices, but there is no choice to be made. The secrets my sisters and I hold like a lifeline are drumming within me, a steady, relentless beat. The secrets are demanding to be free, heard by the world. Yet, I am not ready. I fear I never will be.

Because if they are free, then where does that leave me?

MARIN

She sits with him because she has no place else to go. As the oldest of the three sisters, she has been with him the longest. For some that status would be cause for celebration, the child who had her parents first. For Marin, it is simply more proof that good fortune has to be made—it is not given. She was the first in line for everything—the first disappointment, the first heartbreak. Her sisters, Trisha and Sonya, watched her, learning from her example. When she refused to cry, she told herself it was for them. To show them that strength was the better option. Now, as an adult, when her face remains dry, void of tears, she accepts that the cause is her inability to feel.

Marin crosses one pantsuit leg over the other. She glances at her watch—seven in the morning. Earlier, Raj assured Marin he would have Gia ready and off to school on time. Marin's not worried. At fifteen, Gia sets her own schedule and follows it in exacting detail. Never a minute off. Marin is incredibly proud of her daughter's self-imposed structure, which will serve her well in her career. She applauds herself for her daughter's trait. Since she's always been the same way, it's normal her daughter would follow.

Having climbed the ranks in her finance company to CFO quickly and efficiently, Marin understands there were those who viewed her with contempt. Names whispered behind her back as she chaired meetings and led the company through mergers and acquisitions, one success following another. She worked hard for her place in the world. Others' jealousies or opinions are not her problem, and she will not allow them to constrain her. She knows plenty of women whose self-esteem is based on the estimations of others. They choose the clothes that are in fashion, even if they don't suit their taste. They let their colleagues define the boundaries of their careers. Live their lives according to strangers' rules. Marin congratulates herself for being above the rest. For standing in a place of her own making, for earning her success and creating her perfect life.

Marin took her mother's call about Brent the morning before, while sitting in her office's leather chair. After a few minutes listening to the details, she explained she was late for a meeting. She assured Ranee she would try to stop by the hospital that night, but it had taken her a full day before she finally made it to his bedside.

"Happy birthday to me, Daddy," Marin says. She smooths the hospital sheet over his body. Though he is in his early sixties, his face shows few signs of age.

It's funny, I don't feel older. She pulls her hair back, a nervous gesture from childhood. She's noticed Gia doing the same recently, and makes a mental note to speak to her daughter about it. Nervous habits are a sign of weakness, of vulnerability. Gia can't afford such displays during college interviews. Regardless that they are two years away. As a sophomore, Gia arguably still has time to prepare for soul-searching questions by the interviewers who will determine her future. The time is now to plant the seeds to enjoy the fruits of the tree.

Marin had not told Raj she was coming to the hospital this morning. He assumed she had an early meeting, and she said nothing to correct his assumption. Not a lie, but a truth left unspoken. One of hundreds over the course of their marriage. In an arranged wedding, they came together as strangers, and they went on to build a life with each other. Their daughter was the result.

"Do you remember my first birthday in America?" Marin asks aloud, watching Brent for a sign that he can hear her. None comes; it is the first time she can remember him silent. Unable to afford a party, Brent had taken Marin to the local ice-cream store for a birthday cone. They left Trisha at home with Ranee—Sonya wasn't born yet. Marin's birthday was her special day. Brent told her she could have a double scoop, so she perused all the options carefully. The smell of cream and sugar saturated the air, making her mouth water.

"Hurry," Brent said. He was still in his work clothes. He hadn't found a job as an engineer, so his uniform was soiled with the oil from the gas station where he worked. "Choose."

Marin nodded, but, caught up in the excitement, she failed to notice her father's growing agitation. "May I try this one?" she asked the teenager behind the counter.

"Sure." Bored, he took a tiny pink spoon and scooped out a small amount. Marin savored the melting milk on her tongue. In India, sherbet was the closest thing they had to ice cream. It paled in comparison. Marin had never had anything so delectable before.

"It is wonderful," she said in perfect English. "Thank you. May I try another?"

The boy shrugged, unmoved by her excitement. "Yeah. Which one?"

Marin tried three more before finally deciding on one scoop of vanilla and one of chocolate. "Thank you, Sir," she said to the boy while her father paid. They walked out of the store and started back toward their apartment, Marin licking each side carefully to make sure not even one drop would fall. Daring to take a full bite, she closed her eyes at the taste of the two flavors combined.

"It is so wonderful, Daddy. You must taste it." Marin held her thin arm up, carefully balancing the cone for him to taste. Just as Brent bent down to take a lick, Marin's arm wobbled and the melting ice cream scoops fell out of the cone, splattering on the ground below. Tears filled her eyes, but before they spilled out, she felt the slap across her face. Shocked, Marin glanced at her father in confusion. It was the first time he had raised his hand to her.

"Look what you did," Brent barked. Stepping over the puddle, he continued walking, leaving Marin to stare after him. "What a waste. I never should have bought it for you."

It was an important lesson to Marin, one she didn't forget: never depend on another person for your happiness. If someone had the authority to give, then he or she had the authority to take away.

TRISHA

I recheck the dining room table to make sure each setting is in its place, and I wipe the glassware. Every wineglass is set exactly five inches from the plate. I have used my best silverware, a gift to myself after my wedding. The smell of simmering chicken drifts in from the kitchen. Eloise, our housekeeper, has been with us for the last two years. Though she is not Indian, she has learned to make my favorite dishes. My mother has spent hours patiently teaching her just the right amount of cumin to mix with ginger and red pepper to enhance the flavor of cooked vegetables. As I get older, I find myself craving almost daily the authentic Indian meals I grew up eating. Eric laughs at me whenever I tell him that. Twelve years older, he insists that at thirty I am still a child.

"Everything looks perfect. As always," Eric whispers. He wraps his arms around my waist from behind, his fingers sneaking below my shirt to touch my bare stomach. It is flat, thanks to the hours I spend in the gym. "Are you OK?"

I lean my head back, just for a moment, absorbing his strength before stepping out of his arms to face him. His green eyes fill with warmth and kindness. I run my fingers through his blond waves and rest them on his nape. "I want everything to go right for Mama." I glance around my immaculate house. She is standing by the window, waiting. Resentment starts to rise in my throat, but I swallow it. This is not the time. "She hasn't seen Sonya in years."

"Neither have you."

I fill the crystal pitcher with water, set it in the middle of the table, and take a moment to admire the display. An elaborate celebration to welcome home the sister who abandoned us years ago. Eric watches me, waiting for an answer that I don't have. "It doesn't matter," I finally say. "She made her choice." One I have never understood but have had to accept.

"I look forward to meeting her."

Growing up, Sonya and I shared everything. That she has never met my husband is still difficult for me to believe. I sent her the wedding invitation, called her with the details, but she never showed. Leaving me without a maid of honor. Our oldest sister, Marin, stepped in as I knew she would. And did so without mentioning that she was second choice or that I had waited until minutes before I was set to walk down the aisle to ask her. Marin stood at the altar and later around the fire as I married Eric in two elaborate ceremonies symbolizing both our faiths.

"Mummy is clearly excited," Marin says, coming in from the living room where she was helping Gia with algebra. Each sister uses her own name for our parents. I refer to them affectionately, Mama and Papa, while Marin has never lost use of the traditional Mummy and Daddy. For the life of me I can't remember what Sonya calls them, maybe because I rarely heard her call out for them. "She's been standing by the window for the last hour."

Marin has wrapped her hair tightly into a bun. She stripped off her suit jacket when she arrived, leaving her in a silk shirt and tailored pants that emphasize her slim body, fit from hours of working and stress. She is older than I am by five years, but no one would ever guess we are sisters. Her golden-brown hair, kissed by the California sun, has streaks of blond that genetics fails to explain. Mom swears Marin's deep-green eyes come from a distant great-aunt. Growing up, everyone assumed Sonya and I were the only biological sisters. There were times we were almost identical in looks. Not that Sonya would agree. She swore I was the pretty one. My looks were the reason my parents' friends called me the princess of the house. The only explanation for the childhood I had.

"Shall I serve dinner?" Eloise pokes her head out of the kitchen. Raised in Mexico, she has no family to call her own in the States.

I glance at the slim gold watch peppered with diamonds that encircles my wrist. A gift from Eric to celebrate our fifth wedding anniversary. After his recent promotion to CEO of his company, what once were luxuries had suddenly become necessities. "Her flight should have arrived. Let's wait another fifteen minutes."

"If she decided to come. We don't know for sure she is on the flight." It is Marin's way to be blunt, to say things as they are. Mama turns her face toward us, a fleeting look of pain before she masks it.

"I'm sure she'll be here soon." Mama's voice lacks its normal strength. A pinched smile replaces the full one that graced her face earlier. She pulls her wool cardigan tight around her even though the sun is out and a warm breeze permeates the air. She stopped wearing saris after I got married. Said there was no need to keep up the traditions of the past. If Papa had a problem with the change in her attire, he never mentioned it in front of me. "She called me right before boarding."

"That doesn't mean she boarded." Marin refuses to let the subject drop.

I catch Mama's eye, offering her silent support without alienating my sister. We learned the steps of this dance years ago, my mother and I tiptoeing around Marin's words. It was an unspoken agreement we made when Marin moved back to town. Never allow Marin's way to break the fragile family we have left. Having already lost Sonya because of our past, my mother refused to lose another daughter.

"Well, if nothing else, all of us will have a lovely belated birthday dinner for Marin. Eloise has outdone herself yet again." I hand a bottle of wine to Eric. "Honey, why don't you pour us some?"

With an ease born of practice, he uncorks the bottle and pours the red liquid. As I watch the crystal glasses fill, I remember Sonya and me playing make-believe as children. Whether I was the restaurant owner, hostess, or just woman extraordinaire, I always made sure we toasted one another with grape juice. *To us*, I would say. Never finding a reason to disagree, and happy to be playing with me, Sonya forever followed along. Since she had always been, I assumed she always would be there, standing alongside, waiting for whatever game I wanted to start. As adults, she was meant to be my counterpart—the other half that made me whole. Her darkness to my light, her sadness to my happiness.

I watch my mother wait, her lowered head betraying her heavy heart. When Sonya left, emptiness settled over our lives. Mama rarely mentions her, almost believing if we never say her name then she isn't really gone. I tried to suffocate my loneliness with other sources—Eric, my home, Mama and Papa—but nothing quite filled the void she left.

I learned something important the day Sonya departed: you cannot keep someone who has already left you behind. No matter what I needed or wanted, Sonya put herself first; I was last. For a while, I went through the motions each day. Soon enough, I forgot that there was someone missing. Only now, with the thought of her return, do I recognize anew the cavity left in my being. But I can't show my excitement. If she fails to show, if she disappoints us by maintaining the status quo, then I am left once again, still waiting.

"She's here!" Gia comes running in from the den, still holding the math book Marin bought at an education store. She's a striking replica of Marin, the only difference between the two being the couple of inches in height Gia has over her mother. At fifteen, she looks like a woman. "She's paying the cab driver."

I release a sigh I didn't realize I was holding. Clasping my own hands together, I watch Mama. She turns, having missed seeing Sonya's arrival because she was distracted with the conversation. A sheen of tears covers her eyes before she quickly blinks them away. She straightens her spine, reaching her full height of just over five feet. Stepping quickly to the door, she pauses before opening it. We gather around her, waiting for her to welcome her lost daughter home.

"Mama?" I reach out, covering her hand on the knob with my own. "She's waiting."

"Of course." A small laugh, filled with disbelief. She opens the door quickly, biting her lip at the sight that greets her. "Sonya."

Sonya's hair is longer than I remember, and she is thinner than I have ever seen her. Her jeans and thick sweater seem out of place in comparison to my spring dress. Lines of stress surround her eyes and mouth. At twenty-seven, three years younger than I am, her empty smile is that of someone years older.

"It's been a long time." Sonya hesitates, almost unsure how to react to the reception that greets her. She steps toward our mother, on autopilot it seems, pulling her in for a perfunctory hug. Her arms tighten briefly around Mama before she drops them back to her side. "Marin? It's good to see you." They embrace lightly, their years of living apart creating a greater distance than a difference in age ever could. "Trisha?" She says it on a laugh, her eyes finally filling with emotion. She walks toward me, her arms outstretched. I grab her hand, my little sister, and pull her in tight. "I've missed you." It is a whisper in my hair, her words so quiet they are almost lost.

My throat convulses, the words refusing to come. She is here, after I have spent so many years wanting and wondering. I start to feel the emptiness recede as her presence fills me. As a child I took her for granted. Now I know I will never do so again. My tears fall onto her shoulder as we hold one another. I wrap the palm of my hand around the back of her head, as a mother would hold a child. I bring her in closer, sure if I keep her tight enough she will never leave again. Filled with desperation and relief, I whisper back, "Welcome home."

* * *

To anyone watching, we are a normal family. Food passes around and plates fill to overflowing. The family finishes the bottle of wine as Sonya regales us with tales of her extensive travels. From Alaska to Russia, she has lived in every place imaginable. She tells Gia of riding an elephant in Thailand and flying in a propeller plane over glaciers in Alaska.

"Where did you live?" Gia is enthralled. "Moving place to place must have been hard."

"It was worth it," Sonya says. She avoids meeting anyone's searching gaze. Fiddling with her linen napkin, she folds it into a perfect square. "For the pictures."

"You should have come home." Mama's voice is low, but nonetheless it silences the chatter. "Your travels took you very far away." She immigrated to America from India over twenty-five years ago, but a slight accent remains.

"It was my job," Sonya answers quietly.

"And when you weren't doing your job? Where were you then?" Mama wipes her mouth with her napkin.

A palpable tension settles over the table. Sonya glances at me, unsure. Suddenly I see the little girl who cowered in our bedroom, sure the blanket on our bed would protect her. The one who laughed so she wouldn't cry.

"She's home now," I say. "That's all that matters, right?" Not waiting for an answer, I call out, "Eloise." She pops her head out. "Please bring out the birthday cake and dessert." She has made fresh *gulab jambu*, Sonya's favorite from childhood. Fried wheat balls steeped in sugary syrup. Sonya used to eat at least half a dozen every time Mama made them.

I begin to clear the table. Eric immediately stands to help, as does Raj, Marin's husband. Raj has remained quiet throughout the meal. He often says very little, choosing to let Marin steer the conversations as she wishes. "As soon as dessert is served, we should start to make plans to visit Papa." I stack the fine china carefully and hand the plates to Eric to take to the kitchen. "He is only allowed two family members at a time during visiting hours, but I'm sure the doctor will make an exception for a special event."

"How is he?" Sonya stares at her clasped hands. Both men and Gia are in the kitchen, leaving only us women at the table.

Before I can answer, Marin says, "He's in a coma." Her voice is devoid of all emotion. "The doctor says it doesn't look good."

I flinch, seeing him lying in the hospital bed, tubes keeping him alive. Every morning I visit him as soon as I awake, each time harder than the last. But as the favored daughter, it is my responsibility to return the gift of his love. I accept my duty graciously.

"Is he expected to come out of it?" Sonya has found her footing. She stares directly at Marin, two equals discussing the situation. Watching them, I notice their similarities are striking. Both highly educated, focused on their careers. Neither makes any apologies for her life choices—regardless of whom they hurt. They are both beautiful but neither bothers to enhance their looks. They are my sisters but often I wondered if I was the only real daughter while they were pretending. Like stepchildren, they were never allowed to forget their place: a few steps outside the circle of the real family.

"I'm surprised you care." Marin sits back in her chair, assessing the woman Sonya has become.

I find myself doing the same. If I am honest, we are strangers sitting together. Though we lived in the same house, survived similar ordeals, we have each grown to become our own women. With time we have learned to hold our secrets close rather than share. It is our conditioning, what is expected of a good Indian woman. We learned from a young age not to share our heartbreak, our despairs. It may cause others to view you with a negative eye, think less of you.

"Why is that?" Sonya demands. She straightens in her chair. Refusing to apologize for her escape, she stares without flinching.

"Because you haven't for so many years."

Every instinct demands I call a truce. As if it is my duty to assure both of them that there is no wrongdoing, no matter what anyone believes. Before I can speak, Sonya does. With her words, I shut my eyes, feeling the fragile ties of my family begin to unravel further.

"I could say the same about you," she bites. Her bitterness has become more powerful with time. "I don't remember you looking over your shoulder when you left us behind at twenty-one."

"I got married," Marin argues. "And I came back."

"So did I." Sonya, finished with the battle, turns toward me. "Do they know why he fell into a coma?"

"It does not matter," Mama says, answering before I can. She glances at both Marin and Sonya, relaying a silent message—*enough*. She moves on to me, rewarding me with a smile for always being the stable one. The daughter who never makes unnecessary waves. "It is as it is. We must focus on the future." She stands, finished with their antics and leaving no room for more. "If he does not come out of it, then we must prepare for the cremation, the spreading of his ashes."

"And if he does?" I have to ask the question. I have not given up hope, though I understand why she has. "What then?"

"Then we go back to the way things were."

* * *

I check the lock on the front door and set the security system. Under the illumination of the red blinking light, I walk around my darkened home, straightening sofa pillows and pushing in the dining-room chairs. Eloise cleaned up and left hours ago. Everyone followed her out soon after. Sonya went home with Mama, and Marin and Raj left with Gia. We promised to meet at the hospital tomorrow.

"It went well." Eric sneaks up on me. His tie is undone and his hair disheveled from the unexpected conference call he just finished. "Even under the circumstances." He kisses my neck, pushing my hair out of the way for better access. I moan as he kneads my shoulders, his fingers slowly traveling down my back. His hands settle on my hips and he brings me in tighter. "Are you ovulating?"

For four years, Eric has wanted a child. Twice he was sure I was pregnant, only for me to watch him grieve when my period arrived. Having been raised in an orphanage, Eric is anxious to have a large family. He fell in love with our five-bedroom house and bought it specifically to raise children in. It took us three months to perfect the room down the hall from ours as a nursery. It sits empty, waiting for the cries of a child.

"Yes," I say, though he already has the answer. He has my schedule memorized better than I do. My ovulation cycle and then my period, in their respective orders. My mind wanders back to my family. "Mama and Sonya—do you think they're OK?"

He sighs as his hands drop away. When I turn to face him, his eyes soften. He cradles my cheek in his palm. "Your mom called her. Asked her to come home. They'll figure their way out." He tucks a strand of my hair behind my ear. "You still haven't answered my question from before. Are you OK?"

"She's changed," I say. "Looks older, more tired." *But she's home and for that I'm grateful*, I think.

"She's not what I expected."

Eric has seen pictures of Sonya in the album. Most show a young girl staring silently into the camera. She was always more comfortable behind the lens than in front of it. The last picture I have is the night of her college graduation. Summa cum laude from Stanford. The whole family gathered to celebrate her achievement. But it wasn't enough for

Papa. That night he repeated what he had said so many times before: Sonya never should have been born. But that wasn't what caused Sonya to flee. It was what Mama said later that broke her. Neither of us imagined Sonya would decide to leave us that day. Say good-bye with the plan never to return.

"What did you expect?" I ask.

"Someone damaged." He says it without hesitation, though he has never before offered an opinion on her. "The way you've talked about her all these years—I just assumed she would be . . ." He pauses. "Someone who doesn't know her way." He bends down and brushes my lips lightly with his own. "Unlike you."

"I know my way?"

"That's what I love about you. You're amazing."

I stiffen, though he fails to notice. *I am not amazing*, the voice within me cries. *Look at me carefully—there are scars.* Yet, I am ashamed for complaining. My sisters yearned for love while I received it unconditionally. I was special, loved completely.

"You are so beautiful," he whispers. He unbuttons my dress. Pulling it off my shoulders, he bares me to the waist. His fingers deftly undo my bra, and he cups one breast in his palm, teasing the nipple. "Tonight could be the night."

For a baby. Those are the words he doesn't say. Can't say because he wants it so much.

"Just a minute," I say. He watches me, confused, as I step out of his arms and into the bathroom. I slip my arms back into my dress. The vanity mirror reveals a haunted woman, one who can't see the truth. I ignore her, my hand on my stomach, as I stare at the only truth I know. I take a deep breath and exhale, my decision made years ago.

SONYA

My childhood home holds me like a steel trap. Once inside, I feel the walls close around me, welcoming me like a spider into its web. Mom is busy switching on the lights, having laid her purse down on the cherrywood end table by the front door. A crystal bowl once graced the tabletop. A cherished birthday gift Mom's brother got her in Switzerland. It was smashed years ago. As Mom and I were on our knees cleaning up the shards, she had murmured her belief that the piece was unbreakable.

I close the French doors behind me and lock them. I am always locking doors. Car doors, bedroom doors, even my bathroom door, though I live alone. A few steps farther and I am in the foyer. The house is exactly as I remember it. Sparse decorations scattered against the stark white paint. My parents bought the home when I was still a child. It was time to arrange Marin's wedding, and the small two-bedroom home we lived in at the time would not attract reputable suitors. This place showed the world that we were successful, that we were worthy of having a son from a fine family marry Marin. Apparently it worked, because soon after moving in, Marin was betrothed to Raj, a man she had met only once.

"Your bedroom is the same," Mom says, coming in from the kitchen. She hands me a cup of chai from a pot that is always simmering. "I left it, in case you . . ." She stops, catching herself. She motions for me to follow her back into the kitchen, where she opens the refrigerator. "There is juice, milk, fruit." Pointing to a door down the hall, she says, "The bathroom is there. The shower is fully stocked with shampoo, gel, anything you may need." She points to another door. "Linens, towels in there."

"Mom." I set the chai cup down on the marble island that sits in the middle of the immaculate room. Memories fill the air, of us sitting there, legs swinging, as we ate breakfast. Trisha and I fighting over the Sunday comics as Mom tried to keep us quiet. Dad liked to sleep in on Sunday mornings, and we knew better than to wake him up. "I know where everything is. I used to live here."

She brings her hands together, clasping them in front of her still body. She closes her eyes and nods once. "Of course." She is smaller than I remember her. Her hair is dyed pitch-black from a mix of henna and coloring. Her face, once drawn and tired, seems more alive, refreshed. She looks younger without reason to. "I just thought—because it has been a very long time."

The question hangs in the air between us. It is what I dreaded the most when I packed my bags in New York. I could remind her of the words she spoke to me the night of the graduation. The truth I had always suspected, but never wanted to believe. But that would mean bringing up a past that demands to remain buried. The only acceptable answer is an apology for choosing to walk alone rather than among them. I rehearse the words that tell her it was my only means of survival. My way of living with the memories and still forging ahead. However, the explanation sounds hollow to my own ears. Because my escape only meant her burden became more weighted.

Thinking it safest to say nothing about that, I change the topic. "How have you been doing? In the house without him?"

"It is quiet," she says. "I have never known such silence." She plays with the hem of her cardigan, wrinkles on her fingers that formed since I last saw her. "I play music now. All the time." She gives me a small smile, the first one I have seen since my arrival home. "Music from India. Songs that were in films from my childhood. They sell them now, on CDs labeled *Old is Gold*. Amazing."

I laugh without meaning to. He never liked music. Said it gave him a headache. But this small taste of freedom has brought her a rare happiness. Taken aback at first, she offers another wavering smile before laughing with me. Soon we are both laughing hard, in a way that was always disallowed. Filled with relief and hope. He's not here, and though memories of him permeate the air, we are still able to breathe freely.

"I would love to hear some of the songs." In leaving California and my family, I also left my heritage. No more trips to the temple on Sunday. No Indian clothes for Diwali or Holi. When Bollywood films were offered in the mainstream theaters, I chose another option.

"Yes," she says, excited. "Tomorrow morning, as you have breakfast, I will play them." She takes a step toward me, one of the few times she has ever done so. Without thinking, I cringe. Seeing my reaction, she stops and immediately turns toward the bedrooms. The moment is lost. "You must sleep. Long flight. And tomorrow we have to . . ."

"Go to the hospital."

"Yes. We must go see your father."

* * *

My room is the same as when I left it. The books that offered me my only escape still line the shelves. Grabbing a worn one, I thumb through it. A story of a young man who overcomes great loss to find happiness. It was a favorite of mine. I read it often as a teenager, hoping for clues from his survival to help navigate my own. Running my hands over the spines of others, I realize each one is a survival story. All the characters face insurmountable odds in their quests to find themselves. My legs begin to buckle under me. Whether from the long flight or the weight of the day is difficult to determine.

Settling down on the edge of my bed, I stare at the emptiness around me. How many times did I crave to be away from here, this room, this home, this life? The nights I covered my face with a pillow, hoping to muffle my tears as sounds echoed through the house. I would crawl out of bed and lock the bedroom door, both guilt and fear warring within me.

"Do you have everything?" Mom opens the door, shocking me out of my reverie. Her weathered fingers clutch the doorknob. She doesn't cross the threshold between the hallway and my room, choosing instead to maintain the false distance the line helps to create.

"Yes," I murmur. "Thank you." She never checked on me before. Maybe she was too afraid of what she would find. "Good-night."

She waits and for just a moment we stare at one another, both quiet. Nodding, she returns, "Good-night."

I lock the door after she leaves. Taking the desk chair, I nudge it against the doorknob. It is the only way I can sleep at night. It is the only way I know how to stay safe. That and to keep running. Because as long as you keep running, they can never catch you. *Never get caught. Never, ever get caught.* I repeat the words to myself as I lie down on the bed, searching for the peace that sleep will bring, finding none.

MARIN

Marin watches, her eyelids lowered to slits. The Indian community members mill about, painting her feet with traditional henna for her upcoming wedding. Intricate designs with no significance but patterned to exact detail. Aunts and uncles are gathered, their excitement palpable in the evening air, as younger cousins, with years before their turn to marry, study the scene. They try to understand the joy now and the grief tomorrow. The tears will flow from Mummy; Trisha and Sonya will cling, wishing that it was them instead. And if not, why was she leaving them behind?

Marin had no choice. It had been decided by the date of her birth and the family to whom she was born. She had perused suitors' résumés here and there. Once, she had voiced her opinion. Tossing a résumé down in disgust, she said under no condition would she spend her life with that person. The picture was of a man who she was sure had yet to complete the evolutionary cycle. But it was not an issue. He did not have siblings with graduate degrees. He was not a viable candidate.

"Give me your hand, Beti," Marin's aunt cajoles, calling Marin her own daughter. Lines of age cover her face. "Your feet are finished."

"What?" Marin does not hear. When her aunt fails to answer, Marin questions, "Masi?"

"Beti." Her fingers encircle Marin's forearm, resting inches above a deep indentation. Dead blood rings Marin's tan wrist. Pity spills from her aunt's eyes. "What happened to you, child?" The wedding paste simmers, forgotten, in a pot beside her.

Marin wrenches her hand away, shaking her head. Speaking the story will make it real.

* * *

He lies there, multiple tubes keeping him alive. Marin counts five in all. One in his nose, another down his throat, yet another in his arm. A machine tells her that his heart is still working, sixty beats per minute. She watches the lines on the monitor, the rhythm indicating all is as it should be. Each piece of the whole working together to keep a human being alive. The engineer in Brent would be impressed at the systematic functioning.

There are no flowers in the room. None of them thought to bring any. Cards from well-wishers fill the room. The majority of the Indian community reveres him. They adore him, see him as an example of the true American dream. Having come to this country with nothing, he raised three daughters to have everything. All while teaching them how to be proper, respectable women. They owed him their lives.

"Thank you for allowing all of us to be here," Trisha says. She is, as always, unfailingly polite. The doctor, who just arrived, nods while reviewing the chart. He is one of the best, the nurses assured them upon Brent's admittance. They gush about his skills. Yet, thus far he has failed to give them a reason that their father is in a coma. "Our youngest sister just arrived last night," Trisha says. The self-appointed family spokesperson, she does her job seamlessly. "Sonya, this is Dr. David Ford. Dr. Ford, our sister Sonya."

"A pleasure to meet you. Everyone, please call me David." He holds out his hand to Sonya. His gaze lingers on her. She has brushed out her hair, allowing it to fall around her shoulders. A long-sleeved black cotton top rests atop a pair of slim jeans. Her face is free of all makeup, and the boots she wears are better suited for the New York weather she was living in. Marin's little sister has grown up to be a beautiful woman.

"Doctor." She releases David's hand quickly. "What is the prognosis?"

Though her retreat is obvious, David fails to react. "On the Glasgow Coma Scale, he's registering at a three. In English, that means he's in a deep unconscious state. There is no definitive answer as to when he will come out of it."

"But he will?" Sonya pushes for more.

Marin hears the fear in her sister's voice. Unlike Trisha, Marin understands Sonya's plea. She is asking the doctor to give them hope.

"Not for sure—I'm sorry," he says, misunderstanding.

He looks around, gathering the whole family in his gaze. He is quiet, offering the calm before the impending storm. The battle of life versus death, both respectable warriors depending upon the perspective. But little does he know the war has already been fought.

"Some patients never come out and then the family has to decide to . . ." He pauses, his unspoken words an offer, should they wish to take it.

"Pull the plug." Sonya says it matter-of-factly, without any emotion. She has masked the fear that was obvious to Marin only seconds ago. "And without the machines?"

"Though he is technically in a coma, essentially a deep sleep, his body is reliant upon the respirator and fluids." David slips his hands into his pockets, his white coat pushed back. A stethoscope hangs around his neck. Marin assumes he is younger than she is, but recently she has begun to believe everyone is. "When he was admitted, he was in respiratory failure. The respirator helps his body to breathe." He pauses, trying to prepare them for the news that no family could bear to hear. With a deep sigh and sympathy mixed with apology, he says, "Without the respirator, he wouldn't get enough oxygen."

Sonya listens carefully, analyzing every word. "And without oxygen he would die."

Marin watches her, still smarting from their encounter the night before. Sonya was born after their arrival in America. Their parents had made plans to abort her—she was an accident, after all. A broken condom brought her to life. Cheap latex bought from a discount store in India and stuffed into the suitcase set for the States. Marin heard the story often growing up. In front of Sonya, Brent would repeat the tale, each time laughing louder than before. An elaborate joke no one understood.

The cost of another child was too high, and an abortion was the obvious choice. But Brent was desperate for a son. Using a low-cost ultrasound machine, the community clinic doctor made an educated guess and told them it was a boy. Overjoyed, Brent made the decision for Ranee to continue with the pregnancy, taking extra shifts to cover the cost of the medical care. At the birth, fury filled Brent's face when the doctor announced he had another daughter.

Once born, Sonya became Marin's responsibility while their mother worked in the local factory making children's underwear. Marin changed Sonya's diaper, fed her milk from a bottle, and bathed her when she spit up. Before hitting puberty, Marin was already a mother.

"How long will it take him to die? If they pull the plug?" Gia asks. She's been sitting quietly next to Raj. Still in her tennis uniform from her lesson that morning, she crosses one slim leg over the other. Tendrils from her ponytail fall onto her face, giving the false illusion that she is younger than her years.

"Gia," Marin says, raising her voice to grab her attention. At that specific pitch, her voice sounds exactly like Brent's. "This is not the place for you to speak. Dr. Ford is very busy."

"It's fine." David smiles to ease the sting of Marin's rebuke. "Your question is very important." He is kind to Gia though he does not have to be. "As doctors, we need to know exactly how long the body will survive. It will help us minimize the amount of suffering."

"He will be in pain?" Ranee steps forward, demanding David's attention. She has stayed primarily in the background, listening rather than speaking.

It has always been their mother's way to observe instead of lead. They say a child chooses one parent as a model to replicate. Marin made the decision as a young girl that it would not be Ranee. It wasn't conscious or a process she gave much thought to. In fact, if asked now she would struggle to pinpoint the exact moment. But it was very simple really. Given the choice between strong and weak, it seemed obvious to her to choose strength, no matter what form it came in.

"He will feel the hunger, the loss of breath?" Ranee asks.

"We would do everything in our power to make sure he doesn't. I promise you that." David takes her hand and squeezes it once. Marin catches the interplay.

Ranee nods, turning to Brent's still body in the hospital bed. After his arrival at the hospital via ambulance, they dressed him in a gown—one he would surely hate. Always meticulous with his clothes—every shirt pressed and his pants crease free—he demanded his children be the same.

"He does not like to suffer." Ranee wraps her arms around her small frame.

No, Marin agrees, *he does not like to suffer.*

Marin's breaths become shallow, suddenly harder to draw than moments before. The memories from childhood swim together, as her fingers begin to tingle, each one starting to go numb. Everyone's voices are far away, though they stand right next to her. She shakes her head, trying to clear the cobwebs that suddenly fill it. Closing her eyes, she counts to ten quietly, hoping the exercise will lead her back to normality. When she reopens them, she sees no one has noticed her distress. They're still talking among themselves, their attention on Brent. Lowering her head, she stares at her shoes. The ground beneath her begins to rotate. It is a panic attack, she knows. Though it's been years since her last one, they are always the same. Her heart rate accelerates as her body shuts down. But she refuses it. She will not succumb to its power.

She pulls out her phone, focusing on the only lifeline she knows. Fifty new messages fill her mailbox. Work demanding her attention is her only reprieve from the father who lies dying. She is grateful for the distraction. "Mummy," she says. Her breath begins to even out, but her heart still beats as if she ran a marathon. Almost an hour has passed since she entered the hospital room. Three conference calls have been scheduled since her arrival. Additional homework she created for Gia waits in the car. Math problems guaranteed to keep her in honors next year. "We need to leave. It is late." She motions for Gia and Raj to follow her out.

"We have just arrived." Ranee grasps Gia's hand, pulling her in close. "Let us all stay a bit longer."

"Marin, it is still early." Raj has not risen from his seat. He assures Ranee with a smile. "We will sit a while longer, Mummy."

"No, we will not." Marin swallows a yell. Everyone starts to stare at her but their faces are unclear. Anger at their defiance mixes with the past and creeps into her being. "Raj, I envy your free time, but I don't have the same luxury. I have a lot of work to do and Gia has math problems waiting."

"It's Saturday," Gia says. She looks to Ranee for support. "Sonya masi just came," she says, giving Sonya the traditional name for a mother's sister. "I want to hear more stories."

"You heard plenty of stories last night." Marin cautions herself to slow down, but there is no stopping.

David shifts uncomfortably, caught in the middle of the family drama Marin is creating. A voice whispers inside her head to stop, to let it be. A few more minutes will not hurt. But there is another voice—this one much louder—demanding that her authority not be questioned. Her control will not be compromised. They believe her weak but she is not. She never will be. "Raj, get up now. Gia, let's go."

She walks out, unable to face what she created. Her heels snap against the hospital floor as she rushes down the hall toward the elevators. Pushing the down button three times, she watches impatiently as the numbers slowly light up with the elevator's descent. The steel doors finally open, revealing an empty car. Stepping in, she waits for them to shut. Only then does she lay her head against the mirrored wall, taking deep breaths. A caricature of herself stares back, watching her breakdown with dispassion.

"I am fine," she whispers. Rubbing her hands over her face, she expects to wipe away tears. But her face is dry. There have not been tears since she was young. Straightening her spine, she pulls her hair back. As she gathers the loose tendrils, she puts her emotions in check. Within minutes she is back to how she feels safest. In complete control.

Smoothing the creases in her shirt, she catches her eye in the mirrored doors, and nods once to herself in approval. Pulling out her cell phone, she flips through the messages. Work started for her at five a.m. and usually ended after midnight. When she became pregnant with Gia, she worried how her career would be impacted. In hindsight there was no real need for concern. She worked right up to her labor. A driver chauffeured her straight to the hospital after a board meeting. Five days later, Marin was back at work.

She hands her valet ticket to the small man at the counter, waiting impatiently while he searches for her keys. "It's those, right there," Marin says, pointing to her set among the dozens. He checks her ticket stub against the tag on the key chain. To keep from snapping at him to hurry, she starts to dial her assistant when Raj and Gia come up behind her.

"Were you planning on waiting for us?" Raj asks.

"I told you I have work." Marin takes in Gia and her demeanor relaxes. She runs her hand down her daughter's hair. "You have a test on Monday, Beti. It is important you study, right?" She is about to pull Gia in for a hug when her phone buzzes. Glancing down to see the caller, Marin murmurs, "We have very little time before college applications."

"Yes." Gia steps closer to her father. He slips his arm around her shoulders. "I have to get into a good college."

Marin stiffens at their easy affection, wishing she had the same camaraderie. "Not just a good college," Marin says, texting her assistant to prepare a file. Marin repeats the list of their top choices from memory. "Harvard or Yale will open many doors for you. Brown, Princeton, Chicago, and Pennsylvania are also acceptable, but only if Harvard or Yale fall through."

"Berkeley would be brilliant also," Raj says. His arm still around her, he smiles down at their only child. "I don't know if I can send my little girl across the country for school."

"We don't have to discuss this now," Marin snaps, surprised at Raj's words. The valet attendant has pulled their car up and waits with the door open. "Raj, please drive. I have to return a phone call."

They settle into their seats. Raj pulls out of the garage and onto the tree-lined Sand Hill Road, the road connecting Palo Alto to their home in Los Altos. As he picks up speed, they pass small buildings housing some of the most powerful venture capitalists in the world. After a few minutes of silence Gia asks, "Daddy, what do you think of UCLA? Or maybe a small liberal arts college in Southern California?"

Tension teases up Marin's neck like a spider with claws. The hours of work she endures to pay for Gia to have the best of everything scratch at her eyelids, creating shooting pain. A reminder of the sacrifices she has made so her daughter won't lack as she did. The memories of her own secondhand clothes still haunting, she has always bought Gia designer clothes. Restricted from participating in any after-school activities so she could care for her sisters, Marin insists Gia be involved in as many as possible. Swim team, tennis, dance, and soccer just some of the commitments. Cost has never been a concern, the money irrelevant in comparison to the benefit to her daughter.

When Gia reached school age, Raj researched the local public elementary, but Marin overrode his decision in favor of a prestigious private collegiate school in San Jose that admitted only the elite members of their community. She was steadfast in her decision. At forty thousand a year in tuition, Marin was sure her daughter would get the best education available. Each choice, each activity guaranteed to Marin that she was not a product of her past. That she had broken the cycle of hurt and disappointment, and that her daughter was the future.

"A small college?" Marin shuts off her phone and turns in her seat to face her daughter in the back. "Gia, that is not an option."

"Why?" Gia breaks off eye contact to stare out the window. "It could be a good school."

"Not for you it isn't. Why would you even mention it?" Marin demands. "I don't want to hear about it again."

"It's not a big deal where I go." Gia lowers the window. The wind blows her hair and muffles her mother's voice. "Besides, I want to stay close to my friends."

"Your friends?"

Gia is very social. From a young age she was comfortable with people in a way that Marin still hasn't mastered. She would smile and start up conversations without any self-consciousness. For Marin, whose own social interactions are stilted and short, it was a revelation to have a daughter so rehearsed in social etiquette.

"What friends would want you to sacrifice your future for the sake of themselves?"

Recently, many of Gia's friends had begun to date. When Gia broached the idea with Marin, her immediate reaction was no. It would take away time from her studies. Though Gia kept asking, insisting she should be allowed, Marin refused to change her mind. Marin never dated as a teenager. Their culture demanded a girl be 100 percent pure before marriage. Even one date could taint her reputation and make her an unacceptable candidate for marriage. It was not the cultural concern that made Marin say no; it was this type of situation. Anyone having undue influence over Gia's life.

"No one." Gia answers quickly, without hesitation, and scoots lower into her seat. Searching for a song on her phone, she sticks in her earphones. "Never mind. Harvard or Yale are great. They are still my top choices."

* * *

Marin rubs lotion into her chapped hands. Years of typing have formed calluses that refuse to disappear. Her hair, in a tight braid, falls down her back; her silk nightgown reaches to her feet. Their live-in housekeeper retired to bed hours ago, only after meticulously cleaning up the kitchen. Marin had eaten her dinner at her desk, with hours of work that needed to be finished. The emotional day wore on her, and her body was demanding sleep. But the conversation with Gia continued to replay in her head, keeping any hope of rest at bay.

"You were very tense today." Raj exits the shower into their room, a large towel around his waist. His hair drips droplets of water onto their carpeted floor. Recent years have added pounds to his middle, but his arms and legs have retained their leanness from when they first married. Black hair mixed with silver covers his brown chest, but the hair atop his head has remained its original color. "About Gia."

"I'm fine." She prefers not to discuss it. Their conversation in the car made it painfully obvious to Marin that she had failed to fully explain to her daughter the value of a good college education. She reviewed plans to rectify that immediately. A trip to tour the East Coast and the Ivy Leagues was the obvious first step. Gia would naturally get excited about the campuses and living across the country. Even though she still had a few years, it was time. Marin convinced herself that Gia's indifference was nerves—fear of living away from home. With a game plan in mind, she felt calmer. "We should get to bed. We have an early morning tomorrow."

"Gia's tennis tournament." Raj removes his towel and sets it on the hook. Naked, he slips under the covers and watches Marin turn off the lights. "I can take her if you need to work."

A month has passed since the last time they made love. Raj was the usual initiator, though Marin rarely refused him. The night before her wedding she was taught that sex was a man's right. No matter how successful a woman became, it was her duty to fulfill her husband's needs. It was the only place in their relationship that Marin did not feel in complete control. No matter how often she tried to convince herself that the pleasure was both of theirs to have, she always felt empty and alone afterward.

They had an easy pattern when they made love. Two positions, or more often just one. He finished first, quickly. If Marin needed a release she would guide his hand between her legs. Spooning behind her, he would rub until she found her satisfaction. Sometimes it was quick, but if it took more than ten minutes she would pull away. Her body's failure to respond meant she was not ready. It was a waste of both of their time and of precious sleep to continue trying.

Tonight, however, Marin is not in the mood. She can pinpoint a number of reasons. Work has exhausted her. The hours of reviewing documents, finalizing deals, and instructing her team on projects seemed harder than before. The conversation with Gia. But the scene at the hospital, if she is honest, is the real culprit. The realization that her father might never emerge from his coma—that the man who defined her life was now losing his—jars her.

"Are you wanting to have sex?" Marin asks. Her voice is sharper than she means it to be. Before he can answer or move toward her, Marin says, "It is probably not a good night."

"Of course. No, it is fine."

He is embarrassed. She can hear it in his voice. In all the years they have been married, Marin has turned him away only when she has her period or is ill. Today neither is true. Instead, it is the chains of the past rattling. Trapped in place for so long, they became rusty with age. With Brent in a coma, the lock seems to have loosened, but no matter how hard Marin tries, she cannot free herself of them. She imagines her father's disappointment in her failure to please her husband. She shakes the thought aside and turns to the man she has shared a bed with for years. "I have a lot on my mind," she says as an explanation, though he did not ask for one. "The hospital, everyone there."

"It is not a problem." He shifts, turning his back to her. "Goodnight, Marin."

Humiliated at the panic that envelops her at the thought of her father's demise, she remains quiet. But because Raj doesn't ask, she is spared from forming a response. She keeps to herself that she is scared and alone. That she wants to be held but wouldn't know what to do if he offered.

She lies down on the farthest side of the bed. With his back to her, there is no one left to face but herself. Pulling the sheet over her body, she yearns for comfort that proves inaccessible. Her mind, begging for sleep only minutes ago, now wanders. Everyone was there for her father, wondering, watching, waiting. For what, she does not know. If he lives, then they return to normal. Of course, their normal is not like everyone else's. They each have their role and are exceptional at it. Trisha is the glue that connects the family. As the favorite, she deems it her responsibility to plan the family gatherings. As long as they break

bread together, she has her illusion of a perfect family. Trisha orga-
nizes the holiday get-togethers; whether it be Diwali or Christmas, she
makes sure that no one is left out. When Sonya left, Trisha seemed to
take her duties even more seriously. As if she could fill the void left by
the sister who decided that life was better without them than with.

Marin performs her own role with precision. She is the victory
story, the example of why they came to America. The one they can
point to and say, this is the reason we endured all the heartaches.
While Trisha plays the role of pampered housewife, Marin continues
to exemplify success. And her daughter is the next generation, the one
who doesn't carry the burdens Marin did. She is free to achieve everything—she doesn't need to get away from any anchors.

Tired of tossing, Marin slips out of bed. She can hear Raj's quiet
snoring; he barely moves with her departure. They have never held one
another at night. Both learned soon after their wedding ceremony that
they preferred their own space.

With the events of the day barking at her heels, peace eludes her.
Gingerly, she finds her way down the steps in the dark. In the light
from the moon via the skylight, she pours a cup of milk and heats it.
The steaming cup warms her hands as the darkness brings her a bit of
calm. She has always preferred it to daylight. Secrets stay better hidden
in darkness. Judgments fall to the wayside when there is no light to
shine upon them.

The crystal clock on the mantel shows it is past midnight. A new
day, but it will be similar to other days in the way that only routine can
create. Everyone awake and ready on time. Cooked breakfast grabbed
on the way out. Schedules intermingled as everyone heads their own
way. It was never how she imagined her life would be. But then, she
never imagined anything at all. Her father made all the decisions and
she assumed he would determine the pattern of her daily life also.

She was thirteen when he decided her college major. He had
researched the various careers and determined that finance would give

the best return on his investment. It was irrelevant whether it fit Marin's interests. That it did was lucky, though Marin would never have dared to complain. Any protests would have yielded no sympathy and, worse, might have fueled his anger. It wasn't worth taking the chance. She took her college courses and became an expert in her field. After graduating in two and a half years, she followed up with an MBA. A guarantee for an easy ascension in her career, a career that means everything to her. A livelihood for which she has only her father to thank.

Still not ready for bed, she takes a seat on the sofa. As she curls her legs beneath her, memories from the night before her marriage begin to torment her.

* * *

As Marin watches from the hallway in front of the bathroom, Ranee places an invitation to Marin's wedding in front of a shrine made from pictures of relatives who've died. She turns on all the lights in the house and plays a tape of traditional Indian music.

In the bathroom, Sonya nudges Trisha away from the sink. "This is spooky." She spits out her toothpaste and gargles with the mouthwash. "Are we going to see dead people?"

"Yes. A bunch of dead people are going to come and dance around you. They're going to get closer until they grab you and you're gone. Poof," Trisha teases.

"We're not going to see dead people." Marin buttons her pajamas as she enters the bathroom. "It's tradition. Mummy's family did it when she got married and now we do it."

"But why?" Her fear obvious, Sonya inches closer to Marin.

"It's honoring them. Saying we wish they were here." Marin turns to Trisha. "You need to be nicer to her."

"She's a baby."

"Yeah, our baby sister. You have to take care of her after I'm gone, OK?" A desperate plea for even an insincere acquiescence. Whenever Sonya was ill, Marin had been pulled from her junior-high classes. The nursery school would call to say Sonya had vomited again. Marin would wait in the principal's office, her arms resting on a stack of her assignments for the rest of the day. Her father would summon her with a honk from the parking lot, the used, pea-green station wagon coughing as it waited. The office secretary offered a small wave each time, a smile to conceal her sympathy.

"Whatever. Anyway, you're coming back all the time. Right?" The first vulnerability Trisha has shown, Marin thinks. "Things won't change?"

"It's a little far for that. It'll be hard to come all the time."

"Why do you have to go live with him? Why can't he live here?" Sonya demands. Their bravado gone, they stare at Marin.

"Those are the rules."

"Whose rules?"

"I don't know," Marin snaps. "Daddy found someone for me to marry, and I'm marrying him."

"You don't even know him," Trisha reminds her.

"I met him when we got engaged."

"He could have the cooties," Sonya interjects.

"Sonya, you're too old to think cooties are real."

"He could have AIDS." Trisha starts to brush out her hair. "In science, we just learned that India has the fastest-spreading rate of it. He's from there. He could have it."

"Trisha, we're from there too. And we don't have it, do we?"

"I'm just saying. You should ask him."

"I'll ask him after the wedding."

"That'll be too late. You get it from sex."

"Gross." Sonya's eyes widen. "I know about sex. It's this." She makes a circle with one hand and uses her finger to go in and out.

Marin smacks her hand gently. "Don't do that again."

"Why don't you call and ask him?" Trisha admires herself in the mirror. *"If he has it, then you don't have to marry him."*

"I'm not allowed to call him." Marin looks away.

"I don't want you to go," both Sonya and Trisha say at the same time.

Marin's eyes shut as she pulls both sisters in tight, her childlike arms around their young bodies. *"I know."*

RANEE

She wakes at the first sign of light, which slips through the curtains, teasing her like a gentle feather. Though only a sliver, it brightens the room. A reminder that no matter how much she welcomes the quiet of the night, the day will always follow. Today feels different. She lies still in bed, listening for the reason why. Yet again, she reminds herself that he is not in the house, waiting for her. Her mornings always started with dread. Sure that no matter what time she awoke it was still too late. He always seemed to be up a few minutes before her, angry that his breakfast was not ready.

Once she stayed up all night, counting the minutes until it was proper for her to slip downstairs and begin making chai the way he liked it. At four in the morning, her heavy lids had demanded just a few minutes of closure. She had acquiesced, promising herself only ten minutes of sleep, and woke with a start three hours later when he grabbed her leg.

Ranee knew fear gripped Brent back then. He was afraid of this new world that even after decades still felt foreign to him. Working every day among strangers and colleagues who asked why he smelled like garlic and onion, staples of Indian cooking. Demanded to know why his lips held a sheen of yellow around their rim. When he explained he started his morning with turmeric milk, they laughed and said milk was for kids. This was America and here a man took his coffee black. They brought him a cup and insisted he down the bitter liquid. Every morning after, he filled a mug with it and let it sit on his desk to appease anyone watching.

Brent yearned for the familiarity of India, of living among those who looked like he did and spoke the same language. He tried once to bring a tape player to work and listen to Indian songs with headphones. When the jack accidentally fell out, the songs blared through the office. Teased for hours afterward, he slipped the tape player into his desk drawer and never brought it out again. Brent had lost his life in hopes of making it better. It was a gamble he regretted always.

Ranee shakes the memories away. Those days are behind her. She allows the thought to sweep over her. As it does, she remembers the reason why today feels different. Her daughter is home. Asleep down the hall, in her childhood bed. A prickle of tears as a smile tugs at her lips. Her family finally together again. She wonders at the road Sonya has traveled. Ranee surrendered her own love of adventure when she was married off at the age of eighteen. Her father was sure he had found a good man for her. It did not occur to him to ask if she thought the same.

As she sits up in bed, the covers slip down to her waist. Her hair falls to her shoulders. Peppered with gray, it frames her petite face. Her long eyelashes cover her eyes as she closes them in quick prayer. It's been her habit to start every morning the same way. A few seconds to ask God to protect her children, as she was unable to. The first time was two months after Marin was born. Brent had taken Marin from her arms when she cried for milk. He insisted she was better off with his mother, who lived with them. She knew how to discipline children, he said. Years later, Ranee wanted to ask if his mother had been the one who taught him.

Finishing her prayer, she slips carefully out of bed, her legs covered with the bright orange flannel nightgown she still wears. She bought it years ago at a discount store in hopes it would dissuade him from demanding sex every night. It hadn't worked, but did help to keep the chill at bay afterward. Making her way gingerly to the bathroom, nothing rushes her faster than she wants to go. Once there, she stares at the woman she is now. Older, bruised in places that no one can ever see, but wiser. One piece of knowledge had always eluded her, that life is not what happens to you, but what you make happen. It seems so simple to her now. Yet for years she fell to the floor in tears when she heard her daughters' cries, begging to find that very answer.

She reminds herself again that the past is just that. No matter that every room still holds his scent, the echo of his voice. He is not there. But the walls house his ghost, forcing Ranee to look over her shoulder when she is alone. She dresses quickly, suddenly wanting the company of her youngest more than she wants to savor the freedom of her time.

* * *

She mixes the Bengal gram flour, adding fresh garlic, mint leaves, and chopped spinach. The oil starts to boil on the stove. Scooping two fingers full, Ranee drops the mixture slowly into the heated oil so as not to burn herself. She repeats the process again until all the batter is gone, leaving the bowl empty. Once cooked, she gingerly removes the *pakoras* individually and lays them on a paper towel to help soak up the grease. Removing the frozen mint chutney from the freezer, she runs it under hot water to thaw it. From the pantry she pulls out a tin can full of *ghatiya*—chickpea flour fried into twists. She adds a dollop of mango chutney to the plate before cutting strips of green pepper and washing the seeds out.

The chai starts to boil over on the stove. She lowers the flame under the soy milk mixed with fresh ginger and cumin. From the refrigerator she removes two *methi na thepla*, one of her favorite childhood foods from her home state of Gujarat. Whole-wheat flour combined with fenugreek leaves and other fragrant spices. When the girls were young, she would add minced garlic and bell peppers to get some greens into their diet. As they got older, they began to love the flatbread as much as Ranee did. It became Sonya's favorite; she begged for it every weekend.

Ranee methodically sets the table perfectly for one. Just as she hears Sonya making her way to the kitchen, she pours the chai into a cup. "Good you're up. I have breakfast ready. Your favorite," she says, presenting the plate with a flourish. "Methi na thepla."

"I don't like thepla," Sonya says, looking confused. She glances at the elaborate meal. "That was Marin's favorite. I always liked roti best."

Ranee searches her memory, as a vague picture comes into focus. A young Sonya at the table. She's right; it was Marin's favorite. Sonya would always push the thepla away, asking instead for cereal. If Ranee insisted she eat Indian, then Sonya demanded a plain wheat flour roti, which she could roll up and pretend was a pancake. Now Ranee glances around the kitchen, suddenly unsure. She tries to understand how she could have forgotten such an important detail. "I'll make you something else."

"No, it's fine. This is wonderful. Thank you." To emphasize her point, Sonya dips a piece of the thepla into the chutney and takes a bite. She wipes the mango jelly off her lip before taking a sip of the chai. "You didn't have to do all of this."

"Of course I did. You are home," Ranee says, as if that explains everything. Returning to what makes sense—what comes naturally to her—she starts to clean. With a dry sponge, she wipes the table clear of crumbs that have yet to fall. She pushes in chairs that have not been touched and rearranges the placemats. It is a table for eight. Ranee bought it the day after Brent fell into the coma. He rarely allowed her to entertain the whole family at once. Now, Ranee will have the freedom to do as she wishes. "I thought we could go visit some aunties. They have been asking about you."

In the Indian community, aunties are women friends of the family. No blood connection required. Over the years, the practice offered Ranee some sense of comfort. With little to no family in the States to call her own, she appreciated the semblance the moniker afforded.

"All these years, they say to me, 'Ranee, where is Sonya? She is always on the move, that one.'" Ranee laughs, an insider on the joke. "I tell them, 'One day, you will see, she will come home. Where else can she go?'"

"There's a whole world out there, Mom." Sonya pushes away from the table, her food barely touched. "I imagine there's someplace that would want me."

"But this is your home." Ranee glances around, seeing the home as if it were brand new. In a way it is. The past, no matter how definite, does not have the power to determine the future. The proof is standing right in front of her. How many days had she walked the halls, passed Sonya's room, wondering if it would ever shelter her daughter again? Now, Sonya is here, eating the breakfast she has made. There is no flinching at the sound of his footsteps or cringing before he speaks. There is no fear, and that in itself is proof that they are free of him.

Ranee ignores the sound of laughter that reverberates in her head. It mocks her for believing she has escaped. A fugitive is never free. Though he lies unconscious in a coma, miles away, his memory still smothers the air she breathes. Part of her knows it always will.

"This has always been your home," Ranee argues.

Sonya opens her mouth but no words come. She stares down at her food and fiddles with what's left. "It was never my home," she says quietly. Glancing around at everything familiar, she asks, her voice rising with anger, "Did you convince yourself it was yours?"

Her comment—and her anger—cause Ranee to stagger back, her left arm reaching for the counter for support. Images of India and her homes there dance in front of her eyes. "In my first home," she starts quietly, "I would run along a water bank as the servants washed our clothes in the mouth of the river."

Never having heard any stories from Ranee's childhood, Sonya stops drinking her chai to listen. "What was it like?"

Ranee pauses, thinking back to that time. "Free." She would throw pebbles into the water, earning her a scolding from the servants who watched her. "My mother had five children before me and four after. I was raised by servants who earned a few cents a day."

"I never knew that," Sonya murmurs.

No, she wouldn't have, Ranee thought, never having shared any of her childhood with her daughters. "Do you know my first memory of life?" When Sonya shakes her head no, Ranee begins her tale. "I was three, maybe four. I was running after a bird but it refused to be caught." They share a quick smile with one another. "I stepped on a nail. It pierced my foot, went right through the arch."

"Mom," Sonya's voice fills with pain at the image. "What happened?"

"I cried." Blood had dripped everywhere. Dropping her face into her hands, she had sobbed, sure that the sound would carry and bring someone to her aid. But she had ventured too far. Only trees and the sway of the wind kept her company. "In the distance I was sure I saw my mother stop and stare at me. It was the last thing I remembered before I fell unconscious."

"Was she there?" Sonya asks.

"I never asked. A servant found me and took me home." Ranee takes a deep breath. "This home is the only one I have."

"You could sell it." Sonya starts to clean up. She scrapes all the food into the garbage can before rinsing the plate in the sink. "It's very large for one person."

"You assume your father is never coming home."

"Don't you?" Sonya begins to rinse the sinkful of plates as if she had never stopped. As if she had never walked out of this house and their life seemingly for forever. "Maybe his mind finally understood it was time to turn on himself instead of others."

Ranee hears her daughter's anger. She wants to reach out, to find a way to soothe her pain. But a long time ago she accepted there was nothing she could do. It was their journey to take. Every person had his or her path. Given the chance again, Ranee imagines changing their destiny. Saying no when the green cards came in from America. She could have spoken up and said the land of dreams and opportunity might hold neither for them. That their small village in India was all the happiness they would ever find.

"We do not always understand why people do things," Ranee said, dismissing that memory among millions of others. "But it is not our place to judge."

It was the wrong thing to say. Ranee knew it before the sentence was complete. However, like with so many things in life, there was no turning back. Ranee knew she and Sonya would never be close. Maybe it was the fact that she was the youngest, or that when she was born Ranee was just too tired. Or it could be what Sonya always knew—that they did not want her.

"You certainly never did," Sonya says. "I guess I'm not as forgiving as you."

"You think I have forgiven him?" Ranee always heard that the power of the word was stronger than anything. She wants to ask the person who said that if he or she had ever felt the power of the hand. "I think it is up to God to absolve us. In doing so, he must take into account all that we have done. Not just one act."

"It wasn't one act," Sonya protests. "It was a lifetime of hurt."

"You were not with him his entire lifetime," Ranee says, fighting because she can.

The chants of the gurus from the open-air temples in India start to ring in her head. She can smell the burning incense and hear the bells ring overhead as if she were there. She would watch them from her seat with the other girls on the marble floor of the temple and listen as the gurus taught them about life. Obey your parents, feed the hungry, do good every day, otherwise Lord Shiva may open his third eye and the world will burn. Lessons learned by fear.

"He was not always cruel," Ranee says, hoping to justify her choice to stay with him. "In India, there was a time when he was kind."

"I'm glad you have memories of that," Sonya says, her voice clipped with fury. "But I don't. So I guess I just have to live with what I know."

Ranee watches Sonya walk out of the kitchen without another word. Collapsing into the chair, her mind drifts to the past.

Ranee's father had decided her engagement after a chance meeting with Brent's father. The two men met at a business dinner in rural India. Of the same caste, they learned each was looking for a mate for his child. After discussing formalities, they shook hands on the union. Ranee's father came home and told his wife about the engagement, but Ranee didn't learn about it until a week later, when a servant mentioned it.

The first time she met Brent, three servants accompanied her to the town square. They sat at a table nearby while Ranee and Brent sat opposite one another at an old picnic table. They were shy, glancing everywhere but at one another.

"Ranee is a very pretty name," Brent said in broken English. "It means 'queen,' yes?"

"Yes," Ranee nods. "And to be reborn." They fell quiet again, the noise from the public keeping them company. "Your name, Brent, it is rare."

"Yes," Brent agrees. "My father named me after a friend from overseas. 'A good man,' my father said." He stares at the people around them. "I am happy to have heard the news of our engagement," Brent said. "It was an auspicious occasion for my family."

"As for mine," Ranee lied. In fact, her mother, busy with all the children, had only recently bought sweets to celebrate the occasion. "My siblings look forward to the wedding."

Brent nodded. Staring at his feet, he bent slowly down and ran his hands over the ground. Finding what he was searching for, he picked up a small rock, no larger than a pebble. Laying it between them on the tabletop, he pushed it toward her without touching her. "For you," he said.

Ranee glanced at it in confusion. "I don't understand."

"I hope to give you the world," Brent explained. "This rock is a small piece of it. One day I will present you with more."

Every year after that, until he fell into his coma, Brent would present her with a rock on their anniversary. Each larger than the original one. A few he ordered from faraway places. One from the caves of Brazil, another from the shores of Australia. Ranee never knew how he found them, but each year he would present it to her with a grand display and say, "I'm going to give you the world, Ranee." She always wanted to say, "If you could stop hitting us, that would be enough."

But she never did, and he never stopped.

SONYA

The day of my graduation from Stanford, the sun was shining and there was a slight breeze. Enough wind to cause the tassel on my graduation cap to flutter against my cheek. A distinguished member of the community just told us in his speech that we too could be successful. Life was ours to own. We must forge our path. With Stanford attached to our names, we had the guarantee to blaze a trail with a fire that shone brighter than others did. Now that we had been proven worthy, the future was waiting.

Shockingly inspired by the words, I made the unthinkable decision to declare photography as my vocation. It was always my passion, my escape, but I never dared to dream of doing it full time. I sat in my chair, surrounded by my classmates, and decided to make the once-inconceivable decision for myself. To tell Dad that the law, the profession he chose for me, was not my choice. Never before had I dared speak my mind out of concern for the consequences. I feared his anger, but more so who would feel his wrath.

Later we stood on the grounds of the main quad. I glanced around at my family, who had gathered into a circle. Marin was in her standard suit while Trisha chose a sophisticated summer dress. Mom had on a sari, the tight fit limiting her range of movement. Gia sat atop Raj's shoulders, pulling on his hair and pretending he was a horse.

At first my voice was quiet, gaining strength only as the words flowed from a place deep in my heart. "I've decided to defer my admission to law school," I announced, avoiding Dad's eyes. Clutching my diploma, I struggled for courage. "I'm going to pursue photography."

"No," Dad said, without a second thought. "You will attend law school in the fall, like we decided."

I nearly acquiesced, used to bending to his will. But the sight of Gia atop Raj's shoulders, laughing at the control she was sure she held, triggered something within me. A quick glance at Trisha, who was watching me with concern but not disappointment, strengthened my resolve. "It is my decision to make. I will let the law-school committee know immediately."

He began to laugh, shocking all of us. The sound was not of joy, but instead disgust. I flinched when I saw him narrow his eyes in my direction. Mom closed her eyes, her head dropping in dejection. "You are stupid," he yelled. Unconcerned about having an audience, his face tightened with rage. "I always knew it." A few friends were lingering nearby with their families. At the sound of his raised voice, they turned toward us, watching with curiosity. I felt the familiar shame creep over me, the strong instinct to disappear.

"Please," I pleaded, losing my courage. "I'll defer, just for a year."

"Defer," he mocked. Shaking his head, he announced to all of us, "We should have aborted her when we had the chance."

His words didn't surprise me. Whether he was telling the joke that life played on him when he believed me to be a boy or talking about the additional cost of another child that he resented, I had heard the sentiment enough times over the years to be numb to it. But when he turned toward Mom, who had always stayed silent during his tirades, my heart lurched.

"It was what your mother wanted," Dad revealed to me, letting me know he was not an army of one. "She begged me, but I refused. I should have listened."

Whipping my head toward her, I silently implored her to deny his statement. To tell me she loved me, that I was wanted. No matter that she never protected us, that she stood by and allowed him to hit us. I forgave her, believing her to be a victim right alongside us. But her next words made me realize she was also a perpetrator.

"Right, Ranee?" Dad demanded.

"Yes," Mom answered, her face downcast, refusing to meet my gaze. Her admission, the truth, seared me. "It would have been best for everyone."

*   *   *

It was a mistake coming back. There's no place for me here. I hoped things had changed. That with him in a coma, I could finally find home. But there is no home to be had. Just memories of a heartache that won't heal. The argument with Mom at the house still stings. She has not changed and may never. She's settled into her way of life, and acceptance has followed. I used to watch her when he hit us. Her head lowered, her hands wringing. I believed I hated her for not loving me. Now I realize, more than anything, I hated her for not trying to stop him. At least if she had attempted to do something, I would have known that the sight of us being hit hurt her more than us. That as our mother, she would rather bear any pain than watch ours.

I stare at my father, his breathing steady, stable. It is time to say good-bye. His hands rest on top of the hospital sheet; his fingernails are trimmed, though his hair falls over his forehead. I clutch my camera. A physical extension of me, it is what I trust the most. Like a security blanket, I take it everywhere I go. When I look through the lens, I am sure I will see beauty. No shades of gray to cast a shadow over the image. In that one moment when I shoot the scene, it will be perfect.

Over the years, I learned that it doesn't matter what I photograph. The beauty of a falling snowflake is as powerful as the smile of a young child. I capture what demands immortalization. Like the words from a writer, each photo is its own being, with its own life. I am simply the conduit, the one chosen to take the picture. If not me, then another will pass by and honor the request. It is my fortune to be a part of it, to preserve it.

Raising my camera slowly, I glance through the lens, staring at him. The image blurry, I wait for the automatic focus to correct it. Through my trusted lens I see him, his body frail, and his mind blank. Weakened from age and illness, his face is drawn. The man I believed all-powerful now lies in bed, powerless. Shocked, I lower my camera and stare, watching, waiting for him to rise out of the bed and prove me wrong.

"He's a very lucky man."

I turn, surprised to see David standing at the foot of the bed. Jerking away from the bed, I fear having revealed any secrets. He watches me, his eyes curious.

"I'm sorry, I didn't mean to disturb you."

"No, not at all." I grab the camera as it starts to slip off my lap and onto the tile floor. He had said something before, when he walked in. "I'm sorry—I didn't catch what you said."

"Just that your father is very fortunate." David scans the machines that have become Dad's constant companions. He jots some notes down on the chart. "At least one member of your family is here to visit him every day."

"Other patients? They don't . . ." I leave the question hanging, unspoken.

"Not everyone is fortunate enough to have a loving family," David says, seeming to understand me. "Your father must have done something very right to inspire such loyalty."

I swallow my denial. There is no reason to tell this doctor the truth. For him it is irrelevant that his patient inspired neither loyalty nor love. David's job is to save my father's life. Regardless of whether we want him to live. "How is he doing?"

"No change. I'm sorry." He motions to the camera I am clutching. "You're a photographer."

My camera is top of the line. Having saved for months to buy this particular model, I was thrilled when I could finally afford it. But even with the tools of a professional, I am hesitant to call myself one. My photographs in national magazines make no difference. I am still fighting for approval, though I am no longer sure whose. "I like to take pictures." In hopes of ending the conversation, I try to stuff the camera into my bag, but it proves difficult.

"What kind of pictures do you take?"

There must be patients he needs to see. Something should be more important than wasting time talking to me. My hesitancy in answering must have revealed my thoughts because he says, "I'm giving myself a much-needed break. When you work in a hospital, talking about something other than medicine is the only option for entertainment."

"Oh." The camera finally squeezes into the bag. Sitting while he stands makes me feel like a child. When I rise, I realize he is taller than I thought. I still have to look up at him. "Of anything. People, things, places. Whatever wants to be taken a picture of." When he smiles at my response, the beauty of it takes me aback. I smile back without meaning to.

"Things tell you they want to be photographed?"

It sounds silly put that way, I know. Never have I bothered to explain why I take the pictures I do. It's possible no one has ever asked before. "There's an energy around the piece." I glance out the window that forms one wall. The nurses opened the shades earlier in the day. Searching for words that make sense, I motion him closer to the window. "See that tree. The one in the middle, among the larger ones?" As we stand side by side, our arms touch. "It's the smallest one." The Stanford hospital is set among acres of trees. "The others are blowing in the wind, but the smaller one is protected. It's standing perfectly still, a haven for all the animals whose homes on the larger trees may be destroyed by nature's hand."

"But it doesn't see itself that way," David says.

"No," I say, surprised he follows my thoughts. "It believes itself weak because it is smaller. Less powerful. Maybe nature doesn't trust it to stand up against its wrath and therefore demands others protect it."

"But your picture shows the truth."

I nod. The picture shows what the tree itself cannot see. "Its role as a shelter makes it the most powerful tree of all."

Suddenly, I am embarrassed, though I have no reason to be. But some sense of shame stays with me always. An article I read once said abused children always feel it was a mistake for them to have been born. I don't think the feeling is limited only to those who have been abused. In South Africa I was contracted to do a series of pictures for a news magazine. When I started to take photographs of a man in the town square, he asked me not to. I offered him payment for the photograph, but he still refused. Curious about the reason, I asked him. He answered his skin was too dark. It would shame him to see what he looked like.

"But I was supposed to be a lawyer," I tell David. I glance at my father, who lies interminably still.

"Really?" When the IV machine begins to beep, David pushes a few buttons to silence it. Coolness invades the space where he stood. "Just a warning that the fluid bag needs to be changed soon. The nurses will be in shortly." He is assuring me that my father is receiving the best care possible. I wonder what he would say if I asked him not to change the bag. "Lawyer and photographer—those are two very different professions."

"A lawyer is smarter," I say, my father's voice echoing in my ear.

"I would think the opposite, actually." David leans into the wall. A strand of his hair falls into his eyes. He moves it back mindlessly. "I don't know if a lawyer would be able to see the trees through the forest." He grins like a child.

Maybe it is the lame joke or his silly grin as he makes it, but I laugh aloud. We stare at one another, a heartbeat longer than either one of us should. I look away first. I have to.

"I should go."

"Of course." Reaching the door before I do, he holds it open for me. When I motion for him to go ahead, he says, "Take care."

I watch him leave, the door shutting behind him. I spare a glance at my father. It is the last time I will see him. As I raise my hand in a good-bye, I decide against it. It is useless. His actions, his words, have left an imprint far greater than a simple good-bye can erase. Walking out, I feel the door shut slowly behind me.

TRISHA

She came to say good-bye. She hasn't spoken the words aloud yet, but I see it in her eyes. I know it the way I knew when she was scared as a child but refused to admit it. It's three in the afternoon. I glance out the window as the chai on the stove simmers. The scent of cut ginger and spices fills the air as the milk heats. Mothers pour out of their houses, gathering into groups to make the daily walk to the neighborhood school. The lower grades are dismissed first and then twenty minutes later the upper grades. I know their schedule as if I had my own children.

Sometimes the children will run into one another's homes, creating an unscheduled playdate. The moms will shake their heads in mild frustration but follow their children in, always ready for some tea and talk time. They have never invited me. Why would they? They know there is nothing I can contribute to an afternoon discussion of school gossip about teachers and other parents.

I pour the chai into two china cups, both so thin, so fragile, that one slip and the cups will shatter. I add one sugar to mine, two in Sonya's. She always had a sweet tooth. When we were kids, Papa would buy one box of chocolate mint cookies from Sonya's Girl Scout troop.

Mama would divide the cookies evenly between us three girls. I would take one from my stack and eat it carefully, savoring every bite. Hiding the rest from Sonya became a mission. She would finish all of hers in one sitting. Yet, no matter where I hid them, Sonya would find them. It might take her a few days or even a week, but she would keep searching until she discovered them. From then on, I asked Papa to hide them in his desk, knowing Sonya would never dare to take them from him.

I shake off the memory, reaching into the cupboard for my expensive truffles and other exotic delights I keep for when I entertain executives from Eric's company and their censorious wives. Filling a plate, I set it next to the chai and head back to the living room. She is pacing. A caged animal, she moves on her long legs from one side of the room to the other.

"Here we go." I set the serving tray down and hand her the cup. She takes a sip and nods at me in gratitude. "How have you been?" Small talk—the guarantee against speaking about anything with meaning. A barrier against hearing her tell me what I don't want to learn. "Have you visited old friends? Reacquainted yourself with the town? The weather has been great."

"Your home is beautiful," she says, avoiding answering my slew of questions. Sonya sets the chai down, having taken only a sip or two. "And your husband seems like a wonderful man."

"Thank you. He is." I set my cup down also, next to hers. The handles touch, a union of two pieces so similar that one piece has nothing distinctive to separate it from the other. "He said you were lovely."

"Really?" She shifts in her seat, uncomfortable. "Even though I missed your wedding?"

I had forgotten her way of speaking. Always to the point—never hiding behind walls of make-believe. When we were young, she was the one who spoke about the beatings. Questioned why, and whether Papa had the right. Marin accepted them, said it was just his way. I would never comment. It seemed inappropriate somehow, since I had no experience to speak of. "He understood."

"That I couldn't make it?" She seems surprised.

"Yes," I lie. He never told me he understood. Never questioned why she failed to show. He simply held me and told me how much he loved me. Promised he would always be there for me. I hold up the plate of sweets, offering her all of them. "Try some. You'll really like them."

"No, thank you." She barely glances at them. "I gave up sweets a few years ago."

"What?" There is no hiding my shock. Though the change is minor, it disappoints me that I was unaware. "Why?"

"I was in Ethiopia for a photo shoot." She says it offhandedly. "I had packed a box of real milk chocolates from London—the type you can't find in the States." Her face shows her yearning for them. "I had maybe fifty or so in my knapsack. When I was on location, a child came up to me. Three or four years old. Held out her hand for a piece of the chocolate. I gave her some and soon I was surrounded." Clearly lost in her memory, she continues, "Some of the kids had tears in their eyes as they ate. Over a piece of chocolate."

"Seems an odd reason for you to give it up." She's never offered me details of the places she's traveled. In the few conversations we had over the years, I never thought to ask. It's funny how I forgot that while she was gone she was living her own life. My focus remained on those she left behind and our everyday happenings. On our parents, Marin, and Gia—the only family I had left.

She shrugs her shoulders. "Every time I tried eating sweets afterward, I thought of those kids. I lost my taste for it." She runs her hand through her hair before settling into the sofa. She tries to get comfortable among the ruffled pillows. Out of frustration, she takes three of them and moves them to another sofa before settling into the cushions.

"They're for decoration," I explain. Her lack of appreciation for them stings. There is no way for her to know the hours I spent finding the exact match for the sofa. I am distracted by the casual stack she makes of them. Handmade woven silk pillows thrown together carelessly. Clasping my hands together, I tuck them between my jean-clad knees to keep from reaching out and rearranging them. "A contrast against the solid fabric of the sofa."

Sonya considers my words. She glances at the pillows, running her fingers over the raised stripes interwoven with flowers. Her gaze strays to the sofa, the plain beige fabric that was special-ordered from Italy. The right shade to go with the faux painting and silk curtains in the room. "OK."

Laughter bubbles in me before spilling out. We're choosing to discuss chocolates and pillows after so many years apart. Pillows that she would be surprised to know cost what our parents paid for an entire year of rent for our apartment. She has no clue why they are so important. Even if I tell her that I am forced to maintain an image, an appearance for the society I live in, I am sure she won't care. Just as I cannot relate to her life, she could never commiserate about mine. I wonder if there is anything left between us besides the past. My hands cover my face because the laughter is changing, and I refuse to let her see my tears. I quickly wipe them away, but they flow between my fingers and over my manicured nails.

"Please," she says. "Don't do this."

"Why?" The question reaches far deeper than her leaving. She has still not said the words, but I know it in my heart. The way I know how she sleeps, how she eats, and most important how she lives. Even though I have no idea where home has been for her, I know she is going. We spent hours huddled in the same bed as girls. Without fail, she would curl her body into mine, whether it was searching for heat or the protection of another body during the night. Angrily I would push her away only to cling to her once sleep overtook me. "You just got here."

"There's no reason for me to stay." Her words are a whisper, fear fueling their admission. "He doesn't know I'm in the hospital room. Even if he did, he wouldn't care."

"That's why?" A scream starts to build in me, but I swallow it. "You're leaving because of him?"

"No, I'm leaving because of me."

"What about us?" Through the window, I see my next-door neighbor leave the house across the street. Holding on securely to her young daughter's hand, she looks both ways before crossing our quiet tree-lined street. The houses in this town are large, most built in the last decade. It is a neighborhood of new money inhabited mostly by entrepreneurs who have garnered their wealth via the tech industry. Luxury vehicles sit in the driveways. Hispanic gardeners and housekeepers take their lunch breaks by gathering into a group on the sidewalk or in their trucks to eat tamales. The walls that surround me have become my home, one that I would never have imagined owning, but the indulged child in me would surely have expected. "You never think about that."

"You don't need me," she says. Her voice is barely a whisper, but her declaration is weighted with heartache. "You're fine." She motions around her. "You have everything."

"I have a house." The walls I admired only moments ago suddenly become a barrier between us. "That's not enough."

"It's so much."

It suddenly occurs to me that she is not content with her life. Never would I have argued she was happy. That emotion feels disallowed. With a past molded by infinite sadness, how could she claim happiness as hers? The two sentiments seem impossible to link, and therefore one must take precedence over the other. Yet I believed she had at least reconciled herself with what had happened. That somehow, somewhere she had resigned herself and found purpose.

"Do you want this?" I ask, gesturing around me.

"No," she says. "Not anymore."

"When?" Searching, I can't find a likely time. Never did she talk about the white picket fence or the two point five children. Her dialogue was always of faraway places and people. Which required no more of her than she could give. The stability, the mansion on the hill, that was my pursuit.

"A long time ago." Her head drops; she takes a deep breath. In seconds she seems to shake herself out of her reverie. "It can never be for me. I accept that. This is why I have to leave. I don't belong here. I never did."

"We are your family. Who else do you belong with if not us?" Her indifference infuriates me. Regardless of what happened, we belong together. As a family, we have to get through this. She left us behind years ago. Once was enough. "You don't get to run away again. That's not fair."

"It's not about me," she says. We both know she's lying.

"Why didn't you come to my wedding?" The anger I suppressed on that day rears up, surrounding the empty space between us. Like an art piece come to life, I am beyond recognition. "I wanted you there. I deserved that," I scream. The time for an answer is long past. If she is going to leave again, I need to know the woman she is now. Because never would I have imagined the sister I grew up with would abandon me on the most important day of my life. "Why did you stay away for so long? I needed you."

"Because there was nothing I had to give you." She glances at the wall, biting her lip. "To give anyone." Her eyes cloud over. "I couldn't watch him give you away. Smile as he played the loving father." She stands quickly, knocking the stacked pillows to the ground. She avoids my eyes, but I still catch an unreadable mystery in their depths. "And you letting him." She waits, turning toward me to see how her words affect me.

Something tugs at my brain, a memory. A girl whimpering, searching through the darkness. In the halls of our childhood home, I hear a scream. Terrifying in its intensity, but no one comes to her rescue. She is all alone. I struggle to make out a face, but it is blurred. I shudder, sure it is Sonya I can't see. Shaking away the image, I focus on who she is now, dismissing the past. Now, I fight to hold on to the sister I have lost. "Then help me watch him die. Tell me how to say good-bye."

It is unfair for me to demand such a thing from her. Maybe saying good-bye to him means she has finally found freedom. Her path is not the same as mine. We both accepted that at a young age. She was the one bruised, whereas it was my job to hold her, comfort her as best I could. It was easier than I imagined. When you stand unharmed, you find the strength to help those fallen at your feet.

I reach out. She is the only one I turned to as a child, the one whose tears I would wipe. Whereas she struggled to find herself, I learned to be who he needed me to be. That meant standing in his shadow, allowing him to protect me from himself.

"I can't do this without you." My last appeal, it is all I have left in my arsenal. My eyes shut, sure I will hear the door open and close. Last time she didn't tell me she was leaving. For years, I was positive that a simple farewell would have lessened the pain. Now I know the truth. The courtesy of her good-bye pierces more. Because now I must accept the reality—I don't matter enough for her to stay. "Please."

"Trisha," she starts, the pain in her voice clear. I can feel her struggle, her desire to be as far away from all of this, including me, as possible. When I don't answer, when I refuse to give her a reprieve, I hear her take a deep breath. "I'll stay," she whispers, the decision sounding torn from her. "Help you however I can."

Her words flow through me, warming my heart. She is still the girl I remember. The one I counted on, needed. Just because we were born into the same family did not guarantee we would stand together. With her agreement, we are still one. Opening my eyes, I stare into hers.

They are the exact same color as mine. We are sisters, but a bond far greater binds us. On different sides of the road, we walked through the same hell. "Why?" I ask.

"Because you're my sister," she says, her eyes locked on mine. "And I couldn't have survived our childhood without you."

MARIN

Marin is seven, playing with her friends in the dirt. Cows walk freely among them, eating the scraps of food thrown on the ground and leaving their feces in gratitude. The Indian sun makes the air arid, difficult to breathe. But Marin and her friends are used to it, raised as they were under the scorching heat. There are five girls in all. Neighbors since birth, they have become fast friends over the years. Sticks and stones are their toys; with them, they have created a game of hopscotch and Marin is in the lead. It makes no difference who wins. There is no real way to keep score, and the girls often pad their points. But Marin likes knowing she is winning. She welcomes the feeling it gives her, the sense of superiority. The idea that she can do anything.

"Beti," Ranee calls Marin from the small doorway of their house, modern in comparison to many of the others in the neighborhood. Though their toilet is not connected to running water, they do have a separate space in the house to shower and use as a restroom. Most of her friends still have to walk to an outhouse shared by a number of families. "It is time to prepare dinner."

Marin has recently begun learning how to cook. It is expected of all the girls; the younger you start, the better. The lessons allow her time with

Ranee without her grandmother watching and scolding. Brent's mother lives with them, as tradition demanded, and her arthritis has flared up, causing her to be even more judgmental and critical of Marin's actions. Ranee has told her to ignore the harping, but it is hard.

"Five minutes, Mummy," Marin says, her focus on the game. Three more jumps and she will be the ultimate victor. Scrunching her face in concentration, she eyes the rock she has to pick up without falling over. With all her effort, she makes the leap, but trips over the branch, falling flat onto the concrete. Her nose grazes the ground and begins to bleed. The girls rush to help her. Ranee, having seen the fall, moves as quickly as her sari allows.

"Are you all right?" Ranee uses the edge of her sari to wipe away the blood. When Marin's nose continues to bleed, she pinches the top of it and tips her head back. "What happened, Beti?"

"She was too focused on the rock. Didn't pay attention to the branch," her smug grandmother says, seated on an old wooden chair nearby. "Foolish girl."

* * *

"I'll be home at ten," Gia announces as she grabs a piece of toast. Her backpack overflows with books. Her school uniform, a plaid skirt and pressed white shirt, flatters her slim figure. Two days a week, the students are allowed to wear their own clothes. After a heated discussion about individuality versus conformity at the PTA meeting, the school board compromised. On those two days, Gia often throws on a pair of jeans and a T-shirt. To Marin, her choice of clothes screams indifference rather than a personality statement.

"What?" Marin mutes her conference call. Setting down her chai, she stops Gia before she walks out the door. "Ten?"

"There's a study group for the science test." Gia taps her foot in a seeming hurry to get in the waiting car. She's in a carpool, which frees

Marin from the hassle of school pickup and drop-off. "We'll be at the library."

"Who is driving you?" Marin doesn't recall seeing the test on her calendar. She makes a point to sync Gia's school calendar with her own, and she's careful to keep the nights before due dates and exams free of dinners or family events so she can spend the time reviewing with Gia.

"One of the moms. I have to go," Gia insists, trying to shut the door.

"Have a great day," Marin offers, turning back to her phone. She considers giving Gia a hug, but recently her daughter has started shying away from contact. Not a fan of displays of affection herself, Marin hasn't pushed it. "Good luck studying." But her words are swallowed by empty air. Gia has already left the house.

"That is not acceptable," Marin says, rejoining the conversation on the phone. "Get the reports on my desk within the hour," she orders a senior manager.

Her day started at four this morning—it is now past nine. As she paces her home office, she glances in the mirror that hangs on the back of her door. She's still in her pajamas. A quick glance at her calendar reminds her she has a meeting in an hour at the office. Throwing her cooled chai into the sink, she rushes upstairs and turns on the shower to let it warm up. She quickly grabs a pantsuit and accessories to match as her cell phone begins to buzz on the dresser. "Still have thirty minutes until I'm due in the office," she calls out to no one. Unless it's her secretary, Marin rarely makes time to talk to anyone not on her schedule. But this caller is insistent. Running naked to the phone, she barely registers the number before answering. "Hello."

"Marin? It's Karen, the principal at Gia's school. We need to speak to you. It's urgent."

* * *

"We've had a report of some disturbing behavior," Karen explains quietly. The principal is a short woman, tinier than many of the students walking the halls. Her hair is curly, and she wears glasses that were fashionable a decade ago. Having matriculated from the school herself, she often speaks candidly to the parents about her experiences, good and bad.

A large cherry oak desk overwhelms the office, which is filled with pictures of students past and present. Karen's diploma from the high school hangs on the wall right below her degree from Wellesley in education and her master's from Princeton.

"Drugs?" Marin's voice rises in contrast to Karen's, anger lacing it. Her father's constant fear when they were growing up. "They are becoming too American," he would complain to Ranee. He was sure that somehow, even with the strict regime they lived under, they would stray and humiliate him. Whether it was from dating, drinking, or substances, he was convinced they would lose sight of their way. They never did, but that never swayed his belief they would. That same fear now grips Marin. "Has she been found with some?"

"No," Karen says. She sits back, assessing Marin. Her halo of hair covers the back of the leather chair. "How close are you to Gia?"

"Excuse me?" A shift in energy permeates the room. Karen is suddenly the protector and Marin, unsure what is going on, stands on the outside. "It's time you told me what this meeting is about."

Karen nods, accepting Marin's demand. "During gym class, the PE instructor noticed bruises on Gia's body. Your daughter thought she was alone in the locker room." Karen waits before saying the words that will shift Marin's world on its axis. "They were clear signs of a beating."

The room begins to spin. Marin grasps the handles of her chair. She glances sideways, trying to focus on something. Her blood pressure drops, leaving her dizzy. Images of Brent invade her thoughts. For just a moment, she wonders if he woke up and is responsible. The fear grips her until she reminds herself she just saw him in the hospital, immobile and lost to the world.

"How? When?" The words echo in the room but she can't promise she spoke them. "I don't understand."

"We don't know." Karen softens, seeming to get the answer she was searching for. "We hoped you could give us some insight."

"You think *I* did this?"

Marin spent many afternoons in college reading about violence. The propensity to repeat the pattern. All the fancy verbiage to explain a simple rule—when you are beaten, you beat. You repeat what is familiar, what is programmed into your psyche as normal.

"You think I could beat my own daughter?"

"There are no accusations," Karen says, drawing Marin back. "It is my responsibility to understand what happened."

"My daughter was beaten. Apparently that's what happened," Marin says, trying to find her footing in a changed landscape. "Someone used her as a punching bag. Decided she wasn't worthy of being treated with care or kindness." She drops her head, trying to gather strength but finding none.

"Are you all right?" Pouring a glass of water, Karen sets it in front of Marin.

Marin tenses. Pushing her chair back, she stands. In a heartbeat she changes, returns to normal. The principal's pity is fuel on a fire that has burned from childhood.

"Where is she?" Marin checks her watch. A little before noon. "Her morning classes just ended. She should be at lunch, right?"

Karen glances at the clock on the wall. She fails to mask her surprise that Marin has memorized the schedule. "Um, yes, you're right. The students will be heading to the cafeteria." She takes a step closer to Marin, crossing the invisible boundary between them. "Do you want me to check her out of school for you?"

"No." Marin answers from instinct. She is not ready to face her daughter yet. There would be nothing for her to say. Schooled since birth, she will keep their family secrets within the home. "I'll wait for her at the house after school."

"Of course. You understand I have to file a report with child services. It is my legal obligation."

Karen's words leave her cold.

"And if the abuse happened here then you can understand I will be filing a lawsuit against the school." Marin grabs her purse and moves toward the door. "If not, then I would appreciate your support in keeping my daughter safe."

*   *   *

Marin drops her keys into her purse. She has no recollection of the drive home. Her phone has been buzzing ever since she left the school. A slew of messages from her secretary, frantic to know her whereabouts. She shuts it off before dropping it on the end table. Glancing around, she searches for something, yet nothing offers her a clue on how to move forward.

The clock on the mantel indicates it is past one. Her stomach growls; she considers making herself a sandwich or grabbing a piece of fruit, but she would choke on her first bite. Retreating to the sanctuary of her office, she closes the door behind her. Her computer, always on, beckons. She powers it off without saving the document she had spent the night working through. With nothing left to do, she collapses into the sofa. Clutching a pillow to her chest, she curls her legs against herself. Laying her head down atop her knees, she yearns to weep, but the conditioning is too deep. Instead, memories circle around her, tearing her to shreds without the benefit of tears to ease the pain.

*   *   *

The room is dark. The sun is still shining on the other side of the world. On India. Marin sits up in bed, pulling the sheet tight around herself.

"It is time to prepare." Ranee maneuvers through the bedroom the three girls insist on sharing in the weeks leading up to the wedding. Ranee offers Marin a smile as she shakes Trisha and Sonya from their slumber. She silently waves Marin out of the bed. "Come, Beti. All the clothes need ironing. The family will be here soon."

"What about the food?" Marin asks.

"After you girls went to bed last night, I prepared the meal."

"You have not slept?"

"I will sleep after the wedding." Ranee smiles.

"How are we supposed to iron this?" Trisha asks. Two neatly folded stacks—one of Indian dresses for the girls and the other of Brent's clothes. Atop it lies his favorite suit. A thin gray jacket with matching pants. He bought it for thirteen dollars at a garage sale where it was tagged as new. He had haggled and paid two dollars less than the asking price. Proud of his bargain, he wore it to every occasion since.

"Quickly." Marin unfolds the first dress. "After we finish, we can help Mummy."

"I'm not going to." Trisha makes a face. "I hate cooking."

"It doesn't matter if you hate it or not. You have to learn."

"I don't have to do anything I don't want to," Trisha insists.

"It doesn't work that way," Marin argues, suddenly angry with Trisha. "You need to grow up."

"Says who? Besides, it's my life." Trisha exudes a confidence Marin envies. "I make my own decisions."

"You think I chose this?" Marin drops her head, afraid to admit the truth to herself. "I don't even know him, and now I have to spend the rest of my life with him."

Trisha stares at her sister, Marin's admission silencing her. They busy themselves. Five years in age separates them, but a generation of confusion divides them. Trisha unfolds each piece, methodically shaking it out. She lays it on the board for Marin to iron. The completed pieces she hangs in the plastic garment holder.

"How many are left?" Marin is the first to break the silence. With less than a day left together, she knows neither wants quiet to fill their final minutes.

"Dad's suit and one sari." Trisha touches Marin's shoulder lightly. "Are you excited?" Trisha lays the suit pants on the table. "Everyone here just for you. Being the center of attention?"

"So you wouldn't mind it?" Marin teases her.

"I don't know. But it's not a bad way to end your time here. Right?" Trisha seems to need the answer more for herself than anything.

"I don't know how it's supposed to end. Am I happy that I'm free of Daddy? Or do I spend all my time worrying that you guys are still here?" Marin's gaze is steady on Trisha.

"Don't worry about us." Trisha's voice is sure and strong. "Just be happy. OK?"

The smell of smoke catches them both unaware. In the years to follow, Marin would remember the conversation. The actual piece of clothing would become a distant memory, the burning cheap cotton a vague recollection. But in that moment, when Marin turns to see the charred hole, it freezes them. Their eyes widen in shock, fear tightening their faces. The sudden approach of footsteps leaves them little time to create an excuse. As has been the case so often in their history, there are no alarm bells. No drums or whistles to warn. Rage is random in its frequency. The moments that seem sure to lead to it rarely do. Events to forgive, minor transgressions—those lead to volatility. Unpredictable abuse leaves psychological scars that last long after the physical ones.

Brent's eyes bulge at the sight of the burn. Though it is small, the pants are ruined. Marin stands straight, facing him. There is no other place to escape until tomorrow. She does not look at his face. Not one of them ever does.

"You are stupid with my suit." Brent stares at Marin, anger vibrating off him. "Are only your clothes important to you? You think you are special because you are getting married?"

Marin does not answer. Over time, they have learned it is best not to. His own responses seem to impress him more.

"I am married. I still care about others, including your things. I have paid for this entire wedding, have I not? You do not show the same respect to me. Why?"

His thumb and middle finger encircle Marin's wrist. She stares at his digits. They do not touch. If Marin pulled, one twist of her arm, she would be free. She could step away, say no. This weighs on her, since she has never thought it before.

The first blow lands above Marin's ear. It is from the palm of his hand. Above the ear is his favorite place, that or the side of the head. For Ranee— on the back and in the stomach. Sonya—always the back of the head. Always first with the palm, then, convinced the perceived wrong is egregious, the fist.

"One," Trisha begins to count. It is her ritual, her key for survival. The recipient of the beating is irrelevant. She swears that the hits, no matter how many there really are, never go past eight. It is her lucky number. So she continues. He has never stopped her. Maybe because it has never been her jawbone that connects with his fist. Regardless, she is desperate to reach eight. Because then the violence toward her loved ones will end. And she can return to her reality.

Marin's vision is still intact. After the fourth or fifth one, it will get blurry. Only momentarily. But right then, she can still see. Her head whiplashed to the side. On her wedding night, when Raj caresses her neck, she will wince. Cringe when he goes to kiss her. She will tell him she slept wrong because it was the night before the wedding. Jitters and stress. Just a kink in her neck, Marin will assure him. She will be better soon.

"Two," Trisha continues.

Marin runs through the options in her mind. For the first time, she can stop her father. Take her hand out of his. Explain that she does not belong to him. That tomorrow she will belong to another. But for one day, this day, she belongs to herself. Regardless of their culture and beliefs, having been born to him did not make her his. Stamp his name on hers. But she is not his property. She had not chosen this and does not want it. For once, her wants should matter.

"*Six, seven.*"

Her thoughts ultimately hold no weight. His thumb and finger tighten and come together. He uses her body to balance his. Sonya will joke about it alone in the room and mimic the contortions of his face in the quiet of the night. His lower lip between his teeth and his eyes wide. Like a clown. She will walk around, her arms flailing and feet wide apart. Trisha and Marin will let out small, nervous laughs.

Marin does not feel the final blow. It does not matter anyway. She will never speak about the physical pain. That will subside in time. It is that she could have walked away. She had a choice, and she chose to stay.

"*Eight.*"

It is a lucky day.

RANEE

The first time Brent hit her was three weeks after he started work in the States. An engineer by trade, the only job he could find in America was changing tires at the local gas station. A customer had berated him in front of everyone. Called him a brownie and told him to go back to whatever island he had come from. Brent had nodded, unable to say anything for fear of losing his job. When the man threw a dollar bill at him as a tip, Brent had slowly bent down and picked it up. That dollar would buy them a pint of milk.

When Brent arrived at their cramped apartment later that night, Ranee had been late in starting dinner. He had complained but muttered he would shower first to wash the grime off. When he returned and Ranee was slow to serve the food, Brent had pulled his hand back and hit her across the face. Ranee staggered, reaching back for balance, to regain her footing. Her left hand landed on the still-hot stove. The scar that resulted from her burnt skin was still visible on her palm today. Her other hand had automatically gone to her stomach; she had just learned of her pregnancy. Marin and Trisha stood near the kitchen staring in horror.

* * *

Ranee puts the final touches on the salad while the chicken strips cook. She tosses the dried cranberries with the homemade dressing just as she hears the front door open. A quick glance at the watch that circles her petite wrist tells her it's just before five. Since moving home, Sonya has made a habit of leaving first thing in the morning and returning right before dinner.

"I'm in the kitchen," Ranee calls out when she hears Sonya's footsteps falter in the foyer.

"Something smells good," Sonya says, dropping her camera bag on the kitchen island. Glancing at the salad, she asks, "Can I help?"

"If you could just set the table." They've fallen into a pattern over the last few weeks. Every morning they sit and have breakfast, and in the evenings they cook dinner together. Even if it is just sandwiches, they silently move within the kitchen as if they've been coordinating for years. "How was your day?"

"Fine." Sonya's answers are quick, details often left out. "Yours?"

They are two strangers with a history that serves as the only connection between them. "I picked out new bedding for your room." Sonya is staying. They have not spoken about it, though Ranee is sure that earlier she had made plans to leave. Something changed and for that Ranee is grateful. "The bedding in your room is over ten years old."

"I'm surprised you didn't change it into a guest room," Sonya says softly, grabbing two plates and silverware. "Or Dad didn't convert it into a storage place."

"I would never do that." Avoiding commenting directly, Ranee searches a drawer in the kitchen until she finds what she's looking for. Pulling out a gold necklace with a heart-shaped pendant, Ranee drops it in Sonya's palm. "I found this in my bureau last night. I thought you might want it."

It was the necklace Ranee gave to Sonya for her sixteenth birthday. When Sonya packed her things to move out on the night of her graduation, she had left the necklace dangling on top of her chest of drawers.

Staring at the necklace, Sonya closes her fist around it before slipping it into her pocket. "Thanks."

"When you left, I thought you would only be gone for a short while, so I left it in your room. I never imagined it would be so many years," Ranee admits, fussing over the food. "After the third, maybe fourth year, I took it to my room for safekeeping."

"I left because I had no choice," Sonya says bitingly, taking the bait Ranee subconsciously threw out. "What was said that day—it made everything clear." Sonya shakes her head, anger reverberating off her. After so many years, she can't even pinpoint when it started or where it led, only that it was her constant companion.

They face one another, both clearly wondering how they arrived at this point. Ranee tries to defend herself without destroying the fragile connection she has built with her daughter. "I was scared."

"Of?"

"Of having made the wrong decision."

"You did, Mom." Sonya says, oblivious to the truth Ranee keeps from her. She runs her hands through her hair. "It's the wrong decision to tell your daughter she doesn't matter." The tears choke her. "To tell her she is a burden."

"Sonya." The lit coal in her voice burns her throat. When Sonya was born, her umbilical cord proved difficult to cut. The doctors in the small hospital joked that this one would never leave Ranee's side. "You were never a burden." But Ranee knows it is too little, too late. Sonya's face shows no reaction.

"And yet," Sonya pauses, "you said otherwise at graduation."

Taking a deep breath, Ranee struggles to try to clarify what she meant the night of graduation. "Sonya, when I said it would have been best for you to be aborted . . ." Ranee pauses. "It was the only way I knew how . . ." *To let you go* are the words that remain unspoken. That was the reason Ranee had spoken the truth. She knew it would make Sonya leave, escape. For Ranee, it was the only choice left to make. The only way Sonya could be free.

"Did you mean it?" Sonya asks quietly when Ranee is unable to finish the sentence.

"Yes," Ranee whispers. "But not for the reasons you believe."

Before Ranee can attempt to explain to her daughter why she never wished her born, Sonya finishes the conversation with, "The reasons don't matter. What's done is done. Nothing can change the past." Sighing, she gathers her hair together. "It's best if you and I don't discuss it again."

*   *   *

When you lose someone there is a grieving process. Shock, anger, despair, among a multitude of other emotions. Every one of them wrapping around you like a vise. No room to breathe, to think, or to understand. But what about when someone is alive yet wants nothing to do with you? Is there a mourning process in place then, or do you hold on to hope like a life raft in the abyss? After the fight with Sonya, Ranee's emotions swing erratically. Like a pendulum with no gravity, they shift minute to minute, until she is exhausted from nothingness.

She straightens out the bed covers, smoothing wrinkles she knows Trisha must have attended to once already on her daily visit to Brent. It is past midnight. The hospital halls are eerily quiet. For Brent, it must make no difference; his mind is living in complete solitude. Lost in a world that is void of sense.

In Marin's first year of school in the US, she told Ranee that she'd learned in science class you could tell a tree's age by the number of rings on the stump. Marin yearned to take a trip to Yosemite to learn the ages of fallen trees but Brent refused. Ranee wondered if there was any way for someone to tell her real age—or could people only see the one that the multitude of worry lines on her face indicated?

Ranee learned how to speak proper English from the soap operas on television and how to read it from the newspaper. Since arriving in America, she often thought what it would be like if she brought home pay equal to Brent's. Would that have changed the dynamic of their relationship, or was she destined to live in battle with him as the guaranteed victor?

"I envy you," she said quietly, making sure no one could overhear. The nurses were constantly in and out, as if their noise could be the jarring he needed to awake. "There is no one you have to face for your deeds."

An outlawed practice in India, *sati*, required a widow to throw herself on her deceased husband's burning body during cremation. The assumption was that no woman would want to live without her husband to support and love her. Ranee had seen the practice as a child. Children were not allowed at funerals, but she had sneaked into one. As smoke billowed into the air and sobs were heard, a young widow in a white sari threw herself onto her husband's pyre. Her screams silenced the group as they watched her burn to death. Ranee had covered her eyes, praying for someone to rescue the woman from her demise. But everyone stood in place, watching the widow do the right thing. When the village folk told the couple's orphaned children the news, they fell to the ground sobbing. An uncle pulled them into his arms and explained that their mother had died with honor and they should be proud. They could now hold their heads high because of her actions.

"I won't die with you," Ranee says to Brent's still body. "So many years I wished I were dead that now I choose to live." The argument with Sonya replays in her mind. Her belief that she was a burden. "But she was never a burden, was she, Brent?" The ticking of the clock echoes in the hospital room. Her husband remains the silent companion in the conversation. "None of our girls were. But I believed you when you said you knew what was best. When you told me that I was stupid and you were smart." She lowers her head in shame. "I believed you when you said the stress of our new country was too much to bear. That because you had to stand silent in our new world . . ." She pauses, a sob building. "I convinced myself that in our home you had the right to be strong."

Despair and regret grip Ranee. He was not strong but instead the weakest of them all. Her children were pawns in his game. A voice in her head that sounds eerily familiar to his reminds her that he provided her with a home and food. That he gave her everything when she had nothing. She dismisses the voice, her own finally strong enough to hear.

"But I never knew the full story, did I? Maybe I didn't want to see." In the belly of a whale, Ranee knows she is drowning but is helpless to save herself. "But it was past time for me to save our daughters. I—we owed them that much."

She lays her head on the bed, next to his like she has for all the years of marriage, and weeps. Her *mangalsutra*, the sacred necklace she wears of gold and black beads, falls forward, intertwining them. A symbol of love and marriage, he gave it to her during their wedding ceremony as required by tradition. Slowly, she brings her hands around to the clasp and undoes it, dropping the necklace between them before wiping her tears and walking out.

SONYA

When I left home after graduation, my first stop was Kentucky. I had loved horses as a child, and the song "My Old Kentucky Home" during the Derby always made me feel like crying. Maybe it was the huge hats, a welcome cover from the world, or the sight of the horses running as fast as they could only to end up right where they started, but it was my first choice for escape. I arrived in Lexington and was welcomed by endless miles of thoroughbred farms. White picket fences and grass so green it looked blue. Smiles graced everyone's faces.

I rented a hotel room and car for a week. With no clear direction about what I was doing or planning, I assumed seven days was enough time to figure it out. After researching various options, I started my adventure. Dressed in jeans and a T-shirt, I spent hours hanging off freshly painted fences photographing horses grazing on the grass. At the world famous Keeneland horse track, I snapped pictures of thoroughbreds in flight. Their powerful legs propelled them forward, while their chiseled bodies stayed in perfect alignment with the track. Stall cleaners started recognizing me. At first it was daily waves, but soon they offered me unrestricted entrance to the stalls. With their permission, I was able to capture the horses in peaceful repose, waiting until it was their moment to shine.

Seven days turned to fourteen. I had hundreds of photos, but I still took more. My camera offered a safety I hadn't known before. For the first time in my life, I was in control. But my refuge proved temporary. A horse owner's son noticed me. A few years older, he was handsome and kind. He offered to show me how to ride the ones I admired. English versus Western. We began to spend our days together. When he kissed me, I expected it. The first time we slept together, I told him I was quiet because it was so beautiful. When he told me he loved me, I was lost, falling off a cliff with no parachute. I struggled to say the words back to him, but images of my father strangled any hope. That night I left without saying good-bye. Drove until I found a motel off the highway, hundreds of miles from nowhere. Turning on my computer, I searched the Internet until I found what I was looking for. I read from sunset until sunrise, each account filling an unspoken need within me. Exhausted, I laid my head down on the cheap wood desk and cried.

*　*　*

After leaving Kentucky, I had no idea what to do with the hundreds of pictures I had taken. With no formal training in photography, I had no concept of how to create a career in the industry. Searching online, I found a website where amateurs uploaded their pictures for anyone's viewing pleasure. I did so and thought nothing of them until I received a call from an agent a month later. Linda was with a large management company that represented some of the premier photographers in the country. She asked to see a portfolio. When I told her I didn't have one but was currently in Turkey and could send her pictures I had recently taken, she laughed. "You do that," she said. She signed me, and I've been with her ever since. Through her contacts, I've been hired to work all over the world.

I call Linda days after promising Trisha I won't leave. When I reach her answering machine at the agency I call her cell phone.

"Sonya, sweetie, how are you?" My name has come up on her caller ID.

Linda is quintessential LA. She drives a convertible with the top down; her house sits on the bluffs of Malibu though she hates to swim in the ocean. She has two dogs, Pinky and Princess. She dresses them in identical sweaters, like twins, but somehow is able to tell them apart. Though she sleeps with the dogs nightly, she is a sworn germophobe. Nearing fifty, Linda dresses and looks like she's in her thirties. Swearing that green tea is the fountain of youth, she devours gallons a week. The Botox remains unmentioned.

Linda started her career as an intern at the agency. Over drinks one night she confided that she only had to sleep with two partners before climbing the ranks. That one of them was a woman barely fazed her. When I asked her if she had ever demanded the same from underlings, she winked and told me she would never tell. Linda changed her hair color by the decade. Currently a redhead, in the nineties she was a blonde, but she decided they really don't have more fun. A brunette before that, she has forgotten her natural shade. And since she keeps her weekly Brazilian wax appointment, she said, she'll never find out.

"Good," I answer her over the phone, our connection clear. She was also the first one I called when I decided to come back home. I needed to let her know that I wouldn't be available for any new assignments for a while. Not a religious person, she had nonetheless wished me Godspeed and the best for my father.

"And your daddy? How is he?" she asks me now.

"Still sleeping," I reply, the only answer I have at hand.

"Excellent," Linda does not miss a beat. "The rest will do him good. And your family? How are they holding up?"

"As well as can be expected," I answer. As close as we are, I have never told her or anyone about my past. "Did you get the last set of pictures I sent you?" I ask, eager to change the subject.

"Of the Nor'easter that hit New England? Storm of the century? They were fabulous. I have three papers that made bids for them. We'll play them against each other for a bit."

"Thanks." The money has never excited me much. With no one to spend it on, it sits in the bank. Linda, however, is continually frustrated with me when locale trumps payment for my choice of assignments. She is sure my talent can bring in the big bucks, plus, for her, every assignment's worth is dependent on the commission it pays her. "That's why I'm calling. I need a job."

It is usually the other way around: Linda contacts me with a slew of new projects. She runs down the list until one sounds appealing. I am her favorite client because there are no limitations on where I will go or when. It is easy for me to drop everything since I have nothing to hold me. No husband or children whose schedules will be interrupted by mine.

"Excellent! I have an online magazine that wants pictures of Russia." She pauses as she consults her iPad. Linda has very few attachments in her life but if her tablet could be surgically connected to her, she'd be thrilled. "A paper in London wants to follow up on the rape crisis in India. An in-depth exposé. May require three to six months of time, but that hasn't stopped you before." She sounds pleased. "Which one should I schedule you in for?"

I pause, considering her offer of India. My heritage, my ancestral home. "No," I murmur, keeping my voice light, the panic at bay. Though we went once when I was a child, I've never felt the yearning to return. "Not India. Actually, I need something closer to home." I glance out the window of the café I have been sitting in for the last few hours. With a cup in hand, I have watched as the diverse population of

Palo Alto has found the one thing they have in common—the need for expensive coffee. "The Bay Area, in fact. No traveling."

Linda falls silent, as I expected she might. A question remains unspoken. I wait to see if she will ask it, but in the end I know her decision. Even if it were to save her life, she will not pry into yours. I imagine she has secrets of her own that she holds dear, and she therefore understands others' need to keep their own counsel. Whatever her reasoning, I appreciate her restraint. "Let me see what I find."

* * *

Days have passed since I called Linda. Needing an escape, I drive toward the city and park, deciding to walk along the Golden Gate Bridge. A low fog hangs over the bay, with the sun barely peeking out from behind the clouds. The water is clear but choppy, crashing against the rocks as sea lions cavort nearby. I cup my palms together and blow into them, trying to ward off the chill. Tourists with cameras hanging off their necks bustle past me, pointing and snapping pictures of Alcatraz Island, situated in the middle of the frigid water. Raising my camera, I glance through the lens to see the prison as they do—a fortress that held some of the most notorious criminals of its time. Without taking a picture, I lower it and see it for what I believe it to be—a building that sits empty, with too many ghosts to tell the full tale of the lives that inhabited it.

"Excuse us," a small Chinese man says in stilted English. "Would you mind taking our picture?" he asks, pointing to the large group standing behind him. A mix of young and old, clearly a family that has traveled together. The children are pushing one another while the men and women watch me expectantly, hoping I will capture this moment for them.

"Of course." Taking his camera, I motion for them to stand closer together to fit in the frame. "A little bit more," I say, glancing into the

LCD panel. Behind them, the hills of Sausalito rise up, creating the perfect backdrop for their memento. I begin to snap the picture when a young girl, I would guess her to be eleven, starts to step away from the group. Only now I notice tears have streaked her face, and her lower lip is trembling. I lower the camera to motion her back in, but before I can say anything her mother wraps her arm around the young girl's shoulder. Lowering her head, she speaks softly into the girl's ear. In seconds, like a phoenix rising from the ashes, a smile and laughter fill the girl's face. Nestling into her mother's arms, she lights up for the camera, all her sadness gone with just a few words from the one she loves.

* * *

I arrive home after dinner. Since our argument, I have rarely been home, choosing to drive around for hours, taking pictures wherever I can. I have visited Dad a handful of times. Each time I enter the room, I expect to see him walking around, prepare myself for his reaction upon seeing me. But every time he still lies there, silent, and I leave, waiting until the next time.

"Sonya?" Mom calls out, though there is no one else she is expecting.

"Yes?" I drop my camera bag by the front door. Mom and I have reached an equilibrium. She does not demand to know my comings or goings or what time I will arrive home. For giving me the freedom of my own time, something I am used to, I offer her the security of my presence. They say there is a sixth sense a mother has regarding her children. If Mom has such intuition, she has never used it before. Now, however, it almost feels like she knew I was planning on leaving. Since I decided to stay, she seems happier, relieved.

"The hospital called . . ."

I flinch. Before she can say more, I whisper, my throat convulsing with the words, "Is he awake?"

"No." She is matter of fact, devoid of any emotion. "You left your cell phone in the hospital room. The nurse called me to let me know."

I glance back at my purse. It must have fallen out when I gathered my things. "Thanks. I'll pick it up tomorrow." I start to walk away, toward my room, when she stops me.

"I didn't realize you visited him," she says softly.

I hear the question but don't know how to answer. If anyone had told me I would choose to spend time with him, I would have laughed, assuring them they had no idea who I was. Now I wonder if I know who I really am. "That's why you called me home, right? For me to be with him in his final days?"

"Is that what you thought?" She seems surprised. "I asked you to come home because it had been long enough."

"Not for me it wasn't," I admit quietly, shuttering my eyes when I see her recoil. "I'm sorry."

"Then why did you come?" she asks, begging me for something she may not want to hear.

I pause, trying to find the words to explain to her why I made the decision. How do I tell her I almost didn't come home? That I had ignored the message, even gone so far as to call Linda to set up an overseas assignment. But at the last minute I decided against it and booked a flight home. "To say good-bye," I admit.

I start to leave the room when she asks me, barely a whisper, "To whom?"

I walk away without giving her an answer, leaving her to find her own.

* * *

When Linda calls me back, she does not sound happy. "I came up with three jobs. Three. None of them paying anything near what you are used to."

"It's a short-term thing Linda," I assure her. "I just need something to stay busy while I'm here."

"One is in San Francisco. The local zoo wants to do some damage control after one of their animals got loose and attacked a patron. Pictures of the pretty animals as they are being fed, bathed, etcetera. For a media campaign." Linda is not a fan of zoos, flies, bugs, or anything related. I can hear the disgust in her voice and cannot help my smile.

"Sounds tempting."

"Really?" She sighs. "The next one is in the vineyards north of you. Napa, Sonoma, etcetera. Another media campaign."

"I'm surprised the wineries don't have their own photographers."

"It's from the city councils. For a brochure to attract more tourists during the off season. Again, the pay is not so impressive." I am sure her mind is already calculating the lost commission over the next few months and does not like the numbers. "The last one is at the local hospital. Stanford. They are looking for a photographer for a therapy-type project. Working with patients—sick ones." An edge I have never heard before from her enters her voice. "When I put some feelers out through my contacts they responded immediately, but I told them you would not be interested. Last thing you need is to deal with other people's tragedies when you have your own to handle."

* * *

It is early evening. I can hear the crickets that are always chirping. The Stanford campus is still alive with students attending late classes. I wander near the library, dipping my feet into the fountain in front. Students are seated on the low concrete steps, earphones blaring with music while they study in the warm breeze.

Watching them, I envy their hopes and dreams. Their belief that anything is possible. That the future is theirs to determine, to create.

They are invincible; they are sure. I don't remember feeling like that ever. Even when I had hopes for the future, I knew my past would always walk alongside. My companion for a lifetime.

After letting the hours tick by, I finally drive back home under the guidance of the moon's light. The house is quiet; I assume Mom went to bed hours ago. Feeling restless, I down a glass of warm milk and flip through the TV channels in my room but nothing catches my interest. Lying down, I toss in my bed, uncomfortable with the familiar surroundings. My thoughts wander to the discussion between Mom and me. To all the times I've visited him as he lies dying.

Kicking the covers off, I stretch, hoping to relieve some of the discomfort from the days of doing nothing. Out of habit, I listen for footsteps, for a scream or cry. But Mom is safely encased behind her bedroom door. I think about Trisha and her request. Her need for me to stay to help her say good-bye. I used to wonder how she was doing with our parents. Imagined her catering to them while I was away. She would have done her job perfectly, as only she could.

Shaking off the malaise and the memories, I climb out of bed and switch on my computer. I surf for a few minutes, hoping to distract myself with pictures I have recently taken. When the discontentment lingers, I move on to travel sites, imagining the next place I will end up. I have been all over Europe and to most of Asia. *But never back to India*, a voice reminds me. Rejecting my culture felt like the natural next step when I left home. An announcement to no one listening that I was free of all the chains of my childhood. Having no definition of myself, I refuse to give significance to a place whose only meaning in my life is that it bred my father. That my mother and sisters were born there also holds little weight in comparison.

A tingling begins at the base of my spine. The need that arises when I have gone too long without relief. I struggle against it, hating myself before I begin. But like oxygen, it is my lifeline. My definition of love. Clicking on a few sites, I read until my eyes are weary. When finished, I return to my bed and find the release that eluded me. Soon I feel myself falling into a deep sleep, one guaranteed to be plagued with nightmares from my childhood.

TRISHA

From conception to birth takes approximately nine months. Thousands of sperm search for that one egg. The lucky sperm gets to fertilize it, and if all goes well, an embryo is created. That is just the beginning. Three months of nausea, three months of excitement, and then the final three months of expecting the unknown. Throughout pregnancy, there is both fear and anticipation. You pray for a healthy child without a real concept of what that means. Ten fingers and ten toes offer initial calmness. The first cry assures everyone the baby is alive. After the months of being solely responsible for its well-being, the mother can rest assured she did not make a misstep that took its life.

But the real job—raising them—begins after they come home from the hospital. If done correctly, maybe they grow up to become happy, healthy adults. If not, then all you have is a wish to return to those nine months of obliviousness, when everything seemed possible.

I had one Barbie and one Ken doll growing up; they were my prized possessions. It mattered little to me that she had blond hair and blue eyes, but Marin thought they looked strange. Her dolls from India, cut from wood, had brown bodies. Their hair, black from dye, was braided down their backs. I cared little for her dolls. Though they were a reflection of us, I was secure in the knowledge that mine were truly beautiful.

Every day I would comb their hair, rearrange their clothes, and settle them into their make-believe dollhouse. They were perfect with perfect lives. Every night I would oversee a wedding ceremony between Ken and Barbie, who would live happily ever after. Sonya asked me what happened after they were married. "They have babies, *bewakoof*," I said, repeating the word for stupid that my father called her. "Everyone knows that."

* * *

Eric comes home early from his meeting. I've just finished scheduling dinner with friends from the Junior League. Twice a week, I work with them on community service events. My primary job is to set up the thank-you parties for generous donors. Since Eric and I move in the same circles as many of the donors, the parties become an excuse to spend time with friends.

"An unexpected surprise." I kiss him on the cheek and take his light coat. Shaking it out, I hang it up in the hallway closet. When I turn, he is still standing in the same place. "Is everything OK?"

Taking my hand, he pulls me close. My head nestles perfectly beneath his. He rubs his hand up and down my back and over my hair. "I love you. You know how much, right?"

"You're scaring me." I step out of his arms, wrapping my own around me. "What's going on?"

Eric and I met on a blind date. It was six months after Sonya left. Working as an interior decorator, I was making a reputation for myself. With an eye for detail and a unique ability to bring my clients' imaginings to life, I became a hot commodity. Papa told everyone it was because I never grew up. I was still playing make-believe house.

We dined at a restaurant in San Francisco, overlooking the bay, and munched on bruschetta and a spinach salad. An expensive bottle of red wine was waiting at the table when we were seated. When I told Eric I didn't drink, he told the waiter he would have iced tea with me, never questioning why I detested the smell of alcohol. I assumed since Papa didn't drink I hadn't acquired the taste for it. That night, on my doorstep, Eric asked to see me again. No kiss, no hug. A decision sealed by a nod. I watched him slip back into his car and knew I had met the man I would marry.

"Adoption." Eric pulls out some printed papers, jarring me from my memories. Stapled perfectly together. "I started the process a few months back. Before everything happened with your father." He cups my cheek, his excitement evident. "I wanted to wait to tell you until I had some good news. I know how hard everything has been for you." He pulls out another sheet, showing it to me. It has the name of a woman on it. "This young woman is six months into her pregnancy. She's looking for a couple to adopt her child."

People have children for varied reasons. To make a family whole, to give meaning to their lives, or to re-create themselves, but this time do a better job. I join friends at Little League games or swim meets. Their knuckles clenched, the lines of their face set in worry, they watch for their offspring to validate their existence. But for their child to succeed, the parents have to create a foundation to stand on. To set, by example, what it means to be the best. The children watch your every move, learn how to act by your actions. If you make a misstep, you chance losing their trust forever. I often wonder which of my parents I modeled myself on and which one I trusted.

"I thought we had agreed to keep trying," I say, refusing to take the papers. I turn toward the den, the darkness beckoning me. Early on, Eric had his sperm count checked at the fertility clinic. Since it was fine, we assumed the problem was mine. Though he wanted to attend every appointment I had with the fertility specialist, I assured him it was routine checks and his time was better spent at work. If there was anything life-changing, I would share it with him. "We don't even know what the process will entail. And what about the child?" I start to ramble, my voice rising. "Do we want a boy or a girl?"

"Hey." He reaches out, grabs my shoulders. Turning me to face him, he tips my chin up with his finger. "Slow down. We don't have to have all the answers right now."

"Then why did you bring this home?" I smack the papers in his hand, wishing they would disappear like a fog over the bay in the early morning. "Did you think about discussing this with me first?"

"I thought that was what we were doing."

Eric borrowed his company's private jet to propose to me. We flew to Los Angeles, where he had reserved a table at Spago for lunch. Afterward, he took me on a boat ride into the middle of the ocean. We spent the afternoon riding waves and watching dolphins. It was a perfect day. On the plane ride back, the stars offering us their blessing, he got down on one knee and asked me to marry him. Taking both my hands in his he said, "You are the woman I've been searching for my whole life. Please be my wife and give me the world."

It's impossible to give someone the world. You can show them glimpses of yours, hope they join you in it, but to give them the world means you have to be willing to give up your own. Nonetheless, I was sure I had fooled us both. That somehow, giving myself would be enough. Now he was telling me what I always suspected. I was not enough. He needed more from me. His love was an illusion, a façade that would reveal its true nature soon enough. When my womb remained empty, he would choose between his dream and me. Destiny demanded I would lose.

"It's too soon," I say. Motioning around me at the empty house in our wake, I begin to make excuses. "We don't know how to be parents."

Memories start to filter in, crowding out the conversation.

Darkness falls. A young girl is walking down a hallway. Doors open and close, but no one sees her. Crying out, she begs them to hear her. The words stay lost in her head. There is no audio. Tears stream down her face, creating a puddle as vast as the open sea. In one last act of desperation, she slams her hands against a door, but the impact makes no sound. Falling to the ground, she understands she is alone and will always be.

"Hey," Eric wraps his arms around me, jarring me. "I'm scared too. But we'll be great parents. The best. Any child would be lucky to have you as his or her mother." He kisses my shoulder. "I would have given anything to have been adopted as a child." He assumes I understand his need, accept his decision. "I know it's not the best time, with everything going on with your father. But if we don't move on this, another couple will. This finally might be our chance."

"No," I say, facing him. Fight or flight—both options guarantee I lose. "I can't do this right now. I'm sorry."

* * *

Six in the morning. The sun has only started to peek above the horizon. Dew from the night before blankets the grass. Birds start to awake, chirping the arrival of a new day. The hospital corridor is quiet. A shift change in progress. Nurses hand charts to one another, everyone speaking in quiet tones. Visiting time isn't for another two hours, but they are used to me coming at odd times. A daughter grieving for her father.

"He had a good night," his nurse says. "Vitals were steady."

"Thank you."

I barely slept all night. Eric worked through the night while I lay awake in our bedroom. Maybe he needed distance, though I yearned for his warmth. I hear parents complain that they forget about one another standing under the same umbrella with their children. I wonder what they would say if I told them standing together, without children, can tear you apart.

Papa is asleep. That explanation is my only comfort when I visit him. I believe he is dreaming a wonderful dream, lost in the streets of his beloved India. That he is happy and safe wherever he is. After Papa fell into the coma, I researched the condition and people's experiences. Patients claim to have heard things said in their presence, felt specific people around them. That gives me hope. Papa has to know I have not abandoned him. I will wait forever for him to open his eyes and see me standing here.

I am not foolish. It may seem like that to my sisters, who hate him. They had cause to, I did not. I hated his actions toward them, hated him hurting the sisters and mother I loved. But with me he was a different person. There are a myriad of reasons why I was special. My frailty allowed him to protect me, or maybe because I look like him. A small voice whispers that he simply chose one of us to love and I was the lucky one. Perhaps parents understand their capacity, accept their limitations. They are only able to give so much of themselves to another, to love one person unconditionally. They pick a favorite and the others must fend for themselves. Whatever the reason, I was the one loved. Adored by both parents, I am indebted to them for life for making me the chosen one.

"Hi, Papa." Bending down, I kiss his forehead. After smoothing the blanket over his body, I rearrange his pillow to make him more comfortable. I scan the machines, checking his vitals. Since his admission to the hospital I have become an expert at reading them. What used to be a foreign language is now decipherable. "Did you have a good night?"

Pulling up a chair, I bring it right next to the bed. Holding his hand, I lay my head down on the bed. Exhaustion seeps into my limbs. I want to curl up and fall asleep. We played a game when I was little. The nights when sleep was elusive, he would pick me up and fly me around like an airplane. Through the living room, in and out of the bathrooms, past the den until we returned to the bedroom. While

Sonya lay in bed watching, he would fly me around our room once, twice, until the airplane was all out of fuel. "Time for the plane to land at the gate," he would say, tucking me into bed.

"Me, Daddy, me now," Sonya would yell when she was younger. He would pick her up and play the game, but I knew it wasn't the same. Her plane ride was shorter, quicker, without nearly as many turns or the same level of excitement. She must have caught on too, because after a while she stopped asking.

"Eric is pushing for a baby." The machines are the only sound in the room. "He wants to adopt a child."

Papa loved Gia. It was obvious from the way he played with her. The day of Gia's birth, he arrived at the hospital loaded up with gifts.

"I told him not now." The screeching wheel of the food-service cart as it comes down the hall announces it is breakfast time. They always pass Papa's room. No reason to bring a plate to the man who is dependent on a tube for his sustenance. "Not when you're here, fighting for your life."

The day Mama called me with the news, I was getting ready for our weekly meal. Our plan was for me to pick them up and drive together to sample a new restaurant that had received rave reviews. My cell phone began to buzz just as I was slipping my earring in. "I'm on my way, Mama," I said into the phone, not giving her a chance to speak. Grabbing my keys off the mantel, I rushed out the door, the phone still to my ear.

"He's collapsed, Trisha," she said, interrupting me. "The ambulance is taking him to the hospital."

Her words washed over me. My keys dropped. I stood frozen, paralyzed from shock. Eric came home and drove us to the hospital. We met them in the ER, but the doctors were baffled. He had fallen into a coma with no explanation as to why.

"Please wake up." I pace the tight room. It is as large as my guest bathroom. "How am I supposed to be a mother?" He stays silent. Not a muscle moves or twitches. Picking up his hand, I whisper, "What kind of parent would I be?" His hand stays limp. Left without an answer, I collapse back into the chair and sit, watching him for hours, hoping for a sign. When none comes, I leave the hospital, more confused than before.

MARIN

When an adult has been abused as a child, he or she lives life always expecting the other shoe to drop. That is because it always did. There was never a good day that did not end badly. Sadness always followed happiness, and fear always preempted confidence. A guaranteed emotional roller coaster when you are not the one in control. For Marin, Brent's emotional state always took precedence over hers. Her state of being was dependent on his.

Only three times in Marin's life had she fallen to her knees and asked the heavens for help. The first time, calling on all the deities that Ranee prayed to religiously, Marin had begged not to leave India. No matter how excited her parents were about the new world, she had no desire to leave the one she knew. Her friends, the extended family, were everything familiar. As they packed their entire household, Ranee regaled Marin with stories that she had heard about America. Roads without cows walking alongside. Schools in buildings instead of outside, seated in the dirt. "Everyone owns a car," Ranee had said, laughing excitedly at the thought. Clean air, doctors that don't have to be bribed for care, and most important, Ranee said, kneeling down to face Marin eye to eye, women have all the rights in the world. No matter what Ranee said, Marin knew deep inside herself she did not want to go. But her first prayer went unanswered, and they boarded the plane for the new world, her hand securely in Ranee's, while Brent carried Trisha across the tarmac.

The second time was silently in her room when she was sixteen. It had been a particularly bad beating, and Marin could not take any more. One more incident and she was sure she would die. In fact, she had begun to prefer the idea of death over continuing to live under his roof. Given a choice between her demise and her father's, though, she chose his. Falling to her knees in front of the pictures she kept in her room of Lord Shiva and Ganesha standing next to the Goddess Parvati, she begged for her father to be taken that night. For him to fall asleep and never wake up. She was so sure her prayers had been answered that she stayed awake all night waiting for the morning, when Ranee would announce the good news. Marin imagined the life they would live without him. The freedom she could barely remember from her time in India.

When morning came, Marin waited, clutching her blanket as her heart rate accelerated with excitement. When she heard her parents' bedroom door open, she started shaking with happiness. As her door-knob started turning, she jumped out of bed, ready for the news. Her mother popped her head in, the wariness that had become a permanent mask still there. She asked quietly for Marin to get up and get ready for the day. She said to please hurry; they did not want to make their father angry.

The third and final time Marin turned to God was after she went into labor. Having read all the books and consulted with a number of ob-gyns, she was confident she was prepared for any circumstance that could arise—a breech, uterine rupture, macrosomia. What she was not prepared for was her inability to nurse her crying newborn. Marin tried everything. With the help of the nurses, she was able to get Gia to latch on to her breast and suckle, but no milk came. When it finally did start to flow, it was only a trickle. Not nearly enough to feed her newborn baby.

The first night after Gia's birth, Marin kept her baby with her even when the nurses insisted she would be better off in the nursery. Staying awake, she watched for the first sign of Gia being hungry. Immediately opening her gown, she offered both breasts. Neither filled with milk. Angry, Gia turned to instinct and began to chew the nipple. Marin silenced her cries of pain and watched helplessly as her daughter stayed hungry. After a full day of no milk, the pediatrician gently recommended they supplement with formula. Feeling like a failure, Marin begged anyone who was listening for her body to produce sustenance for her daughter. Her final prayer went unheeded, and within weeks Gia was on formula full time. Back at work, things went as Marin commanded.

* * *

Twenty-four hours have passed since Marin's meeting with the principal. She has taken the day off from work, called in sick for the first time in her history with the company. She does not tell Raj the real reason, nor has she spoken with Gia about the situation. She is afraid to say anything. In truth, she has no idea how to take the next step. Nothing in her life had prepared her for this moment. The one where you ask your child who beat her. She considered confiding in Raj, telling him what she had learned, but the decision seemed to make itself. Raj left for an unexpected meeting in Los Angeles that morning. His return date wasn't set. Which left Marin and Gia alone, together, with no suitable time to broach the subject.

The clock on the mantel strikes nine p.m. Over the years, Marin became deaf to the sound, but now she seems to hear every second passing. As if time is counting down and she has little left of it. What used to matter to her now seems irrelevant. Her stately mansion with a pristine yard and columns that wrap around the deck. The deadlines, the stock prices, her investment portfolio. The definition of her success feels absent, having lost its urgency.

The house is dark. Gia is at another study session for a science exam. Marin knows she will get an A on the test. She cannot pinpoint when her expectation of good grades became Gia's. When Gia accepted that her grades validated her. An A versus a B—one step on the spectrum and yet miles apart in meaning. Exceptional versus satisfactory. Standards set by society that first Marin and now Gia bows to. Marin could not fathom her daughter bringing home anything less than perfection—her name on every honor roll means Gia has flown over the bar and landed on her feet.

The front door opens and closes, signaling Gia's arrival home. Marin hears the drop of the backpack in the foyer, the jingling of keys as they are pulled out of the lock. The crack beneath her door reveals that light is flooding the house. Following a habit from childhood, Gia hits every switch as she makes her way through the house. Marin waits for her name to be called, but she is not summoned. She is not the first one her child seeks out. Gia has no desire to share her day, to reminisce about happenings at school. For a second Marin wonders what Gia would say if she did ask. *The day was wonderful, but somewhere along the way I was beaten, and I don't know why.*

Gia is in the kitchen, rummaging for food. Marin can hear the sound of her munching on an apple as she takes the steps up to her room. Taking a deep breath, Marin clasps her hands together in prayer for the fourth time in her life. She doesn't fall to her knees or lower herself to the ground to show the gods she is beneath them. They say with humility comes supremacy, but Marin has no interest. Today, she will stand side by side with whoever demands a place next to her. She will not ask, but instead command the right steps toward the path she needs to be on. She has learned the hard way that a request can be denied. For all the unanswered prayers of her past, today she will rely on herself, not leaving anything to chance.

"Gia," Marin opens her office door and calls out. Her office is dark. The sun set hours ago and the moon rose, but Marin had not moved from her place on the sofa. Now that she has she can feel the stiffness set in. She wonders if it is what rigor mortis feels like. A body with a mind of its own. Having lost any reason to live, it becomes immobile. Like her father. "I need to see you."

"Yeah?" Gia, still in her school clothes, makes her way down the stairs. "What's going on?"

"Come in, please. We need to talk." Marin switches on the table lamp. With the room full of light, she watches as Gia takes a seat on the sofa Marin just vacated. "How was school?"

"Great. But I have a test, so I should probably study."

"I thought that's what you were doing?" Marin asks.

"Are you OK? You look different." Marin realizes that Gia has registered how her hair is tangled and that she is wearing the same jeans and T-shirt she had on last night.

"I'm fine," Marin lies. She is not fine. She is scared and unsure, but mostly angry. Furious at whoever did this to her daughter. She must tread carefully. If she alienates Gia, she chances losing more than she bargained for. "How was school?"

Gia lets out a small laugh, filled with incredulity. Stealing a glance at the watch on her wrist, she mutters, "Great, Mom, as always. But seriously, I have to study." She stands to leave and makes it to the door before Marin stops her.

"Sit down. I'm not done talking to you." It is harsher than she wanted, but having never been on this ride before, she is unsure where to hold on to assure their safety. "I will tell you when we are done."

"Wow." Gia rolls her eyes and retakes her seat. "OK. Is Dad home?"

Her savior, Marin realizes. The one who will protect Gia from Marin. "He left for a meeting this morning, remember?"

"Right." Gia does not look happy. "I totally forgot." She starts to tap her foot before something occurs to her. "Is this about *Dada?*" She uses the traditional name for grandfather. Brent insisted it was Gia's first word.

Gia melts into the sofa, concern covering her. Seeing her, Marin suddenly remembers the little girl she was. She would cry when she scraped her knee and demanded ice for every injury, no matter how small the bruise. Marin lowers her voice, yearning to reach out but unable to do so. "Are you all right?"

"Yes, of course I am." Gia's visible anger dissipates at Marin's softening. "Mom, please talk to me." Gia's lower lip starts to tremble. The unknown frightens her more. "Has Dada taken a turn for the worse?"

"You love him." Marin knows her daughter loves her grandfather. Gia has never experienced his violence, never even witnessed it. Since her birth, Brent would spend hours playing with her. After her delivery, he stood staring into the hospital nursery window at his only grandchild. When Gia came home, he would tickle her feet, calling everyone to watch how she laughed in response. He never came over without a toy in hand. Marin would watch them, wondering how different life would be if that was the man she had known growing up.

"He's my grandfather." Gia fiddles with the pleats on her skirt. She has no idea about the history between Marin and Brent. "I don't want to lose him."

Brent was the only grandfather Gia knew. Raj's parents still lived in India. When he came to the States to study at university, his family stayed behind, hoping their son would return home. When he married instead, they visited yearly. For a while, they considered moving and living with the family, but their advanced age made that impossible.

"Is he all right?" Gia repeats.

"The same," Marin answers. Done with the delays, she says, "Your principal called me into her office yesterday."

"What about?" Gia seems furious. "My grades are fine."

"I know they are." Marin chooses her words carefully. Her greatest strength, forging her way to the end zone and winning the game, now has no value. "This is about you." Marin checks to see that the door is shut. If the housekeeper is nearby, Marin doesn't want her overhearing. "Take off your shirt."

"What?" The shock on her face tells Marin it is the last thing Gia expected. Her mistrust is palpable. "No way!"

"Now!" Marin snaps, furious to see the chariness in her daughter's eyes. A distrust Marin never earned accompanies it. In the silence that follows, Marin tallies each of their breaths. The showdown continues, leading them toward an end neither of them can predict. But Marin is tired of waiting, of wondering.

"Are you searching me?" Gia takes a step toward the closed door, her only escape. "What, you think I have drugs on me or something?"

Marin wishes it were drugs, rather than her daughter beaten. It was possible the principal was wrong. Surely the PE instructor exaggerated what she saw. Most likely she misidentified the student. Because a child of Marin's could never be hurt that way. Marin has done everything to guarantee the abuse is behind her, not in front. It is the reason she has kept it a secret. Hiding it deep in the closet, without exposure, keeps everyone safe. Gia is meant to reach for the stars, not fall beneath them.

"Please don't argue with me," Marin says.

"I'm not arguing," Gia replies. "I'm just not taking off my clothes," she says with resolve. She reveals a confidence born of having been rewarded with all the best in life. No matter that it was Marin and Raj who provided her with the material comforts she has become used to. The sculpture has been created, and now the sculptor has to face her creation. "You can't tell me what to do."

"Yes, I can." Any hope of compassion dissipates. They stand facing each other. Mother against daughter. A reflection of each other, yet a world of doubt separating them. Resentment and annoyance creep in. "Now, Gia."

"No." Gia reaches for the doorknob, ready to flee. "You won't tell me what's going on, and now you want me to strip? Forget it."

She wrenches the door open, but Marin slams it shut. A battle of wills and anger begins. Marin starts to unbutton Gia's blouse herself. Gia, too shocked at first to stop her, allows one button to get undone before she pushes her mother's hands away.

"Don't touch me," Gia yells.

The skin bared so far is untouched. Relief mingles with fury at Gia for fighting her. Marin grabs her by the shoulder to hold her still while attempting to unbutton more. Desperate for this to be over so she can return to work, so she can make up for the hours of production lost. Just as she undoes another button, Gia pushes her, hard. Staggering back, Marin barely keeps from falling.

Marin will relive the next moment hundreds of times in her head. Rethink each step and imagine it differently. Wonder which options would have been wiser, smarter. Wish that it had occurred to her to stop and think before destroying the only thing that really mattered to her—Gia's love. But hindsight is a vicious thing. It mocks you with what should have been done. Teases with how things could still be. When left with ashes, you wonder how you could have prevented the fire. But introspection is not Marin's friend. Instead, blind fury propels her. With one hand holding Gia in place, she pulls back her other, slapping her daughter with all she has.

The silence that follows drowns out Marin's regret. Her arms fall to her sides, too weak to hold up. Before she can utter an apology, Gia begins to unbutton her blouse. One at a time, while holding fast to Marin's gaze. She clearly accepts that she can't fight Marin any longer, yet her eyes fill with defiance. A need to take back control. Slowly, she spreads apart the lapels of the starched white shirt, the last barrier of innocence against the horror.

"Is this what you wanted to see?" Gia demands, allowing the shirt to fall down her arms. Bruises, some black and blue, others green, decorate her body. Two on her abdomen, framing her belly button. Gia loved playing peekaboo with her belly button as a toddler. Raj had found a flap book that showed different babies showing their belly buttons. It became Gia's favorite game for weeks. Her shirt up and then down, laughing in fits when her belly button was exposed.

Two more bruises on Gia's back. From her own experience, Marin determines that the ones on the back are older. As a teenager, Marin would wonder what her maximum number would be at one time. Just as the old ones would fade, new ones were created to replace them. Ten was the max. The magic number. Four is apparently Gia's.

"Who did this to you?" Marin longs to reach out, to enfold Gia in the security of her arms. But when your mother never offered you comfort, you are unsure how to give it to your daughter. "Who hit you?"

"You just did." Gia pulls on her shirt and buttons it, hiding the bruises. Finished, she palms the cheek Marin slapped. "Seconds ago."

"Gia." Marin is adrift with no compass to steer her. She graduated high school at sixteen and college at nineteen. When she was hired in finance at the age of twenty, she swore she would never be lost again. She believed herself free, capable of being her own beacon. "I'm sorry."

It is the first time Marin has ever apologized to her daughter. Whether it is for the bruises that mark Gia's body or for the slap, neither can say for sure. Regardless, it shocks Gia. Her eyes fill with tears. She wipes them away quickly. Tucking her shirt back into her skirt, she meets Marin's gaze. "I should get to my schoolwork."

"Not yet. Please." Marin reaches for her daughter's hand, but Gia pulls away. Accepting the gulf she has created, Marin asks her to join her on the sofa. When Gia refuses yet again, Marin pleads, "Were you in some kind of a fight?"

"No."

"Was it . . ." She pauses, struggling to say the name aloud. A desperate reach for all the imaginable ways the bruises might have come about. Raj? The possibility occurs to her only in the darkness that has descended. It would seem impossible on its face. He was the loving father, the gentle giant incapable of hurting his beloved Gia. But the world saw Brent differently too. No one would have ever guessed what he was capable of. The monster he became when no one was watching. "Did your dad do this?"

"No!" Gia finally drops onto the sofa. Her eyes wide, she pleads silently with her mother to believe her. "Never. It's not possible."

No, Marin knows, it is not possible for Raj to do such a thing. But she just did, she realizes. Gia couldn't say the same about her. Not anymore.

Tapping her feet, Gia is clearly anxious to be anywhere else. "I have to go."

Her patience worn thin, Marin snaps, "We're not going to do this anymore." She will not play twenty questions with her daughter. Not when Gia knows the answer but refuses to tell. "Tell me now."

"This is my life." The sofa no longer a refuge, Gia stands, walking toward Marin's desk. She picks up a picture of herself when she was five. She had won her first trophy by coming in third at a swim competition. Her parents, bursting with pride, had taken an entire roll worth of film.

Marin takes the picture from Gia's hand, glances at it. The picture epitomized what Gia's life was supposed to be—success at every turn. "Gia."

"There's nothing to tell." Without another word she walks out, leaving Marin to stare into the empty space.

SONYA

I drive around town, going everywhere but here. Yet, without meaning to, I arrive at the same place. Usually I sit in the parking lot of the hospital, staring at the building that houses my father. Sometimes, when I can't help it, like today, I go in. I fight the instinct to see him. Part of me refuses to believe that he's sick, unable to move or speak. My visits assure me he is still paralyzed, unable to attack. It's jarring to see, to accept. His power was all encompassing, his hold over us complete. If someone had told me that this would be the way we concluded our story, I would have laughed. Said it was impossible. I was destined to always be at the end of a never-ending line for happiness, and he . . . well he was the one who demanded I stand there.

"Why?" I ask him for the first time in my life. It never occurred to me to ask as a child. I accepted his violence like other children accept love—as an assumed part of their lives. Only when I left for Stanford did I consider not everyone was raised as we were. It seems almost naive to me now, but when beatings are a normal part of your upbringing, you don't question them. It may have been too much for my psyche to acknowledge before eighteen that I had been put on the path of abuse while others were given the hand of love. That's still true now. I fear what would happen if he opens his eyes. If he regains the ability to hurt me when I am already ruined. "Why did you take so much away that wasn't yours?"

"Good to see you again."

I have missed David's arrival. Suddenly self-conscious, I scoot back, allowing him room to do his checkup. I scan his face to see if he overheard me, but he gives no indication he has. "Do you need me to leave?"

"You're fine." David uses his stethoscope to listen to my father's heart. I watch him silently, wondering about the results. He checks his pulse, watching the monitors for any sign. Making some notes on his chart, he glances at me. "He's the same."

"Still no idea what could have caused this?" I want a reason. I need to know that he is not going unpunished for everything he did. I want to hear that he is suffering, that as his body began to fail him, my father felt the same fear and agony that we did every day of our lives.

"We'll continue to run tests, but right now all we can point to is the diabetes. His insulin levels had dropped dangerously low."

"Is that normal?" I ask.

"He was fairly healthy for his age. No smoking or drinking." He scans the chart again. "Said he walked for exercise." He looks up at me, an apology in his gaze. "The longer he stays in the coma, the fewer answers we have."

He starts to leave, to tend to other patients that need him. I glance down at my father, suddenly not wanting to be left alone with him. Having kept to myself for so many years, I find I am yearning for conversation. "Were you his regular doctor?" I ask before I can censor myself.

"No." He looks puzzled that I wouldn't know that. "I'm an attending. His regular physician is an internist. We're staying in touch about his condition."

"That's good." I feel new to polite conversation. I have never been good at it. I read somewhere that abused children often have social anxiety as adults. Whatever the terminology may be—all I know is that I feel safer away from people than with. "Thanks."

He starts to leave again but seems to reconsider his actions. Stopping, he watches me. "Your mom mentioned your dad's condition would bring you home from your travels. She asked if he would be better by the time you arrived. I'm sorry we weren't able to make that happen."

"She said I would come home?" I stop him, stand in his way. I am shocked she would say anything about me. "When?"

"A few days after his admission." He glances at me, trying to understand my reaction. "I hope I didn't speak out of turn."

"No." I step back, out of his way. "I'm just surprised." I cross my arms around myself, hoping to ward off the chill that is in the air. "What else did she say?" It feels odd to ask a stranger for insight into my mother's thoughts.

"Mentioned you traveled all over the world," he says gently. "She was clearly very proud."

He misunderstood. Mom has always hated my travel. My travel meant that I was lost to her. That she had one less daughter to mother, and for her, the role was all she had left in a life that ceased to make sense the first day my father hit her. "Not as much as you would think. It's for work."

"Photography?"

"Yes." I think about all the places I've been, but more than that, all the places I have never been. "For pictures."

"Where have you traveled?"

I can't tell if he's asking to be courteous or if he's genuinely interested. "I know you're busy. I didn't mean to keep you."

"No worries." He glances at his watch. "I'm actually ahead of schedule today. Shocking, just so you know. I make a habit of being late." He smiles and I can't help but return it.

"Europe, Asia, all over the US," I say it without pride or thought. My travels mean little to me. The places blend together, faces of people I have met lost in a sea of those I have left behind. Where I am matters little, only that I am no longer where I was. I haven't decided where I will go next. Not back to New York, where I received the call about Dad. Find somewhere that had no memories to haunt. "What about you?" I ask, trying to be polite. "Do you travel often?"

"Not as much as I used to. I have to be here, for my patients." Though he stands still, his eyes wander, taking on a faraway look. "I used to write for *Let's Go*. That was the last time I traveled like I would want to."

"You went to Harvard?" I had used *Let's Go* guidebooks dozens of times when I arrived at new destinations. Written by Harvard students, they became my go-to for how to travel on a budget. "For undergraduate or medical?"

"Both." He motions around him. "But California is home. The Bay Area's pull proved too strong to resist when it came time to decide my residency. What about you?"

"Stanford." Speaking of mundane things such as travel and life is a novelty I cannot take for granted. When you leave as many places as I have, you have little in common with those who remain. "You went to high school here?" I imagine we are near the same age.

"The Monroe School. Down the road actually."

The school tells me a lot about him. A man born into success, offered the very best from a young age. The parents of the children who attend often talk about their private jets and front-row seats at world events. That he mentions it without boast or pride says what kind of man he is.

"What about you?" he asks.

"Gunn High School." Consistently ranked as one of the top high schools in the country, the campus often felt like a natural precursor to Stanford. "In Palo Alto."

"Great school. I have a lot of friends who graduated from there."

We don't compare names of those we knew. It is useless to do so. I lived in my own world in high school, cut off from the community because I had to be. I could never bring friends home. My father's behavior was too unpredictable to trust. If anyone witnessed his loss of temper, the reputation I had carefully cultivated would have been tarnished. He was always on his best behavior with the Indian community and his coworkers. He relished his image as a powerful man, benevolent to his children, doing everything for them. Our school friends were of no significance to him, so he cared little if he was cruel or demeaning in front of them.

"Then on to Stanford." He is clearly impressed. "What hall did you live in?"

Excited about the full experience of college, most Stanford students choose to live on campus, and those who do pick one of ten dormitory houses. After the first year, a student decides to continue living in the same hall or to move on to an upper-class residence. Your hall is a critical part of your experience as a freshman. One that I almost missed out on. "Roble Hall. I moved in a few months late," I admit before I remember to censor myself. "Dad wouldn't allow me to live on campus before then."

"Why?" David fails to hide his shock.

Unwilling to give up control over me, Dad refused to allow me to move into my assigned room. "I don't know," I lie, not able to explain. I had begged my father to allow me to live in a hall, but he repeatedly refused me. Finally, I went to the dean of the school and explained my situation. A firm letter was sent to my house stating that unless I abided by the rules of the school, my admission would be reviewed. Unwilling to chance such a humiliation in front of his friends, he relented.

"Maybe he wasn't ready to let his little girl go." Grabbing his wallet from his back pocket, he opens it to reveal a photo of a young girl, maybe six years old. "As the father of one, I can imagine how hard it would be."

"She's beautiful."

"I give my ex-wife credit for that." He holds my gaze. "And you? Do you have any children?"

"No. I've never been married." His question reminds me who I am. Who I will always be. "Not even a boyfriend."

He tries to mask his disbelief, does not ask why. Likely the best conclusion he can come to is that my travels are to blame. I am a mistress to my photography. My viable excuse to every man who gets too close, who demands more. The darkness that is my companion leaves little room for the light of love.

"How old is she?" I ask, changing the subject.

He lights up. It was my childhood envy—watching fathers love their daughters.

"Five." He fiddles with the stethoscope around his neck. "Her name is Alexis. My ex and I have joint custody."

"You're very lucky." The words aren't perfunctory. The picture showed a beautiful girl with a smile that warms the heart. Children are my favorite to photograph. There is a beauty in childhood innocence.

"Where are you traveling to next?" he asks, tucking the wallet back into his pocket.

"I haven't decided." At his confusion, I attempt to explain, "I pick a place I've never been, and hope I find what I'm looking for."

"Which is?"

Not answering his question immediately, I attempt to explain. "Two years ago, I spent time at a monastery in China. Lived with the monks, watched their daily life. Every day they woke at the same time, ate the same meal." There was an odd comfort in the repetition. "Sitting side by side, they would meditate for hours." Their faces held a contentment I rarely saw again. "But they were completely removed from the world."

"Solitude?" He guesses, seeming surprised at the thought.

"They seemed happy," I say, a note of defense in my voice. The square footage of the room starts to shrink. I have revealed too much, making myself vulnerable. I consider walking into the bathroom to my right and locking the door. A viselike grip encircles my throat. My father's body lies still under the pristine white sheet. I had forgotten about him, but like a dark shadow he looms above me, always there, always watching. "I should let you get back to your patients." Not waiting for him to leave, I do, knowing I will be back, because I have no choice.

* * *

I meet Trisha at a secluded park in the hills of Saratoga. It was a narrow drive on a one-lane road that circled the mountain before climbing toward the peak. There, overlooking the town and its neighbors, we find a patch of grass and settle in. Because it is the middle of the day, there are only a few hikers and some ambitious mothers with their toddlers in tow. Otherwise, we have the area to ourselves.

Welcoming the shade from a large tree, I lean against the trunk watching as Trisha unpacks a light lunch, laying it out on the plaid tablecloth as if we are readying to eat a five-course meal.

Hiding my smile, I compliment her on the spread and take a bite out of some still-warm French bread. "This is delicious," I admit. She sets out a bowl of fruit and a container filled with what looks like crushed olives. "Is this an olive spread?" I ask, reaching for a butter knife.

"Tapenade," Trisha corrects before realizing how she sounds. Giving me a sheepish grin, she says, "Sorry."

"Tapenade it is," I say, assuring her no harm done. Taking another bite, I savor the olives mixed with peppers and garlic. "Thanks for this lunch. I was expecting Danish and coffee."

"You remember?" Trisha asks, surprised. When Trisha was fourteen, she watched *Breakfast at Tiffany's* for the first time. Deciding Audrey Hepburn was her idol, she insisted on eating Danishes and drinking decaf coffee for a full year.

"I can still taste it. You made me eat that stuff with you," I say, shuddering. "To this day I cringe at the sight of a Danish."

"Sorry," she says, though I have the feeling she doesn't mean it. We eat in silence, listening to the leaves rustling in the breeze. When we were young, it was rare for us to be in each other's company without talking. To do so now makes me realize that we have both grown up but still find comfort in spending time together. "What was your favorite place to live?" Trisha asks quietly, surprising me. The few times we spoke over the years she never asked me where I was.

"Seychelles," I answer without hesitation. "A small island in the Indian Ocean. Has a population of about ninety thousand." I remember sleeping in a tent on the beach, waking every morning to the sounds of the ocean crashing against the shore.

"Were you lonely?" she asks, looking horrified.

I want to explain to her that loneliness isn't remedied by people around me, that my loneliness is an integral part of me. But by admitting that to her, I would be welcoming questions I don't have answers to. "Yes, I was."

"I can imagine." Taking some grapes from the bowl, she munches on them. She offers me some, and I take a handful. After setting the bowl back down, she stares into the forest. "There's a mother looking for parents for her newborn," she shares. "Eric wants to adopt the child," she murmurs.

"That's wonderful news?" I ask, assuming it would be.

"Maybe," she says softly, but her face says otherwise. As I start to prod her for more, to ask why she doesn't have children when that was all she ever wanted, she points behind me to a bird walking nearby. We both watch as it comes closer to us. "I think it is hurt," Trisha exclaims. Jumping up, she walks slowly toward it, bending to scoop it up in her palm. "It's the wing."

On closer look, we see a small cut on the side of the wing. I spent over three months on an African safari for endangered animals doing a photo shoot for *National Geographic*. There I learned that an injured wing will heal in time, but the bird's greatest threat was the danger in the wild in the meantime. "It needs food," I say, starting to crumble the bread.

"Let's build it a nest," Trisha decides. Cradling the bird in one palm, she frantically starts to gather materials for a makeshift nest. I watch her curiously before she motions me to help. "Come on!"

For the next fifteen minutes we put together twigs, leaves, and grass and build the best nest we can. In between laughing, we argue about how to make the nest into the most luxurious bedding possible. Finally satisfied, we situate the new home in a circle of trees, protected from any prying eyes. After filling the nest with food, Trisha gently lays the bird down, but not before it gives Trisha a few hard pecks in gratitude. Rubbing her broken skin, she asks me, "You think it'll work?"

"Yes," I say with a surety I suddenly feel. "She's going to be fine."

"It's a she?" Trisha teases me.

"He's going to be fine." When she gives me a look, I throw up my hands in mock surrender. "It's going to be fine."

Laughing, Trisha and I watch the bird settle in. As we start to walk away, she nudges me with her shoulder. "We should do this again."

"Definitely," I say, already looking forward to it.

TRISHA

In India, a woman's marriage means she is moving from one man's house to another's. Both men chosen for her, one by an act of God, and the other by the father. As dictated by Indians' belief system, the men, the father and the husband, were two sides of the same coin. Both owned you and could do with you what they wished. But what happens when the woman wants her freedom?

Twice as a child, Sonya called an ambulance to our house. The first time, playing hooky from school, she waited for Mama to get up. When Mama stayed in bed, Sonya, eight years old, climbed in with her. Finding her unresponsive, she called 911. After running a number of tests, the doctors concluded Mama had simply blacked out. No one thought to mention the hit to the head the night before.

The second time was when Mama started vomiting and didn't stop. Sonya, eleven, had again feigned illness and stayed home from school. The ambulance sped Sonya and Mama to the nearest hospital. The doctors made Sonya wait in the reception area with an angel helper who gave her crayons and paper, assuming coloring would alleviate her gut-wrenching fear.

Inside, unbeknownst to Sonya, they were pumping our mother's stomach. She had swallowed a full bottle of sleeping pills that morning. Afterward, when the social worker asked her why, she replied, "I was tired." That was the last time Sonya stayed home from school. Connecting the dots, she decided it was safer for her to be away from home, where at least there were no lives she had to save.

* * *

The lights are off in the house when I arrive home. Eloise will have already cleaned up, leaving me a plate of food in the oven. I have started spending more time at the hospital, with Papa. After my visit today, I drove for hours.

"You're home." Surprised, I see Eric standing in the dark, his eyes unreadable. "Where were you?"

"You're home," I say. When he stays silent, waiting for an answer, I tell him, "I was driving around." I search for the light switch. Once I find it, I hit it, but the light only flickers, casting us in an eerie glow.

"It's not working," Eric says, coming closer. His voice is hard. "Driving around for six hours?"

"Of course not."

I am not afraid of my husband. I know women who are. After giving up work, they may decide that the breadwinner makes the decisions in the home, their autonomy lost in favor of security. Others simply give up the ordinary fight. Believe themselves safer that way than fighting battles they might lose. Friends tell me I am lucky. They say I married an extraordinary man, one who gives me the lifestyle others dream of while allowing me complete control. He cedes to my every wish, my every want. In return, I offer him myself.

"Then where were you?" he demands, his words like ice.

"I was with my father." Reaching a table lamp, I hit the switch, flooding the room with light. Eric's hair is disheveled, his tie undone.

He's wary, a hawk circling the field. Closing the distance between us, I reach out but he steps back. "Eric, what's going on?"

"How is he?"

"The same." My footing, already unsteady, is shakier with Eric's demeanor. "He just lies there," I tell Eric. "No matter what I say to him, he doesn't answer."

"That must be hard." Eric watches me, his stance unflinching. "To be in the dark." From the end table, he grabs a sheaf of papers. He tries to hand them to me but I refuse. "The adoption forms. I filled them out."

He flips through the pages until he reaches the last one. "Everything is set. It just needs your signature here and here"—he points to two flagged spaces—"and I'll get my attorney to start the process."

A process. In India, children are born for many reasons. In the villages, it is for labor. Boys outweigh girls in importance. Boys are able to help in the family's business, whether it is farming or shop keeping. No one judges the family when the boys begin working at a young age. Girls, however, present a liability. Dowries must be saved for each daughter born. A payment to the boy's family for accepting their daughter in marriage.

"A child is not a process." Sweat starts to trickle down my spine. "Not a decision to be made lightly." Images of my father holding me beckon. His love unconditional, constant. "We have to discuss this, think about it."

"I agree." He throws the papers down on the table. A deep swallow. A sheen of wetness covers his eyes. "I thought that's what we had been doing. All these years, when we talked about having a baby. Decorating the nursery. Believing you when you told me the fertility specialist said it would happen."

"It will. There's just a lot of stress right now." Something is wrong. I rack my brain for the answer, search for the words he wants to hear.

"With my father, Sonya coming home." I reach for him but he steps back. "I just need time."

"Is that why you're on birth control?" From the table drawer, where the adoption papers are, he pulls out a sheet of paper. My heart starts to race. I scan it quickly when he hands it to me. A letter from my doctor. I am past the date to replace my IUD. The coil I had inserted years ago to prevent a pregnancy. Since the day I vowed to love and honor Eric till death do us part. "For time?"

Some moments in your life you wish never happened; you would do anything to take them back. They make you realize you are not all-powerful. That there is a force stronger than you at work. In those moments, you fall to your knees and abdicate all sense of power. Offer your hand and ask for help. If you are lucky, you will feel the touch of something or someone to help you rise. If not, you stay kneeling, left all alone.

"When did you get this?" he asks. There is no use denying the facts. With all the stress of the last few weeks, the appointment slipped my mind. I have always kept it before, never missed a date. Being diligent, I was sure he would never learn my secret.

I start to count. One, two. In my head I race, wanting to reach eight. My lucky number. It has been years since the need has arisen. I had almost forgotten about my escape. One where reality shifts until returning to one I can live with. Where I am happy and safe.

"You lied to me." He waits for an answer. Offers me the courtesy of a chance to explain my betrayal. "You made a fool of me."

"No." His pain crowds the room, inching over me until I can't breathe. He's told me the stories—growing up alone in an orphanage, yearning for a family to love. I knew his pain but dismissed it without reason. Now, he's demanding to know why. Words race through my head as I search for the exact ones that will end this nightmare. But even as I dismiss one excuse after another, I know there is no justification that he will accept. "It was not about you." Three.

"Then who?"

He stares at me as though we have just met. I am desperate to remind him I am the woman he married, the one he loved above all else. We wrote our own vows. He told everyone who came to bear witness that I was the most important person in his life. That I was his dream come true.

"Being a mother, I don't know, it just . . ." I went to my doctor a month before our wedding to get the IUD implanted. It guaranteed I would never bear a child, though all the while Eric yearned desperately for one. "My family," I try again, the only explanation I have. Four.

"When I met you, I thought your commitment to your parents was commendable. Daddy's little girl, always will be." He laughs at himself, at both of us. "I was fine with it. Believed it proof how much you valued family."

"I do." But what is the value of a family when it is a kaleidoscope of broken glass? Each turn, each twist, is just another view of shattered pieces thrown together. When raised with the belief that you are perfect within an imperfect world, you fear one day you too will fall from grace. "You know what they mean to me."

"Yet, you don't want one of your own," he accuses.

He's waiting for an answer. A reason why I would have lied to him. I imagine telling him about my family—the facts that he has no idea about. I have given him a fantasy to believe in, a reality based on a story I have created. If I told him my father, the man I love with all my heart, beat my sisters and Mama, then it would alter his view of me. Because what does it say about me to love a man like that?

"No," I start and then stop. How do I explain that in the maze of my existence, if I turned even slightly one way or the other, if I became someone other than who I was, then I too chanced being pierced? In telling Eric, I would have to pull aside the curtain and reveal all the ugliness that makes up my existence. Then he would have to ask the question, the one I refuse to answer—did Papa love me because I'm a reflection of him? "I don't want children," I admit quietly.

He blinks away the heartbreak shining through his eyes. A wall comes down, his love lost with my refusal to reveal the truth. "I deserved to know that. I could have lived with that." His head drops in defeat. "I can't live with you lying to me. I deserved better. I gave you better."

Six. Seven.

"What are you saying?"

Eight.

"I'm saying I want a separation."

MARIN

Every nine seconds, a woman is assaulted or beaten in the United States. Marin can repeat the statistic from memory. Since her discovery of the bruises on Gia's body, she has researched all the facts. One in ten girls admits to having experienced physical violence in her dating relationship, a one-year study found. The majority of teen abuse occurs in the home.

Since their conversation, Gia and Marin have avoided one another, Marin vacillating between shock and outrage. A perfect life mapped out is fallen to shambles. When Raj returned, Gia stared at Marin silently, wondering whether she would reveal her secret. For Marin, a lifetime of keeping them made the decision easy. She acted as if nothing was wrong. So, they continued, Gia and Marin acting out their fairy-tale life while Raj remained oblivious.

Marin tried twice more to approach Gia, demanding to know how the bruises came to be. Both times Gia shook her head no. Told Marin it didn't matter. "I'm fine, Mom." But she was not fine, and Marin was at a loss about how to make it better. But as if she were a child, the decision was made for Marin.

Two days after their confrontation, Gia is preparing to leave for school. As she reaches up to grab the cereal box from the cupboard, her shirt sleeve falls back, revealing a fresh bruise on her arm.

"What is this?" Marin breathes, but she already knows. The grip of a hand around the forearm, tight enough to hold the person in place for a hit across the face, or one in the stomach.

"Nothing, Mom." Gia quickly covers it with her sleeve. Leaving the cereal, she starts to move out of the kitchen when Marin stands in front of her.

"If I peel your shirt back, there'll be a fresh one on your torso, right?" Marin knew it was the way it worked. Before the old bruises could fully disappear, a new one would emerge. Almost as if the abuser needed to see his or her artwork on display. To mark the beaten as owned, possessed, for anyone foolish enough to intervene.

"No," Gia says urgently, dropping her voice. "Why would you say such a thing?"

Because I've been there, Marin almost says, but as always, she holds back, keeps the truth hidden. Brent was brilliant—his bruises were a secret well kept. And Marin, like Sonya and Ranee, became his accomplice, ensuring no one ever saw.

"Gia," Marin starts, but it is too late. With a wave, Gia goes through the front door, a smile plastered on her face as if it were sewn on. Shutting the door, Marin sinks against it, her breath coming in gasps.

"Gia left for school?" Raj comes down the stairs, his chai steaming. At the sight of Marin on the floor, he rushes toward her, dropping the cup along the way. The spiced chai seeps across the marble floor toward the carpet. Marin watches it in slow motion, wondering absently how they will remove the stain. Reaching for her, he demands, "Marin, what's happened?"

She stares at him, her husband, but a complete stranger. She has never told him about her past, her childhood. There was no reason to.

It was over, she was sure. What purpose was served in telling him? She would not live in the past when she could control the future.

Her husband is not her confidant. She has never told him about her stresses at work or career concerns. They never share dreams, or intertwine their lives. Gia is the string that binds them together, and with their child broken, they have nothing to hold on to.

"Gia has bruises on her body," Marin admits, pulling her hand out of his. "On her stomach, her back, and now her arm."

"What?!" He steps away from her, revulsion filling his face. "How the hell did she get those?"

"I don't know."

It is an odd thing to share burdens with another human being. You imagine it will lessen your own burden, ease some of the ache that sits in you like lead. But it almost does the opposite. Seeing Raj's reaction only brings home the enormity of the situation. Turning away from it, she focuses instead on the chai that has fully soaked into the carpet, leaving an odd-shaped stain.

"An illness? They can start with bruises, right?"

Marin welcomes the idea, chiding herself for doing so. When would a parent ever choose a disease for their child? "She's not sick, Raj," Marin says. "She was beaten."

He turns toward her, fire raging. A man lost, he attacks the closest thing available. "Did you do this?"

Standing slowly, she faces him—her partner, her husband, and now, when they are both desperate, her enemy. She wants to lash out, to show him that she is her father's daughter, but she refuses. "I didn't touch our daughter. Did you?" Turning the tables, she enjoys his look of horror.

"No." He stares at Marin, both of them outsiders in their own home. "I didn't." He drops his face into his hands, his agony like a virus marching through the home, filling every space and crevice available. "Never."

"Then it's time we found out who did."

* * *

Raj and Marin have never worked together. When Gia was born, they carved out separate hours during the night to tend to her. Since she was on formula, they each took a three-hour shift. During the day, Marin would work while Raj played with her and vice versa. When they went to restaurants, Marin ate her food quickly while Raj walked Gia, and then Raj ate his. Marin saw couples working together, playing family games, both parents coaxing their child to eat. The partnership felt foreign to her, no part of her desiring to replicate it.

Now they stand on the same side, facing a situation neither ever dreamed of. What parent would? "Has she given any indication whom it could be?"

They have settled in Marin's office, she in her leather chair, and Raj on the sofa. "No. I asked, begged her, but no answer." Marin doesn't tell him about the slap.

"What did the school say?"

"They didn't. Karen seemed as shocked as we are."

Raj nods, processing the information. "We need to meet with the school administration. Discuss all the possibilities."

He has calmed down, taken a step back to view the situation objectively. When Marin's parents selected his résumé, listing all of his qualifications, Marin was impressed. Holding advanced degrees in both engineering and math, he had climbed the corporate ladder with both his social skills and knowledge base. He had proved himself a capable leader. Though not as ambitious as Marin, he held his own. Marin had never sought out his expertise or called on his skills, but now she found herself grateful for them.

"It has to be someone at the school," he murmurs, thinking. "She's been studying late night?"

"Yes, for exams." Marin goes through the list of Gia's friends and their parents in her head. All the steps that were impossible to see days ago now are clear. "Let me contact her friends' parents. If Gia won't tell us who did this, maybe they will."

"Let's wait," Raj says, the voice of caution. "Gia could end up hating us if we go behind her back. We should try coaxing it out of her."

Now that Marin had a game plan, she hesitated about not putting it into play. Her instinct demanded she pick up the phone, overriding Raj's concerns, and call the parents to set up a time to talk. "I already tried that."

"But I haven't."

What he doesn't say is that sometimes Gia is willing to confide in him instead of Marin. The resentment comes rushing back. It takes Marin a moment to temper it, to remember their objective, and not focus on the course. "Fine. Once she shuts you down, we can take step two."

"This isn't a competition, Marin," Raj says simply, staring at her.

"No," Marin agrees. "It's our daughter's life."

They try to work for the rest of the day, but find themselves wandering the house, desperate for a distraction. Marin's normal five-minute shower turns into twenty. She lingers under the hot water, wishing the spray could wash away the ache that has become permanent in her heart. Leaning against the cold tiles, she watches with detachment as the soap bubbles circle the drain before disappearing from sight. She reaches for the shampoo before remembering she has already shampooed. Twisting the knobs, she increases the hot water, welcoming the scalding sting. When her skin begins to shrivel from the heat, she turns on the cold, blasting her body with the arctic water. She refuses to stand back, though. Accepting the self-torture she is inflicting feels good. She wonders if Gia felt the same pain when she was hit. If her mind cried for the torment to stop while her body acclimated itself to the pain. Maybe she is her mother's daughter and stood silent while her body was beaten. Marin turns toward the tiles, hitting her head against them, wishing for tears to rush down her face.

"Marin?" Raj calls into the bathroom. "It's almost time for Gia to be home from school."

"I'll be right out." She quickly dresses, pulling on jeans and a T-shirt instead of a business suit. She pulls her wet hair back and clasps it together with a pin. Slipping her feet into a pair of loafers, she rushes downstairs to wait with Raj.

Gia arrives home on time. Her backpack thrown carelessly over her shoulder, she waves to her friends still in the car as it pulls away. Raj opens the door before she can insert her key. "Dad!" Gia smiles at the sight of him. "You scared me."

"Hi, Beti." He takes her backpack and sets it down in the foyer.

Gia notices Marin standing there, both of them staring at her. She swallows, shaking her head in clear disgust. "You told him?" she accuses Marin.

"Yes." Marin imagines reaching out, enfolding her daughter in her arms, but instead chooses to stand in place, her arms lying limply by her side. "I'm sorry."

"Great." Gia pulls her hand away when Raj reaches for her. "It's not anyone's business."

Before Marin can yell, demand to know whose business it is if not theirs, Raj says, "When you are hurt, it is our business."

"I'm not hurt," Gia cries out, begging both of them. "I'm fine, I promise. It's not a big deal!"

"Who says?" Marin demands, losing patience. "Bruises on your stomach, on your back." She reaches out, grabbing Gia's hand and pulling up her shirtsleeves to reveal the most recent. "A new one on your arm. Are you stupid enough to think this is right?"

"You forgot the one on my face. When you slapped me," Gia says coldly, silencing the room. She cups her own cheek, facing Marin head on. "Did you remember that one?"

Marin does not look at Raj but can feel the anger vibrating off him. The truth she has failed to reveal. "I never meant to hurt you."

"No, no one ever does." Gia grabs her backpack and starts to head up the stairs. "I have homework."

"Gia." Raj's command stops her in her tracks. She pivots on the stairs to face him. "Last chance, Beti," he says, love lacing his words. "Who did this to you?"

"Please, Daddy," Gia whispers. She grasps the banister with her other hand. Marin can see the whites of her knuckles as she holds on tight to the only thing she can. "I'm OK. Please let it go. For me." With that she turns and runs up the stairs and into her room, slamming her door shut.

They convene in Marin's office. First, they call all the parents they are friendly with. Marin has spent her career making decisions that affect thousands, and yet, these calls are the hardest she has ever made. Each is answered by voice mail. Marin asks the parent to call back without explaining why. Marin hangs up, no closer to an answer than before.

They are on a road with no exits, no danger signs to warn them. It's hard not to storm upstairs and throw open Gia's door, demanding answers. But Gia is not the one to give them. She has made her decision clear.

Raj starts to snap his fingers, demanding Marin's attention. He holds his cell phone to his ear. "Yes," he says to someone on the other line, "this is Raj. How are you? We definitely need to catch a game." He makes small talk for a few more minutes. Marin jumps out of her chair and stands alongside him, listening. "Marin and I have a favor to ask of you." Raj falls silent, listening. Seconds later a smile breaks onto his face. "Tonight is perfect. Thank you." Hanging up, he beams at Marin. "The Ahbrams. Eight o'clock tonight."

* * *

They don't tell Gia where they are going. There's no reason to. For now, she and they stand on opposite sides. She is drowning, choosing to swim in the ocean against the currents while Marin and Raj are desperately searching for a life raft to save her. Fear propels Marin. She knows in her heart that no matter how hard she and Raj try, if Gia chooses to drown, they will be helpless to do anything but watch her.

They arrive at the house fifteen minutes early. They've been here numerous times over the years for parties, playdates, and barbeques. The Ahbrams live in Palo Alto, on a hill overlooking the city. Robert is the CEO of a start-up company, while Michelle is an attending physician at the teaching hospital in San Francisco. Their daughter, Amber, has been a good friend of Gia's since grade school.

Marin feels humiliation creeping over her as they stand on the doorstep after ringing the doorbell. Years of keeping her childhood shrouded in secrecy makes sense. How do you demand the respect of your peers when you stand in the shadow of shame? Warring with herself, she offers a halfhearted smile when Robert opens the door.

"Raj, Marin, welcome." He ushers them in, inviting them into the closed den where they can have some privacy. Michelle, waiting, embraces Marin. "Robert said Raj sounded very serious on the phone. Is everything all right?"

Marin and Raj did not discuss the steps to this dance on the car ride over. Instead, Marin spent the few minutes staring out at the darkened sky, searching for the North Star on the horizon. On a half chance, she hoped it would guide her way. "Thank you for having us over."

"Of course."

They take their seats, Robert and Michelle on the chairs while Marin and Raj keep a distance between them on the sofa. Glancing at him, Marin struggles to remember the last time they sat together or sought out a physical connection other than their occasional sexual encounters.

"We've had some disturbing information about Gia," Raj begins, only to stop. He swallows.

"Has Amber revealed anything unusual about Gia?" Marin steps in, her gaze intent on both Robert and Michelle. "Anything that would be cause for concern?" When the couple exchanges a look, the hairs on the back of Marin's neck start to tingle. Her pulse becomes erratic. "What? Please tell us," she says, struggling to keep her voice light.

"They're not as close as they used to be," Michelle begins, almost apologetic. "We haven't known how to approach you about it. Amber mentioned the girls don't spend as much time together anymore."

It was the last thing Marin expected to hear. She could admit that she didn't keep track of Gia's social life the way she did her academic one, but she just assumed Gia remained friends with the group she had always been with. Amber was one of her closest. "I don't understand. Did they have a falling out?"

"Amber never said. Just that Gia and she weren't friends anymore."

Marin searches her brain for a reason, an explanation that makes sense. She knows girls at this age are prone to form cliques, to decide based on arbitrary reasons who belongs and who doesn't. Marin herself had been kept out of all the popular cliques when she was in high school. Her speech still heavy with an accent, in addition to her secondhand clothes bought from Goodwill, Marin was the easy choice for an outcast. When her father forced her to take extra classes during the summer so she could graduate high school early, she had welcomed the decision. It allowed her to attend university sooner, which proved to be much more welcoming and inclusive than high school.

"Gia never mentioned it?" Robert asks, searching both their faces.

"No," Raj answers, his face troubled. "Was there anything else that Amber said?"

"I'm sorry, no." Michelle seems to search for the right words. "I don't want to pry, but would you feel comfortable telling us what's going on? We've known Gia since kindergarten. If there's anything we can do to help—"

Before she can continue or Raj can answer, Marin interrupts, "She's fine, thank you. We really appreciate your time." Marin stands, her action directing Raj to do the same.

"If there's anything," Robert says, both he and Michelle seeing them out, "don't hesitate to ask."

Raj gets in the driver's seat, while Marin settles into the passenger side. Just as Raj starts the car, the front door of the house opens and Amber runs out. She stands on the steps, under the light of the front porch, watching them. Marin, noticing her, immediately unbuckles her seat belt and opens the door. "Give me a minute," she instructs Raj. Rushing up the steps, she reaches the girl in seconds. "Amber, how are you?"

"I'm fine, thank you." She is smaller than the other girls in the class. Her hair is in a braid, and though some of the girls have started to wear makeup, she is free of any. "My mom said you came over to talk about Gia?"

"Yes." Marin tries to rein in her anxiety. "I had no idea you two weren't friends anymore."

"Yeah," Amber says, shrugging her shoulders. To Marin she still seems like the young girl who used to come over for sleepovers and would cry for her mom in the middle of the night. The girl who Gia swore was her best friend for life. "It sucks."

Marin nods, unsure how to move forward. Since this situation began, everything has felt new, without a roadmap to guide. "Gia is not herself. I was wondering if you knew anything about that," Marin says, trying not to reveal too much.

"Is she in trouble?" Amber asks, her eyes wide.

"No," Marin says, her nerves fraught. "Why aren't you two friends anymore?"

Amber clearly fights telling her the truth. Her eyes dart away, staring at the trees swaying in the front yard. She still has on her school uniform. She plays with the pleats of her skirt, thinking. "The boy Gia is dating . . ."

"Gia's dating a boy?" Marin steps back, trying to keep the shock out of her voice. She pauses, staring at a space above Amber's head. "Who is he?"

"I don't know him that well. He's new." Amber's face falls. She is hedging, not telling Marin the complete truth, Marin is sure. "I think that's why we aren't friends anymore."

Thanking her, Marin heads back to the car. Raj backs out of the driveway and turns onto the main street before asking, "What did she say?"

"Nothing," Marin lies. A vine, stripped of its leaves, wraps around her, binding her arms and legs, paralyzing her. As she takes a breath, seeking strength to free herself, it tightens around her throat and face, cutting off all access to oxygen. With a life built on a foundation of lies, adding one more is seamless. "She just asked us to say hello to Gia for her."

RANEE

Most of her hours she spends alone now, though she never imagined she'd prefer it that way. Raising a houseful of children makes you forget what your own time means. For some couples, when the children leave home and start their own lives, it is a blessing. More time to spend with your spouse, to rekindle the romance that was lost through the years. For Ranee, it simply meant increased loneliness. Alone with Brent in the house, she used to daydream about leaving. It mattered little where or how; she just wished to be gone.

Ranee often wondered if Sonya was happier far away than she had been with them. So many times, she picked up the phone to dial her daughter, only to lose her nerve and replace the receiver. She knew she had no right to seek advice from the daughter she betrayed. The one who escaped because Ranee had failed to offer her a haven.

Since she had married, Ranee prayed twice a day. Every morning, she repeated the Nimantran, a mantra of verses asking for forgiveness, protection, and humility in life. She added her own words afterward. Specifically, requests of guidance for her daughters, forgiveness for her lack of action, and kindness from her husband. At night, lying next to

Brent, hearing his breathing, she only had one prayer: that she and her daughters would survive to see another day.

When she was young, her parents took the family on a pilgrimage to Palitana, eight hundred and sixty-three temples atop Mount Shatrunjaya. Over seven thousand feet above sea level, it took a full day to climb. People from all over the world came to pay homage, believing it to be a place of victory, where one conquers enemies. Pilgrims offered gold and silver in return for blessings of good health, marriage, and security.

Ranee took a train with her parents and siblings from their hometown and arrived at nightfall. Staying with friends, they all slept in one room on the floor. Ranee curled up next to one of her brothers for warmth. The next morning, her mother woke them while it was still dark to get dressed. They packed *naan* and *chevda*—a mix of spicy rice flakes, lentils, and nuts—for the trek. Ranee was shocked the first time she saw chevda being sold as Hot Mix in grocery stores in America.

The sun was just rising over the mountain. Even from far below, Ranee could hear the bells tolling and smell the incense and roses wafting down the grassy hill. Hundreds of Dalits, untouchables, working in pairs and dressed in loincloths, carried those too old or feeble on *dolis*, swing chairs, up the stairs. After about an hour of climbing steps in the heat, Ranee yearned for the luxury. When she innocently asked her mother if she could sit in one for the rest of the journey, her mother laughed and told her it cost a thousand rupees per person. They were not about to spend that money on her because she was tired.

Chastised, Ranee continued climbing with her brothers and sisters. Along the way, they stopped to drink the fresh coconut water sold at regular intervals. After punching a hole through the hard skin, they tipped the coconut and let the water drip into their mouths. Afterward, Ranee's dad broke it open so they could feast on the milky white meat inside.

The memory of the temples that awaited them still takes Ranee's breath away. Carved from solid stone with marble pillars, the open temple was filled to capacity with well-wishers. From every walk of life, people stood side by side in saris and *salwar kameezes*, gently swaying to the songs sung by the gurus. The lyrics paid tribute to the marble statues depicting the various gods the temple enshrined. Lord Shiva, Goddess Parvati, their son Ganesha, and his daughters Lakshmi and Sarasvati were among the dozens of life-size figures.

The pillars served as the only enclosure, leaving the wall-less temple open to the warm breeze from nature. Ranee closed her eyes, letting the music and the wind wash over, cleansing her innocent soul. In that moment, Ranee was one with a being she had never met. Loved in a manner she had never known, and assured of her life in a way that no matter how hard she tried, she could never be certain of again. She made a promise to herself that day, one that haunted her since, to always remember the message conveyed—the world was waiting for her to live.

* * *

Ranee arrives at the gathering of the Indian community on time. A family has requested a *puja*—often commissioned for auspicious occasions—to celebrate the building of their new house. In a puja, the gurus spend an entire day in prayer and then call friends and loved ones of the family to join in to bless the occasion. Ranee has attended hundreds of them over the years. The pujas also serve as an excuse to socialize and enjoy dinner together while the children play. It is common in the community to meet every weekend for dinner, to play cards, or to watch a movie at the house. Any excuse to spend time and to make the memories of loved ones left behind in India less stinging. A surrogate family built by those who came from the same homeland.

"Ranee!" Nita, the host and a good friend, comes over immediately after spotting her. "How are you?"

"I am well." Ranee slips off her shoes at the entrance of the celebration. The temples in India required everyone to leave their shoes outside before entering; people believed that they could feel Earth's vibration through the structure's floor, transmitted via the feet. The practice was centuries old. They followed the ritual in their homes too, since nearly every Indian had some form of a shrine within the house. "How are you?"

"I think of you every day." Nita offers her a hug. "I stopped by to visit Brent last week. My heart is breaking for you, my friend."

"Every day I pray," Ranee says, dropping her head, never having revealed their secret to anyone. "But God does not always hear our prayers."

"No," Nita agrees. A number of women join them. "He is mysterious in his ways."

"But we have no choice but to keep asking," another friend interjects. "If we do not ask, then how will God know our requests?"

They all murmur their agreement. "It is always the strongest and best that suffer," Nita says, clasping Ranee's hand in her own. "As if God knows that you have strength the rest of us lack."

A polite way of explaining her heartbreak, Ranee thinks. Nodding her head, she accepts their condolences with graciousness. A common belief among Indians is that if you spend too much time around someone experiencing bad luck, their energy can transfer to you. Their bad luck may become yours. If you are invited to a wedding and have an unexpected death in the family, no matter how distant, you must decline the invitation. It was why her decades-old friends came to visit but never stayed. Before Sonya came home, friends made sure there was dinner waiting for Ranee at the house. In the mornings, another friend would bring breakfast. A carousel of meals constantly available but no one to share them with. It was why Ranee never revealed her truth to any of them—if they knew her misfortune, they would cease to be her friends.

"It is with the strength of your friendships that I am able to continue every day," Ranee returns, offering each of them a warm smile. "Without all of you, where would I be?"

The guru starts to ring the bell, motioning for everyone to gather around. The men take their seats on the floor on one side, while the women sit on the floor on the other side. The genders refrain from intermingling while in prayer to keep the air pure. Once everyone is seated, the guru begins the prayer.

"We are here to bless the new home of our friends Nita and Sanjay," he says, adding melted butter to the small fire in the pot. Over a small statue of Lord Ganesha and Lord Shiva, he pours milk and water, following it with a sprinkle of rose petals. "Let there only be happiness in this home, prosperity, and great health. Let God smile on this home and its owners. No one deserves it more."

The mantras continue, the guru calling on each deity to bless their home and to repel any misfortunes. Ranee wishes it were so simple. So often, she longed for a simple prayer to change her course in life. If only the deities were all-powerful—like a child with a simple request, she could ask them to bequeath the gift of a perfect life. But Ranee knows it is not so. Helpless to offer her daughters the childhood they deserved, she acknowledges there is no magic wand or prayer to erase the mural of her life.

With that knowledge comes her acceptance that to have the life she wants, she has to repaint the painting. Redefine the rules and reject all the beliefs she had been raised with. She has no need to honor the husband who dishonored her. To continue fearing the rejection of her community means living the life they accepted. But since it is all a lie, what does that make her if not a liar?

Ranee closes her eyes, allowing the memory of standing atop the mountain in India and the songs of the gurus then to intermingle with the songs being sung now. The same incense smell, decades apart, brings tears to her eyes. Surrounded by strangers, then and now, she welcomes the knowledge that she belongs because of who she is, not what they need her to be.

She used to have a recurring dream after she married—one where she fell out of the temple and down the mountain. It was a free fall, past the thousand steps and everyone climbing them. She kept falling and would awake with sweat covering her body. After Brent's admission into the hospital, she had the dream again. This time, she landed in someone's arms. When she turned to thank the person, she came face-to-face with herself.

As the fire burns and the smoke billows around them, Ranee smiles. Hidden by the haze, she is secure in the knowledge that she is finally living and somehow, she is sure, the world is watching.

SONYA

I spent four months in a gang-infested neighborhood for my first assignment as a photographer. I watched as young boys were initiated into their new families at the age of nine, some even younger. Each one trained in warfare before they reached puberty. They carried guns like appendages, and shot their weapons with the expertise of those who had been shooting their whole lives. Infractions as simple as crossing the wrong street could be cause for execution. Boys who had once been friends now fought like archenemies.

One of their leaders was hunted down for taking out an opposing leader. A hit was put out on him with a reward for the first one who could offer his bullet-riddled body. When he was cornered, two of his underlings stood in front of him like a shield and took the bullets instead. The leader escaped the carnage and hailed the two boys as heroes. At their funerals, their mothers laid themselves over their caskets and begged for an explanation. None came. As I stood in the procession of mourners, I wondered why children so easily accepted it as their place to absorb the sins of their elders, even if it meant losing themselves in the process.

* * *

I arrive at the hospital with my portfolio in hand. Pictures from all over the world. I find the Human Resources Department easily, and wait to meet the department chair. I interviewed for the other two jobs first. Both wanted to hire me, but the work was only for a week or two. I needed something longer. When I told Linda the news, she bit her tongue and notified the hospital immediately that I was interested in getting more information. No promises I would accept, she warned them. They set up a time for us to meet. In the meantime, I researched as much as I could on photography as a means of therapy; there was not much to be found. But bundled in with other creative endeavors, such as music and even video games, it had shown promise in helping patients increase their endorphin levels and help fight the illnesses invading their bodies.

When I drive into the parking lot, it feels odd to be here for a job rather than for my father. My need to see him wanes with each day. There is nothing I want to say to him; I know if he was awake, he'd have no desire to see me. My only purpose in remaining is for Trisha. Once she no longer needs me, I will move on.

The Human Resources Department is large and fills an entire wing of the hospital, with people in and out of offices. Everyone here is dressed in suits, not the hospital scrubs and white coats you expect to see on the floor of the hospital. "Sonya? I'm Sean." A tall gray-haired man approaches me with his hand outstretched.

"A pleasure to meet you." His grip is firm, filled with warmth.

"I have to tell you," he says as he motions me into his office, "when I received the call from your agent, I was floored. Someone of your caliber being interested in this position—well, I don't have to tell you what a coup it would be for us."

"Thank you." I have never gotten used to the praise my work elicits. When Linda receives feedback, she forwards me the e-mails or letters. I usually delete or trash them without reading the words. The few times I tried, it proved impossible to believe they were talking about me. "I would love to hear more about the opportunity."

"Our board just passed a budget for out-of-the-box therapy." He hands me documents to review. I glance at the glossy brochure about the hospital, touting its achievements. "Innovation in health care. We, of course, have art therapy, music, even video games in Pediatrics. But photography has made headlines recently, and since our hospital is always on the leading edge in health care, we decided to see what we could do."

"What would the position consist of?" Returning the documents to him, I lean back in my chair. I am unsure about this step. More than just about the decision to stay, I worry about working with people. All my assignments before have been me, alone, behind the camera.

"Working with patients, teaching them about photography. Our first focus will be on Pediatrics. Children may benefit the most from it right now. Usually they haven't had much exposure to cameras, prints, the entire process of photo-taking. We hope it will open another world to them in a very simple way."

That's the beauty of photography. One picture, taken a thousand miles away, can make viewers feel as though they are standing in the same place. Their imaginations can take them on a journey without ever leaving their house. A collage of photographs can create a whole new experience, and allow people to enter places they couldn't have imagined going. I have never underestimated the power of a picture.

"Your agent mentioned that your father is currently a patient here. I took the liberty of finding him and learning who the attending doctor is."

"Dr. David Ford," we both say at the same time.

"David is one of our best," he says.

"So we've been told."

"He's also on the board of directors. When I told him you were interested in the position and would be coming in today, he was understandably thrilled. Asked if he could give you the tour himself."

There's a knock on the door just as he finishes speaking. David pops his head in, smiling at the sight of me. "Sonya, wonderful to see you again."

I stand automatically to return his greeting. "Pleasure to see you again, Doctor."

"I thought we agreed on David." He turns his gaze toward Sean, a perfect professional. "Sean, the hospital owes you one. If we can hire Sonya, we would look pretty brilliant."

*   *   *

"I may not be the best fit for the job," I warn David as we walk alongside one another down the hall. Doctors and nurses pass us, each one offering a greeting. He is well liked, respected by his peers. "This was just an exploratory meeting." He pushes the "Up" button when we reach the elevators. "Where are we going?" I ask.

"Wait and see."

He is playing and enjoying it. His happiness is infectious. Caught up in his excitement, we take the elevator up two floors. Stepping out, I am overwhelmed with the colors. Walls covered with every shade of the rainbow. Murals of balloons, zoo animals, every creature imaginable painted with precision. Large enough to catch a child's eye and offer them comfort.

"Whoa!" David grabs my wrist and pulls me back as two young boys go screeching past. Embroiled in a fight to see who pushes the elevator button first, they barely notice us.

"Sorry." Their mother runs after them, a blur of blond hair pulled into a ponytail, jeans, and a sweatshirt. "You would think after giving blood they would be a little tired."

"Not a problem." The fraternal twins continue their battle, pushing one another in their mission to get into the elevator first. "Don't forget your mom, boys," David says.

When they dutifully hold open the door, their mother gives David a grateful smile. As the doors close, I turn toward him. "Pediatrics, I assume?"

"One of the floors. This one is primarily oncology."

I follow him down the hall toward a glass window. Behind it, a dozen children play in a small room. Most are bald, and all of them have tubes in their bodies. Their ages are mixed, and I imagine they all are older than they look. They are laughing, enjoying the assortment of toys available. They take no notice of us standing, staring. Maybe they are used to adults watching them, searching for a sign that they are on the mend. I can imagine doctors like David jotting down notes. The patients' every behavior critical. The way they share toys or handle conflict an insight into the state of their health. Or maybe they just don't care who is behind the window. It is irrelevant to them whether they are passing or failing an unknown test. Because they are already facing the greatest battle of their lives. One that determines if they will be the ultimate victor or the greatest loser.

"You want me to take pictures of them?" I ask.

"With them," he corrects, waving to a young boy. He turns toward me but my eyes remain on the children. "Did Sean mention various forms of therapy to you? Such as animal therapy?"

"Yes." Studies showed that an animal's unconditional love helped to heal what medicine could not. I often wondered what it would have been like if I had one growing up. Would a dog or cat have been strong enough to diminish my pain? "It can work miracles."

"Yes." He seems pleased by my knowledge of it. "We are searching for additional ideas to help patients heal or at least get on the path."

"You believe photography is the answer?" Photography was the only answer I found. Spending hours looking through the lens saved me from turning my eye inward and focusing on my own life and loss.

"Art in any form is powerful. The children have plenty of crayons and paper for their artistic endeavors. But we have never offered photography. I would be fascinated to see what effect it has." He points out a little girl whose new growth of hair barely covers her head. She walks slowly so as not to topple the attached IV stand. "She loves looking at picture books. Imagine if she could take some of her own."

"Teach a class?"

"That might work better for the adults. With the children, maybe gather a few at a time and show them the basics. The hospital will of course provide the cameras and supplies."

"A printer. They would love to see their pictures right after they take them." Ideas start to crowd in my head. "They could create a book of their photographs. Something to take home with them." Those who survive to see their homes again.

"Is that a yes?" He rubs his hands together, a mixture of excitement and relief. "We'll deal with some human resource formalities and then you can start immediately."

"Wait," I say, trying to slow the train down. "Don't you want to see my portfolio?"

"When Sean told us your agent called, the board researched your work," he admits. "The pictures are brilliant." He motions toward the children. "We would be very lucky to have you."

"Thank you." A child, maybe five, catches my eye. He has stacked his Lego bricks into a tall building. After showing everyone his feat, he pulls one arm back and with a swift chop tumbles them all to the ground. A human instinct, I muse. Destroy that which we have built.

"I had no idea who you were or the quality of your work when we last spoke." He looks contrite. "I feel foolish."

"Please." His admiration sends a slow tingle down my spine, where it intermingles with fear, a hellish symbiosis. I can't be sure if it's knowing my father is in his room below us lying near death or having enjoyed the last few minutes of conversation with David, but the feelings overwhelm me. Remind me of what I can never have. Never be. "I appreciate your kindness."

"So what do you think?" He holds on to his stethoscope, pulling it tight around his neck. He glances down at his feet before meeting my gaze. "It's great work if you're interested."

Turning away from the children, I step out of their line of sight. It makes no difference to them, but it keeps me from seeing their suffering. That is the most difficult part. Children, blameless from birth, harmed for no reason. Whether their pain comes from the hands of a parent, a stranger, or God, it is impossible for me to accept. Innocents, never schooled on how to fight, still just learning how to live, have to be strong and wise just to survive. Maybe that is my undoing. I have never learned. How could I when I am still running? "Let me think about it." I start to walk away, dread settling inside me like a lost friend. As I pass the window, I see the young boy raise his hand in celebration, all the Lego bricks lying at his feet.

*　*　*

"We should sit down for dinner soon," Trisha says, setting out her daily dishware. It's just the four of us—the three sisters and Mom. It's Saturday night and the first time we are all having dinner together in a while. We are cautious with one another, as if we are afraid of disturbing the balance we have created.

"Eloise made your favorite, Mama. Of course, it's not as good as yours, but she used your recipe." Trisha brings out the *baingan bharta* dish and sets it in the middle. She ushers us toward the table, insisting we take our seats.

"You're wearing saris again?" Trisha stops, staring.

I take in Mom's outfit. Today she chose to wear a green sari. It is not one I recognize, but from the simple design along the edge, I can tell it is old. The newer ones have strips of gold or silver thread, and the colors seeping together are vibrant, alive, as if to keep pace with the Bollywood films that have saturated the market. The green dye of Mom's sari is worn, faded from too many washes. There is no sparkle in the color, no decorations to enhance its appearance. It is simple, and yet Mom looks beautiful. Her hair is pulled back and held with a gold clasp. Gold hoop earrings and a simple gold chain are the only jewelry she wears. I can't help but notice her mangalsutra is missing from her neck.

"You stopped?" I ask, surprised.

"Yes," Mom answers quickly.

"Why?" Everyone stares at her, waiting for an answer.

"After you left and Trisha got married, it didn't seem important to keep up appearances anymore," Mom says quietly.

"Appearances of what?" Marin asks.

Mom says nothing. When the silence lingers, Trisha speaks up. "Who wants wine? Marin? Sonya?"

She has an odd, frenetic energy. Her makeup is flawless and her outfit pressed perfectly. The house is clean and welcoming, but something is amiss. She avoided my eyes when opening the front door and has avoided me since. When I tried to help her with the meal, she ushered me out of the kitchen.

"Red, please," I say.

"Right. Of course." She hunts through her cabinet for the wine opener. Opening each drawer, she fails to find it. "Where does he keep it?"

Her hands are shaking, and she is flustered. Lost, like a child, she searches obsessively. I have never seen her this way before. The sight of it unnerves me, makes me realize that her stability is my foundation. Even when I was traveling, knowing that Trisha was back home, living a normal life, gave me the hope I needed to keep going. At least one of us was doing more than surviving.

"What's going on?" My words cause Mom and Marin to look up, to watch Trisha with new eyes. When Trisha fails to respond, I join her, standing side by side. I can feel her nervousness, her fear. "Hey, what's up?"

"Nothing," she whispers. Her eyes close, her long lashes veiling the truth. "Everything is fine." She pushes past me, rejecting my help. She starts to pour water in everyone's wineglasses. "Let's eat."

We do as we are told. When Marin got married, Trisha assumed the role of matriarch. Since Mom never owned the position, it was open and Trisha was the obvious choice. We followed her rule, her decisions, like chicks to a hen. Mom fell in line like the rest of us, relieved that someone other than my father had some semblance of control.

We eat our meal in silence. The fresh garlic naan is warm. We use it to scoop up the baingan bharta—eggplant *sakh* mixed with fresh tomatoes and onions. I take a sip of my lentil soup, the lemony aftertaste lingering on my tongue. The meal is delicious, as I expected. Trisha rarely does anything wrong. It's comforting to know that someone in my life knows what they are doing.

"I'm going to accept a position at the hospital. As a photographer," I announce. It feels odd to me to confide my plans to anyone. But after leaving the hospital, I drove around, considering my options. Since it was the only one I had, the choice was made for me.

"For how long?" Trisha asks, her joy clear.

"As long as I'm needed," I say, leaving open to interpretation who needs me. From Trisha's glance, she knows I'm speaking about her. She nods to me once, her face filled with gratitude.

"Your father's condition is unchanged." Mom wipes her mouth with her napkin. She makes no comment about my announcement. The curry leaves an orange stain on the pristine white linen. "I don't know how long the insurance company will pay for his care."

"He will come out of it soon," Trisha says. She pushes her plate away, most of the food untouched. "I was with him the other day. There was improvement."

"What?" Marin, who has remained aloof most of the meal, lowers her fork to stare at Trisha. "What did you see?"

On the spot, Trisha clasps her hands together. The air-conditioning kicks on, causing the chandelier above us to sway slightly. "There was nothing to see. I just know."

"Of course," Marin mocks. "You just know."

"What does that mean?"

Trisha and Marin's relationship vacillated between combative and impersonal growing up. Marin resented the love and attention showered on Trisha when she was the one who brought home the top grades and succeeded beyond everyone's expectation. But her battle to replace Trisha was a losing one. Our parents would never see Marin or me the way they viewed Trisha. Marin must have accepted that at some point. Decided the battle was no longer worth fighting. It was why I was shocked when she made the decision to return to California soon after she married.

"Just that it must be nice to know everything, that's all," Marin says.

Her face is drawn tight. Her usual control replaced with worry, anxiety. Lost in Trisha's discomfort, I failed to notice Marin's. I see now what I missed before. Dark circles color the skin beneath her eyes. There are lines of age that weren't there just a week ago. She is holding herself together, but barely.

As children, we were each lost in our own hell. That became our excuse not to ask the other what had happened when she was crying or quiet. The question was moot anyway. Most likely we had seen the hit or the insult. Witnessed the altercation that resulted in a one-way beating. We knew never to interrupt—to stand up for our loved one. It could only lead to a more severe beating—or worse, he could turn on us. Somehow, we convinced ourselves that one person beaten was better than two.

Now there is no reason to remain quiet. It is easy to forget that I am allowed to ask why she is sad. This is new territory for me. With trepidation, I turn toward Marin, assuming that whatever is bothering Trisha will right itself because it has to.

"Marin? Is something wrong?" I realize neither Gia nor Raj have joined us for dinner. "Gia and Raj? They couldn't make dinner?"

She flinches. Dropping her spoon, she shakes her head no. "Gia had to study." At the same time, her mouth draws into a tight line and her hands fist atop the table. "Everything's fine."

"You are lying."

We all turn toward Mom, shocked to hear her argue. She was always the first one to accept our insistence that we were fine. Even as our faces would begin to swell with dead blood, we would assure her that we had moved past the incident. His sobs from the bedroom— because he always cried after hitting us—were more important than what he had done. She welcomed our strength, used it to buoy her when she had none of her own. Then she would leave us to comfort him, because it was what he expected her to do.

"And if I am?" Marin stands, dropping her napkin over the remainder of her food. "What business is it of yours?"

She needs someone to attack. Her fighting stance, the venom in her words, makes it clear. Mom is the easiest and most vulnerable. We watched her beaten so many times, it seems natural to watch it in play again. I have no instinct to come to her defense. I turn toward Trisha, assuming she will end this war before Mom loses the battle, but she remains quiet. A glaze covers her eyes, protecting her from what is about to happen.

"I am your mother. If not mine, whose business is it?"

She is not backing down.

"No one's," Marin answers.

So, something is wrong. Marin has just admitted as much. We are at a crossroads. As children, we were forced to share our lives by default. Dad made sure all of us were pieces in his game. No one was allowed to opt out, to choose not to play. There were no teams, so our only role was to comfort the loser of the day.

As adults, we each took our own path. Even living in the same town, it is obvious that Marin and Trisha never take the same road. Their lives never intersect. If not for the forced family functions, their worlds would remain separate and apart. The only bond that binds them now is the blood that courses through their veins. That, and being two of the only five people in the world who know about the life we lived.

"Maybe it is our business." Trisha comes back from wherever she had gone. She reaches out, covering the top of Marin's hand with her own. Only for a second, but enough time to have everyone staring at their joined fingers. She echoes Mom. "Who else's would it be?"

"You don't want to know." Marin slips her hand out from beneath Trisha's. She starts to stack our dishes, irrelevant whether we are finished eating. "It would ruin the perfection you work so hard to preserve."

"Don't you mean it would ruin the image you so desperately try to maintain?" Trisha shrugs, indifferent to Marin's intake of breath. "Honestly, Marin, you shouldn't bother. Everyone stopped caring years ago."

After an assignment for the *New York Times*, I spent time in their stacks, going through old photographs. The ones that were too fragile to preserve had been scanned and copied. The originals were kept for historical purposes. Like a scattering of light snow, pieces of print fell into my hands. Images taken in a moment offered the only window into another generation's life. I stared at their faces, their poses revealing little of their struggles, their hopes, and disappointments. They stared into the camera, allowing only what they wanted to be exposed.

Seeing my family now, I wonder if we are any different. Each one of us portraying only what we allow. Like statues inside a snow globe, we are frozen, emotionless to anyone watching. No matter what happens, we will not visibly break, even if we are shattered on the inside. But when did we decide to keep our secrets from one another? When did our circle shrink to one, leaving the chain that connected us broken irretrievably? But each one of us was the weak link. The chain was bound to break.

"We're trying to help," I interject because the bridge we are walking on is about to collapse. Mom turns toward me, watching me with interest. "Let us."

"You're trying to help?" Marin laughs, a cruel sound filled with emptiness. "All these years, you disappear and now you think you can come in and save the day?"

"No, I don't." I say, fully aware of my own limitations. "I'm asking you to let us in, to help you shoulder whatever is going on." I offer the only reason I have. "You did the same for us, when we were kids."

She collapses back into her chair, defeated. Almost to herself she asks, "Why did I let him hit me? Why would anyone allow herself to be hit?"

It is not what I expected. None of us saw that coming. Mom disappears into her chair. Trisha, the only one with a response, answers, "Maybe it was meant to be."

"Spoken from the girl who was never hit," Marin says with a bite. "How fortunate for you. The rest of us didn't have that luxury, did we?" She looks to me for support.

I stop myself from speaking aloud the resentment that simmered over the years—the envy toward Trisha. But the relationship we share, all the times we stood together, overshadow any other emotion.

"I guess I was lucky," Trisha says, barely blinking. She empties her glass. Her reasoning sounds rehearsed, something she has repeated to herself.

"Or maybe no one saved us." Marin turns her gaze to Mom, betrayal filling the room. "That is a mother's job, right? To protect her children? Even animals know something that basic. They protect their young, fight to the death if necessary for their safety."

"Is that what I should have done?" Mom asks. "Given up my life for the sake of yours?" She pauses, considering. Coming to her own conclusion, she nods, "Yes, maybe that is what I should have done."

As a child I vacillated between anger and gratitude for her inaction. Because even though she failed to stand between him and us, she was at least there to stand beside us. As a child desperate for some semblance of love, I rationalized that as enough. Besides, we were still alive. None of us had died at his hands. That had to count for something.

"Too late now. You never even tried." Marin throws back. "If you had attempted, maybe . . ."

Twice, Dad put Marin in a dark closet for hours because of her grades. While I sat outside the door, whimpering for the heartache I imagined she was enduring, Marin stayed deathly silent inside. Mom, her mouth clenched shut, continued to prepare dinner. Only her eyes flitting toward the clock on the wall every few minutes, counting the time as it passed, gave any indication of her concern.

"But I didn't."

Marin's question and Mom's response hang over us like a bomb ready to explode. I read once that we don't choose our families, or our childhood, but we choose our future. As if that one choice can help ease the heartache of a childhood gone wrong. I wonder if I would choose my sisters as my friends, if I would make the conscious decision to confide in them, spend time together, trust them. Would I be able to accept the responsibility of carrying them when they fell? In truth, can anyone really be counted on to help when all is lost?

"It doesn't matter anymore, does it?" I ask. They are the only words I have in my arsenal. I have nightmares of Marin in the closet. But in my dreams she is crying, and Mom is desperately trying to save her. "He can't hit you ever again."

"No, he can't." She glances at her watch, time having stood still for the last hour. She straightens her hair, fixes her shirt. In a matter of a few steps, she returns to the executive she is. Any signs of vulnerability have disappeared, leaving the rest of us to wonder if we imagined it. "Dinner was wonderful, as always," she says to Trisha. "Can I help clean up?"

"Eloise will do it," Trisha says.

"Then it's time I head out."

She pushes her chair back, only to be halted by Mom's words. "You never told us what was bothering you."

"Nothing I can't handle." We watch, the three of us, as she walks out the door, shutting it quietly behind her.

"Are you all right?" Trisha asks Mom quietly.

"Of course."

It is difficult to imagine how she could be. Maybe Marin attacked Mom before. In the years that I was gone, there may have been numerous confrontations like the one I just witnessed. Seeing Mom's reaction however, I doubt it. She is shaken, saddened by the clash. With tired hands, she reaches for her purse and shawl. The beauty that had emanated from her earlier has disappeared. All that is left is an old woman, aged before her time.

"I should go. It is late." Turning to me, she asks, "I will see you at home?"

"Yes, I'll see you there."

Trisha and I watch her walk out the same door Marin left through only moments ago. We are both silent, the only two left in the room. She starts to clear the table. I help her, both of us quietly working. It is not like Trisha; normally she is the one who fills the silence. After one of Dad's episodes, it was her job to change the conversation. To return all of us to the time right before the violence. She became an expert at it. With a smile, she would seamlessly restart the interrupted conversation. While Mom comforted Dad, or left to deal with her own cuts, Trisha would nurse us with an alternate reality.

"You'll have to get on Eric's case," I say, trying to lighten the mood. I fill the sink with the dishes. "A dinner without wine is unacceptable."

"You're right." Trisha wipes her hands on the dish towel. "Let's make up for it."

"What are you talking about?"

"Come on." She grabs her purse and keys off the end table and walks out the front door. When I don't move, she sticks her head back in, crooking her arm for me to follow her. "Let's go!"

* * *

University Avenue is Stanford students' main thoroughfare for bars and off-campus dining. It also hosts the elite venture capitalist crowd of Palo Alto when they want to unwind. The combination of money and brilliance offers a distinctive crowd in every establishment. Trisha routes us to one off the main street. It is small but that doesn't stop people from crowding the corners and spilling into the courtyard in the back. Men and women dressed in casual business clothes drink alongside students sporting Stanford gear, carrying backpacks. I follow Trisha to the counter, where we find two empty stools.

"What can I get you?" The bartender looks barely old enough to be serving us. As he waits for our orders, he waves to some friends who've just entered.

"Two glasses of your most expensive red." Trisha pulls out her credit card and slides it toward him. "Start us a tab, please."

"Are we planning on getting drunk?" I ask.

"Why not?"

I watch her as we wait for our drinks. When they are finally served, Trisha toasts me with her full glass. Without waiting for me, she takes a deep swallow. She winces, the wine burning her throat.

"Because you don't do that." I take a sip of mine. It's a dry Cabernet. I prefer a Pinot but don't say anything. "You never touch your drink at home."

Drinking to oblivion was not something any of us sisters chose to do. When you have no control as a child, there is no reason to cede it as an adult. Trisha is worse than I am. She avoids alcohol completely. She swears the smell nauseates her.

When we were kids, Dad would sometimes leave the house when he was truly angry. He would return hours later with a brown bag, supposedly with a bottle of liquor inside. The irony was that he never drank, so the threat was meant to scare us more than anything. As if to say he could get more violent with alcohol in him than without. I always believed it was the memory of those nights that turned Trisha off drinking.

"Then let tonight be the night that changes." She finishes the glass while mine remains full. She motions to the bartender for another. Glancing around, she sees everyone, as if for the first time. "Busy night." Trisha lingers on a couple holding one another. The man's arm is around the woman's waist. He bends low to hear what she says over the roar of the crowd, offering her a smile in response. Trisha turns back toward the bar, facing the rows of bottles and the mirror on the wall. Her reflection stares back at us, offering no revelations. She fingers her wedding ring, the large solitaire glittering under the glare of the overhead lights.

"Should you let Eric know we're out?" When he wasn't at the dinner, I assumed he was still working. When Trisha continues to stare at her ring, I ask softly, "Trisha, where's Eric?"

"Gone." Trisha nods her thanks when the bartender refills her glass.

"On a business trip?" I shake my head no when he tries to refill mine.

"Moved out." She avoids my eyes while relaying the news. She empties half of her second glass. "A few days ago."

I stare at her, sure she is joking. "Trisha?" When she doesn't answer, I grip her upper arm and turn her toward me. She rotates her face away, staring at the bottles that line the shelves behind the bar. Her deep swallows are the only indication I have she is telling me the truth. "Why?" I ask, sadness settling deep within me. She was the one who was supposed to be okay. The one whose compass was set, her way guided.

"No reason."

A well-dressed man in his midforties interrupts us. He takes the stool right next to Trisha's. Already nursing a mixed drink, he is clearly not at the bar for another. I roll my eyes when he swivels toward us, his gaze roaming over Trisha's left hand before landing on mine.

"I'm Zach."

"We're busy," I reply, as rudely as I can.

"Not nice," Trisha scolds me. She thrusts out her hand to shake his. "I'm Trisha. And you are?"

"Zach," I remind her.

"Can I buy you ladies a drink?" Zach asks, keeping his gaze on Trisha. Apparently, he has decided the less sober one is the best chance he has tonight. "What are you drinking?"

"I'll have what you're having," Trisha decides. "Bartender?" She tries to snap her fingers, succeeding in making no sound at all.

My sister is not only drunk but rude as well. I lean past her just as our friend Zach gets the bartender's attention and orders us a round of drinks. "Listen, Zach, I really appreciate the drinks, but this is not a good night."

"You'll have to excuse my sister." Trisha pushes me back onto my stool and runs her hand through her hair. Her feeble attempt at flirting would be hilarious if it weren't so sad. "She just got back from a far, far away place. Worlds away. She isn't quite herself yet."

"Really?" Zach inquires, feigning interest. "Where did you travel?"

"New York." I try to reach for the drink before Trisha. She proves faster than me and downs it in two gulps. Her eyes bulge as it burns going down her throat. A small part of me is glad for her pain. Maybe it will stop her shenanigans and she will tell me what is going on. "Great city. It's like a whole other world." If Zach has caught on to my sarcasm he doesn't let on.

"I travel there for work quite a bit. I'm in sales."

I want to point out that I didn't ask, but that would mean continuing the conversation with him, and no purpose would be served. Instead I take out my wallet and pay for the two drinks he just bought us. I slide my untouched one toward him. "On me. Enjoy." Grabbing Trisha's hand, I pull on her hand. "I'd better get my sister home."

"I don't want to go home," Trisha moans, the alcohol taking effect. "Eric . . ."

"Eric?" Zach asks.

Zach has started to become an annoyance, and my sister a liability. "Eric is her husband. Hence the ring you saw on her finger when you sat down. He apparently just left her, which is why she's drinking herself into oblivion. That information may not matter to you, but this will: Neither my sister nor I will be sleeping with you tonight. She won't because she's three sheets to the wind and will most likely spend the night vomiting. I won't because I have absolutely no interest in you. No offense."

Zach gets the message, thank goodness, and turns his stool toward the person on his other side. Not without taking the drink I slid his way, however. Sighing, I hold on to Trisha's hand tight. She is surprisingly strong. Gathering all of our stuff, I somehow get us both into the car and head toward her house.

"He's not coming back, you know." Trisha lolls her head toward me. There's a sheen of water over her pupils. "Packed all of his stuff."

"Why did he leave?" I take the highway toward the hills of Saratoga where Trisha lives. "You guys seemed like you had it together." When she doesn't answer me right away, I take my eyes off the road to glance at her. She's staring through the front windshield at nothing. "Hey." I reach for her hand, giving it a gentle squeeze. "Talk to me. What happened?"

"Do you want children?" she asks.

"Children?" It's not the question I expected. I have never allowed myself to imagine children. I loved the ones I came across in my years in the field. I learned that no matter what country I was in or the conditions of the local economy, children all over the world had the same thing in common—they wanted to spend their lives laughing. I was amazed at the lengths they would go to play a game or a joke to reach their goal. When I spent time in Congo, I watched young girls and boys using their firearms as play swords while training for the front lines of a war. They laughed as they played, oblivious to the live weapon in their hand. "I don't know."

"You don't know?" Trisha mocks my answer. "Everyone knows," she says. She grips the door handle even though I am going below the speed limit. "Children are the source of all happiness. The happily ever after." Her voice, high from the alcohol, suddenly drops. "But you have to have a husband first. Or a wife." She glances over at me, coming to a realization. "Are you gay?"

"No," I say quietly, "I'm not gay."

"Because now that I think about it, I've never seen you with a man." She is reviewing the years, trying to find a time when I brought home a guy or mentioned a date. She will come up empty. "Wow," she says. "Are you a virgin?"

Sex is not a topic openly discussed in Indian households. There is a taboo around the concept, as if it were a dirty word. When I got my period, I remember my mother dropping her head in disappointment. She told me quietly she would let Dad know. I wondered why it was important to inform him when it was my body. My sisters and I followed Mom's example and never mentioned the word. Since we weren't allowed to date, there was never a reason to broach the subject or discuss the implications.

"No, Trisha, I'm not." I ward off the uncomfortable feeling, the fear that grips me. My secret will remain hidden, I assure myself. "But we're not talking about me. Why did Eric leave?"

"Children," she says, thankfully forgetting about my sex life. "He wants children."

"Don't you?" I still remember the years of her playing with her Barbies. Her nightly ritual of wedded bliss followed by a family. The only definition of happiness she knew.

"No," she shudders. Wrapping her arms around herself, she sinks into the seat. "I couldn't."

"You have problems with infertility?" Of all the things, I never would have expected this. When you view someone to be perfect, it is hard to imagine any imperfections marring their life.

"No." Trisha is quiet. I glance at her to see if she is falling asleep, but her eyes are wide open, staring at nothing. "He thought we did."

She is speaking in circles, taking the conversation around without an endpoint. "What happened, Trisha?"

When we were kids, Trisha and I used to play a game of hide-and-seek. But she changed the rules every time we played. Sometimes I would have to count to ten before seeking her, other times to fifty. But the rule that infuriated me the most was that if I found her too fast, I lost. She used to say the game had not really been played. As if it were my fault that her hiding place was easy to discover. We would start over, with her hiding and me counting. I didn't realize until I was older that the rule was never used when we reversed position. No matter how quickly she found me, she still won the game.

"I have an IUD," she finally admits, too lost in her alcohol stupor to censor her admission. "So that I wouldn't get pregnant."

I reach her house. Pulling into the driveway, I keep the car running. The headlights illuminate the house, a mansion by anyone's standards. The yard is immaculate and a small white fence lines the tulip garden. A "Welcome" sign adorns the door, as does a brass knocker to announce one's arrival. "He wanted it out?" I ask, trying to make sense of her words.

"You can't change what you don't know," she says, staring at her home. "I lied to him, Sonya. But then he found out and now he's gone."

MARIN

Five steps before she reaches the school, Marin stops, unsure. The day is beautiful, warm, and breezy. Quintessential California. The weather offers a false sense of security—with so much beauty you assume nothing bad can ever happen. Her childhood was proof that wasn't true. Nonetheless, she convinced herself. Fell for the false sale. Now, she knows for sure. It is not just the dark that brings out the darkness. Daylight has its own form of hell.

Marin doesn't allow fear to make her falter. Reaching the front door, she walks in with a confidence she doesn't feel. A lesson learned from childhood—if you put on a good show, people will believe. Marin lost track of the visits to the nurse for pain in her stomach when she was a child. A simple examination would have revealed the bruises, but the school nurse accepted Marin's insistence she was learning to digest American fare.

"Marin." Karen is in the office when she enters. "I'm surprised to see you here."

After returning home from Amber's, neither Raj nor Marin mentioned their visit to Gia. That night they fell asleep with a gulf between them. Enough room for the heartbreak that had settled into their lives.

"Gia forgot her science book," Marin says. She had actually pulled it out of Gia's backpack seconds before she left for school. It was the only excuse Marin could create to follow through on her plan. "Since she has science after lunch, I thought I would drop it off."

"Of course." Karen holds out her hand. "We'd be happy to take it to her."

"I'm fine. It'll give me a chance to say hello," Marin continues the lie seamlessly.

Karen glances around them, cognizant of other parents in and out of the office. "Why don't we speak in my office?" Once there, she closes the door behind them. "I've been meaning to call you but wanted to give your family some time."

"We appreciate it," Marin says, holding her cards close. "As you can assume, it was a shock." Always a professional, she keeps her words clipped and sure.

"Of course. You spoke to Gia?"

"Yes." Marin weighs her options, each one weightier than the last. There is no right answer here, she is sure. Instead, she chooses the easiest, the one to get her where she wants to go. "She refuses to tell us anything."

"I see." Karen fails to mask her disappointment. "I was hoping for more." She goes behind her desk and opens a drawer. Pulling out a Rolodex, she flips through it until she finds the card she is searching for. Handing it to Marin, she says, "An excellent child psychologist. One trained to deal with abuse. I would highly recommend you call her."

Marin takes the card and tucks it into her purse. She has no plans to call a psychologist or psychiatrist to help her with her daughter. She will handle this herself. "Thank you," she says. "I appreciate the reference." She glances at the time. "Now, if you'll excuse me, I better get this book to Gia before lunch is over and classes resume."

"Marin," Karen says, coming to stand beside her. "I mentioned to you last time I was required by law to contact child services."

With all that happened that day, Marin has forgotten.

"As an administrator it is my first priority to protect the children in the school," Karen continues. "I would never try to overstep my place—"

"Then don't," Marin says, not allowing her to finish.

"A social worker contacted me. They wanted more information." Karen doesn't acknowledge Marin's directive. "I told them what I knew. What I believed."

"Which is?"

"That I don't think her parents are at fault. But someone hurt Gia." Karen lowers her voice. "They mentioned they would be contacting you very soon. They need to know who did this."

"Then we agree," Marin says, softening her tone so the interaction doesn't become combative. "When I find out who did this, and I plan to, I will make sure and let you know. Until then, I appreciate you providing my daughter with the best education my money can pay for."

A diverse student body fills the hallways. Pouring out of their classrooms, the ninth through twelfth graders search until they find their friends. They head en masse toward the lunchroom or outside to eat. With the weather permitting it year round, most students chose to eat outside on the tables under the trees. Gia's last class before lunch is literature. It is with her favorite teacher, a man who has published a number of short stories in journals. As Marin nears the classroom, she spots Gia standing right outside of it, her hand enclosed in a young man's. Taller than Gia by a number of inches, his blond hair is a contrast to Gia's brown. A handsome face filled with confidence. He's laughing at something Gia said. He moves down, brushing his lips over hers.

"Gia!" Marin's yell reverberates through the hallway, stopping everyone. Students stare, first at Marin and then at Gia. The small student population guarantees everyone knows one another. An unexpected drama in the middle of another normal day catches their attention, and the normally boisterous students fall quiet. Aware of the potential scene, Marin plasters a smile on and lowers her voice. "Sweetheart, you forgot your textbook at home."

"I did?" Gia drops the boy's hand immediately. Stepping away, she begs him with her eyes to leave. "Which one?"

"Science." Marin leans down to offer Gia a quick hug. Gia winces when Marin's hand brushes her arm. "Gia, aren't you going to introduce me to this young man?"

Disappointed there isn't a show, students scatter. Gia glances around, making sure they no longer have an audience. "Uh, this is Adam." She steps even farther away from him, as if the last few minutes never existed. Starting to walk away, she waits for Marin to follow her.

"Nice to meet you, Adam," Marin says, ignoring Gia's cue. Holding out her hand, she waits for him to shake it. Already knowing the answer, she asks, "Are you in the same grade as Gia?"

"No." He glances at Gia, a silent message passing between the two of them. "I'm a senior."

"And you're new?" Marin prods, demanding answers.

"Yes. My family just moved here this year." Sticking his hands into his pockets, he leans back against the lockers. "From Florida."

"Well, welcome." Marin smiles, a false one meant to disarm. "I'm thrilled Gia and you have met. Obviously, you've become closer than she let on." Marin gives Gia an indulgent smile, assuring them she's in on their secret but approves wholeheartedly. Gia, who has returned to Marin's side, returns a weak one. "Tell me about yourself, Adam, since Gia has failed to."

Adam raises his eyebrows, confused. "I play basketball." A bell rings overhead, reminding the students lunch period has begun. Pointing to the clock, he says, "The bell is my cue. I should get going."

"Of course." Turning toward Gia, Marin offers a half-disapproving look. "I'm sorry Gia hasn't introduced us earlier. But no worries, we can make up for it." Leaning down, Marin whispers into her ear, "See you later, sweetheart." Not waiting for any further discussion, Marin leaves them, walking briskly out of the school and back to her car.

"I have a study session tonight," Gia calls out, sharing a glance with Adam.

"Right. Study hard," Marin says, giving nothing away.

* * *

Almost Gia's dismissal time. Marin has waited impatiently. Work failed to keep her occupied. Without telling Raj of her plans, she gets into her car and drives to the school and parks at a distance. From her vantage, she'll be able to see Gia without being detected. When the final bell rings, students pour out the front door. The younger classmen head toward rides while the upperclassmen go toward the parking lot where their cars are parked. Marin spots Gia immediately. Her backpack is thrown carelessly over her shoulder. She is surrounded by her friends, some of whom Marin doesn't recognize. Relieved, Marin watches them walk toward a waiting car. Seconds later, Adam exits the school. Marin assumes he calls Gia's name, because she turns. Marin sees the struggle on Gia's face before she says something inaudible to her friends. Soon enough she turns toward Adam, slipping her hand into his. Waving good-bye to her friends, Gia gets into Adam's car and they drive off.

Driving a safe distance behind them, Marin watches as they pull in front of a house in Redwood City, a few miles north of their home. It's large, with a well-kept yard and luxury vehicles parked in the road. The neighboring homes are similar in style and square footage. Adam pulls into the driveway and both exit the car. From Gia's behavior, Marin can tell she's been here before. Gia waits while Adam unlocks the front door with a key. Following him in, Gia shuts the door, not catching sight of Marin sitting in her car a few doors down.

Marin watches, waiting. One hour turns to two, until soon enough the sun sets and dusk falls. Marin doesn't leave her place, her eyes focused on the front door. Nearing ten p.m., Gia's curfew, Adam exits the house first, followed by Gia. They get into his car and start to drive. Marin quickly starts her own car, increasing her speed to reach home before they do. Once there, she pulls into the garage, shutting it quickly behind her. She sprints into the house just as she hears the jingle of keys in the front door. Smoothing her hair back, she goes into her office to wait. When the front door slams shut, Marin steps out of her office to see Gia locking up.

"How was studying?" Marin asks, watching Raj come down the stairs at the sound of the door.

"Good," Gia says, avoiding her eyes. "I should get to bed."

"Do you want anything to eat?" Raj asks, his eyes curious.

"We grabbed a bite." Gia starts to move past Marin toward the stairs.

"Who dropped you off?" Marin asks casually, already turning back toward her office. She makes no mention of Adam or the revelation at school.

"One of the moms."

Not even a breath to consider the lie or a pause to wonder if telling the truth is better. When Gia was a child, Marin always knew how to tell she was lying—Gia would tap her left foot. First it would be sporadically, but as Gia continued the lie, it would get faster. Unable to control it, she would cover her left foot with the right, hoping to quiet the movement.

Over the years Gia had mastered the urge and almost rid herself of it completely. Marin hadn't seen the action for quite a while. She assumed it was because Gia had stopped finding reasons to lie. Now she understood Gia had simply learned to be a better liar.

"Good." Marin stops, turning toward both Raj and Gia at the same time. "I almost forgot," she says, stopping Gia's escape. "When I dropped off your book today, the principal pulled me aside. Mentioned that legally she has to contact child services when a child has been abused."

"What?" Raj swallows, his mouth forming into a thin line.

"I wasn't abused," Gia whispers, her eyes wide. "Did you tell her that?"

"I couldn't tell her anything, since you won't tell us what happened," Marin replies easily, refusing to soften at the sight of her daughter's distress. "A social worker will be contacting us soon to get more information. Visit the home to understand the situation."

"What does that mean?" Gia asks, fear in her voice.

"It means if they think your father or I are the reason you have bruises, then they can take you away and put you into a foster home."

Part of Marin welcomes the look of horror on Gia's face. Now maybe Gia can understand the hell they have been living through. One thing Gia has always taken for granted, Marin is sure, is the comfort of her life. The thought of anything else is destabilizing.

"But that's not true." Gia tenses, withdrawing into herself. She drops her head, hiding from them. Seeming to come to a decision, she wraps her arms around herself. "My friends and I play this game. It's stupid." Gia glances at Marin, who is listening intently. "I knew you guys would be mad so I didn't mention it."

"What?" Raj looks to Marin first before settling his gaze on Gia. His voice getting louder with anger, he demands, "What the hell kind of game?"

"We hit each other to see how much pain you can endure. The one who cries uncle last wins."

"Which friends?" Marin demands, watching Gia carefully. She considers Amber then dismisses the thought. An innocence still lingers on her. Something that Gia no longer has.

"Why does it matter?" Gia demands.

"Who came up with the game?" Raj interjects, giving Marin a warning glance. One that implores she tread lightly.

"It's something kids do. To keep things interesting." Gia turns toward Marin, begging her. "Can you tell them that? The social worker?"

"Are you telling us the truth?" Marin demands. She had read stories of teenagers hurting themselves—cutting, choking, and now beating one another up. Furious at Gia for participating, her tone is biting. "Or is this another lie?"

"I'm telling the truth," Gia says. "I promise."

* * *

Night has fallen. The window in Marin's office reveals the stars in the sky. She lies on the sofa, not having moved since Gia offered her admission hours ago. They have left the cleanup for the housekeeper, and Gia has gone upstairs to finish her homework. Marin said nothing to Raj about Adam. Gia gave her a grateful glance as she said her good-nights.

Marin replays the day's events and Gia's admission in her head. Marin knew all of Gia's old friends. They come from upstanding families. As does Gia, Marin thinks. Going through the list, she tries to imagine which one would play the game. One name after the next she mentally crosses out.

A fleeting image, a whisper in the woods, brings to mind Adam's hand encased in Gia's. He had refused to leave Gia's side at the school, held on tightly to her hand. His look reminded Marin of one she had seen her entire childhood. It was from someone who believed they owned you and could do with you as they wished. The lie Gia so easily spoke about whom she was with. Gia going to his home. Both of them all alone for hours. Their relationship an elaborate secret. Images start to crowd in her head—all of them leading toward the inevitable truth.

Gia isn't lying to save herself, Marin realizes with a start. She's lying to save Adam.

Nausea rises up, gagging her. She rushes to the adjoining bathroom just in time. Holding on to the toilet, she retches until her stomach is empty. Sweat lines her brow, and her body shakes from the convulsions. She falls back against the wall, grabbing the edge of the toilet to support her. He has beaten Gia, Marin is sure of it. There is no question in her mind that he has raised his hands to her daughter more than once. Why and how don't matter anymore. All that's important is that Marin is going to destroy him. Take him apart for having harmed her little girl. Only then can she assure Gia's safety in a way she had never been able to guarantee her own.

TRISHA

On the night before Marin's wedding, the lightbulb flickers as the electricity sizzles; the crickets chatter among themselves. The three sisters stand together, one shoulder against the other. Ranee, a fragile barrier, stands between Brent and the girls.

The night air is cool after the damp summer rain. Brent struggles with the key, cursing in Gujarati when it fails to give. "Did you spray the WD-40 like I told you?" he demands.

"Yes," Ranee lies. In the midst of finalizing wedding details, she has forgotten.

"It didn't work." He yanks the key, slamming his fist against the door.

"The rain always expands the wood. Here, let me try." She hopes to calm him.

"You think you are stronger than me?" He laughs—the only one. "Stupid."

The girls continue in silence, watching. He alternates between trying the key and hitting the door. A raindrop falls. Soon, a light shower begins. They use the veils of their saris to cover their heads.

"Got it." The click of the lock and he throws the door open. He steps quickly in ahead of them all. They are slow to remove their heeled pumps in

the entryway, each still on a high from the hours of dancing and socializing with their friends in the Indian community.

"Girls, change your clothes, fold them, and bring them to me. I will put them back in the suitcase." Ranee prods them along. The saris are fashioned from silk she received as a wedding gift. Brent had commissioned a tailor weeks later. A lovely surprise from when his heart was still kind.

"I want to wear mine to bed, Mama," Trisha declares. Fascinated by the vibrant colors, she revels in the way it makes her feel.

"No, Beti," Ranee cajoles. "These are special. Meant only for wedding celebrations. When it is your time, you will be allowed to choose."

"Well, I want this one." Trisha twirls and dances through the foyer. Their home is immaculate on the inside. An engineer with two master's degrees, Brent is thorough and organized. His home life must follow suit. "I look beautiful in it," Trisha announces, confident. She's enthralled by the grace and splendor she perceives in herself. She just turned fifteen, is on the brink of becoming a woman. Her lean thighs have yet to mimic the curves of her breasts, which are bound tight by the form-fitting deep-red blouse. The silk stops below the edge of her bra, leaving bare her flat stomach to below the belly button. The free-flowing skirt ties above the bones of her hips, elegant to the rim of her ankles. The translucent sari wraps around her, meticulously tucked in, then like a beaded shawl thrown carelessly over her shoulder. "Everyone was staring at me."

"No one was," Brent snaps. They stop, all of them. Not by thought but reflex. Animals trained to tremble at their owner. "Is this proper? There is a need to be looked at?"

These are not questions. Trisha's face shows her deliberation. A decision whether to answer or remain silent. She fears either choice, not for herself but for the others. Ranee inspects him from a distance. An immediate survey to gauge the situation.

"Yes, Trisha, you are correct."

"What?" Brent snaps his gaze toward Ranee.

"An auntie at the garba was telling me how beautiful Trisha looked. Her mastery of the steps to the stick dance. She of course takes after your youngest brother, dear."

The girls wait. They have no other option.

"Marin, Sonya—you are both on my side of the family. But Trisha, you are your father's daughter." She takes each step one at a time. With a full belly laugh, she creates a diversion. A smile graces her face. From deep within her, she finds a reason. An illusion for them all.

"My brother named you," Brent reminisces. Lost in her game, unaware of the play. *"He was the first to hold you."*

The girls know the story. It is a tale repeated over the years. Lost in the memories of another time, the only time Brent was happy. *"You were in New Delhi, Papa,"* Trisha says.

"I was. The monsoon had flooded the streets. The trains could not move."

"You telegrammed that you had hired a rickshaw. Driving all night you would arrive by morning." Ranee passes Trisha to move closer to him. *"In the middle of labor, and I am calling friends of friends. To keep you from danger."*

"I needed to see my second-born enter this world. Be the first to give her the drink of sugar water." He reaches Trisha, but she is not afraid. He caresses her hair and pulls her into an embrace.

"Your brother thought of the name you would like best," Trisha prompts him, sustaining the flow of the story.

"Yes, I listened to your mummy and stayed put. Waiting anxiously for the news."

"We could not lose you to the floods. What would we do without you?" Ranee asks. *"You arrived in Rajkot two weeks later. Your suitcases filled with gifts for Marin and our new child. Trisha, all you cared for was milk from my breast, and your father had spent thousands of rupees on toys for the two of you."*

The memories tease them, reminding them of a different time. Yet, they had left everything behind. Now all that remained was a bastardized mockery of the past.

"They told me." Brent's gaze fills with warmth and love. "Your mummy had the servants wire notes daily to the hotel. Your mind—sharp like my father's. A blessed future . . ." His voice trails off. His face is awash in anger. "It is why I made the sacrifice to come to America. A pauper in this country when I was a raja in my own."

He releases Trisha, his fists tight. "Opportunities for my daughters, I explained to my mother. An education they cannot receive in India. She begged me to stay, her oldest son." Brent's face fills with obvious ache. "I did not listen. I left my family and my life to better my children's."

"Your sacrifice can never be repaid." Ranee exhales and then motions her girls toward their room. "Daughters, never forget your father's gift to each of you." She caresses his back, a rare initiated touch. "Soon we will celebrate as never imagined. Our first child's wedding to a maharaja. An engineer of Brahmin caste. The gods are proud of the sacrifice you have made. We have been rewarded with giving our daughter to an upstanding family of class and value."

"Trisha will be next," Brent says quietly, staring at his middle daughter. "Soon, she will leave us."

"Yes, and she will be even more fortunate than her sister," Ranee agrees. "What more could we want?"

* * *

I can count the exact number of days since Eric left. While planning my wedding, I often daydreamed about our marriage. The house we would live in, the cars we would drive. I could feel the kisses we would give one another before heading to work and hear the conversations at dinner discussing our day. My mind laid everything out in exact detail. Everything except the separation. I made no accommodations for that intrusion. But now that it is real, I am helpless but to accept it. To welcome the loneliness with open arms and find a way to live alongside it, accommodating the stranger in my home.

I think of Mama and her feelings about living alone. Funny, I never thought about it before. Never wondered how she adjusted to her own empty house or if she could swear someone was calling her name but then be met with silence. I walked into Eric's empty closet the other day. He left a few things behind: a sock with no match, shirts he hasn't worn in years, and a pair of running shoes. The shoes fascinated me the most. I sat down in the middle of the walk-in and stared at them. I could see him lacing them up as he prepared for a run. Returning after a long one and then jumping into the shower to wash up. Back then, I knew when he left that he was coming back.

It's the daily occurrences that I miss the most. The events that failed to register once they became normal parts of coexisting. Emptying his pockets of extra change, setting his wallet on the bureau, or throwing his clothes into the hamper only to miss and have everything land on the bathroom floor instead. I accepted him in my life as if he had always been there. Now, I wonder how I will ever live without him.

Sleeping together was the easiest. Almost as if a bed were meant for two rather than one. When Eric would awake early for a meeting, I'd feel his absence within seconds. The emptiness made sleep impossible. I was used to another body in the bed, always had been. A childhood filled with Sonya curling into bed with me made it easier to share space. With my husband, there were no fights for the blanket, no side that was his or mine.

"I want to make love to you," he would whisper in my ear. No matter where we were, in the den paying bills, or warming up hot cocoa, he would slip his arms around my waist and pull me in tight. Never able to resist him, I would turn into his arms, always ready, always wanting. We rarely fought but when we did, I was always first to acquiesce, to give in. It felt easiest. After watching a lifetime of fighting, I did not want friction. Peace became my motivation, and I did everything to maintain it.

Eric's clout in business rarely spilled over into our life together. He had no reason to show his power with me. I took to being an executive's wife as if I had been preparing for it forever. The clothes, the money, the social circle—all of it felt normal, right to me. Born to be a wife. My stomach tightens now at the thought. When did his vocation supersede mine? I easily accepted our traditional roles though no one demanded I do so. *But*, a voice reminds, *I never allowed the one role that would have solidified my place—that of a parent.*

Needing to escape the confines of my home, I grab my keys, race to my car, and start driving. Without planning to, I end up at the only place that has always been safe, that has always been mine. I pull into my parents' driveway and kill the engine. Even now, I still think of it as their home, versus hers alone. Though Papa may never step into the house again, it will always be the home where he gave me everything.

Out of habit, I use my own key to open the door. Before Sonya came home, I was the only one of the three daughters who still had one. Even when Papa updated the locks, he made sure to make me a copy. Said it was important I have one in case of an emergency. When the true emergency arose, my key was useless. There was nothing I could do to keep Papa safe.

"Trisha!" Mama says, surprised. She is on her way downstairs. She is still dressed in her pajamas, and her hair is flowing around her. "What are you doing here, Beti?" She takes the few extra steps to embrace me. I hold her close, tighter than I ever have before.

"I thought we could have lunch," I say, finding an excuse.

"At ten in the morning?" She takes my hand, enclosing it in hers. It is warm and though my hand is larger than hers now, I hold on firmly, welcoming the security. "Let's sit."

She leads us to the living room, where framed pictures of the three daughters and Gia line the shelf above the fireplace. All the pictures of Papa are gone. I remove my hand from hers, glancing around the room, suddenly seeing it as if for the first time. Every trace of him has vanished. The basket he kept his newspapers in. The case for his reading glasses. His slippers that were always tucked beneath the sofa he favored. All of it gone. I turn toward her, fury filling me. "Everything, Mama? You didn't leave one trace for us to remember him by?"

Before she can answer, I start opening the writing-desk drawers. Unable to sleep, I would come downstairs at night for water and he would be sitting here, reminiscing over pictures from India. I would climb onto his lap and he would tell me stories of his childhood, of his home when he was happy. Each opened drawer reveals what I already suspected—all of his childhood pictures are gone. "Where are they?" I demand, turning on her. "All of his photos?"

"Why?" she asks, gently. "What need do you have for them?"

"He's my father!" I scream at her, the first time in my life. "You may believe he's never coming back, but I don't." I want to hit her, to hurt her like I saw Papa do so many times. I want to see her afraid so she can understand the fear gripping me. "He's not dead."

"No." She is calm in a way I have never seen her. "But I hope he does die."

My knees buckle; my legs weaken. I sink into the sofa, my head in my hands. "What? Why?" The question is ridiculous, I know. But I ask nonetheless. I am sure the physical abuse stopped after we all left the house. With no children left to rile his anger, I assumed he had no reason to lash out. "He stopped hitting you, right?"

"Yes." She answers me matter-of-factly, as if we are in a courtroom and her answers are rehearsed. "The last time was the day Sonya left."

Shocked, I raise my eyes to her. The day still haunts, reminds each of us how easy it was to walk away. None of us had ever considered it before, so when Sonya did it, it was a revelation. "Why?" It made no sense. Sonya was never his favorite, not the one he needed. Why would her leaving affect him?

"Because that was the day I told him I wanted a divorce."

Looking at my mother now, feeling dread and shock, and trying to process what she just said, I respond, "You asked him for a divorce?" I stare at her. "What happened?"

"He beat me, worse than all the other times," she admits conversationally, as if we are talking about the weather. "Then he cried and told me that he had spent his entire life supporting me, providing for me, for you girls. He said he had made mistakes, lots of them, but he was sorry." She pauses, a faraway look. "It was the first time he said those words to me. He told me he didn't know how to love, that he was learning."

"Then why?" I plead, moving past her admission as I used to move past the physical violence. I am an expert at it, storing the occurrence in a small box in my brain where it can't hurt me. "There's no reason to rid the house of him." I am begging for myself. With my own home in shambles, this one is the only stability I have left, the house and the memories of my time here.

"He lied, Trisha," Mama says. "He wasn't sorry. He never was." She sits down next to me, wrapping her frail arm around my shoulder. "You know that."

Her words cause me to flinch. Unable to understand why, I push away from her. Standing, I pace the small room. Music filters down the stairs. Old Hindi songs. A small *diya* burns in the makeshift temple on the edge of the kitchen. Homemade ghee fuels the flame. Inside the steel shrine sit pictures of all the gods we pray to. Out of deference to Eric's faith, Mama added a small statue of Jesus when we got married. My childhood home, the one where I grew into the woman I am today, starts to close in on me. My mother's words feel like a sword, though I have no idea what she is talking about.

"Then why did you stay?" I demand. I see my reflection in the mirror on the side wall. Instead of the perfectly kept woman I am used to seeing, I gaze at a child in distress. A girl is screaming. Her hair in disarray, her face stained with tears. Her eyes are closed, refusing to see. I shake my head, trying to dislodge the image, but when I reopen my eyes, I see she has opened hers. She stares at me. I turn away, unable to look at her anymore.

"Because I believed him," she answers. "Just like you did."

I have to get out. My sanctuary has become a prison. I grab my purse and am ready to bolt when she asks, "Why did Eric leave?"

Of course Sonya would have told her. Though we knew to keep our secrets from the outside world, sometimes we forgot to keep them from one another. They served as a reminder that no matter how much time has passed, we can never truly escape the darkness we shared. "Because I wasn't enough," I say.

She grabs my hand as I am about to leave. Holds tight. "Why didn't you want children?"

Sonya is not home, I am sure of it. That night when she stayed with me, held my hair back as I vomited, and then curled into the bed with me while we slept, I had never been so grateful to have my sister back. But now, if she were home, I would turn on her, furious that she revealed too much. "Since Sonya has all the answers, why don't you ask her?"

"Your sister loves you." Mama pauses, accepting her next words as truth. "You are the only one I am sure she loves." She takes both my hands in hers, faces me. "Please, Beti," she whispers, "tell me. Why didn't you want children?"

"Maybe I'm just like Papa," I tell her, wondering if the reason is real. "Maybe I don't know how to love."

SONYA

"Can you take a picture of me?" The little girl, Tessa, bounces on her hospital bed. She is the fifth patient I've worked with today, and so far the youngest. The others were almost teens. Most stared at me, bored, until they had the camera in their hands. Then, like magic, they began to photograph whatever they could find. Soon, they were chasing down laughing nurses, begging for just one more shot.

"How about you take some by yourself?" I open her tight palm and gently lay the camera atop her cold fingers. I still feel like a stranger in this hospital. My official badge hangs off my suit pants. After wearing jeans and T-shirts the first few days, I used some saved money on more grown-up wear. Splurging on fitted work dresses and pantsuits, I updated my closet for the first time in years. As promised by Human Resources and David, I was supplied with a number of high-end digital cameras and a photo printer for each floor. "You can do it."

"What if I break it?" Tessa stares at the camera in her hand, her desire warring with her fear.

"You can't break it," I assure her. "But if you really don't want to . . ." When I try to take the camera back, her fingers reflexively curl around it. I suppress a knowing smile. "How about you give it a try?"

She takes a picture of her toe, giggling all the while. Then follows it up with one of her knee and a thumb. Two elbows and her shoulder later she is almost finished. Right before she hands the camera back she takes one of her IV. "All the parts of me," Tessa says. "Did I do it right?"

"Perfect." I envision her final picture and wonder about how easily she accepts a needle in her arm as an extension of her. A necessity forced on her by those trying to save her. "How about I print these out and we can make a picture book for you? Title it *ME*." With a tired nod, she agrees. As I gather my materials, Tessa climbs slowly back under the covers. Flipping through the channels like a seasoned pro, she settles on some cartoons. Wanting to say more but unsure of what, I leave without a word.

"There you are." David catches me in the hall. "How's it going?"

After accepting the position, I sought him out to let him know. He was thrilled. Since I started, we run into each other a few times a day. He stops me every time, making an excuse to talk. He'll ask to see the pictures the children have taken or want to know what they had to say. As I repeat their adventures, many of them concocted in the young patients' imaginations after hours of lying in hospital beds, he watches me. His eyes soften and he leans closer to hear me carefully. I have come to look forward to these moments; there is safety in our interactions. In the halls, among the hospital staff and patients, I am sheltered. In that haven, I am free to appreciate him. To admire the respect the staff has for him, the gratitude from his patients and their families. He accepts it all with humility, never basking in the credit bestowed on him.

David rarely asks me about my father—how I feel about him. I appreciate that. There's really nothing I can say beyond that we are waiting. Just waiting. It is impossible to imagine my own father acting anything like David. My father's desperate need for control, for respect, was proof of his weakness. An adult bully who made his children into his victims. A man like David could never build a rapport with a man like that. They are from two different worlds, and if my father wasn't lying in a coma upstairs, I am certain their paths would never have crossed.

Today David has on a suit and a tie with a picture of Elmo stealing cookies. He is always impeccably dressed, his suits cut to fit his lean form perfectly. "Nice tie."

"Thanks." He pulls it forward to give me a better view. "Present from my daughter." He relieves me of a few of the cameras I'm juggling to hold. "Are you free for lunch?"

"I was heading upstairs to print out the pictures."

"Have you already eaten? My treat."

The rumbling of my stomach gives me away. I roll my eyes at his knowing smile. "Fine, but my treat. You did get me a job, after all."

We put the cameras safely behind the nurses' desk and head toward the cafeteria. "Everyone is raving about your work. I'm the star of the hospital for having convinced you."

"Everyone?" I tease. "This must be a small hospital."

"Word gets around fast." He holds open the door, allowing me to enter first. "And as a thank you for finally getting me my long overdue sense of importance, I offer you wrapped sandwiches." The cafeteria has a number of sandwiches, fries, salads.

"Wow, you really know how to treat a woman right," I return, picking from the salad bar. As promised, I pay, though he argues and promises the next meal is on him. We eye the full cafeteria—not a free seat in sight. "Looks like everyone is hungry."

"Come on. Let's eat in my office."

I follow him back out and we ride the elevator silently upstairs. Inside his office, there are more pictures of his daughter from her birth on. Framed photos line the ledge against the window. His mounted degrees are set evenly on the wall behind his desk. Rich leather chairs and a plush sofa are our choices for seating. I pick one edge of the sofa and am not surprised when he joins me. "Nice office."

"I had to kill someone to get it, but please don't tell." He grabs two bottled waters from a miniature refrigerator, opens one, and hands it to me. "They frown on those types of things."

"Picky, picky." I take a deep swallow from the bottle. "Do they expect you to be perfect?"

"That's what I've been saying." He chuckles as he takes a bite of his food.

We eat in comfortable silence, both happy to fill our stomachs. He passes me an extra fork when my plastic one breaks, and I offer him one of my paper napkins when his falls to the ground. Finally sated, we finish off our water and gather the trash. "That was nice, thank you."

"You paid, so thank you," he says.

He takes the trash from my hand, our fingers touching. I'm the first to pull away. I glance at my watch, an excuse to break eye contact. "I'd better get going."

"The children will be eating right now," he murmurs, glancing at his own watch. "We still have a few minutes." He motions for me to retake my seat. Unable to come up with an excuse to refuse, I sit down. "Have I told you how thrilled I am you took the job?"

"Only a few dozen times," I say, "but don't let that stop you." On a more serious note I say, "It's been more fun than I thought."

"Working with sick children?" He gazes at me questioningly.

"They find joy in the simplest things," I say, trying to verbalize my feelings. "We forget that as adults." There's something in his look but I can't quite make it out. Almost as if I have passed a test, as if he were waiting for me to say the right words but I did better. It pleases me while at the same time makes me want to run. The dichotomy of my life—want what I can never have, reject it because I am too afraid.

"They didn't choose this fight," he says, "so they try to remember what it was like when they weren't losing."

That makes sense. How many times did I yearn for normality in my childhood, only to have the expectation shattered when faced with my father? My needs became secondary to his, so much so that in time I forgot what I ever wanted. "What made you want to be a doctor?"

"Both my parents were," he shares. "I grew up in hospitals, around their friends—all of whom were doctors, by the way." He smiles easily. "I never knew anything else."

It's hard for me to imagine being so confident about your life at such a young age. To know that you belong. "You're lucky," I say sincerely. "Not everyone has such a clear vision."

"You didn't." It's not a question.

"No." I struggle not to reveal too much. "Growing up—there were more questions than answers."

"You were supposed to go to law school."

I tense, forgetting I had told him that. I start to shake my head, to tell him that, no, there was no conflict, no scars to hide, but he interrupts me before I can say anything.

"The world is very lucky you chose photography instead. You have a true gift."

"I think it chose me." I never imagined the joy I would get from taking pictures. From memorializing events and places with a snap of a camera. When I see the pictures I've taken, I stare at them in wonder, amazed at the beauty that has been captured forever. "I had no choice but to say yes." Seeing the numerous awards David has won and the honors bestowed on him, I walk over, running my hands over the crystal accolades. "But I don't save lives. Make people whole again. That's the real gift."

When I take a picture, it's a multiple-step process. First, I view the scene with my naked eye. Assess the surroundings, the light, the scene to make sure everything is perfect. In a professional shoot I have the benefit of added light, but out in the field, I am dependent upon nature or circumstance. Once I have finalized the details, made sure my focus is clear, I look through the lens and start snapping. With digital, I have no worries about film or the cost. I can take hundreds of pictures, quickly, capturing every second of movement. Once I have as many as I need, I upload them onto my computer, analyzing each one to find perfection.

On rare occasions, something hidden finds its way into the picture. A person passing by, or an animal in flight. A child playing or a look between friends. Something I missed, because I was so focused on the vision in my head, reveals itself in the picture. With the unexpected addition, I am mesmerized. The picture has a new life, one I would never have foreseen. It changes the story; what I had hoped to say becomes altogether different. The new story is superior, told in a way I couldn't fathom. Those are the moments when I especially love what I do. When the picture becomes the storyteller and I am the recipient of the story it tells.

"A matter of perspective," David says, bringing me out of my thoughts. He comes to stand next to me, his warmth filling the empty space. He pauses, watching me carefully, gauging my reaction before he says, "Your dad's condition is unchanged."

I am between the wall and him, with no place to run. "Yes," I agree quickly. "But we appreciate everything you're doing."

"Checking his vitals every day?" He leans against the wall, effectively trapping me in. "Don't mention it." He stares at a space above me. Trying to find the right words. "I'm sorry I haven't been able to give your family more answers."

The truth lies unspoken between us. My father's death would not change my life, but his living would. I wonder what further damage he can inflict if he lives. I am already torn, and he can't tear apart much more. But his death would leave me as I already am—irretrievably broken.

"Maybe there aren't any," I say, treading water. I have no place to hide, to flee to, without going past him. "Sometimes that's life."

It is how I soothe my soul—my explanation for why tragedy was mine when others lived a life filled with tranquility. When I was young,

I would watch nature channels, fascinated by videos of a cheetah or tiger crouched, waiting. When the time came, it would run toward a herd of animals, increasing its speed until it had joined those running for their lives. In a heartbeat, it would attack, choosing one while sparing the rest. The others kept running, the instinct to survive strong. Was there any way for the lost one to live another day or was death simply its destiny?

"Do you believe that?" he asks.

"I have to," I say, brushing past him to find my own space. I look around, envisioning the room expanding, a hole that I can slip through and disappear into forever opening up in the middle of the floor. "Otherwise, how do you find the will to keep going?"

It's past time for me to return to what I know best—hiding behind the camera so I control the vision the world offers me. But David's next question stops me. "You all love him so much," he says, oblivious. "What did he do that was so right?"

I spent an entire night watching Trisha drink herself into oblivion because she refused to have her happily ever after. I listened to her call out for Eric in her sleep, her heart broken because her mind knew what her soul refused to believe—that he was gone. I coexist with my mother in a home that houses so many secrets the walls are filled with them, and yet it is the only shelter she trusts, the one she returns to night after night. And Marin, my own flesh and blood, has evolved into a woman I barely recognize.

"He made our life his own," I say, the only answer I have.

*　*　*

"In my day, we didn't have such fancy things." William turns the camera over in his hand, inspecting it from every angle.

At seventy-two, he is my oldest patient. Having just finished dialysis, he's cranky. I helped him into the chair next to his bed and handed him the camera. He refused it at first, saying he had no time for such things. I thought about leaving him, trying another day, but the way he turned toward the window, staring at nothing, made me try one more time. With a grunt to let me know he was doing me a favor and not the other way around, he held out his hand.

"It's a digital camera," I explain. "No film needed."

"Really?" He glances at me, the first hint of a smile on his lips. "I've got kidney failure, not Alzheimer's," he says. "I know what digital is."

"Right," I say, amused at having been thoroughly put in my place. "You have one at home?"

"No." He hands the camera back to me, his voice dropping. "Can't afford it." He reaches for the wheelchair nearby.

"They're easy to use." I roll the chair over, holding out a hand to him. Refusing my help, he struggles to rise from the sofa. "Just focus, click, and you have your picture."

"What would I want to take pictures for?" He barely stands before starting to stumble. Again, I reach out to help him, and again he refuses my overtures. It's a dance with no definitive steps. "Nothing I need to see again." He finally settles himself into the chair.

"How about those flowers?" A bouquet of fresh carnations sits in a glass vase next to the plastic water pitcher. A "Get Well Soon" card has fallen to the floor. "That would make a nice picture."

"Why? So I can remember them after they're dead?"

I suppress a sigh, a deep one. This was the part of the job I wasn't prepared for. I fear people. Having never understood what made my father tick, what made him react as he did, I am wary of others.

"No," I try, "so you can enjoy them forever."

"Haven't you heard?" He points to his IV. "I haven't got forever."

"None of us do," I say without thinking.

His gaze sharp now, he turns it toward me. "You make it sound like a good thing."

I look through the lens and focus the camera before handing it to him. "No, just inevitable." When he resists my efforts, I lay it gently in his lap. "But why not make the best of it while we can?"

He takes the camera and looks through the lens. From the other side I can see his worn eye blinking rapidly, trying to adjust. "You're too close," he says, bringing the camera down. "Move back so I don't get your whole face in it."

When he still struggles, I say, "Here, try this." I reach around him and show him how to adjust the lens. "Better?"

"I guess." He starts snapping pictures, one after the other. First he takes a few of me and then, bored, moves on to the water pitcher, the bed, and some of the outside through the window. Finished, he hands the camera back to me. "Congratulations, I'm healed."

Suppressing a smile, I point to the flowers. "You missed those."

"No, I didn't," he says, adjusting his tubes like an expert.

I reach over, rearranging the stems and petals. "You're missing a wonderful opportunity." Glancing through the lens, I bring the flowers into focus and adjust the center so they fill the screen. Once the picture is taken and printed, the flowers will have a whole new power—the ability to brighten any room. I snap a few photos and then glance at the LCD panel to review them. One especially is breathtaking. I try to show it to William, but he waves me away.

"I'm all finished for the day," he says, turning his face.

"OK," I murmur. "I'll print them out for you and make a book."

I'm about to gather my things when he barks, "Don't bother with the flower pictures."

"You don't like them?" I ask, surprised.

"Not much to like," he murmurs. With only a few options available in the small room, he climbs back into his bed.

"Let me help you." I quickly move back to his side, but he rejects my offer again. The flowers have the hospital's gift store sticker on them. "I can take the flowers downstairs. See if they have another arrangement."

"My daughter bought them. Won't be happy if she sees that."

He turns on the television, trying to ignore me. Unperturbed, I bend down to smell them, inhaling their fragrance, a contrast to the sterile smell of the room. "Nice of her. They're quite beautiful," I say, aware he's watching me. "Your daughter doesn't know you hate carnations?"

"They were her mother's favorite." He drops the remote. "Guess she thinks it'll help me to remember my wife."

"Your wife . . . ?" I leave the question hanging, wondering.

"Died a year ago." He is angry, at me, at everything, from what I can gather.

"I'm sorry." This is my cue to leave, to drop the subject. Nothing is gained from getting too close to people. From sharing secrets, dreams, and hopes. When you give a piece of yourself to someone, count on them to hold it safe, you become vulnerable. You depend on them, but they may not be the person you expected, the one you were sure could carry you. Then the disappointment becomes a burden to bear. It is better to keep yourself at a distance, never getting too close. I retrace my steps toward the door, ready to leave.

"Never thought I'd find love like that," he says, challenging me. "When you do, you don't ever want to lose it." He turns off the television and turns away from me. "Thanks for the pictures."

I shut the door quietly behind me. Nurses and doctors fill the hallway as they move in and out of patients' rooms. Families come and go, some with balloons in hand, while others, weary from months of visiting, simply come as they are. I watch them, wondering about the love that binds. In the name of love, people do extraordinary things. Sacrifice their time, money, even themselves for another. Parents dedicate their lives to raising children, work endless hours to provide; siblings love their sister or brother as if they were one instead of two. Here in the hospital, I see love displayed every day. Family members offering whatever they have in the hopes it is enough to heal.

I always wonder how one gets lucky enough to find unconditional love. Perhaps I drew the short straw and came to my father so he had someone on whom to inflict damage. Or maybe, given the secret I hold deep within me, I am no different than he is. My soul must be as dark, if not darker, to be who I am. A woman who, though no longer beaten, needs the memory of the beatings to survive.

MARIN

She plans and then executes. It's what she does best and the only means to maintain control. She has not shared her revelation with Raj or Gia. If she needed help, maybe she'd run the options by Raj, but she's confident enough in herself not to bother. She fears he would slow her down, question each decision. Gia's life is at stake, and for Marin that is enough reason to follow through.

Her first step was to hire a private investigator. She couldn't take the chance of Gia spotting her or learning of her intentions. The investigator was easily able to take the pictures Marin needed for proof. Almost daily, Gia went to Adam's house after school. When it was time for her to come home, he'd drop her off a few houses down, guaranteeing they avoided discovery. The game Gia professed they were playing wasn't happening. None of her friends were hitting her for fun. Gia was being abused, and worse, she was going back for more.

The PI performed a background check. The information he garnered was what put the next step of Marin's plan in motion. "He was charged as a juvenile for assault," he said when they met.

"On whom?" Marin had set up the meeting at a coffee shop in San Francisco, away from any prying eyes.

"A former girlfriend." The investigator slid a sheet of paper toward Marin. "The victim's name has been redacted, but all relevant information is there. Your boy likes to punch girls."

Marin read through the information as quickly as possible. "How did you get this?" she demanded, glancing up. "Juvenile records are supposed to be sealed."

"You hired me because I'm the best. You're getting what your money pays for." The investigator took a swallow of his coffee. "He was sixteen when he was charged. Got a slap on the wrist and some community service."

"Bastard." Marin glanced at the pictures he had printed out. Gia's hand in Adam's. His arm around her shoulders, holding her possessively. Most of them in front of his house, a few at school. "They don't go out much."

"No. In my experience, abusers like to do their work at home. Keeps it from getting messy."

Marin started to agree before catching herself. She knew well the benefits of hiding the hitting from the prying eyes of the world. The fewer people who knew, the safer the abuser was. "Anything else?"

"Like I said, he was sixteen when he was charged." The investigator leaned back in his chair, assessing her. "You don't get the same kiddie treatment as an adult."

"I don't understand."

The investigator reached over and pointed to a line on the sheet. Adam's date of birth. "His birthday is in a week."

He would turn eighteen. He could be tried as an adult. The wheels in Marin's head turned and soon everything fell into place. Thanking him for his service, she returned home and took the steps she was sure would destroy Adam. She called child services and set up an appointment. At that meeting, she offered them the necessary proof and her thoughts. Together they laid out the details and follow-up plan. The social worker agreed to arrive at their home at a scheduled time to start the process.

"Gia, Beti, the doorbell is ringing. Can you get it?" Marin calls out now. It's two in the afternoon on Saturday. Marin cleared her schedule and Gia's to make sure they'd be home. "Who is it, honey?" Marin calls from her office, waiting for the answer she already knows.

"Mom!" Gia's voice holds the fear Marin expected. "Come out here."

Marin takes her time, refusing to show her hand. She leisurely glances in the mirror in the bathroom before heading out. "What is it?"

"Mom, this is a social worker." Gia's hands are clasped in front of her, the fear obvious on her face. "I thought I told you . . ."

"Gia," Marin gives her a warning glance before stretching out her hand to the woman she's already met a few days before. "I'm Marin, Gia's mother. How may I help you?"

"Deborah. I'm from child services. We received a report from the school of potential abuse." She runs her eyes over Gia, an initial assessment of the situation. "I tried calling but didn't receive an answer, so I took a chance and stopped by."

"I see." Marin shows practiced surprise, but Gia is too scared to notice. "Why don't we speak in the living room?" Marin leads the way. Glancing at the clock on the mantel, she does a quick calculation. She has about an hour before Raj is due home from his tennis game. "I explained to the school that my daughter was participating in a game." She waves a hand toward Gia, who nods in agreement. "Not a very wise one, but you know kids these days."

"If that's the case, then I won't have to be here long." Deborah pulls out a notepad and pen. Turning toward Gia, she says, "I'll just need the first and last names of the friends you've been playing this game with."

"Why?" Gia asks, her voice low.

"To verify the story. Names?"

Gia glances at Marin, her face begging her mother to intercede. To save her. *That's what I'm doing.* "Give her the names, sweetheart."

"I can't." Gia swallows visibly. "I don't want them to get into trouble."

"I see." Deborah shuts the notebook. Her gaze intent on Gia, she seems to have come to a decision. "I need to see the bruises."

"What?" Gia flinches, as if she's been scalded. "No."

"We can do it here or I can get us an appointment at the local trauma center. But I need to see the bruises." Deborah meets Marin's eyes; a silent message passes between the two.

"She can't do this, Mom. Right?"

"I'm afraid she can, Beti," Marin says. "Let her see the bruises. You don't want to go to a hospital, do you?"

As a child, Gia used to love the cartoons with a cat chasing a mouse but always failing to catch it. It was hilarious to her that a measly rodent could so easily outsmart a creature known for its conniving ability. Now, Gia seems oblivious to her role in the game. Her face shows her worry that she is running out of options; the match is over. She slowly pulls off her T-shirt, revealing a plain white bra. There are two fresh bruises, Marin notes.

Her face hard, Marin watches wordlessly as Deborah takes out a small camera and begins taking pictures of the discolorations. "For the file," Deborah explains, noting the size and shape of each one. There are seven in all. Fresh ones mixed with those almost healed. A mural of pain. Finished, she instructs Gia to put her shirt back on. "Can I see your legs, please?" Gia lowers her head as she pulls up her skirt. Black and purple line her upper thighs. From kicks, Marin knows, her gut churning. When you are lying on the ground and they can't pummel their fist into your stomach, they resort to kicking, as if breaking an animal. Two more pictures, a few more notes, before Deborah is finished.

"What now?" Marin demands, unable to face her daughter.

"I create a file. Do some investigation." Facing Gia, she asks, "Is there anything you want to tell me? Now is the time."

"No." Gia's face crumbles. "Please, can't you just let it go? I'm OK." To Marin she pleads, "Mom, please."

"It's not your mom's decision. No one is allowed to beat you. It's against the law." Deborah stands, her job finished, for now. "I'll be in touch."

"What happens?" Gia asks, her voice small. "To the person that did this?"

"That depends," Deborah replies. "The final decision is up to the courts."

Marin makes sure Gia spends the rest of the weekend in the house. No hanging out with friends or leaving the house to see Adam. She confiscates Gia's phone under the pretense that she wants to upgrade it. She'll have it back in a few days, she assures her daughter. The only landline in the house is in Marin's office, used mainly for the fax. Left without a means to contact Adam, Gia sulks in the house.

"There were fresh bruises?" Raj demands, pacing back and forth in Marin's office. Marin has updated him on the visit, leaving out her part in the situation. "What now?"

"We wait. Gia still won't give names, so I assume there will be an investigation."

"My god." Raj drops into the sofa, his head in his hands. "How did this happen?"

"Does it matter?" Marin asks, dismissing the nagging feeling in the pit of her stomach. "It's happened and it needs to be fixed."

Something in her voice causes Raj to look up. "What are you saying, Marin?"

Marin schools her features. "Only that we have to support Gia and help her through this."

"I was thinking maybe we should pull her out of the school. Surround her with a new group of friends."

"No." Marin's response is visceral, straight from her gut. She will not allow Gia's future to be compromised. "We deal with this and move on. The best thing for her is consistency. To be surrounded by what's familiar. Putting her in a new school would hurt more than help."

Raj watches his wife carefully before responding. "I'll agree with your decision for now. But the matter is not closed."

Soon enough it will be, Marin thinks. Soon enough.

* * *

Marin cancels all her appointments for the day. Her secretary, getting used to the unexpected vacation days, says nothing. Marin's first call after speaking to her secretary is to the private investigator. "I need you to do one more job," she instructs. After giving him the details, she slips into a suit and meets Deborah at her office.

"Thank you for stopping by Saturday." Marin gives the woman a grateful smile, one of the few she's ever shown. "Gia had no idea we had spoken."

"It's my job to fully investigate the situation. I must say, you're playing a risky game." The social worker leans back in her folding chair, eyeing Marin. Marin knew she had fulfilled her obligations as a social worker. She had opened a full-scale investigation, run down each possibility. Karen had informed Marin that the social worker had stopped by the school, interviewed her and the PE teacher. "But I commend your dedication."

"She's my daughter," Marin says, as if that is enough explanation. "I kept her home all weekend. No contact with anyone besides me and her father."

"Not with Adam?"

"None. I made sure she had no access to the boy. She's back at school today."

"You're sure she'll go home with him after?"

"Guaranteed." Marin could tell from Gia's anxiousness all weekend that she was desperate to tell Adam what had transpired over the weekend. The visit from the social worker had scared her. "My investigator is ready to take pictures."

"Pictures of him in the act will prove he's the one beating her. Bruises are only circumstantial evidence." The social worker watches Marin carefully.

"Then let's expect pictures of him in the act."

Marin thought through each step and came up with the plan in detail. Experience with her father afforded Marin inside knowledge of how Adam's mind would work. Fear of the social worker's visit would drive him to desperation. With no other outlet, he would default to his preferred one—hitting Gia. He would convince her that it was her fault. She should have lied better, hidden her bruises more carefully, done anything that would absolve him and put the blame on her. Not only would she expect the beating, she'd convince herself she deserved it.

"He just turned eighteen." Deborah holds Marin's gaze. "He'll be charged as an adult."

"I'm very aware of that." Marin is anxious for the next step. "Let's move this forward."

It is the longest twenty-four hours Marin can remember. That night, she forces herself to work while waiting for the sound of Gia's arrival home. Raj, still in the dark, is busy at work. Marin finds herself rereading documents only to forget every word she just read. Giving up, she turns off the computer and sits in her chair, waiting.

The jingle of keys is the first thing that fills the silence. Then the front door opens and shuts. Marin jumps up, ready to bolt out of the room, when she hears the soft crying. Small gasps in an attempt to hide. Marin leans her forehead against the closed door of her office, steeling herself. Only when she is ready does she walk out, prepared to face her daughter.

"Gia." Marin's voice betrays none of the emotion she feels. "Are you all right, Beti?"

"Yeah." Gia quickly wipes at her face, wincing when she lifts her arm. "I'm just tired." She moves toward the stairs, ready to make her escape. "I'm going to go to bed."

"You were out late," Marin says, stopping her. Glancing at her watch, she murmurs, "Almost ten. You were studying?"

"Yes." Gia doesn't hesitate. "For a quiz. With friends."

"Which friends?" Marin asks, sharper than she meant to.

Gia lowers her eyes, taking the stairs quickly. "A study group."

"Gia." Marin's voice leaves no room for argument. Gia slowly turns, facing her mother. "I . . ." The words catch in her throat. From here she can see her daughter's pain, feel her fear. But she is helpless to heal it, to offer the words of comfort that will ease the tangled snare she's trapped in. Instead she says the only thing that comes to mind. "Are you ready for the quiz?"

"Yeah. Of course I'm ready." Not leaving room for anything else, Gia rushes up the stairs and into her room.

* * *

Marin waits in the car for Deborah and the police car. She awoke at the crack of dawn, made her own chai, sipping on the creamy milk until she felt her gut settle. An hour later, she heard Gia's alarm clock go off and then the sound of her showering. Leaving the kitchen for the security of her office, she stayed there until Gia finished her breakfast and left for the day. Then she drove to the school and, from a spot hidden in the distance, watched all the students enter.

"Are you ready?" Deborah taps on the closed window of Marin's car.

"Yes." Marin joins her on the street, both watching as the patrol car parks alongside them. "I have the pictures."

Late last night, the investigator e-mailed Marin the pictures of Gia and Adam at Adam's house. The last few Marin could barely glance at. The curtain had been open so the PI was able to get shots of Adam striking Gia, her face streaked with tears. Marin had immediately e-mailed them to Deborah, who agreed it was time to move. Neither woman wanted Gia going home with him even one more night.

Marin hands the prints to one of the officers. He reviews them before nodding once to Deborah. "Let's go."

Marin follows them silently into the school, where she points out the office. Karen has already been notified by the district attorney about the officers' visit. "They'll be breaking for lunch soon," Karen says upon their arrival. "I'll bring them to the office."

Though it's only minutes later, it feels like forever when Karen finally returns with Adam and Gia. Both look confused until they see the police.

"No," Gia says first, not noticing Marin. "He didn't do anything." The officers ignore her while reading Miranda rights to Adam. They pull his wrists behind him and cuff him. Adam stares ahead, his jaw tense. "Please let him go," Gia begs, staring first at Karen and then Deborah for help.

"Enough." Marin steps forward, catching Gia off guard. "Stop now." Gia, clearly shocked, falls silent. She watches with tears as Adam is led out of the office and the school.

"We need you to come with us," Deborah says gently, breaking the silence that had descended. "Your mom can drive."

"Go where?" Gia looks at Deborah and Marin, her face pained and scared.

"To the hospital. We need to make a record of the additional bruises on your body."

SONYA

When I was a teenager, Mom and Dad took us to Disney World in Florida. From there, we drove through Alabama, Mississippi, and Louisiana to Texas, before boarding a flight back to California. Dad loved driving and said the open roads of the South were like no others. Along the way we met many people, in restaurants, at the hotels. Everywhere we traveled, people were wearing crosses around their necks. We could see large churches from miles away. "Jesus Will Save You" was spray-painted on stop signs. At a gas station, a woman was passing out Bibles. Bored, I took one. She told me as long as I accepted Jesus Christ as my savior, I would be saved from the inferno, and, better yet, I could help save my loved ones. "What if I don't accept him?" I asked, curious.

Mom did diya every morning, and we stood around her while she prayed for us to be safe and protected. We visited the temple on certain holy days and for celebratory events, but otherwise religion played a very small role in our lives. Maybe Mom had a hard time believing in a God who would allow us to live the life we had.

"Then y'all going to spend the rest of eternity in hell," the woman answered with a rare surety.

On the road again, I wondered aloud if there really was a hell.

"No," Dad answered with complete confidence. "There's no such thing."

With hours on the road to reflect, I thought about his quick answer and could only come to one conclusion: he dared not believe in a hell, otherwise he had to know he was destined for it. But if I didn't do as they said, if I didn't accept this savior as mine, maybe I was headed for the same place. I knew the answer before it came to me—if my burning in hell meant my father would spend the rest of his soul's life swallowed by fire, then I was sure it was worth it.

*   *   *

It is David who pages me to tell me the news. Every day at work I slip on a little pager in case of an emergency. It's standard issue for all employees. I wanted to laugh when they gave it to me but held back. As if there would be a photography emergency. I was surprised when I started to get calls from nurses a few weeks in. Pediatric patients asked for me, wanted to take pictures, took delight in their creations. Though I was scheduled to leave work at four, I often found myself staying past dinner to meet all the requests of the day.

When I receive David's page, I assume he has a patient he wants me to work with. He seems to know the needs of the children outweigh those of his adult patients, so he rarely contacts me. Every time he does, I feel a jolt when his name shows up on the little screen. I always ignore the sensation, stamping out any feelings to keep our relationship completely professional. I use the nurses' desk phone to call him.

"You caught me," I tease, as soon as he picks up. "I was going to sneak out early today."

We have started to meet up with one another two to three times a week in the early evening. With few people left on the floors past dinner time, we grab a bite to eat together. Usually in the cafeteria, or if it is already closed, we munch on whatever we can find in the vending machines. We keep our conversations light, away from anything too serious. He never pushes me or asks for more than I am willing to say. It guarantees the impromptu meetings can continue. I won't be forced to run as long as he gives me nothing to run from.

"I'll believe that when I see it." David's voice holds an edge I haven't heard before. "Are you busy?"

"What's going on?" I start to have trouble breathing. It's been two days since I last visited my father. When I had a break between patients, I would beg myself not to go see him; there was no point. No words were strong enough. Even if I just sneaked briefly into his room, it calmed my nerves to see him still lying there—almost dead. "Is it Dad?" If he has awoken, then I will leave tonight. I won't see him. I will stop by Trisha's—say good-bye. She will understand. She will have to. I have my escape plan mapped out. My mind whirling, I barely hear David's next words.

"It's not your father. It's your niece."

I run when David finishes talking. He doesn't have details. Only that Gia is in the Trauma Unit and has asked for me. The sound of my heels hitting the sterile floors thunders in my ear. I wait impatiently for the elevator to arrive. When it refuses to, I run into the stairwell and down the flights to her floor. My badge is enough to get me past the security desk protecting the identity of the patients inside. Uniformed officers are in and out, a sea of blue among the walls of white.

"My niece, Gia, was just admitted . . ." I demand at the nurses' station. When my name is called, I turn around to see Marin as I have never imagined her. Her arms are crossed over her rail-thin body, her body tense. Instead of her normal suits, she has on jeans and a jacket. Circles underneath her eyes show hours of sleep lost. I rush toward her. "What happened?"

"Gia asked for you," Marin says, ignoring my question.

My face betrays my shock. Gia and I barely know each other now. When she was born, I was enthralled with her. Her unabashed happiness, delight at every turn. I didn't know a human was capable of such joy. When I left, I gave up any hope of us having a relationship.

"She said she knew you worked here. Wanted your support." She glances back, toward the closed curtain. "I didn't know how to get ahold of you so I contacted Dr. Ford."

"I'm glad you did." I want to reach for her hand, the one with the nails digging into her forearm, but I don't. "What happened?"

Before she can answer, a doctor I don't recognize pulls the curtain back to reveal Gia standing in a hospital gown, her face washed with tears. Another woman, not a hospital employee from what I can gather, stands nearby. The doctor motions us in. I glance at Marin for approval, but she is focused on her daughter.

"There are some new bruises," the doctor says. "I've read the notes from Deborah and agree with her assessment of the older bruises. Gia's ribs are also fractured. She's lucky they weren't broken."

"Any internal damage?" Marin's voice is steady, a contrast to her demeanor.

"I can run further tests, but from my initial exam I don't believe so."

I stand, listening in shock. When I meet my niece's eyes, I see what is as familiar to me as living—fear.

"Once we get the all clear, you can take her home. I'll make sure the police get my report immediately."

Marin nods, any words of thanks seeming out of place. The doctor walks past her, leaving just the four of us.

"I'm Deborah." The woman I don't recognize reaches out to shake my hand. "The family resemblance is striking."

"Sonya. Gia's aunt." It is odd to say. I haven't been anything to anybody for so long, the words sound foreign on my tongue. I move toward Gia, unsure where else to go. "Are you all right?"

"No, she's not," Marin answers instead. "Her boyfriend has been beating her up."

In shock, I drop my gaze, unable to look at her. I stare at the floor, willing the nausea to subside. The story is not over as we had hoped. It didn't end with our generation. Innocent, untouched by Dad's violence, and yet here Gia stands, bruised and broken as if she had been raised under the same roof as us. Before I can speak, before I can fathom what words to utter, the curtain is pushed aside to reveal a hurried and distraught Raj.

"Tell me now," he says, going straight toward his daughter.

I walk out, unable to bear witness to their heartbreak. First their voices are loud and then a whisper. Raj's voice holds the tears that Marin's speech never will. I want to walk away, to be as far away as possible, but my feet refuse to move. Gia asked for me. I cannot run, not today.

I've never been to the Trauma Unit. There was never a need for me here since patients don't come to stay. The wing houses doctors and nurses who care for victims of rape, assault, anything that can be dealt with medically within hours, though the scars might last a lifetime. After their traumatic event, victims often yearn to stay within the confines of safety the hospital corridors offer. Here, no one can hurt them again.

"How is she?" David asks gently, coming to stand right in front of me.

His concern cuts through my thoughts. I didn't see him arrive. "Beaten, bruised, ribs fractured," I whisper, staring at nothing in the distance.

"Damn it." He runs his hand through his hair. "Did they catch the person?"

"It was her boyfriend." Shame fills me at revealing this new family secret. One that can be added to the skeletons already spilling into our lives. "That's all I know." My legs start to buckle beneath me, but I refuse to let them. Instead, I lean against the wall, amazed that no matter how hard we try, we can never seem to wash the grime of my father's touch from our existence.

"Sonya." He doesn't touch me. Taking a step closer, he comes as near as I can allow. "What can I do? Anything at all. Name it."

I want to ask him to stop trying to save the man who created this. The one who left a trail of broken wings in his wake. To just let my father die so we can continue living. Instead, I shake my head and push back the curtain, reentering the hell we have been fated for.

* * *

I follow them home, to their palace that feels like a prison. Gia chose to ride with her father. Marin said nothing as he helped her into the passenger seat and leaned over to buckle her belt, as if she were a child. Slipping off his jacket, he covered her with it, though the car was already warm from the midday sun.

Their home is only a few minutes' drive, in the hills of Los Altos. Marin pulls into the garage first, and then Raj. I leave my car in the driveway and wait, like a stranger, at the front door for them to allow me in.

"Do you want something to eat?" Raj asks Gia, all of us standing in a circle in the foyer, offering her a ring of protection that is too late.

"No." Gia's face is downcast, her eyes refusing to meet anyone's. "I just want to go to bed." She reaches toward her neck, the movement clearly a habit. When she touches bare skin, she looks up, her face becoming frantic. "My necklace. It's gone."

"What?" Marin looks at Raj, her concern minor in comparison. "Did you drop it?"

"They made me take it off for the X-rays. I think I forgot it there." To Raj she pleads. "I need my necklace, Daddy. Please."

"I'll call the hospital in the morning. See if they can find it." Marin dismisses the issue without further discussion, her mind clearly elsewhere. "Gia, we need to talk about what happened today."

"Dada gave it to me," Gia bites out, ignoring Marin's dictate. She finally meets her mother's eyes. "I can't lose it."

"If we weren't in this situation, you never would have lost it," Marin returns, a cold edge in her voice.

"Marin," Raj retorts, his voice holding a warning that fails to back her down. "Not now."

"Is there a better time?" Marin demands, seemingly having forgotten my presence. Her anger is understandable. For so long, my sister has fought to create the perfect life. Gia was Marin's future and now it lies in shambles around her.

"I'll go get it," I say, interrupting the dead silence that has descended. "The necklace," I explain when Marin turns to me in confusion. I am a voyeur watching a family's breakdown, unable to help. "I can drive back there now and find it." I meet Gia's eyes, hoping to convey warmth and love for the niece I barely know. "How about that?"

Gia nods. "Thank you. He gave it to me on my thirteenth birthday. Told me it would bring me luck." Her reminiscing reminds me she is still a child, her innocence destroyed way too young. "It's my favorite."

I can't help myself; I look to Marin, trying to reconcile the man Gia is talking about with the one I know. But Marin avoids my eyes, as if she is fully aware of the dichotomy but has failed to find an explanation. "I'll call you as soon as I find it."

* * *

The necklace is right where Gia thought it would be. In my hand it feels light, a gold chain with a figurine of a small bird in flight. Tucking it into a pocket of my purse, I text Marin to let her know I have it and will deliver it first thing tomorrow.

Restless, I begin to walk the halls of the hospital that have become so familiar to me in a short period of time. The corridors are already emptying out, the night staff not nearly as large as the day. Bored on one floor, I take the stairs to another and then another, walking until my feet are exhausted. At last I come to where I have been headed from the beginning, the hallway that houses David's office. Each door is closed, shut for the night. I know I am foolish to seek him out and chide myself. Turning to leave, I hear his door open.

"Hey." David says, shocked to see me. "What are you doing here?"

I was hoping to find you, a small voice whispers in my head. But a louder one, the one that dictates every move I make, refuses it an audience. "Gia forgot her necklace in Radiology," I mumble. "I came back for it." I pull it out of my purse, to prove to him that I wasn't searching for him, that I wasn't, for the first time in my life, hoping for a lighthouse in the storm. "I was just on my way home."

He doesn't mention that Radiology is three floors down. That there is no reason for me to be on this floor or that Radiology closed over an hour ago and if I were on my way home I should already be gone. He says none of this but instead, "Come with me."

"Where?"

He motions for me to follow him into the elevator, where he uses his badge to swipe a security strip allowing him access to the roof. We stand a few feet apart, both silently watching the floor numbers light up until the doors open. He steps out first, reaching back with his hand for mine. I glance at it and then at him. His eyes, patient, unwavering, wait for my decision. I think of Gia, her pain, and feel helplessness wash over me. Slipping my hand into his, I cross the threshold of the elevator and onto the roof.

"Watch your step," he says, leading me toward the edge of the roof where there are cement blocks to lean against. Keeping my hand tucked into his, he uses his other one to point toward the sky. "When I was little, my dad used to bring me up here. When he would lose a patient or had a bad day, we would sit in this very place and he would point out all the stars. He even knew their names."

"Now you do the same," I say, knowing without a doubt he does.

"Makes me remember I'm not all that." He offers me a small smile, holding my gaze. "Sometimes things happen that don't make sense."

Tears fill my eyes, but I refuse them. Breaking his gaze, I tug my hand from his. I point to a cluster of stars. "Cassiopeia."

"Her husband Cepheus," he points out.

"There's the Big Dipper." I rotate, taking in as much as I can. "And Orion."

"You know your constellations." His voice holds admiration.

"Doesn't everybody?" I ask, tongue in cheek. We both fall silent. I can feel his eyes on me, watching. "She's fifteen," I finally whisper. "Just a baby."

"We have girls younger than her come into the Trauma Unit." He offers me medical statistics to explain we are not at the end of the road, no matter what we believe. "The drama in the relationship, in the abuse, attracts them. A warped definition of love." He bends down, holding my gaze. "Gia's going to get through this. Your family will get her through this."

He is sure as only someone so naive could be. I imagine telling him that it is impossible for us to get through this. That abuse is cyclical, in our genes. No matter how hard we fight, we can't escape it. I know; I've tried. "Yes."

"Sonya." My name sounds torn from his lips, as if he's absorbed my pain and made it his. "I'm sorry." The physician is gone, replaced by a man. "Your father, Gia." He reaches out, brushing an imaginary strand of hair off my face and over my ear. "No one deserves so much heartbreak."

"What's the worst thing that has ever happened to you?" I demand, still feeling his fingertips on my face. For just a minute I need to know we are not the only ones hurt, that others know the definition of pain.

His confusion is obvious, but he answers me nonetheless. "I lost my grandmother and grandfather when I was fifteen. One illness after the next." He resists the details.

"You loved them?" I ask quietly.

"Completely." He looks toward the sky, as if searching for them in the distance. "They took care of me when my parents worked. They were like second parents."

"I'm sorry," I offer, meaning it.

He steps toward me, gauging my reaction. When I make no protest, he takes me in his arms, allowing my head to nestle under his. Rubbing his hand slowly over my back, he says, "I said this before, but it bears repeating. Whatever I can do, say the word."

My body relaxes under his touch. For the first time in my life, I feel safe in a man's arms. The thought frightens me more than anything. I know what I need to do, to say, but I allow myself a two-minute reprieve. Enough time to enjoy what he's offering, knowing I will never have it again. We were never supposed to cross this line; I was never allowed to know this. That I initiated it, searched for him, shames me. But Gia's situation brought forth too many memories, with them a yearning to be safe when only danger lurked.

When he runs his hand down my hair, offering me sympathy and the hint of more, I know my time is up. Stepping out of his arms, I stare at him, readying myself for the moment he hears the truth and walks away. "You want to do something?"

"Anything."

"Let my father die," I beg. Turning away, I head toward the elevator, feeling his disgust all the way home.

RANEE

She waited one day before going to Marin's home, needing the time to process what Sonya had told her. Gia—beaten. Ranee stayed silent, emotionless, as Sonya conveyed the details. Only in the privacy of her own room did she fall to her knees and weep for her only grandchild. With shuddering breaths, Ranee relived the image of Gia's birth, her toddler years, growing into a beautiful young woman. Now that beauty is forever scarred. Without seeing her, she could imagine the bruises that covered her body, the excruciating pain of a fractured rib. She knew every emotion Gia was feeling because she had felt them herself—the shame that comes with being beaten like an animal.

When she finally arrives, she comes without calling. Marin opens the door after the first ring of the bell. She's dressed as Ranee has rarely seen her—in yoga pants and a T-shirt.

"How is she?" Ranee asks, moving past her daughter into the foyer. She has decided to wear a traditional salwar kameez for the visit, needing something familiar to get her through this. Paired with slim cotton pants, the multicolored, embroidered shirt reaches past her knees.

"Sleeping. Locked in her room." Marin closes the door behind her. "Sonya told you."

Something in her voice sharpens Ranee's gaze. "You expected her not to?"

"I wasn't sure what to expect. It's not like we have a protocol." Marin shrugs her shoulders. "Gia's fine."

"That's what I would have thought before receiving such news." Ranee moves toward the stairs. "I will go see for myself."

"Mummy." Marin's voice holds desperation, an edge Ranee hasn't heard since she was a child. When Ranee turns to face her, she sees Marin pull all of her hair back in a nervous gesture, gripping the strands. It was what she used to do when she came home with an A-minus or B-plus on a test, knowing Brent would soon unleash his violence. When there was nothing else to hold on to, she held on to herself. "She's fine."

"Yes." Ranee's stance softens. "She will be."

Ranee knocks softly on her granddaughter's door before opening it. Gia is bundled under the covers, though it is warm in the house. All the lights are off. There is an uneaten sandwich on the end table and a glass of milk. Ranee walks over and sits down on the bed, laying a hand atop Gia's head, which peeks out from under the covers.

"Leave me alone," Gia murmurs, anger lacing resignation.

"Is that any way to speak to your *Mumji*?" Ranee asks, using the traditional name for maternal grandmother that Gia calls her.

Gia lowers the blanket and turns to stare at her grandmother. Her hair is knotted and her face blotched from tears. When Ranee switches on the bedside lamp, Gia blinks, trying to adjust from the darkness to the light. "What are you doing here, Mumji?"

"I came to see you."

Sitting up, Gia lowers her face and pulls up her knees, like a child. "Mom told you."

"Actually, it was your Sonya masi." Ranee runs her hand over Gia's hair, trying to smooth what she can. "She is very worried about you. All of us are."

"I'm fine."

Ranee wants to smile. She can hear in Gia's voice the same insistence she heard in Marin's. Their similarities are striking, though neither mother nor daughter can see it. "That is not what I see."

"You wouldn't understand, Mumji," Gia says, for the first time speaking back to Ranee. "It's teenager stuff."

"When did you start dating? Hmm?" Ranee cups Gia's cheek in her palm. "I don't remember the family meeting to give approval."

Fighting a smile, Gia fails. "I don't need the family's approval."

"Ah, see that is where you are mistaken." Ranee can remember her own family and the struggle whether to approve her meeting Brent in the open, with chaperones, before their marriage. Her mother feared her reputation would be tainted. Taking Gia's hand now, she lightly traces the veins with her finger. "Feel the blood? That is the same blood that is in me, in your mother, in Sonya masi, in Trisha masi. So whatever you do, whatever happens to you, it affects all of us, because you have our blood." She holds Gia's face gently in her palms, staring directly into her eyes. "Your mother and her sisters came from my womb and you came from your mother's. You are ours, my darling."

Gia allows a lone tear to fall. "I love him so much. And now . . ."

"He hit you. He hurt you. How is that love?" She asked herself the same question for years. But Brent was able to convince her because she had already convinced herself.

"He was sweet. He would slip notes inside my locker, telling me how beautiful I was." Gia's face fills with the memories, showing the first signs of happiness. "He's gorgeous, Mumji. And popular. All the girls wanted him but he wanted me." Gia tightens her fingers around Ranee's hand. "He didn't care if I was smart or perfect, he liked *me*."

When Marin was first born, she would cry when she needed something, like all babies do. If she was hungry, or if she had soiled her cloth diaper, she would begin with a whimper and if Ranee did not respond immediately, it would turn to a full cry. As she got older, Marin always used her tears to get what she wanted. Until Brent started to hit her. Then Ranee never saw another tear fall.

"And when he hit you?" Ranee asks.

Gia drops Ranee's hand immediately, shuttering herself off. "He's new at school. His parents expect a lot out of him. He doesn't mean to hurt me. He loves me." Gia pauses, waiting to deliver the blow that Ranee could never have expected. "It's not a big deal. Besides, Dada used to hit Mom, right?"

With Gia's revelation, Ranee falls silent. She stares at her granddaughter, wondering how and when she learned the truth. She tries to ask, but the words never make it past her throat. Each syllable sticks, blocking any noise. She pats Gia, as if she were a wayward child, and makes her way to the door and out. She goes down the stairs slowly, each step a descent into hell. Her hand grips the banister in her fear she might miss a step and tumble down.

She stands on the bottom step, trying to remember the last few minutes when Marin walks out of her office. "Mummy?" Marin rushes to her side. "What's wrong?"

"She knows," Ranee whispers, unable to meet Marin's eyes. "She knows."

Marin doesn't need any further explanation. It is the secret they have kept for so long, each one of them holding it like a prized possession. "No. There's no way." Even now, her voice drops, fearing Raj may overhear. "It's not possible."

"She told me." The step beneath her seems to give way, causing her knees to weaken. She reaches for the mangalsutra around her neck, belatedly remembering she has removed it. "She said it was not a matter of concern, since the boy hit her like your father hit you."

"No!" Marin's anger vibrates off her, filling the space between them. "I need you to leave." Marin glances around, desperate. She walks to the door, flinging it open. "Go."

"She's my granddaughter." Ranee stands her ground. She can see her daughter's fear beneath the anger, the anguish propelling her. "I won't leave."

"You told her."

Ranee jerks back, as if Marin had slapped her. "Never." Ranee wraps her arms around her waist instead of reaching out. "Why would I do such a thing?"

"To hurt me." The statement is final with no room for argument, a verdict handed down from a lifetime of evidence. "There's no other explanation."

"You're my daughter." Ranee will weep later, in the privacy of her own room, where there is no one to bear witness. "I would first hurt myself before hurting you."

"Maybe I could believe that if you ever stopped him. If you ever cared that I was hurting." Marin meets Ranee's eyes, allowing no further argument. "You didn't, but I do care for my daughter. There's nothing more for you to do."

Ranee nods, accepting the sentence without argument. "If you need me, I am here." Without anything else to say, she walks out.

* * *

For hours, Ranee sits in the dark, staring at the pictures spread out before her. In the shadows, she can barely make out the faces, but there is no need. She memorized them all years ago. There were one or two pictures of her parents, whom she barely saw after she married. They never came to visit her in her new home. With young children still at home, they were grateful to have one less mouth to feed. Ranee only went back home three times. Twice to introduce Marin and Trisha after they were born, and the third time to say good-bye. That time, right as Ranee was leaving their house, her mother brought out an unworn sari, expensive for its time. It had been gifted to her in dowry by her parents, and she offered it to Ranee.

"Something to remember me by."

"I will see you again," Ranee had said, insistent. "America is not so far away."

But her mother was not listening, her attention already on one of the other children. A year after their arrival to America, Ranee received notice that her mother had passed on and her father had married a widow from a neighboring village. Ranee took the sari from her closet and tucked it away in a drawer so she wouldn't think of the mother she barely knew.

There are pictures of the girls' childhood birthday parties alongside dozens of Brent. He loved having his picture taken when they traveled. Like a child, he would hand the camera to Ranee and slip in next to the three girls, whether it was standing in front of the Grand Canyon or the monuments in Washington, DC. Marin's and Sonya's smiles turned into thin lines as they stood rod still, afraid of doing anything to rile his anger. Only Trisha seemed relaxed, unafraid of his presence.

Ranee roams over the other photographs, realizing there are none of her. She checks again to make sure. But she was always the one behind the camera, instructed by Brent on how to focus and aim for the right shot. Never did he ask to take one of her, her beauty emblazoned forever on paper. The irony was the daughter he hated the most was the only one who shared his passion for photography.

"What are you doing in here?" Sonya flips on the light, squinting to help her eyes adjust. "Mom?"

"I saw Gia." The wound still open and bleeding, Ranee has no idea how to stop the gushing blood. "She knows."

"How?" Without further explanation, Sonya understands.

"I don't know." Ranee takes the pair of scissors she had sat down with and begins to cut. With precise strokes, from every picture, she begins to remove all traces of Brent. "Marin thinks I told her."

"You didn't."

Ranee looks up, nipping her finger with the scissors as a result. "Is that a question?"

Sonya glances at the mutilated pictures, taking her time. "You have no reason to tell her."

"Yes." Ranee starts to gather up all the images of Brent. "Gia had permission to be beaten." Ranee drops the pictures into the trash, a lifetime of memories torn to shreds. "I gave it to her."

Sonya glances toward the door, making clear her yearning to be elsewhere. "Maybe she just needed an excuse." She kneels down and begins rifling through the pictures, the faces staring back at her a collage of heartbreak. "I used to hate the birthday parties."

Ranee is genuinely shocked. "Why?"

"I had to pretend to be happy."

Suddenly Ranee needs to know the answer to a question she has always wanted to ask but never dared to. "Do you wish we had aborted you?"

Sonya doesn't look up, doesn't show any shock at the question. "Yes," she says simply, "I do."

"I'm sorry." Ranee drops her head down, lost in her own home, the revelations of the day too much to handle. "I'm so sorry."

TRISHA

When I was in second grade, there was a girl, Melinda, who used to torment me daily. Whether it was about my hand-me-down clothes, my braided hair, or the cheap bag Mama said I had to use as a backpack, she was relentless in her teasing. I wasn't the only one she picked on, however. Nobody unfortunate enough to come to her notice was left unscathed. Melinda was one of the popular girls. With that status, she enjoyed the support of a loyal and large entourage. Her friends were quick to attack whomever Melinda chose that day. If you were the victim, you had no choice but to listen to their taunts. The others didn't come to your aid out of fear they would be next.

I was so grateful when, in the middle of the year, a teacher overheard Melinda making fun of the roti and sakh I had brought for lunch. The teacher warned Melinda never to say such things again or she would be sent to the principal's office. The reprieve was my blessing, and I continued happily through second grade, safe in the protection of the teacher's warning. But it was not to last. Melinda's mother fell ill and died a few months later. Suddenly, Melinda could do no wrong. A victim of circumstance, she now had a halo over her head.

We were warned to be extra kind to her, to show her empathy, to be good friends. Letters went home telling our parents about the situation. Playdates with Melinda were encouraged, dinners dropped off at their home welcomed. I expected Melinda to become a new person, to be humbled by her loss. But if cheetahs don't change their spots, then cruelty within humans has no chance. Melinda returned to her evil ways and for two years made my life hell. Only when her father moved them out of town did I get my freedom. But I learned an important lesson I have never forgotten—with weakness comes great power.

* * *

As soon as I heard about Gia, I considered texting Eric. He always had a soft spot for her and would want to know she had been hurt. In the end, I refused to use the excuse to reach out, no matter how much I yearned to. At a loss about how to help Gia, I went shopping. Hours I spent perusing aisles of knickknacks, trying to find just the right things that would brighten Gia's day. A few stuffed animals, tons of chocolate, some newly released CDs of her favorite artists that I recalled her talking about, and a diary, among other things.

I drop by without calling. My mistake, since no one except the housekeeper is home. I leave the basket with a note for Marin to call me, knowing she won't. If it wasn't for Mama, I never would have known what happened.

As I'm settling back into my car, my phone buzzes. I'm expecting Mama, and my heart rate accelerates when I see it's Eric.

Do you have time to talk?

Yes, I do. Absolutely. Like a schoolgirl, I text back in seconds.

With our lawyers.

The phone drops onto the leather seat. Sweat lines my hand, dampening it. He wants to make the separation permanent, no going back. Unable to text back, I drive. Aimlessly at first, then to run irrelevant errands. I pick up dry cleaning and then groceries for one. Arriving home, I see a forgotten embossed invitation to a charity luncheon on the counter. Glancing down at my outfit, I decide my slacks and summer blouse will do. Leaving the milk and eggs on the counter, I head out, anxious to make it on time.

"Trisha," they exclaim on my arrival, "we weren't expecting you!"

No, I imagine they weren't. Bad news spreads faster than good as a rule. Everyone knew that Eric had left the house, but no one knew why. They would have made guesses, finding proof in their own minds to support their theories. No one could have imagined the truth. "I wouldn't have missed it," I say, faking a smile.

I sit with my friends around a table, laughing at whatever they say. We talk about mundane things, the weather, local fashion, and Hollywood gossip, as if those lives affected ours. A few catty comments about locals, but nothing too abrasive for fear it may be repeated and credit given. Checks are made out for a local charity, the flavor of the month. I take out my checkbook, ready to donate as I always do, and ask the name of the charity.

"It's the shelter in San Francisco for women and children victims of domestic violence," a friend from years past tells me, signing her own check with a flourish, her manicured nails perfectly done. "God, I can't imagine what those people go through. Can you?"

No, I want to say, keeping up the illusion I have created, but I can't. Instead, I start to write but my hand begins to shake. My father is lying in a coma. Eric wants me gone from his life forever. My niece— our future, beaten. No straw breaks the camel's back. Instead it is an avalanche. I stare at the wine goblet and wonder what it would feel like to throw it against the wall. Disturb the perfect setting I have lost myself in. Glass doesn't break cleanly. It shatters into a million pieces, making it impossible to put back together. Leaving the glass untouched, I stand, the check unwritten.

"Yes, I can imagine," I say to the group, shocking them into silence. My friends for years, but not one of them knows as I was sure there wasn't anything to tell. "I know what they go through because I watched it my entire childhood." A tree that falls in a forest doesn't make a sound because no one is there to hear it. Believing that, I hid my past, sure it didn't exist if I didn't speak of it.

"Trisha, what are you talking about?" another friend asks, staring at me like I'm a stranger. "That's impossible."

I had tried so hard to make it seem as if it were, but I was fatigued by the act. The façade was harder to maintain than I realized. I had convinced myself that if I mastered the part, if I was queen of the stage, then I would become the person I was playing. But the mask has started to slip and no matter how hard I try, I can't seem to keep it in place. Accepting the past that belongs to me I murmur, "I wish it were." Meeting their shocked gazes, I stare at the friends I called my own. "My father beat my sisters and mom our entire childhood." Sure I can feel their disgust, I turn away, wondering if this is how Sonya and Marin feel every day of their lives.

"I'm sorry," a friend whispers, covering my hand with her own. "We never knew."

Caught off guard by her sympathy, I lower my head in shame for where I come from, where I'm standing, and for not knowing where I'm going. With nothing left to lose, I return to my empty car and continue to drive aimlessly.

* * *

It is a formal conference room. Upon entering, I immediately notice the drapes and fabric of the chairs. The table is expensive, cut from cherrywood. Eric is already seated with a woman dressed in a suit. She is a partner at the firm, I'm sure. He wouldn't settle for any less. Power demands power—the rules of the game are set.

"Where is your lawyer?" Eric demands, the first words he's spoken to me since he left our house weeks ago.

"I don't have one." I am not trying to be obtuse or difficult. It just seems superfluous to me when we haven't decided what the next step is. "I thought we could talk."

"I'm not paying five hundred dollars an hour to my attorney for us to talk," Eric bites out.

I try to gather my senses. This is not the man I knew, the one I married. The man whose smell still permeates every room of our house and reminds me of a time when I was happy. "Then why are we here?"

"To discuss the settlements of the divorce." His attorney takes over, talking to me as if I'm a wayward child, needing to be spoken to slowly and with explanation.

"You want a divorce?" I ignore her, staring at my husband instead. "That's it? We're over?"

"I think it's best if we keep the conversation to details about finances and division of property," the woman says, ice in every word. "Eric is prepared to be very generous with alimony. I understand you have no means of income."

She sees me as a kept woman, one who is easily bought and dismissed. Whereas she is someone used to taking over, to being in charge. But I am not in the mood to be taken charge of. "We're over?" I ask again, ignoring her, facing Eric. "Because of a child?"

"Because you lied to me," Eric answers, no longer able to stay silent. "Because I trusted you."

You lied to me, I want to yell, fighting back tears. "You told me you would love me no matter what," I say, throwing his words back at him. I ache to tell him that his belief that a family makes everything perfect is flawed. But I stay silent, remaining the holder of our secret. He can never learn that every scar, even those invisible to the naked eye, was once an open wound. "I guess we both lied."

"If that's how you see it," he says. "There's nothing left to say."

We have reached an impasse. There is no turning back, no retreat that will make this right. The game is set, the final hand ready to be played. My father's voice whispers in my ear, a memory from long ago that I had forgotten. I was playing with neighborhood children, each of us riding our bikes. I had yet to fully grasp the basics and kept falling off, fear driving me to be cautious. Enough teasing and I couldn't help the tears that flowed. Escaping into the house, I ran right into my father's arms. With a gentleness saved only for me, he wiped them away and said, "You are so special. Don't ever let anyone convince you otherwise."

"You're right," I say, returning to the present. Turning away from him and facing her, I show her who I really am. "There's no need for alimony. I'll be moved out of his house by month's end." I push my chair back, ready for it to be over. Walking toward the door, I look back to see Eric staring at me silently. I want to say good-bye, but I don't.

* * *

I end up where I have never left—beside my father. I sit next to his bed, his chest rising and falling in perfect synchronicity with the respirator. I take his hand in mine, his cold seeping into my warmth, chilling me. I had hoped for the opposite—he had been the shelter from the storm, the one safe place I could rely on. When your anchor becomes unmoored, you are left to the whims of the vast ocean, unsure where it may lead you but forced to hold on nonetheless. "I have no one left," I say to him. "I'm all alone."

I wait and wait, watching for anything to give me hope. A sign that will lead the way, guide me to an answer for a question that remains unasked. But my road remains unpaved, with no marker to give me direction. But then history has proven that the events that uproot your life, the ones that remain so deep in the recesses of your mind that you can't even imagine them, let alone fear them, are the ones that come without warning. No compass can lead you away from them, no alarm can caution you. They happen, and when they do you must make a choice—allow the wave to wash over you until there is nothing left but blessed blackness or fight with everything, even if in the process of struggling to survive you fill your lungs with salt water.

"I thought that's why I stayed," Sonya says quietly, arriving just as I spoke aloud.

"What are you doing here?" I ask, standing quickly, uncomfortable she heard me.

"I work here," she reminds me.

"No," I motion around the room. "Here. In Papa's room." Her uneasiness clearly matches mine, both of us wary. She glances around, as if avoiding my question. But I don't let her evade the question. "You're here to visit him," I say, realizing.

"Yes."

Saying anything else would be a lie, I can tell. She doesn't bother, since I have known from childhood all of her telltale signs of lying. I used to catch her when we were children and hold it over her like an ax ready to fall unless she did my bidding. Fearing repercussions from my father, she always danced to the tune I played. Now I wonder if I too wasn't a puppet, like all of them, the strings visible to everyone but me.

"How did it feel?" I say, softening as shame fills me. I think of the luncheon, charities set up to protect families like mine. "When he hit you?"

She takes a step back, ready to run. It's a question I never asked, didn't dare to. Hearing the truth would have changed Papa in my eyes into a man I couldn't conceive. Even as I saw him beat them, I convinced myself that wasn't really him. It was a mirage fueled by anger or disappointment and maybe, maybe it was just as much their fault as it was his. If only they could be more of what he wanted, needed, then they too would be safe.

"Like there was nothing left of me but the imprint of his hand," she says, her voice a mere whisper above the roar in my ears. "He owned me. I was a vessel for his rage."

"Then how are you surviving without him?" I ask, instinct driving the question. I know Marin and Sonya's legs were cut from beneath them. They learned to walk with prosthetics, the true part of them taken away by force.

Something flitters across her eyes, a story untold. A secret she won't tell. "By trying to forget."

The young girl is walking down the hallway, her hands limp by her sides. Her throat is raw, her screams having gone unheard. The darkness is now welcome to hide the sins of her soul. There is only empty air all around her but she still can't catch her breath. Gasping, she tries to remember her name, but even something as simple as that escapes her. She tries a door and finds it open. Finally, since every other one has been shut to her, refusing her refuge. She enters the pristine bathroom but the light has gone out.

Blackness causes her to stumble, hitting her head. Feeling wetness on her face, she touches her forehead. Even in the night, she can see the blood marking her hands. She hits the light switch, then she turns on the water, washing it off. Taking a hand towel, she wipes her temple, removing any residual proof of her wound. After, she throws the towel in the sink, watching with detached fascination as the blood seeps from it and swirls around the drain until disappearing from view. Once the water runs clear, she splashes some on her face, until she can recognize the face in the mirror.

I let go of Papa's hand, a shiver running up my spine. Wrapping my arms around me, I ward off a chill. I have lost my footing. Thoughts of Eric, Papa, Gia—ghosts of the still-living—circle. Feeling my grip on sanity start to slip, my body begins to shiver.

"Hey," Sonya says gently, her hand slowly covering my own. "You're OK." Cradling my hands in hers, she pulls me close with her other arm. And then, for the first time in our lives, we reverse our roles.

Now she is the one holding me tightly, our clasped hands still between us, a bridge vulnerable to collapse. "Trisha, you're going to be fine."

Sonya is the sister I have loved because I had to. She arrived after me and followed me around like a puppy dog. Looked up to me, no matter what I did. All the childish cruelty that only children can create never swayed her reverence. She was in awe, and in her eyes, I could do no wrong. How many times, I wonder, did I take advantage of that? I've lost count of the times I accepted her worship as my right. Now, I realize that, for all the times I convinced myself she was fortunate to have me in her life, maybe I too was lucky.

"You don't know that," I whisper, sure she is wrong. I lay my head on her shoulder, the little strength I have acquired over the years seeping out of me. My father, my pillar, lay dying, but the one holding me up is the little girl I believed had never learned to stand.

"Yes, I do," she says, insistence lacing every word. "Because you're the strongest person I know."

"You're wrong," I tell her, wanting to pull off her rose-colored glasses. They no longer provide me with the reflection I have become used to seeing. Of someone perfect. "See me. See *me*." My tears soak her shoulder. "I have nothing left."

"You have you." Her words allow no room for argument. "You are the girl who kept us playing, no matter how bad it got. You are the woman who became the glue for a family torn apart." She pulls inches away from me, holding my gaze. Her eyes are wet with tears. "You are the sister who made me believe it was worth living, no matter how many times I wanted to die."

Letting go of her hand, I slip mine around her waist, more grateful than words can convey. We both stand there, holding one another, two pieces of a puzzle that has never been put together. But for the first time I see what I never had before; my little sister has a well of strength. With it she offers me a light to escape the nightmare I cannot seem to wake from.

SONYA

I change into running clothes and slip my earphones into my ears. It's past six in the evening. After my conversation with Trisha, I need to escape, to get as far away as possible. Since I can't run away like I used to, I have found this is the best alternative.

Throwing my things into a locker, I stretch before making my way through the halls of the hospital toward the exit. Once outside, I breathe in the fresh air. Choosing a path around the hospital and toward the familiar Stanford campus, I start off slow to let my muscles warm up. The sun is starting to set, taking with it the warm blanket that had settled over the region.

I make a loop around the campus before taking a route through it. The buildings I once took classes in, along with the well-known walkways, beckon me in a way I never believed possible. The familiarity that was once stifling now feels welcoming. I shake it off, refusing the emotion any influence. Turning my music louder to drown out any thoughts, I continue the run for another half hour before my body begs me for a reprieve. Sweat pouring down my face and dampening my shirt, I finish the final stretch of the run at a slow jog, arriving back at the hospital nearly two hours after I left.

Heading straight for the showers, I let the warm water cascade over my body, relaxing my tight muscles. The events of the last few days, Gia, my conversations with David and then Trisha, replay in my mind. Leaning my head against the cool tiles, I yearn for the pain to dissipate, to disappear like the steam enveloping me. But it is a childish wish, a hope that can never reach fruition. Accepting reality, I turn off the water and get dressed in the empty locker room, pulling my wet hair back as I walk out.

"Did you have a good run?"

I start at the sound of David's voice. Glancing up, I see him standing in the large break area past the men's and women's locker rooms. His white coat off, he's rolled his shirtsleeves to below his elbows. His eyes are tired, his face drawn with worry.

"I'm sorry, I didn't mean to startle you," he says, seeing my reaction. "I saw you leave earlier for your run. I was hoping to catch you when you got back."

"Are you following me?" I ask, sounding harsher than I mean to.

"Yes," he answers without hesitation, a small smile tugging at his lips. "I'm only pretending to be a doctor. My real job is to watch your every move." Giving me a quick wink, he lowers his voice. "But please, whatever you do, don't tell the patients. That would ruin my reputation."

Having been thoroughly put in my place, I can't help but grin back. "Your secret is safe with me."

"Excellent. I owe you one." Turning toward the coffee machine, he grimaces when he sees all that is left are hours-old coffee grounds at the bottom of the carafe. "If I make a new pot, will you join me?"

I shake my head no. "I need to head home."

"Right." He turns back toward me, forgetting about the coffee. Holding my gaze, he says gently, "I was hoping to talk to you. Hence, the stalking."

Feeling the familiar unease, I step toward the door. "There's nothing to talk about."

As I move past him, he reaches out, his hand gentle on my arm, stopping me. "What you said the other day. Can we talk about it?" Gently pulling me toward him, he dips his head to stare at me. "Why do you want your father dead?"

"It doesn't matter," I say, pulling my arm from his. The warmth of his touch still lingers. Without thinking, I rub the spot, trying to erase the tingling. His eyes follow my movement, narrowed in question. "You wouldn't understand."

"Try me."

"No," I almost yell, needing to get out. The oxygen levels in the room drop, and I can't catch my breath. "You have everything," I say, pointing around me. "Your life is good."

He laughs, the sound hollow. "What does that have to do with anything?" He shakes his head in confusion. "You matter to me."

"Don't care," I beg. "About me, my life." I pause, struggling to explain without revealing too much. "Please, just let it go." When I leave, I don't look back. But I know, without a doubt, that he's not following me.

MARIN

Days have passed since the arrest. Gia has remained in her room, eating only when they take her food, and showering every other day. She refuses to speak to any of them. Even Raj has been stonewalled, Gia's despair shutting her off from those closest to her. Marin is tempted to march in and throw off the covers, order her daughter to get up and return to the living, but she holds back. She will allow Gia five days to go through whatever process she needs to before demanding she return to school and her life. Five days feels benevolent, more than necessary. But Raj insists. A full week off to mourn the man who beat her.

On the last day of Gia's self-imposed exile, Marin is at her desk working when the call comes in. Sleep has eluded her. Instead of wasting time tossing and turning, she spends every night working. When her body demands a reprieve, she lies down on the sofa in her office and closes her eyes for a few minutes. But thoughts of Gia cause her heart to race and adrenaline replaces the exhaustion, forcing her to return to work or chance a panic attack.

"Yes?" Marin answers the phone on the first ring, without bothering to check the caller ID.

The detective on the line asks what would be the best time for some questions he has for Gia. Anytime, Marin answers. They agree to after lunch. Leaning back in her chair, Marin stares at the flickering computer screen, the blue haze creating a halo over her desk. The thought of Adam behind bars gives Marin a sense of completion, of closure.

"Raj?" She leaves her office to search for him. Finding him in his office on the other side of the house, she closes the door behind her. "A detective is coming to ask Gia questions."

"What kind of questions?" he demands.

He has tried over a dozen times to talk to Marin privately about what happened. How the steps played out that resulted in Adam's arrest at the school and Gia's subsequent trip to the hospital. Each time, Marin sidestepped him, her answers vague and quick. When he pushed, she pushed back, demanding to know why it mattered when the end result was what they both wanted. Raj finally gave up, but a silence descended between them, leaving them farther apart than they already were.

"I don't know, Raj," Marin bites, lack of sleep causing her to lose patience. "I'm not a psychic."

"Yet, you seem to have all the answers," Raj murmurs, returning to his seat behind the desk, dismissing her.

"What does that mean?"

"Nothing. I'm just surprised you thought to include me in this when you failed to in everything else."

"If that's your way of trying to say thank you for saving your daughter from the boy who was beating her . . . you're welcome." Marin slams out of the office. Taking the steps two at a time, she throws open Gia's door and hits the light switch with more force than necessary. "Get up," she orders, pulling the covers off like she had yearned to days ago.

"What?"

Gia's hair is tangled, the brown and gold strands in knots. Her face is swollen from tears, and she has lost weight. Her eyes are empty, searching for something, finding nothing. Marin, taken aback at the sight of her daughter's state, pauses, wondering what the right thing to do is. But conditioning from years of practice takes over, and she defaults to what feels normal.

"A detective is coming to ask you some questions." Marin starts to rifle through Gia's drawers, pulling out a respectable top and jeans. Walking into the adjoining bathroom, she turns on the shower to warm. "You need to get dressed."

"I don't want to talk to anyone," Gia says, lying back down and pulling the covers over her head. "Leave me alone."

The words trigger a reaction Marin is too tired to censor. Pulling the covers off again, Marin raises her voice. "Get up now." Each word spoken slowly and precisely, leaving no room for argument. "Do not push me."

"Why?" Gia asks, throwing her feet over the bed. "Will you slap me again?"

"I already apologized for that," Marin says, refusing to allow her daughter to provoke her. "You will look respectable in front of the detective."

"What does it matter what he thinks?" Gia continues, insistent on getting a reaction. "Or is how other people see you all that matters?"

Marin has never confronted Gia about what the girl knows of her mother's childhood. Fear kept her from saying anything. "Watch how you speak to me," she says instead. Marin takes a step closer, knowing her move could be perceived as threatening. "Whatever you think you know, whatever story your teenage brain has conjured up is a lie. There's nothing there. I don't have to pretend to be anything. Everything I am, everything I provide for you is from my hard work. You can thank me anytime." She calmly walks over to the bathroom, pushing the door open. "Now."

Moving past Marin, Gia walks into the bathroom and shuts the door. Rooted to her spot, Marin waits, listening for the signs of her daughter stepping into the shower. Once satisfied, she leaves to get ready for the meeting.

* * *

"Thank you for meeting with us on such short notice." The detective, Greg, takes a seat on the sofa in the den.

"Anything we can do to help the process move along faster," Marin says from her seat on the chair. She avoids Raj's sharp look. "What's the next step?"

"We need a statement from Gia about everything that happened. From the beginning to the last incident."

He's young. If Marin had to venture a guess, he just earned his detective badge. Marin wonders if teenage domestic violence falls at the top or bottom of the promotion ladder. A prelude to real violence—except for their family, this was not a foreword; it was real.

"There were no incidents," Gia says, looking down at her hands. "I don't want Adam to go to jail."

"That's not the information we have," Greg says, glancing at Marin.

"Then you have the wrong information," Gia says with a gumption that surprises Marin. In another circumstance, she might actually feel pride in her daughter's comeback, but right now it only fuels her simmering anger.

"Answer him, Gia," Marin barks, startling everyone with the vehemence in her voice.

"Why don't you?" Gia says. Seeming to accept she's already lost the fight, she comes back with the only thing she has left—defiance.

Greg retrieves an envelope from his bag and starts to pull out pictures. Laying each one on the table, he faces Gia and Raj. "Photographs of your bruises. You remember them being taken?"

"Yes," Gia murmurs, cringing at the sight of them. Raj visibly tenses next to her, his jaw clenched.

"And these?" Greg lays out another set, the ones from when Marin hired the detective. Dozens of Gia and Adam in front of his house, each one clearly date-stamped. "You acknowledge they are of you." Gia nods. Greg takes out the final few, offering them to Gia. "These are the ones from the night before the arrest. The two of you together." He pulls out the final pictures, hesitant in handing them over. "Here are the pictures of him hitting you."

Raj takes the pictures from Gia's hand, flipping through them, flinching at the ones that show Adam hitting her. Swallowing, he blinks back tears. Dropping the pictures, he starts to turn away when he notices the date and time stamp at the bottom of each photograph. "Who took these?" he demands, his eyes on the detective.

"A private investigator," Greg says, oblivious to the storm brewing.

"Your office hired the PI?" Raj asks.

"No, we did not."

"I think we need to focus, Raj, on the next steps for our daughter," Marin interrupts, stopping the line of questioning. Gathering the pictures into a stack, she hands them back to the detective. "Do you need an official statement from Gia?"

"Yes." Greg turns to Gia. "This young man hurt you and we have the proof. If there's a trial, you will be subpoenaed to take the stand."

"What do you mean if there is a trial? He will be going to jail for what he did to Gia," Marin says, interrupting him. Everything she did can't have been for nothing.

"His lawyers may advise him to plead it out. If it's a first offense, he could get some community service and a fine," Greg cautions.

"So he won't go to jail?" The relief on Gia's face is palpable. "He'll come back to school?"

"From my experience, he won't be allowed to return to the school you were attending together. The DA will likely request a restraining order," Greg explains. "It's standard procedure when there's a domestic violence situation."

"So he wouldn't be allowed near our daughter again?" Raj asks.

"That would be the intention." The detective watches Gia carefully. "No matter what, this will stay on his record forever. His life will never be the same." Greg looks to Marin, trying to reassure her.

"What if he violates the order?" Gia asks.

"He goes to jail."

Gia drops her head in her hands. "But he didn't do anything." She starts to beg anyone who will listen. "He didn't mean to hurt me. It wasn't his fault."

I am doing this for your own good. Brent standing above Marin. He was so large and she felt so small. She would nod; she had no choice. It was her fault; he made sure she knew that. If only she were smarter, prettier, a better student. Straight As weren't good enough. Where were the A-pluses? Why did another student get two awards when she only got one? *It's your fault. It's your fault.* A mantra in her head, beating her harder than his fists.

"He did it before," Marin bites out, shocking all of them into silence. "He beat the girl before you. Made her his own personal punching bag. Was it her fault too? Was it?"

"How do you know this?" Raj asks quietly, staring at her.

Marin lifts her chin, refusing to apologize or hide from the fact that she saved her daughter's life. "I hired the private investigator. He researched Adam's past and provided me with the information."

Raj nods, disappointment weighing him down. "Without telling me." He rubs his neck with the palm of his hand. "This was a public record?"

"No," Marin says. "It was a sealed juvenile record."

Gia glances between her father and mother. "You did this?" she asks, picking up the stacked pictures. "You had me followed?" She stands, dropping the pictures onto the floor, allowing them to scatter everywhere. "Do you know what you did?" Tears start to flow down her face. "I was a nobody until Adam liked me. The perfect school, the perfect life you created for me? I hate it. Adam . . ." She swallows, trying to get the words out. "He made me popular. He made people like me. He made me important! And now . . ." Gia wipes at the tears. "Everyone hates me. They hate me, Mom. Are you happy? You got what you wanted."

"That is never what I wanted," Marin says, standing to face her daughter. "I did what was best for you. Do you have any idea what could have happened to you? You were ruining your life. I saved you."

"No, you didn't. You left me with nothing and I hate you. I hate you so much." Not waiting for anything more, she leaves them, running up the stairs and into her room.

* * *

Marin stares at her own reflection in the bathroom mirror, not recognizing the woman who stares back. Tired from the events of the day, she grasps the counter, yearning for support from the only thing that will offer it. Gia disappeared to her room. When Marin started to enter, Raj came out and quietly told her to leave their child alone. Saying nothing else, he left her standing there, staring after him.

Marin can hear him getting ready for bed. Rubbing lotion into her dry hands, she walks out, tired of the silence. "We need to discuss Gia returning to school on Monday," Marin says, slipping off her robe to reveal her satin pajamas.

"You believe that's the priority right now?" Raj demands. He puts down the book he's been reading in bed and turns to Marin. "Her return to school?"

"What else would be?" Marin slips beneath the covers, grateful for the king-size bed that allows for distance between them. "We agreed to one week off."

"That was before she knew what her mother did to her," Raj says. Deciding that small distance wasn't enough, he slips out of the bed Marin just entered to begin pacing their room. "Before you betrayed her."

Marin had overheard Brent once telling Trisha that only the best got ahead in America. The smartest survived; everyone else was left behind. Marin refused to leave her daughter behind. "And what would you have done?" Marin asks slowly now, facing her husband across the divide of the bed. Her face is frozen, with no cracks. "Continued to allow her to drown?"

"You should have discussed it with me," Raj says, fury filling the space between each word. "She is my daughter too!"

Marin laughs, finally understanding. "This isn't about what I did, it's that you didn't think to do it." Her father's words echo in the room, the ones he uttered every time she didn't come home with the highest grade: *Everyone is the competition. You are only the best if you are better than others.* "You can have my reward. I don't need it. Just don't stand there and pretend to be up in arms because I somehow betrayed her. I saved her!"

"Who are you?" Raj demands, staring at Marin with horror. "Do you really think this is about credit? About who gets the prize?" He sighs, a sound filled with emptiness. "I am talking about our daughter trusting us. Believing in us. She was hurting and you just hurt her more."

Marin, tired of the conversation, accepts they stand on separate ends of an abyss with no means to reach the other side. She grabs her robe and slips it on. "I'll sleep in the guest room."

"That's your answer?" Raj meets her at the bedroom door, blocking her.

"Get out of my way." Marin cautions herself to take it slow, to breathe deeply. In all the years of her marriage, she never once feared Raj. Never believed him capable of behaving like her father. But right now, in the heat of their argument, she feels a twinge of fear and hates herself for it. "Now."

"Not until we finish this discussion." Oblivious to the fear gripping her, to the reasons behind it, Raj stays where he is. "You owe me an explanation."

"No, I don't. I owe you nothing." Marin grasps the doorknob, ready to hurl the door open and into him if necessary. "I need to get some sleep so I can think. For too long I have left my work unattended while I dealt with our daughter. If you want to help, be involved; make sure tomorrow she finishes up any homework she missed during her week off." Opening the door, she forces him to either step back or chance her hitting him with it. He steps to the side, finally, watching her leave.

SONYA

I continue to work, arriving each day on time, and staying for hours after my shift is over. The patients have started to get to know me. The young ones, who after chemo treatments are desperate for a distraction, ask for me by name. I spend the longest time with them, explaining in detail the intricacies of photography, offering the only means I have for them to escape.

Since our charged encounter, David and I pass one another in the halls, not stopping like we did to talk or grab a bite to eat. It's what I expected and what I wanted, yet it hurts more than I imagined. I hold my head up high, refusing to cower when we run into each other. Now, as I am talking to a nurse about a pediatric patient, he walks by, both of us aware of the other, even in this crowded hall.

"Doctor?" The nurse stops him. "Can I bother you for a minute?"

"Of course," he answers smoothly, dropping a patient's chart at the nurses' desk before approaching us.

We nod to one another before she asks him a series of questions regarding a patient. All the while, I can feel his eyes on me, watching silently as he answers her. Oblivious to the tension, she thanks him for his time.

"Sonya, if you have a minute? There are some new board initiatives I wanted to discuss with you," David says, surprising me.

He is lying; I am sure. But if I refuse, it will seem odd. "Of course."

He glances at his watch. "I have one more patient to see. Why don't we meet in my office in fifteen?" He offers the nurse a warm smile. "That will give the two of you a chance to finish up your conversation I so rudely interrupted."

"I called you over," she says, buying what he is selling. I want to roll my eyes, but keep the childish gesture to myself. "Thanks again, Doctor."

"So fifteen minutes, Sonya?" he asks, leaving me no room for argument.

"I'll meet you there."

I arrive before he does. When I knock, there is no answer, so I wait outside, pacing the hall. I remind myself that he has no hold over me, no control, no matter what I revealed to him.

"You're likely to wear out the floor." He watches me as he walks down the corridor. "How are you?" he asks, reaching me.

"Great. What did you want to discuss?" I'm angry for having been manipulated into the meeting. I almost didn't show, but I knew it was useless. At some point we would have to talk. Better now than later.

"It'll be better in the office." He unlocks the door and motions me in.

"Tell me," I demand, refusing to go in. I lower my voice when I hear a door down the hall opening.

"Do you really want to do this here?" he asks, his gaze searching mine. "Where anyone can hear?"

"Fine." I walk in, my arms crossed—my only show of self-protection. "What did you want to discuss?"

"How are you?" he asks again, shutting the door behind him.

"Like I said, great." Anger pushes me to be impolite. "The discussion?"

"I'd like to ask you out to dinner," he says, taking me in.

Of all the things, I never expected this. Disgust, maybe even pity, but nothing other than that. "You're asking me out on a date?"

"Yes."

I want to laugh, but I fear the sentiment may not go over well. "No."

"No, I'm not asking you out on a date or no, you won't go out with me?" he asks, his eyebrows lifted in curiosity.

"Both. You were there when I told you to leave this alone? When I asked you to let my father die, right?" I shrug my shoulders. "I could have sworn it was you."

"It was me. Unless there are other doctors from the hospital you're spending time on the roof with."

He's teasing me. If the situation weren't so ridiculous, I would smile. "Then what are you doing?" I tell myself I don't want the answer, I don't need the answer, yet I wait for it.

He gets a faraway look. "I can't stop thinking about you. You're always on my mind." He grimaces. "I've missed you. Not great for patient care. But I know you need time." He rubs the back of his neck, a gesture he makes when he's under stress. "With everything you have going . . . Gia, your . . ." He catches himself. "How is she doing?"

"Hiding." That was the update I received from Mom this morning. She called Marin at least three times a day and had stopped over repeatedly to check on her granddaughter. "From herself, the world, I guess. They are moving forward with charges."

"Good."

The fight goes out of me. I drop my hands and lean back against his desk. "It doesn't bother you that I want my father dead?"

"I'm trying to understand." He takes a step toward me. "Tell me why. Tell me about yourself. About why you and your family visit the man you hate every single day."

"Over spaghetti and garlic bread?" I mock.

"Talk to me." He reaches for me, leaving only a few inches between us. His palm cradles my head, allowing me a second to refuse. He waits for an answer, his eyes holding mine. "You are so beautiful," he whispers. I shake my head, but his lips are already on mine. They are gentle and kind and everything I can't have. I lift my hand, ready to push him away, but he grasps my fingers in his, holding them between us like a precious child. When he deepens the kiss, I can't help the moan. I return the kiss, tired of fighting him and my feelings. My other hand sneaks around his back, bunching his white coat into my fingers.

He trails kisses down my cheek and over my throat. Pulling me in tighter than I have ever been before, his hands caress my back, lingering over my hip. My head falls to the side, his touch holding me close. I fist one hand into his hair when he gently pulls the tail of my shirt out of my pants and touches my bare skin. His hand slowly crawls up my back, beneath my bra strap, his thumb caressing the side of my breast.

"David," I murmur, the sound so low I wonder if I said the word aloud.

"Give us a chance," he says, whispering in my ear. His lips find mine again, more gently, both of us holding on as tightly as we can.

His words are the reminder I need. Pushing him away, I straighten my clothes, avoiding his eyes. "I can't," I try, pleading with him to understand.

"Why?" He reaches for me again but I sidestep him, moving to the other side of his office.

"You don't know me." I will myself to end this now. Because in the last few weeks I have come to look forward to the time we spend together and I can't afford that vulnerability. "We could never work." That's a lie and we both know it. Whenever we grabbed dinner together at the hospital, time flew by. Any silence between us was comfortable.

"I know you are an incredibly talented photographer," he says, dismissing my argument easily. "I know that you can make sick kids laugh even as they are lost in their illnesses." He takes a step toward me, reaching out to brush my hair. I step back, out of reach. We play a chess game without a king. "I know your mom told me you would never come home, but I'm damn glad you did."

Some instances in life create a bread trail to a moment that alters everything. It is impossible to imagine the crumbs or pay much notice to them. Only in retrospect do you stop and wonder how you missed the obvious signs. When I met David, our eyes mirrored the mutual attraction. Spending time with him, that has only deepened. Yet it can't be more than a passing entanglement. Another loss from never having learned how to win.

"When you have a patient come in with symptoms of cancer, what do you do?" I ask, desperate to get through. "Run tests?"

His confusion is clear at the change of topic, but nonetheless he answers the question. "Of course. Conduct a full physical history, take blood, order further tests if necessary."

"And once the diagnosis comes in?" I need him to understand. It is the first time it has mattered to me. "You determine the stage of cancer?"

"Yes." His gaze holds mine, unwavering. "We hope it's the first stage so they have a fighting chance, but obviously patients can be in the later stages."

"Can you heal them?" I have attempted to recover. Taken whatever steps necessary—read the books, visited a therapist. But like a landslide, the memories bury me, diminishing any hopes of survival. "Those in advanced stages?"

"We try and hope, but no, not always." He is patient, waiting for an explanation.

"What do you tell them then?" I had a therapist once describe me as broken. Said the solution was to put myself back together. I asked her how that was possible when there were pieces of me my father had taken and never returned.

"To live their life out as comfortably as they can."

That option is tempting. To accept that nothing will be as you imagined. That control was never yours, no matter how much you convinced yourself otherwise. "If you and I went out, we would have dinner a few times, catch a movie. I would laugh at your jokes and you would listen as I told you about my experiences traveling."

"Sounds normal, appealing even." He takes a deep breath, his frustration clear. "I'm not sure where you're going with this."

"We may start to care about one another." Like a daydream, I see us holding one another. Sharing each other's lives and passions. Trusting the other one to always be there. "I may fall in love with you."

He stays silent, watching me. "And I may fall in love with you."

Tears well up but refuse to fall over. They stopped years ago. My hands begin to shake and suddenly I am very cold. "That would be a mistake. Because like your patients with advanced stages of cancer—I have no hope. I have no future, not one that you would want to be a part of."

"Why don't you let me decide that?"

"Because I'm broken and I can't be fixed." I see Trisha, sitting on her sofa. Reaching out to me. Lost in a sea where a storm is always brewing. "And if I go out to dinner with you it would end with me having to run. And I can't do that. Not right now. Not until my father dies."

"So that's it. You've decided we can't take the first step because there has to be a last one?" He slams his hand against his desk. "That sounds like a cop-out to me. Bullshit." He takes my hand, holds it even as I try to pull away. "I'm not a romantic. It's probably not allowed in my profession." He rubs his thumb against my palm. "But the first time I met you . . ." He drops my hand, running his hand through his hair.

"What?" It is self-flagellation, me asking him to elaborate. To finish the sentence when the decision is made. I am sure of what he wants to say. He felt something when we shook hands, that we both fantasized about more. Sometimes, if you're lucky, you meet a stranger who holds the piece of you that has been missing. "You felt something?"

"No." He holds my eyes. "I saw more." He glances at the shut door. "When I first went to medical school, I gorged on the science. Every action had a reaction. The blood had to follow a certain path in the body, the brain so powerful, any modern computer should fall to its knees in awe. I was sure every question had an answer—a scientific answer." He stops, his eyes shifting as if remembering.

"What happened?"

"I started seeing patients. Real people with real problems. And suddenly A didn't have a straight path to B. Two plus two never equaled four. Bodies weren't always a science experiment." He takes a deep breath. "I had to see past the disease to the person. Hardest thing I've ever done."

"Not many doctors would bother," I tell him, his words drawing me to him.

"I wasn't so impressive." He shakes off any admiration. "I screwed up more times than I want to admit." He smiles, as if begging me to understand him. "But I learned you have to know the patients. Understand what they're telling you past the illness."

"How?"

"Their mannerisms, physical appearance. The people they have around them. All of it, put together, you see whether they will survive the disease. Or not." His voice takes on an edge. "There are those who come in and you know nothing will beat them. Those are the ones to admire. To learn from. The illness is a side note. They can and will fight anything. And win."

"So when we met?"

"I saw a winner."

My father labeled us when we were born. Marin was *dohd-dai*, overachiever in Indian. Trisha was *mathajee*, a goddess on Earth, and I was bewakoof, the stupid one. After enough years of hearing the label, you assume it is true. Believe that when someone says something with enough confidence, they know what they are talking about. Especially when it's the person God entrusted you to.

"You're wrong," I say. David shakes his head, seeming confident he is right. "I'm not a winner. I can never be." I move toward the door, wrenching it open.

"Why?"

"Because to be a winner, you have to have something you're fighting for." Like a snake disturbed, my father's words rear up, echoing through my head, filling my empty soul. "I have nothing."

I leave work immediately and drive for hours. From Palo Alto, I go down to Los Altos, passing Marin's house and then driving by Trisha's. I don't stop at either, just need a reminder of who lives behind the walls and the memories that bind us together, no matter what physical barriers separate us. From there, I drive past my high school, my route taking me in circles around the Bay Area. My hometown has never felt like mine, but then nothing else has either. The only thing I can truly hold on to, that will never leave me, are the invisible scars from the abuse.

The memories start to fill the space in the car and in my head. I can feel the tingling in my stomach, the yearning in my soul. Shaking my head, I hit the radio, blasting it loud enough to drown out the recollections, but it's not strong enough. Nothing ever has been. David's face appears before me, a vision calling for me, but I can't see him. I won't. He cannot be my savior. He is too pure, too good for someone like me.

Seeing the exit for 280, I cross two lanes to take it. Ignoring the sounds of horns blasting at me, I speed up, desperate to escape the demons that accompany me. My heart rate accelerates, fast enough that I fear it may beat out of my chest. I zip past the evergreens, oblivious to the beauty that led this to be labeled the most gorgeous highway in the country. I can still feel David's kiss on my lips, the warmth of his arms around me. My heartbeat seemed to match his, and when he called me a winner, I yearned to believe him, to accept his label as the truth and my father's as a lie. But the past refuses me such an allowance. Who I really am is my constant reminder of what I can never be.

Heading into San Francisco, I drive past the bay and down Van Ness Avenue. I enter the famous Pacific Heights neighborhood. As students at Stanford, my friends and I would spend afternoons walking around on a constant quest to find the best Thai restaurant in a city with a competition among hundreds. Without fail, we would always end up in the prestigious locale, admiring the block of Victorian mansions and the views of the Golden Gate and the bay. We would argue which one of us was most likely to end up buying there once we had our own careers. I always remained quiet, a sixth sense telling me I was likely the last one to buy or settle down anywhere.

Now I continue past without stopping to admire the architecture or historic buildings. I keep driving until the area changes from luxurious homes to boarded windows and graffiti-covered structures. Finding what I am looking for, I pull into an empty parking space, turning the wheels toward the curb and putting on the parking brake to keep the car from rolling down the hill. I walk into the dive bar, the darkness and smell of cheap beer enveloping me, cleansing away any reminders of David and his touch.

"What'll you have?" the bartender asks when I slip into a stool at the bar. He has a front tooth missing and a sheen of dirt beneath his nails.

"Shots of whiskey and keep them coming," I say, pulling out my credit card and sliding it toward him. I glance around, my eyes finally adjusting to the darkness. Cheap window covers allow only a sliver of the daytime sun to peek in. It is a rare sunny day in San Francisco, the fog that normally blankets the city having burned off hours ago.

The bartender sets down a full glass in front of me and leaves the bottle. I take the shot down in one gulp, welcoming the bitter liquid as it burns my throat. I pour myself another, the knot in my stomach finally loosening. My hand tingles, the one David held as he kissed me. I scrub at it, trying to erase his mark on me.

"I don't think I've seen you in here before," a man to my left says.

My first instinct is to do what I always do, tell the guy I'm not interested. That there's no way in hell we'll be sleeping together. But my reflexes are off, rubbed raw from my moment with David. "First time."

"I'm Chris." He takes the seat next to me. In the dim lighting, I guess him to be a construction worker. "I'll have what she's having," he tells the bartender. "You are?"

"Nobody," I answer, downing another.

"Nice to meet you, Nobody." He swallows his shot. "Are you from around here?"

"No." I close my eyes, hearing David's words in my ear, his touch on me. It is the first time another man's presence has crowded out my father's. "How about you?"

"Live down the street. Just finished up a job." He points to his hard hat on the stool next to him. So he's in construction. "Little early to be drinking that much, isn't it?" he asks, pointing to my bottle. "Something happen?"

"Are we going to share sad stories?" I ask, meeting his gaze.

"Don't have to," he answers, his gaze holding mine. "Just making conversation."

"I'm not the best conversationalist," I say, remembering the hours David and I spent talking to one another. Thoughts of him flood me and I hate myself for what I want, what I can never have. The tingling at the base of my spine begins again, crawling up my back like razors ready to draw blood. Nausea hits me as the alcohol saturates my empty stomach. I forgot to eat lunch again, I belatedly realize. I glance around, searching for something but I have no idea what.

"Are you OK?" Chris asks, interrupting my train of thought.

"Do you have porn?" I ask, the alcohol buzzing in my ears. I close my eyes, trying to recall the last few stories I read.

"Is that a trick question?"

"The kind where . . ." I trail off, unable to say the words out loud. I swallow, scared, so completely scared, but left with nowhere to hide. "Where they hurt women?"

"No." He stares at me, and I see what I always saw in my father's eyes—disgust. "I don't."

"That's OK." I stumble out of the bar and into my car. Curling up in the backseat like a child, I allow the tears to finally flow, the sobs wracking my body until all that is left is the vision of my father.

RANEE

With all that is happening in their lives, they are rarely able to come together as a family these days. To do so now makes Ranee want to celebrate; she cannot, as it is not a joyous occasion that gathers them. Trisha has organized the house into separate sections and assigned each of them tasks. She has planned for one full day of packing and will schedule her movers for later.

"The boxes are there," Trisha says, pointing to a stack, "and the tape there." She is dressed in sweats and a T-shirt, her hair pulled into a ponytail. To Ranee, she looks like a teenager trying to pass as an adult. "Let's go, people," she says, clapping her hands together.

"What do you want us to pack?" Sonya asks, dressed similarly to her sister. Hands on her hips, she glances around. "How will we know what belongs to you versus Eric?"

"It's labeled," Marin announces, pulling out a stack of books from the shelf. Each one has a sticky note with Trisha's name. "Every single thing."

"No point making the job harder than it has to be," Trisha seems to defend against any unspoken judgment. "Besides, I would hate to take anything of Eric's." At her own mention of his name, her lips thin out and her face tightens. Only Ranee notices the subtle shift and catches the sadness that crosses her daughter's face before she masks it. "The sooner we're done, the better."

Trisha called Ranee a few days back to tell her the news that they were moving forward with a divorce. Shocked, Ranee demanded answers, but Trisha's terse reply was that it was for the best. She asked if her mother would help her pack her few belongings. Not only did Ranee agree, but she immediately contacted Marin and Sonya to enlist them.

"There's not a lot of stuff that's labeled yours," Sonya says, going through the music and only finding a few CDs with Trisha's name on them. "He bought all the rest?" She indicates the shelf still filled.

"I bought them, but after we got married," Trisha explains vaguely, not meeting anyone's eyes. "Since they were with his money, they're his."

Everyone falls silent, staring at her. Marin finally breaks it, stepping closer to Trisha. "Are you telling me that anything bought after marriage Eric says belongs to him?" Marin shakes her head. In seconds, she transforms into the executive that she is, assessing the situation, unhappy with the results. "I'm going to call around, find you a better divorce lawyer."

"That was my decision, not his." Trisha finally faces her sister. "He wanted to be generous with alimony, split everything in half. I refused."

Ranee closes her eyes, praying for guidance. "Why, Trisha?" She wrings her hands together. "What will you live on?"

"I'll be fine." Trisha insists. Finished filling a box with her shoes, she tapes it closed. "I'm going to look for a job."

No one says a word, each one fully aware that Trisha hasn't worked in years. Silently, they return to their packing. It is easier than they initially imagined, since so many of the household possessions were bought after Eric and Trisha took their vows. Ranee watches her three daughters carefully, seeing them for the women they are, and also the women they could be. She imagines a trapeze artist walking a tightrope across a large gulf, desperate to reach the other side but unsure if she'll survive to make it.

"He wanted the divorce?" Ranee asks, taking a seat on the sofa for a minute of rest. Time has passed quickly as each one worked diligently on the task at hand. She pours them all glasses of iced tea, choosing the cool drink over her preferred chai. "Because of children?"

Trisha whips around, her glare warning Ranee to let the subject drop. "It just didn't work out," she says mildly, her voice rising, a hopeless attempt to protect the truth. "Marriages end every day."

"Without a reason?" Marin demands, joining the conversation. She finishes labeling a box "Dishes and Plates." The china from the marriage is left untouched in the cabinet. "You two always seemed so in sync."

Ranee hadn't confided in Marin the information Sonya had given her about the real reason for Eric and Trisha's separation. With Gia's situation, Ranee was sure Marin had enough to deal with. But it was hard to keep the truth from her oldest. To Ranee, another secret felt like yet another skeleton.

"We wanted different things," Trisha answers coolly. A few beats later, she asks, "How is Gia?" The change of topic is abrupt, clearly not fooling anyone. "She's back at school?"

A week has passed since Gia returned to school. Ranee stopped by the morning of her first day back and stood by while Marin and Raj awkwardly went through the rituals of early morning preparation. Ranee listened as Raj chatted about the weather, ignoring Marin as she silently rechecked Gia's backpack to make sure all her finished homework was in the appropriate folders. Gia gave Ranee a hug good-bye before slipping into the car for Raj to drive her to school. Marin immediately returned to work, leaving Ranee to see herself out. She called that afternoon to check how Gia's first day went, but Marin coldly replied that it was fine and she was in her room studying.

"Yes," Marin answers, now the one to avoid everyone's eyes. "She appreciated your gift basket."

"You gave her a gift basket?" Sonya asks, a smile hovering. "Really?"

"It seemed appropriate," Trisha says, defending herself with a shrug.

"What was in it?" Sonya asks, dropping the tape roll and scissors on the box she was packing.

"CDs, some books, I think," Trisha pauses. "Maybe hot chocolate, body wash."

"Just what she needs," Sonya says. "Some yummy-smelling soap." Sonya starts to laugh, fueled by the ludicrousness of the situation.

Ranee opens her mouth to scold Sonya, to tell her that the thought is what counts, but before she can utter a word, Trisha starts to laugh. At first it is small, almost as if in embarrassment, but soon she is doubled over with it. Marin watches in shock, but soon enough she joins in, the laughter contagious.

For just a moment they are young again, all three of them, laughing like they did in their room late at night, bonding over the pain that no one else could understand. A decision to laugh instead of cry, to survive instead of let go. There was no past and no future, just now. As Ranee watches them, she wishes she could hold them in this place forever. Where they remember how to laugh with one another, to find joy even when sadness is the dominant emotion. But it is not meant to last. Just as Ranee begins to hope that they are once again tied together, that maybe there was a right after all the wrongs, Trisha's laughter turns ugly, bitter. As if remembering the surety of her life is shattered, she stops abruptly, shaking her head in obvious disgust.

"I guess I should have done more research, tried to figure out what to give a girl like Gia," Trisha says.

"What does that mean?" Marin demands, her own laughter coming to a halt.

"Why wouldn't she tell you what was happening to her?" Trisha demands. "Hard to figure out." Trisha stacks a box atop another. "Don't you think?"

Marin slowly approaches Trisha without breaking her gaze. "You don't want to know what I'm thinking right now."

"Gia is a teenager," Ranee interrupts, coming to stand between the two of them. "It does not always make sense why they do what they do."

"I just think—" Trisha begins, but Marin interrupts.

"I think my daughter is none of your business," Marin lashes out, clearly ignoring Ranee's attempt at diplomacy. "And you'll understand my hesitancy to accept any advice from the woman who can't have any children of her own." Hands on her hips, she has the stance of one ready for battle. A thought seems to occur to her, the revelation clear on her face. "Is that why Eric left? Because you couldn't have children?"

"I didn't want any," Trisha says slowly, her words laced with venom. "Good thing too, huh? Given the track record of our ability to mother."

"Everything my daughter is, is because of me," Marin throws out.

"Including the bruises?" Trisha demands. The words are whispered, said so quietly that Ranee isn't sure anyone heard. But when Marin grabs her purse and moves toward the door, Ranee accepts that she did.

"Good luck with the move," Marin says.

Ranee wants to call out, to beg her daughter to stop before it is too late, but the words stay stuck in her throat. Her only option is to watch her family tear themselves up from the inside, until nothing but fragments remain of who they could have been. Just as Ranee starts to turn away, to accept the inevitable, Trisha reaches the door before her sister.

"Marin," she says, her face filled with apology, "I'm sorry. That was uncalled for." She lays a palm against the wood, curling it into a fist as if she can hold on. "I love Gia. I love you. I'm just not in a good place right now." She steps forward, her body tense, almost preparing for a rejection. When none comes, she slips her arms around Marin's shoulders and brings her sister in for an embrace. They stand in silence for only a few seconds before Marin steps away. Opening the door, she walks out, shutting it quietly behind her.

* * *

Ranee walks through the darkened home, running her hands over the polished wood and fine furniture. The three of them finished packing the rest of the house in silence and then made a simple meal of potato sakh with naan. No one brought up what had happened between Trisha and Marin, preferring to pretend rather than confront. With so much they were already dealing with, selective amnesia felt easier. Sonya left soon after.

Ranee and Trisha quickly cleaned up after dinner. Trisha had released Eloise from her duties soon after Eric walked out, so the two of them were left to deal with the dishes. Once the kitchen sparkled, Trisha murmured that she was going to go lie down for a while. Ranee simply nodded, watching her daughter wearily climb the stairs toward her bedroom. She decided not to leave, an urge to remain with Trisha stronger than the desire to escape to the security of her own vacant home.

As the night sky falls, casting the room into darkness, Ranee chooses a seat in the den, glancing around at her daughter's choice of décor. Simple but elegant, a statement on how far she has come from the humble home she was raised in. Ranee is the first to admit she does not have an eye for decorations. It seemed pointless to decorate a home that felt more like solitary confinement. But Trisha clearly had no similar notions and chose to make the most of her house. She allowed it to become the vessel for her dreams, the place where she made reality fit her vision of a life well lived.

But she rejected the one thing that promised her everything—a child. The irony does not escape Ranee. Her children bound her to the man she was forced to marry, while Trisha's refusal to have a baby caused her to lose the man she loved. In the deafening quiet, Ranee imagines she can hear Trisha's cries on the bed upstairs. Her weeping for the castle that has crumbled around her. Oblivious to the truth, she never knew the castle was built from a lie—a grenade meant to explode.

The truth, when she learned it, leveled Ranee. In a moment of vulnerability, Brent had uttered the words that Ranee was sure would stop her heart. That they didn't shames her even now. Because his revelation, the one that no mother should imagine, let alone hear, is what makes women fall to their knees and wail, wonder how they could have failed so completely.

Brent whispered his secret not to make it better, or to seek justice for his deeds. No, he confessed to unburden his own soul. For all the sins he had committed, this was the one he did not want to take with him to the other side. He hadn't been feeling well, knew something was off. Wondered aloud if his time was near. When Ranee agreed it might be, he had dropped his head, gripped the armrests of the chair he was seated on, and admitted a wrong Ranee had never conceived. When he was done, when he laid his head back against the chair and closed his eyes, Ranee walked out and didn't return home until hours later.

Since then, she'd rehearsed the words, created the perfect scenario to tell Trisha the secret no one knew. But no setting seemed right; no combination of words fit together to make sense. Maybe now, Ranee thinks, the time has arrived. Without planning, without preparation, maybe the moment has finally come to admit the occurrence that Trisha needs to hear. Has the right to know.

Heroes are not born or created. They become so in the passing moments of life. When something or someone demands you be more than you have been, when you must put aside your own needs and what is best for you to fight for another, no matter the cost. The past, the day-to-day living becomes irrelevant. All that matters is that instant when the ticking of the clock is louder than an ocean's wave hitting the rocks, when time does not stand still, but slows, every second longer than the last one. This is when the decision becomes the only thing you can hear and see. When the choice falls out of your hand and fate intervenes. When your life is no longer yours but conjoined with another's, each dependent upon the other to survive and thrive.

Ranee stands and walks toward the stairs, prepared to take each one, but her courage fails her. Today is not the day. Ranee was not born to be a hero or a savior. She is not ready and wonders if she ever will be. Knowing that Trisha has mapped out her own life, fully aware that she holds the pen to help Trisha redraw the lines, Ranee is nonetheless too afraid to tell the truth. Instead, she walks to the front door, following the same path her other two daughters did before her, leaving Trisha all alone.

MARIN

Brent insisted Marin take Home Economics in high school. Along with Calculus and Biology, he was sure the class would fully round out her résumé. Marin didn't mind. They scrambled eggs, a food Marin never had before, and ate it with toast and jelly. She was used to roti and pickled turmeric root every morning; the American breakfast staple was a novelty. Marin devoured the meal, savoring the unique tastes. Afterward, as they were cleaning up, the students started playing a game.

"If you could be any kind of fruit, what would you be?" one of the girls asked aloud to no one specifically.

"An apple, because everyone loves them," one girl replied.

"A tomato," one of the guys said, "because it's a stupid question."

"Well, technically, a tomato could be considered a fruit, so thank you," the girl who asked the question returned.

They went around the room, Marin murmuring "Grapes," but offering no reason when it was her turn. But when another girl said pineapple, Marin paid attention, curious about the choice. "Because it's prickly on the outside and impossible to cut through. But once you get to the fruit, it's worth the trouble," the girl explained. "So don't always believe what you see."

* * *

Marin eats alone at her desk. She and Raj have barely spoken to one another since Gia returned to school. The prosecutor assigned to Adam's case keeps them abreast of any updates, but the backlog means things move slowly. Marin tries to temper her need for the process to speed up, wishing she could control it like she does her work. She's refocused her energy on her job, grateful that their family life has returned to some semblance of what it used to be. The only difference now is that Raj and Marin take turns picking up Gia from school every afternoon, having lost trust she'll be honest regarding her whereabouts.

"Three o'clock?" Marin is on the phone, attempting to reschedule a meeting she missed while dealing with Gia's situation. "I'll have to get back to you." Hanging up, she searches for Raj to see if he'll be able to switch pickup duties. She finds him in his office, staring out the window. Knocking once on the open door, as if they were colleagues instead of married, she catches his attention. "Can you get Gia today? I have a call I need to take."

He doesn't answer her, offering her a cursory glance before returning to staring out the window.

"Raj!" Marin loses her patience. "Can you get Gia after school today?"

He remains silent, instead holding out a sheet of paper for her. Marin stares at it in his hands, refusing to take it. "What is it?" she demands.

"I found it a few days ago. I think it's time I share."

Moving forward on legs that barely hold her, Marin takes the paper. Something in his eyes, in his voice, gives her a sense of foreboding, a wish to be back in her office, overwhelmed with work. At first glance she recognizes Gia's handwriting. It starts with a paragraph about love and loss. About being all alone. Marin reads through the words quickly, Gia's heartbreak laid out in detail. It is the last few words that cause Marin to stumble, to wonder when it all went wrong, when she had planned it so perfectly to go right. Gia's soliloquy speaks of life and wonders if death is not easier. If maybe life isn't meant to be lived, that somewhere it had to be easier than it was here. Sure she can't be everything everyone wants her to be. That in the end, she just wants to be herself, but fears that it will never be enough.

"Where did you get this?" Marin demands, finally finished.

"I found it in her diary. It was dated three days ago," Raj says quietly, still not meeting Marin's eyes.

"You searched her room?" Marin asks, needing someone or something to blame.

"This from the woman who had Gia followed? Who raised her hand to our daughter when she was already covered in bruises? Who decided to humiliate her in front of all her friends and classmates by bringing in the police to arrest her boyfriend?" He finally turns his head to stare at her, the air filling with his disgust. "You dare to stand in judgment of me?"

"I did it all for her," Marin says, her breath shallow, uneven. "I did what I thought was right for her life."

"The life she doesn't care to live." Raj stands, tearing the paper out of Marin's hands. "I have followed your lead for years. Trusted you knew what school was best for her, what activities. The focus on her grades trumping all else. I have abdicated all decisions, trusting you completely. I now see my mistake."

"You think you know better than I do?" Marin holds back an expletive. "Let's be realistic."

"I am," Raj says quietly, his demeanor more serious than Marin has ever seen. "She's hurting, and as much as you had hoped sending Adam to jail would solve all our problems, it hasn't. We're pulling her out of school immediately. Giving her some time off."

"We will do no such thing," Marin says, the room closing in on her. Her daughter's success, the routes that would define her place in the world, start to erode, washed under a tsunami, left only with debris. "I won't allow you to mess with her future."

"She has no future," Raj spits out. He shakes the paper in Marin's face. "This is all she has. All she is."

"We'll send her to a therapist," Marin decides, remembering the card thrown carelessly into a drawer. "Karen mentioned someone. I can set up some appointments for after school."

"You don't get it, do you?" Raj demands, narrowing his eyes. "This isn't a discussion. I've made my decision."

"When did you start to believe it was yours to make?" Marin demands.

"When I realized you were making all the wrong ones for her." Raj folds the paper carefully and slips it into his top desk drawer. "If you have a problem with my decisions, too bad. You have no choice."

"That is your first mistake," Marin says, her mind whirling. "I always have a choice." She finally sees what she hasn't been able to. What she has avoided since the first night of her marriage. "If you and I can't agree on Gia, we have nothing left." She begins laying out the steps in her head. Separate rooms, separate bank accounts. Whatever it took to separate their lives.

"You want to split?" Raj barks, his words ripped out. Clearly filled with incredulity, he stares at her.

Marin knows they are lost in a maze, one with no exit. Every turn they make is the wrong one, every corner leading to more darkness. If there was once a way out, it no longer exists, having been destroyed by their distrust, the belief that each one knew better. Hubris in its purest form, the price to pay higher than anyone could calculate. She doesn't respond.

"It's that easy?" he asks, quietly.

"When it comes to my daughter, everything takes a backseat. Including us."

Raj's shoulders slump; he seems to accept her decision without a fight. "If that's all we are, then I've been mistaken all these years. I thought we had a marriage. I now see it was just a charade." He stills when his phone begins to ring. He takes the call, turning his back on his wife.

* * *

It's raining. The Bay Area has four seasons—sunny, sunnier, rain, and rainier. Today the rain comes in sheets, blinding anyone who dares to venture onto its war path. For Marin, it is a welcome distraction from her life. She sits in her car, the windshield wipers at full speed but failing to stop the water from covering the glass. Staring at her phone, she wonders whom she can call.

Her contacts are filled with numbers of colleagues and subordinates, none of whom would care to hear about her woes, since she has never bothered to hear theirs. Births, deaths, weddings, and joyous occasions—all of them she's glossed over with a few perfunctory words before returning to the task at hand. Not once did she bother to ask the people these things happened to how they were feeling, if there was anything she could do. Now, when she is in need, no one will offer her a hand, an ear to listen. She is alone because she refused, over the years when it counted, to walk alongside anyone in their time of need.

Reincarnation is an established tenet of Hinduism. As children, Marin and her friends would play a game where they would guess who and what they were in their previous lives. From princesses and movie stars to cockroaches—the lowest reincarnation possible—they fantasized about all the possibilities.

"You had to be a man," one of Marin's oldest friends said as they sat in the safety of her mud-and-brick home, staring at the monsoon raging outside.

"Definitely," the rest of them agreed.

"Why would you think that?" Marin demanded, playing with her braided hair. "Are you saying I look like a boy?"

"No," they assured her. "But you don't let anyone tell you what to do."

"Why should I?" Marin demanded, sure of herself. "Just because I'm a girl doesn't mean anyone is the boss of me."

Marin hated the inferior status of women in their culture. It was standard practice; men controlled women. Males were assumed the superior sex, smarter, wiser, and more powerful. Women, no matter what age, were required to obey and follow their dictates. Cover their heads in respect, ask for permission to leave the home, with opportunities for higher education few and far between. It was the reason Brent gave everyone for leaving India, the sacrifice he made for his daughters. Better educations so they could have better lives.

Marin assured her friends that day that even if she were a man before, she would never be a man again, not in any future lives. When they demanded to know why, she answered with all the confidence born from not knowing, "Because that's the easy way out. I like the hard way better, because then you know who you really are."

Never would she have predicted how hard it would get, or how Brent would hold his position as man of the house over her like a burning flame, ready and willing to scorch her if she didn't obey. His threat so powerful and so effective that if asked again who she would reincarnate as—a man or a woman—Marin would say neither. She would rather not be reborn at all.

RANEE

She was born to give birth. That and to keep house. From the time Ranee could remember, she was taught all the intricacies of making a home. From doing laundry and the proper way to fold it, to making roti perfectly round. She and all the other girls she knew were enrolled full time in the school of homemaking from the moment they uttered their first word.

Ranee would listen as her brothers spoke about school, what they had learned and the games they played. They would bring home books that Ranee yearned to read but didn't know how. After begging her older brother for hours to teach her, he gave her a basic lesson. With it, she taught herself the rest. Sneaking the books with her to the outhouse, Ranee would use the few minutes of privacy to devour as many chapters as she could. As they got older, their books became more sophisticated. The stories were of places Ranee had never been, countries Ranee dreamed of visiting.

After their arrival in the States, Ranee's constant exposure to women who were confident both in their careers and their places in the house gave Ranee a different perspective. Whether in television or real life, Ranee watched them like a voyeur. Admiring their suits, their confidence, made her wonder what it would be like to be in control. To be the one who made the decisions, who forged the path of her and her daughters' futures, instead of it all being laid out for them.

She never told anyone of her wishes, not even the women she called friends in the community, for fear of their reaction. As time wore on, the dream seemed to fade farther away. But on Sonya's birthday a few months back, it became obvious; the decision didn't really need to be made, just followed through.

Once Sonya left, Ranee had no reason to celebrate her birthday. The day passed quietly, until the silence became deafening. Brent was seated in his favorite chair, reading the newspaper. His eyes had started to give him trouble, a side effect of the diabetes that ravaged his body. The doctor had prescribed drops, but he also used Visine to help with the redness.

"Ranee," he called out, refusing to get up, "bring me my eye drops."

Normally, Ranee would have rushed to do his bidding, anxious to keep him happy. But the day was weighing on her. Another year without her youngest.

"Do you miss her?" Ranee asked, needing to fill the emptiness.

"Who?" Brent asked, not bothering to glance up.

"Sonya," Ranee bit out. "Our daughter."

Brent lowered the paper slowly, clearly agitated at being disturbed. "Why are you asking me this today?"

Shocked, Ranee stared at him. "It's her birthday." Ranee had left her a voice mail, but unlike every year past, Sonya did not return the call. Normally the sound of her voice assuaged the heartache, but today Ranee didn't even have that. She tried twice more, but still no answer.

Realization dawned on Brent. Dismissing the importance, he raised his paper again, squinting to make out the words. "It was her choice to leave, Ranee."

Fury propelling her, Ranee pulled the paper out of his hands. She saw his anger simmer, knew her action was fuel on fire. Maybe she was looking for a fight, something to make her feel again since numbness had taken over. "Again and again, you told her she was a mistake." When Sonya left, she had taken a part of Ranee. "She had no choice."

"You think it was because of me?" Brent shakes his head, not bothering to give Ranee his full attention. "It was hearing the truth from you—that you didn't want her. That was the reason she left."

At times Ranee felt like a small fish in the vast ocean, no boundaries or limits to where her life went. She was at the mercy of each wave, each surge leading her farther away from where she was before. In between, she had to survive. But she couldn't deny Brent's words. She had pushed her daughter away. With so little of herself left, she had offered Sonya nothing. But by telling her child she wasn't wanted—and not telling her the reason why—she drove her away.

"It was to save her," Ranee finally spoke up, needing to admit it aloud. "You would have destroyed her if she stayed here."

Turning his gaze toward her, Brent assessed her before letting out a low laugh. "That was the decision you made? Having your daughter hate you?" Dismissing her, he murmured, "When Sonya chose photography over law I knew she wasn't intelligent. Now I know where she got it from." Letting her know the discussion is over, he motioned toward the kitchen and reminded her, "My drops, Ranee. I'm having difficulty reading."

"Yes," Ranee said, her mind starting to turn. "You need your eye medicine. If you went blind, how would I see?"

TRISHA

I wait on the sofa, one leg crossed over the other. I threw on a pair of slacks and a blouse after showering. The house is still, as though it has already accepted its fate and is mourning the loss. A family that never came to fruition. I assume Eric will sell it or maybe live in it, hoping to fill it one day with the children he wants. The thought of him with another woman, holding her, tightens my stomach. He has been mine for so long I can't imagine him being someone else's. But I know he may one day be. I have no say in the matter. I gave that up when I had the IUD implanted.

The doorbell rings, startling me. The watch that he gave me tells me he is on time. We have not seen one another since that day in his attorney's office. All communication has been via the woman who now speaks for him. My first replacement, I realize. How easy it was, I muse. I rise slowly, taking each step as if it were my last. Opening the door, I soak in the sight of him. It is the end of a workday, so he has on a suit and tie. He looks everything that I know him to be—strong and sure.

"Thanks for meeting me here," I say, welcoming him into his own home. "I know you preferred your attorney's office but—"

"This is fine," he says, interrupting me. His steps are hesitant, his hands thrust into his suit pockets. He no longer wears his wedding ring—it was the first thing I noticed at the attorney's office. "Since you've refused any type of alimony, her services seem superfluous."

"Right." We take a seat on opposite sofas, facing one another like strangers. I can still remember making love on them when they first arrived. Eric teased that we should christen them and was surprised when I readily agreed. I had stripped first, enjoying the burn of desire in his eyes as he watched me. "How are you?"

"Fine." Always the gentleman he asks, "And you?"

"Good," I lie. I wonder what he would say if I told him I hadn't slept more than a couple of hours each night, the bed too empty to sleep peacefully in. That I wonder daily what it would feel like to have had a child, to be a mother. To have given him what he wanted so badly, and in the process taken the step that I feared so much. "I've packed everything that was mine." I motion to the few boxes that are stacked in the foyer. "Anything we bought after the marriage I left."

"Where are you going to live?" he asks.

"I signed a month-to-month lease for an apartment in the city." I don't meet his eyes. "Until I can find something more permanent."

"Right."

We both fall silent, the pain in the room palpable. I yearn to reach out, to have the right to hold him like I used to. I never imagined the choice I made would lead to this. But only because I assumed he would never learn the truth. The secret was meant to be hidden forever, as they all are. The voice inside my head that has become louder in recent months starts to laugh, amused at my naïveté. *No secret stays hidden forever*, it whispers. *No secret*.

"How's work?" I ask abruptly, trying to quiet the murmuring.

He laughs bitterly, his face showing fatigue at the game. "Do you really care?"

"Yes," I say, taken aback that he would think otherwise. "I know how much your career means to you."

"Having a child with you meant something to me too," he says, the pain raw. "But that apparently didn't matter." He stands, finished with the farce. "Why did you want to meet?"

"To say good-bye." The words sound foreign to my ears. "To give you the keys to the house. To tell you I'm sorry." I turn my head, staring out the window. Swallowing the lump in my throat, I try to find the words. I will myself to stop, to let it go, but I can't. He was my husband, the man I meant to stay with forever. That I was wrong, that it was my fault, makes me feel foolish. "I never meant for this to happen, for us to say good-bye." Wringing my hands together, I admit, "I would have done anything not to hurt you. I loved you." Finding no reason to keep it from him, I tell him what I can barely admit to myself, "I still love you."

"Then why?" Eric pleads, his defenses clearly gone. He comes to stand before me. Holding my shoulders, his question is ripped out. "We had everything. You were my love, my life."

"I don't know," I whisper, his touch reminding me of another time. Another place. Another man.

"You are my life," the voice whispers in the dark. She had been sleeping. She was sure she imagined it until she felt the hand on her shoulder through the thin material of her nightgown.

Without meaning to, I wrench out of Eric's arms, wrapping my own around my much slimmer frame. There is no longer joy in food, three meals a day feeling more like a chore than anything. My body has paid the price, withering away. My clothes hang off me, my belts never tight enough.

She awakens slowly, sure it is Sonya sneaking into her bed again. At fifteen, Trisha isn't as quick to welcome her anymore. It is the night of Marin's marriage. Trisha feels older, more mature. Too mature to have her little sister sleep with her. "You're the only one I love," *the voice continues, the hand moving from her shoulder down her arm.*

"It's done," I say, trying to push him and the memory away at the same time. I shake my head, back and forth, trying to rid myself of the vision. But it holds me in its grip, refusing me a reprieve. "It doesn't matter anymore."

"That's it?" Eric shakes his head, clearly angry for having tried.

She's walking down the darkened hallway. No one responds to her silent cries. They are filled with horror and sadness, too loud for anyone to hear. She bangs her fists on the wall, hitting until they are raw with pain. One door after the other she tries, unsure of where she is. What was once familiar is now foreign, her home alien. Finding one door unlocked, she wrenches it open, only to discover it is a linen closet. Leaving the door ajar, she searches for another. And another until she enters a darkened bedroom. She falls to the floor, so exhausted from her search for a haven. She cries into her hands, her sobs echoing in her head.

"Trisha?" *Sonya's young voice breaks through the sound of the cries, her arms surrounding. Fear laced into every word.* "What happened? Why are you crying?"

"Can you at least tell me this?" Eric asks, jarring me back to the present. A muscle jerks in his jaw. "You knew about my past, the loneliness . . ." He pauses, hurt. "Why didn't you want a child?"

"Because they always get hurt," I finally answer, the truth searing me.

* * *

I sit in front of Mama's house, the engine idle. I stare at the front door for what feels like an eternity, too afraid to go in, but more afraid not to. Thoughts haunt me, tugging at my brain. I try to push them away, desperate to forget, but they refuse to go. *Now, it says. Now it is time.* I shake my head, but time is not my friend or my ally. If it were, then maybe I would have more of it.

I finally step out of the car, the metal casket no longer providing me a reprieve. I don't use my key, the house suddenly feeling like a stranger's home instead of mine. I ring the bell and wait, sure that Sonya will be in at this time of the evening. I ring again. And again, my fingers sitting on the bell.

When Eric left the house, disgusted with me, I followed, jumping into my car, all the packed boxes left in the foyer. I could feel him watching me from his car, his love turning to hatred, two sides of the same coin, each emotion a worthy opponent of the other. I drove straight here, needing answers and sure that only Sonya could give them to me. What I can't remember, she must. As if the floodgates have been opened, I can see her sitting on my sofa when she came to say good-bye. *He plays the loving father. You let him.* Her words repeat in my head, her eyes searching mine for a sign of recollection.

"Trisha?" Mama answers the door. "What are you doing here, Beti?" She steps back, motioning me in, but I stand rooted to the same spot.

"Is Sonya home?" My hands are shaking. "I need to speak to her."

"No," Mama says, staring at me. I imagine everyone doing the same thing, trying to understand the train wreck I have become. "What's wrong, Beti?"

"When will she be home?" The sun is getting ready to set. The mosquitoes have begun to bite. As a child, I was always their target, my skin swelling with welts. "Because you are so sweet," Papa would say.

"It's late."

Mama takes my hand, ushering me into the house. I allow her to do so, too weak to lead myself. "Soon. Come, we will have a cup of chai and you can tell me what has happened."

I want to laugh. Her solution to everything, as if chai can fix the world's woes. Yet, hadn't I done the same thing? Offered Sonya a cup of tea when she came to say good-bye. Included a bag of hot cocoa in

Gia's gift basket. I wonder how many other habits of Mama's I have made my own. When did I become her reflection and Papa's creation?

"No chai," I murmur, searching. The cries that have been muted until now are suddenly loud, searing me with their desperation. I watch in slow motion as Mama walks into the kitchen, pours the cup I refused, and sets it in front of me. I can barely make out the steaming milk or decipher what she is saying. Without a word to her, I walk out of the kitchen and toward the stairs.

"Trisha." Her yell breaks through the barrier, but I ignore it, other voices louder. She follows me, her breath on the back of my neck.

I say nothing to her, climbing the stairs quietly, lost in another time, another place. My fingers grip the bannister, each step harder than the last. Reaching the top, I walk down the hallway, my hand sliding alongside. I reach my room first, flinging the door open. It is the same as I left it years ago. The last time I spent the night here was the day before I got married. That evening, everything seemed possible. The only thing missing from my life was the presence of my little sister, but I wouldn't allow that to mar my good day. I had two dresses laid out on my bed, my red sari and a white wedding gown. Both I had spent hours shopping for, insisting everything be perfect for when I married the perfect man. No matter that Eric was white and older. He loved me as I deserved to be loved.

"Why did Papa let me marry an American?" I ask, my mind whirling. I know she is behind me, watching. "It went against our culture, his dictates."

Papa never uttered a word of anger when I told them with trepidation that I had fallen in love with a white man. "Never marry a BMW" was the mantra of the Indian community. Black, Mormon, White—the three unacceptable marriage partners in our culture. I was sure my announcement would be met with fury and disappointment, that it would be the first time I would feel his wrath. I had prepared myself for the worst, but when he simply dropped his head and nodded his acceptance, I was left speechless. He walked out of the room and the discussion was over.

I stare at my room now, changed completely from that night, when I was still fifteen. Redecorated, a gift for my sixteenth birthday. I was allowed to choose whatever theme I wanted, whatever bed I desired. Everything in the room was trashed, replaced by new. Sonya stood by, watching in envy, as I chose the color to paint the walls and picked a princess theme décor to match my mentality. I kept the room that way for a year, until my friends began to tease me. I asked Papa if I could change it one more time, and he readily agreed. I went with a more mature theme, neutral spring colors that have remained to this day.

"He let me change the décor," I murmur. "Buy everything new."

"Yes." She nods.

Her answers are quick, to the point. As if she fears saying too much. I step out of my bedroom and back into the hall. She follows me silently, a guide to a labyrinth with no way out. In the hallway, I slide my hands along the wall, remembering doing the same thing years ago. The red paint on my colored nails starts to drip over my fingertips and down the back of my hand. The paint turns to blood. I yank my hand off the wall, sure I have left a stain, but only pristine white stares back at me. I stare at my fingers but there is no longer any blood.

"I was crying," I say, lost in another time. "I screamed."

"I didn't hear you," Mama says, anguished. I pivot toward her, watching with odd detachment as she wrings her hands together. She refuses to look at me, her tears falling off her face and onto the floor. Like an old woman, her body has shriveled into itself. In front of my eyes she seems to have aged by twenty years while I am stuck in a time warp. "I never heard you, Beti."

"The bathroom," I exclaim. There was blood in the bathroom, in the sink. I can see it now, swirling with the water. Throwing open the door, I stare into the sink, but only sparkling porcelain stares back. "There was a rag. I cleaned the blood with it." Opening the drawers I search for it. But they are bare. I grab the trash can, sure I threw it in there, but it stands empty. The laundry basket is the same. "Where did it go?" I demand.

"It's gone," she says, reaching for me, but I push her away. I don't want her hands on me. I start to rub my arms, feeling the heavy weight of something else or someone else on me. "I never saw it."

"Where did it go?" I demand, sure she is playing a game with me. The memories flood my mind, erasing the line between yesterday and today. Lost in a vortex, my mind throws me from place to place, refusing me reality to hold on to. "It was right here."

"I don't know," she whispers.

"Sonya may know," I exclaim. I rush toward her room and open the door. "Where is she?" I demand when my search comes up empty.

"She's still at work, remember?"

"You're lying!" I scream. "She's just a kid."

"She's a grown woman," Mama says quietly. "So are you."

She must be joking. I am only fifteen. Still a child. I have pretended to be a woman, like all teenagers do. But deep down I am still a young girl, waiting for when I am fully grown and dreading it at the same time. "Why are you saying this?" I cry. "After what happened, how can you do this to me?"

"What happened, Beti?" Mama asks.

I start to tell her what I remember, vague images filtering through a dark curtain, but something in her eyes stops me. A revelation that what I will say is not a surprise, not a secret I have kept from her, from myself, but instead the other way around.

"You know?" I am on a swing, flying so high that I fear I may fall. One moment I am the woman she says I am, and in the next second I am just a teenager. I vacillate between the two, neither one feeling real to me.

"Yes," she admits, lowering her head. "Not then, but recently."

"How?" I demand. Shaking my head, I push past her back to the bathroom. There, I stare into the mirror, the image staring back at me changing. The girl with her hair strewn haplessly and tears streaking her face evolves into a woman I no longer recognize. "What's happening to me?" I demand, grasping the sink for stability. "What happened to me?"

"You don't remember?" she asks.

"Tell me!" I scream again, hearing it echo in the empty house.

"He came to you late at night, after Marin's wedding. He started drinking after all the guests left."

I can smell the liquor now. He had never drunk before, always threatening it, but never following through. But that night he reeked of it. Cheap liquor mixed with the smell of wine. I made the distinction years later, the smell of both still causing my stomach to churn. I was fast asleep. I had started sleeping in my own room, insisting Sonya sleep in hers. He whispered the words in my ear, waking me with a touch. His hands down my arm, pulling the blanket slowly away. I clutched at it, fear paralyzing me.

"You are the only one I truly love. You know that, right? It is why you are so special to me. Why I treat you differently."

Why I never beat you, were the unspoken words. The ones he didn't utter, but made sure I understood. As he lifted my nightgown, the thought reverberated in my head. I was the lucky one. The special one. That's why he wasn't beating me. And when he finally bore down on me, I was grateful that I was still safe from his fists. If this was the cost of being protected, then it was a small price to pay.

"What did he do?" I demand, everything moving faster and faster. The first time we went to an amusement park, I repeatedly rode the teacup that went round and round, laughing as everyone complained how dizzy they were. Only after, when I climbed out, did I realize the effect. Holding on to the side of the ride, I fought for everything to stabilize and failed. I vomited seconds later, the purge finally giving me the steadiness I craved. "Tell me!"

"It doesn't matter," Mama starts, obviously hiding the truth. We had learned to appreciate our lies like a veil over our lives, each untruth stronger than the facts. I loved playing with her saris as a child, using the end as a veil like women were required to in India. Always fascinated by the mystery it represented, I see it now for what it is—an excuse to keep a woman in her place, her beauty and power hidden from the world.

"It matters to me," I yell. At the same time I demand an answer, I want to run from it. Now I understand Sonya's instinct, her desire to keep moving. When faced with what has happened, when you have no choice but to live with it, it seems wiser to sink rather than swim. "Tell me!"

"He raped you," Mama whispers, each word sounding as if torn from her throat. I take two steps back, her admission repeating itself over and over in my head. I was blind for so long that now I wonder how I will ever learn to see again.

"How did you know?" Maybe she is mistaken. I still hold on to the chance that maybe it's all a dream, that I was confused. That the fiction I created, built a life on, is what is real, and she is spewing a lie.

"He told me." She reaches for me again, and this time I am too weak to fight her. His admission makes it real. Her petite body fits against mine. "A few months back, he told me everything." Her tears start to soak my blouse as I stand completely still. "He hadn't been feeling well. Wanted to confess. He said he'd been living with the guilt ever since that night." She steps back, facing me. Cradles my face in her frail hands. "I'm so sorry, Beti. I'm so sorry."

RANEE

Three months had passed since Sonya's birthday. Brent was getting weaker over time. He had gone to the doctor's but was not a fan of them telling him how to take care of himself. Because of his diabetes, they insisted he limit his sugar intake. He refused to give up on his vice and assumed he would be fine. But time proved him wrong. He started to feel worse and began to fear for his health.

"Ranee," Brent called out one early morning. They were scheduled to have lunch with Trisha later that afternoon. Ranee had started to clean the house while Brent rested in his favorite chair.

"Yes?" Ranee swiped the counters clean, removing the few specks of dirt.

"Can you get me a glass of water?" he asked. Only recently had he begun to ask rather than tell.

Ranee took her time, secure in the knowledge that he could do nothing but wait for her. Filling a glass with lukewarm water instead of the cold that he preferred, she handed it to him and started to turn away when he said, "Trisha—every time we see her she is happy."

"Yes," Ranee agreed. Trisha had made it. Untouched, she was the one Ranee could point to and say something went right. "Her life is everything she wants it to be."

"Yes." Brent laid his head back, releasing a deep sigh. "It is good."

Something in his voice tugged at her, made her stop and stare. "She was the one who was never hurt," Ranee said, the words an accusation. "She was the lucky one. Happiness is hers to have."

Opening his eyes, Brent didn't respond to her statement directly. Instead, he watched her, fear filling his features. "What do you think happens to us when we die?" he asked.

The question took Ranee aback. She rarely gave death a thought when life took so much of her energy. "I don't know. I imagine we face our creator, have to explain our actions," she said, jabbing at him however she could. "Give a reason for hurting the ones we did."

"And if there is no reason?" Brent whispered. "If it was a mistake you never imagined making?"

It was a question Ranee never believed Brent capable of asking. Staring at him, wondering if he felt regret for all of his actions, she asked, "Then why did you do it?"

"You know?" Brent whispered, his round eyes large in his weathered face. "How?"

"I was right here," Ranee bit out, wondering if he was losing his mind. "Every single day, when you hit me and my two girls, I was standing right here!" she said, her voice nearly a scream.

Closing his eyes, he turned his face away, relief washing over him. Ignoring her outburst, he said, "Never mind."

There was something he wasn't telling her, Ranee was sure. She knew it the way she knew what was coming minutes before he started hitting. The way she knew that if there was ever good in his heart, it was long gone. Fear gripped her, pushed her to take a seat across from him. Staring at the man who once held her life in his palm, she demanded, "What did you do?"

"It doesn't matter," Brent whispered. A lone tear fell from his eye over his cheek. Too weak to wipe it away, he let it linger, the wetness leaving a trail.

"It does," Ranee pushed, fighting against the voice in her head that demanded she let it be. For her entire life she had let things go. Suddenly, a force greater than the beaten voice demanded she act. "Tell me or I swear on the mangalsutra I wear around my neck that I will leave you right now to die alone."

"There are some things better left unsaid," he said quietly, his breath ragged.

"For whom?" Ranee demanded, the room closing in on her. Taking a step toward him, she towered over him. "For the first time in a long time, I want to hear you speak."

He glanced at her, seeming to gauge whether she was serious. Ranee watched as he opened his mouth, but no words came out. He wrung his hands together; hands that were once so powerful were now weak and frail. "Please," he begged, the first time in his life. Ranee stared at him before making her decision. Knowing he could not follow, she reached for her keys and started to walk out of the house. "Ranee," he called out.

Refusing to turn, she demanded, "Tell me."

"I drank the liquor I brought home."

"The bottles you threatened us with?" Ranee turned to stare at him. She still remembered the dozens of unopened bottles she would throw out. Stepping closer to him, she dropped her purse on the counter. "When?"

He struggled, something Ranee had never seen him do. "The night of Marin's wedding." Refolding the paper, he shifted in his seat. Rubbing his hand over his face, he refused to meet Ranee's stare. "I drank all of it."

Ranee racked her brain, trying to remember that night, but she couldn't. Exhausted from the day's events, she had fallen into a deep sleep. "Did you come to bed after?"

"Not ours, no," Brent answered softly.

A slow buzzing started in her brain. From the base of her neck, rising to the top, drowning out every other noise. She felt the pounding between her eyes and at her temples like a bulldozer. The room began to spin. She clutched her mangalsutra, but it burned her fingers. Letting it go, she stared down at her hands. Small red hives started to pop up on her arms. Her vision began to blur, but she refused to let it—for the first time in her life, she had to keep her control. When her focus returned, the first thing she saw was the fire poker on the fireplace. For just a heartbeat she imagined walking over, pulling it out of the holder, and bashing him with it.

"Whose bed?" she demanded but already knew the answer. The only one he loved.

"Trisha's." He started to sob, the sound reverberating through the house. "I never meant to do that to her."

"You raped her," she said aloud, still in disbelief. Tears coursed down her face, drenching her neck and shirt. Everything in Ranee wanted him dead, but she knew he was already dying. Left with no other way to hurt him, she walked away, though she promised him she wouldn't. Grabbing her purse, she left the house and drove around for hours, with no place to go. When she returned, she found him collapsed on the ground, his breathing erratic and his mind gone.

SONYA

"Do you believe in miracles?"

"Excuse me?" I am behind the nurses' desk, storing the cameras for the evening.

"Divine intervention." The nurse is inputting information about a patient into a computer. "An act from somewhere out there"—she waves her hand toward nothing—"making everything right."

I have never thought of miracles, never believed they were mine to have. If there were such a thing, then I wouldn't have had the childhood I did. "I don't know," I say honestly, leaning against the station. "Do you?"

"Didn't used to," she comments. "But after last night, I'm starting to wonder."

"What happened last night?" I ask, searching my brain for news I may have heard but not registered. David was right; information spreads like wildfire in the hospital. Good or bad, everyone seems to know events as fast as they happen. "I think I'm out of the loop."

Over the last few weeks, I've started to make friends. It's a new concept for me, given the last years of my life. Friends were the casualty of my nomad existence, a necessary loss for my survival. But now, seeing these same people every day, watching them dedicate their lives to helping others who are suffering, I realize that the world is not just black and white. It isn't just my suffering and the darkness that became my umbrella versus those who seemed to have everything right—instead, there are shades of all the colors, each one seeping into the other, changing the landscape, an evolution of the human soul.

"Tessa died last night."

I stop, my hands gripping air. She was the little girl I worked with when I began. Who titled her book *ME*. I saw her regularly after that, and she seemed to be getting better, stronger. "What happened?" I ask, dread settling in me like a lost friend.

"She sat up, asked us to call her family." The nurse stares at me, her face filled with wonder. "They arrived immediately. Tessa started naming members of her family that had passed on. People she had never met before. Told her mom and dad that those people were there, that they would take care of her." The nurse continues to input information into the computer. "She said everything was going to be all right."

I don't want to listen anymore. I want to leave the conversation, go back to taking pictures, believing in what I know to be real. "What did they say?"

"They listened. They held her. She closed her eyes, and a few minutes later her heart stopped." The nurse shakes her head in seeming confusion. "It was a code blue. They did everything to resuscitate her."

"Where was the miracle?" I demand, my heart breaking, angry at life's unfairness. Tessa was young, just a child. She had just started to live, the future unwritten, waiting for her to decide on the story she would tell. There should be a rule somewhere, somehow, that happiness is the default, the fallback for every situation. Every turn, every twist should lead toward a better beginning. There's no light at the end of the tunnel; instead, the entire path is paved with sunshine.

"She came back to life. Minutes after they pronounced her dead, she came back."

I don't respond, have no answer. I have never wondered about more than here and now . . . it is all I have had the capacity for. If there is a life after now, a profound reason for what happens today, then I have missed the memo or purposely ignored it. Either way, I have no opinion on life after this one. But the breath I hold, the sadness I swallow, leaves my body in one swoop. She is alive. For now, she is still alive.

"Do good in this life so your karma allows a wonderful life next time," Mom used to tell us. Karma was both a threat and a beacon; the life lived now would determine the future.

I leave the nurse, still shocked by the previous night's events, and make my way to Tessa's room. I know it by heart, her room just a few hallways down from where I am. It is late, so I know Tessa will already have had dinner. Most likely her parents have left for the night; with other children at home, they can only be spread so thin. I listen at the door for voices. When I hear none, I quietly push open the door. Peeking in, I see what I need—Tessa sleeping peacefully, her skin healthier, her vitals better than ever before. Nodding to myself, I start to close the door quietly as David approaches.

"So you heard?"

Though the hospital is large, it is nearly impossible to avoid someone. Similar patients, same diagnostic areas—all of it leading to an eventual encounter. Being near him, in the quiet of the hallway, I automatically go to our last encounter, when I almost lost myself with him and after.

"Yes," I say, stepping away from him. "It's a miracle."

"That's what everyone's saying," he responds. I watch him, his movements, the way he speaks, all of it feeling familiar in a way that it shouldn't, that makes no sense.

"She's going to be all right?" I ask, afraid of the answer. If I were God, my first decree would be that once you have a miracle, nothing bad can happen. After a magic hand has touched you, after you have been deemed special, there is no going back. Forever after you are blessed. My second would be that everyone is worthy of their own miracle. "The cancer?"

"We think so," David answers, somehow understanding my deeper question. "What happened, what she said, can only give us hope."

Like a rainbow after a tornado, I think. I was in the Southwest for a photo shoot when a mile-wide tornado ravaged the community. I took shelter like everyone else, waiting for nature's evil to pass. Sirens blared; thunder clapped around us as the winds screamed their power. For ten minutes, we stood frozen, waiting without any other option. When silence descended, everyone ran out, trying to calculate with their eyes the irreparable damage done. As people scattered, searching for loved ones, someone cried out, pointing toward the sky. Every face lifted in dread, sure it was another twister, but instead a multitude of colors spanned the horizon, offering beauty in the face of despair.

"Then it's a good thing." I search for a way out, anything to avoid a repeat of what happened with David. I can't lose myself like that again, if only because I fear I might not find my way out twice. I start to walk away, the only thing I know how to do, when he stops me.

"I miss you."

He says it where anyone can hear. I look around, fearing an audience. The hallway is quiet. "You can't miss what's not yours," I say, lashing out, trying to hurt.

"You're right," he agrees. "Doesn't seem to stop it, unfortunately."

I look into his eyes and see in them the sadness we both feel.

"I was never supposed to be here." I start to say more, to fight a battle that hasn't begun, when a nurse moves past us to enter Tessa's room. Using the excuse, I flee, the only answer I have.

MARIN

They are seated around the dinner table, each at an equal distance from the other. The meal completed, they stare, first at each other and then at anything that holds their interest. Raj is the first to speak, reaching across the table for Gia's hand. "How are you doing, Beti?" he asks.

"I'm fine, Daddy," Gia says, pulling her hand away after a second. "Everything is good."

Her demeanor contradicts her words. Her hair lies limply around her shoulders. There are dark circles beneath her eyes, and her nails, usually painted and trimmed, have been bitten to the skin. "You don't look fine," Marin says, her voice harsher than she meant. "You look terrible."

"Thanks, Mom," Gia says, not meeting Marin's eyes. "Really appreciate it."

Marin bites back a retort, her instinct screaming to tell Gia to get in line, to shape up. That her drama needs to come to an end now. Marin imagines telling Gia that if she dared to behave like Gia when she was a child, she would have been thrown against the wall in seconds without a chance to explain.

"You're lucky that we—"

Before Marin can say the words she's thinking, Raj interrupts. "Gia, I found this in your drawer the other day." He looks defeated, like a father searching. "You can understand how worried we are."

Gia reads the top line before letting the piece of paper slip from her fingers. "You went into my room? Searched through my things?" She drops her head. "How could you?"

"I am your father," Raj says gently. "How could I not?" He comes around to her side, taking the seat next to her. "I have been so worried about you. What can we do, Beti?" Taking her hand once again in his, he says, "Tell us. Anything, just say the word."

"I don't know," Gia whispers, the tears falling.

"Then why the tears? Hmm?" Raj slowly wipes them away, as if Gia were still a child. "Tell me."

"I miss him," Gia admits. "All the time."

Adam. The thought of him brings bile to the surface. Marin swallows it but it rises again, leaving bitterness in its wake. "Have you no sense?" Marin demands, staring at Gia, seeing a stranger instead of her daughter. "You miss the boy that hurt you?"

"He loved me."

"No, he did not!" Marin berates her, slamming her fist against the table, startling both Raj and Gia. "Do you have any idea what love is?" Marin stands, ignoring the warning bells going off in her head. "Love is good. It's . . ." Marin struggles to define the emotion. "It's working to give you the best life, a superior education. Everything I didn't have, you do. That's what love is."

"No, it's not," Raj says quietly. He shakes his head in clear disappointment, turning away from Marin and back toward Gia. "We've done something wrong and it needs to be fixed. Somewhere along the way, we lost you and we need to find you. We need to get our girl back." He pauses, shuts his eyes, and takes a deep breath. "Do you want to leave school for a while? Take a break, use some time to heal?"

"I can do that?" Gia automatically glances at Marin, as she is the one who will withhold permission.

"No," Marin says, but Raj overrides her, his voice louder than hers.

"Yes, you can," Raj says. "If that's what you want."

"I'm sorry, I thought we already discussed this," Marin interjects, feeling the anger boiling over. Since their last conversation, she and Raj have avoided the topic of a separation. However, Raj did move his things into the guest room and now sleeps there. Other than co-parenting, there is little left for them to speak about. "She will not be leaving school."

Raj stands, facing Marin. "If that's what she needs right now, yes, she will."

"I won't allow you to destroy her life," Marin says. "If you want a battle, you've got one."

"Meaning what?" Raj asks slowly.

"Gia and I will move out. I'll fight for full custody and the right to make all decisions about her life," Marin warns. As soon as the threat comes out of her mouth, she knows it's what makes the most sense. She and Raj are at an impasse, and his ideas will only lead to long-term harm for Gia. Marin can't allow it, even if it means taking Gia away from her father.

"I would want to live with Dad," Gia says quietly. She rises from her seat, coming to stand right next to her father. "My wishes would count, right?" When Raj nods, she continues, "Then that's what I want. I don't care if it's here or somewhere else. I want to stay with you, Dad. Please."

Marin staggers back, the shock destabilizing her. "Gia, what are you saying?" she pleads, feeling a type of fear she hasn't felt since leaving her father's home. "I'm your mother. You belong with me."

"I think I would be better with Dad," Gia whispers, not meeting Marin's eyes. "OK?"

Her question is directed to Marin, but it's Raj who answers. "Sure, sweetheart."

* * *

Marin arrives in Brent's hospital room late at night. She left the house after Gia's declaration, driving first to her office at the company's headquarters. She closed her office door and sat staring at the walls for hours. She reviewed all her options and even placed a call to a number of divorce lawyers, setting up times to meet next week. But some quick Internet research proved her fears correct: at the age of fifteen, Gia's choice would take precedence. Once she told a judge she preferred to live with her father, there would be no reason not to let her do so.

Marin wondered how everything had gone so wrong. She had it all, everything laid out in exact detail, and now, without any choice in the matter, it was all crumbling around her. She had never loved Raj, she could see that now, but she had accepted their roles, their place, in each other's lives. Understood that under the dictates of their Indian culture, the marriage was forever even if only on paper.

Now, nothing seemed certain. The concrete foundation she had built her life on was cracked, leaving her life susceptible to collapse. For Gia, Marin had strived for perfection but was deceived by the illusion. There was no excellence to be attained. No superiority to hold over those less accomplished. In offering Gia the world, Marin stole her daughter's sense of self.

After leaving her office, finding that the walls that once offered her a reprieve felt like a coffin, she arrived at the one place she never would have thought to go. She sat in the hospital parking lot for over an hour, begging herself not to go in. It was too late for answers; too much had happened to try and scrutinize. Besides, she was not one to lie down on a sofa for a stranger to analyze. In doing so, she'd be admitting there was something wrong, and she refused to make such a concession. No one knew better than she how to chart her life. No matter what happened with Gia and Raj. No matter what the future held.

But she ignored her own words. Under the light of the moon and the glare of the fluorescent ER lights, Marin found her way to the hospital's front door and inside the sterile walls. Taking the empty elevator to her father's floor, she made her way to his room. It seemed like only yesterday she had walked down a separate but similar hall, leading Gia to the Trauma Unit. Yet, it was not yesterday. If it were, maybe she could undo the steps that followed. Change the course of her life and chart a new direction. Find a way to keep Gia as her own instead of losing her to circumstance.

* * *

"You won," Marin says to her father as he lies very still under the white sheet. "I thought I could beat you, show you that I wasn't yours to rule, but I was wrong." She takes the seat next to her father's bed, refusing to touch him. "All those years, you controlled me with an iron hand, but I convinced myself that in time I would prove I was stronger, smarter than you."

After the first time he hit her, soon enough it became a regular occurrence. Marin never expected the violence initially, always believing she could do something wiser, earn a better grade to avoid the beating. But no grade was ever good enough, no behavior acceptable. It wasn't until two years after their arrival in the States that Marin learned a very important lesson on how to deal with her father.

They had just arrived at an Indian function celebrating Navrati followed by Diwali—the festival of lights. Over nine days, the members of the Indian community, dressed in their finest attire, would gather to dance with sticks. Most of the women wore saris, while the girls wore *chaniya cholis*—ankle-length skirts and short blouses that left their stomachs and arms bare. A sheer shawl thrown over their shoulders and tucked into the back of the skirts was the only other covering. Each outfit had fake jewels threaded through, making the girls sparkle as they danced. Around statues of the Goddess Lakshmi—the patron of wealth—they would twirl. Diyas lit the room, and incense permeated with a rose essence burned. It was nine days of beauty, filled with hope and a sense of community.

As a child, Marin still yearned for the celebrations in India, where the country shut down for the festivities. The streets would fill with those reveling in the occasion. Caste, color, and gender became irrelevant in the face of the joy. Marin would spend the nine days with her friends, and they rotated at whose house they stayed the night. Brent would tuck fifty rupees—a fortune—into Marin's palm and tell her to go have a wonderful time.

Vendors lined the streets, their carts filled with sweets and toys. For Marin, the money was enough to keep her pockets filled for all nine days. Her friends envied the amount, their own fathers giving them only ten to twenty rupees. Marin was always quick to share, unable to enjoy her windfall if her friends suffered. The nine days of celebration were something Marin looked forward to all year, the happiness filling every part of her.

She assumed the celebrations in America would be the same, if not better. The first night, when she realized they were limited to the inside of a rented hall and that the festivities lasted only from evening to midnight, Marin lulled herself to sleep with memories of years past. It was only in the second year that Marin fully understood the difference—and what her life was now compared to what it had been.

After getting dressed and eating dinner, they all herded into their station wagon and Brent drove them the short distance to the church hall the Indian *samaj* had rented out for the occasion. After they parked in the lot, Marin jumped out, ready to run in and lose herself in the sea of hundreds of people in attendance.

"Marin," Brent said, stilling her.

"Yes, Daddy?" Marin asked, wondering, hoping, for just a moment, that he was about to slip some dollars in her hand to buy succulent Indian sweets that some of the ladies sold to raise funds.

"I have a reputation to maintain. Remember that," her father said as he lifted Sonya from her car seat.

"Yes, Daddy," Marin said, her hands clasped in front of her, anxious to be on her way.

Marin spent the night playing with friends she had made within the Indian crowd, many of them having nothing more in common than the color of their skin. But like all children, they found whatever similarities they could as an excuse to play together. The night went quickly, Marin finding happiness in the game of hide-and-seek they played, while the adults and teenagers danced in the main hall. When her friends tired, they found an office in the back hall. Sneaking in cans of soda and bowls of *ghatiya*, they snacked while they played.

Two of the boys began to wrestle, knocking over three cans of soda. As the caramel color seeped into the beige carpet, they ran out of the office, refusing responsibility. Others followed, leaving Marin and one other girl. Ready to flee themselves, they were caught at the door by an adult who saw the stain.

"I expected more from you," the man said, calling out for Brent and the other girl's father.

"Please, Uncle," Marin began, using the moniker as a sign of respect. Sweat started to line her blouse and upper lip. Fear made her voice tremble. "We were not at fault. The boys were playing and . . ."

Before she could finish, Brent arrived. He saw the stain and stepped forward to reprimand her, but then the other girl's father arrived and assessed the situation. "Marin could never do such a thing," he said. "Marin," he continued, coming to lay his hand on her shoulder, the only acceptable touch from a man to a girl. "My daughter was telling us just the other day what an outstanding student you are. Have I heard correctly that you are skipping two grade levels?"

"Yes," Brent answered for her. "The principal contacted me recently to recommend it."

"Brent, you just arrived in America. We have been here since before our children's births, and yet we are not able to accomplish the success you have in such a short time." The uncle offered Marin another smile. "You are an example to the rest of the children in our community. How fortunate for us that you are here now. Our children now have someone to look up to and learn from." He shook Brent's hand, using his other to motion toward the stain. "This is not a child who would make such a mistake. Tell me, what is your secret?"

"I sit with her every night for her studies," Brent said, offering a smile to Marin for the uncle's benefit. "Her success is our validation for coming to America."

"And she should be applauded for it, my friend." He motioned for Marin and his daughter to follow. "Come, I will buy you whichever sweet you prefer. You have earned it."

Marin lays her head against the back of the chair next to Brent's bed, the memory of that day washing over her. She enjoyed a plateful of delectable Indian sweets that night, thanks to the uncle and Brent both buying them whatever they wanted. But more important than the sweets was the lesson of the night. The one that came with Brent's apology to her.

"I'm sorry," he said, one of the first and last times Marin would hear the words from him. "The uncle was right. Someone with your accomplishments would never make such a mistake." Lost in thought, he murmured to himself, "It is all a game, Marin. Life, I mean. You must know how to win it. That's all that matters."

The message was clear—as long as she was accomplished and the world knew it, she was safe. No one would dare touch her. She was special because she was successful. That night, she made herself a promise. Never again would she be anything but the best. It was the only way to guarantee complete control over her life, to win the game.

"Here is my success, Daddy," Marin murmurs now. "Gia wants to live with her father." Marin hears her daughter's declaration again and again in her ears. "She doesn't want me." Marin catches her breath, each passing second making it more difficult. "I've done everything for her. My success was supposed to be her beacon, but it wasn't enough. I wasn't enough. She doesn't love me."

Her weight too heavy to bear, Marin slides off the chair and onto the floor. On her knees, she lays her head down on the floor, the tears that have been dry for her entire life now flowing. At first they are slow, but soon enough they turn to sobs. "I don't know what to do." Like a dam that has burst, Marin can't stop the tears. Sure she has lost her daughter, Marin accepts she has nothing left in a life that was destroyed years ago.

TRISHA

I lie in Sonya's bed, both of us flat on our backs next to one another. Our hands are clasped together as we stare at the ceiling. In the silence, you can hear our breaths, hers steady, mine loud, ragged.

"What did I say? That night," I finally ask, needing to know.

After Mama told me everything, I collapsed on the floor and sobbed into her arms until the past slowly slipped away and I finally returned to reality. I was no longer fifteen, but I didn't feel thirty either. I felt older than my years, and yet I couldn't help but wonder how much of my childhood got frozen in time after the assault. How much I lost living in the shadow of what he did to me. I was his favorite, and only now do I realize the high price I paid for that preference.

"That he had hurt you. When I asked how, you said he had touched you. That he took you." Sonya squeezes my hand tighter, the memory hurting her. "I didn't understand until years later what you meant."

"Why didn't you say anything?" I ask.

"I did. That night, you fell asleep in my bed. The next morning you woke up and acted like nothing had happened. When I tried to say something, you dismissed me, told me I was stupid." Sonya turns her face toward mine. "I was confused, not sure if you made it up or just didn't want to talk about it."

"I forgot," I admit, trying desperately to remember that night and the following day in full detail. "Everything. I don't even remember our conversation."

"Can you blame yourself for that?" she asks. "You were his princess."

"He's a monster, isn't he?" I say, the words sounding foreign to my ears. "All of you knew that, but I didn't see it. Refused to see it." I feel like a fool. "I was his girl, the special one." Glimpses of that night filter through my memory like dandelion seeds floating through the air. Just as I hold on to one, another floats by, grabbing my attention but causing me to lose sight of the one I just saw.

"When I was little, I was so scared of monsters under my bed," Sonya says. "But when friends started describing the monsters they thought lived under their beds, I realized my description was of Dad. He was the monster I feared," she reveals. She lets go of my hand and rises up on her elbow, leaning her head on her palm. Her hair flows around her. She had come back home late and was surprised to see me and Mama sitting in the hallway, our faces drawn from grief and shock. "What are you going to do?"

"I don't know," I answer honestly. In a matter of weeks, my entire life has changed from what it was, what I knew. I'm drained, exhausted, and helpless to find an answer. "I still don't remember everything," I admit, almost ashamed. I wonder how far I've gone to protect myself from pain.

"Maybe that's a good thing," Sonya muses, lying back down. "The mind is very powerful. It knows what we can't handle, what we can't process." She twines her fingers with mine again. "What he did to you, Trisha, why would you want to remember?"

"You know what's crazy?" I hesitate to say the words, to say out loud what I feel. "I still love him. I can't relate the father I remember with the glimpses of memory of that night. It feels like a movie reel, like it's not really me it's happening to."

"You disassociated," Sonya says. "It's pretty common in cases of abuse." She speaks slowly, hesitantly. "You separate from the incident or situation; convince yourself it's not you. It's a protective measure. A survival instinct."

"Is that what you did?" I ask, for the first time wondering how she survived a lifetime of horror when I barely survived one night of it. "Disassociated?"

"Sometimes I wish I had," Sonya says after a long pause. "Maybe it would have made it easier, I don't know." She gets off the bed, taking a sip of water from the glass she brought in for me. "I stayed in the moment, absorbing everything he did, making it mine."

"How do you know so much?" I ask, wondering again what she did with her time when she was away from us. "When did you become so brilliant?"

"I'm not," Sonya says, showing me a glimpse of vulnerability. "I just did some research, learned a few fancy words." She offers me the glass of water. I take a healthy swallow before setting it down on the end table next to the bed.

"You must hate me," I say, my throat feeling like sandpaper. "When we were growing up. Everything all of you had to face"—I pause—"while I stood by, untouched."

"Sometimes I thought I did," Sonya admits, her words not surprising. "But you weren't doing the hitting, were you?" She stares at the ceiling, fighting tears. "You were always in the same boat as us, just standing on the other side."

"I blamed you," I admit, shame coursing through me. She turns to me in shock. "All of you. Maybe if you were just more of what he needed . . ." I admit. "Am I a monster? Like him?" The fear rears up from deep within me. It's what drove me to create my perfect life. To hide from Eric all my truths. The reason I refused to have children.

"Maybe that's why I was his favorite. Why he loved"—I nearly choke on the word and his definition of it—"me. Because I'm just like him."

"Is that what you think?" Sonya asks quietly. Sitting down next to me, she takes my hand in hers. "You think if you had a child, you would hurt him or her like he hurt us?"

"Who says I wouldn't?"

"You do," Sonya says it with such definitiveness it takes me off guard. "You make that choice, just like he did."

"You honestly believe that it's that easy?" I shake my head, unable to accept what she's saying. "We walked through darkness. How do you find the light?"

"Wherever you can." Sonya plucks at the bedspread, avoiding my eyes. There's something she's not telling me. I wonder how far our web of secrets has been woven and whether we will ever be able to fully untangle ourselves from it.

"Are you afraid?" I think of her travels, her love of photography. It dawns on me that my sister is talking from experience. She found her light the only place she knew—as far away from us as possible, trusting the world through the lens of her camera more than through her own eyes.

"Every minute of my life," she admits. Stepping away from me, she lets me know the discussion is over. "What are you going to do?" she repeats.

"I don't know," I admit, still not having an answer. "I honestly have no idea."

* * *

When I am not sleeping, I lose myself in the garden. Mama has an array of flowers in the back that the gardener tends to every week. There were tulips a few weeks ago, and now there are roses among the fruit trees and green foliage. There's a small waterfall to the side, an addition Mama sanctioned after Papa fell into the coma. The water flows over the rocks, the noise drowning out the sound of my own thoughts. I sit and stare at the presentation, the beauty available for anyone wishing to bask in it.

Each stem of the rosebush intertwines with the others, a medley of splendor. Like life, it is exquisiteness intermixed with thorns. A prick if you touch without caution. People often make the mistake of believing the rose's magnificence is just in the flower, failing to see the whole picture. But the thorn is there to protect, to keep the rose safe.

Once upon a time, I too would have clipped the barbs before arranging a bouquet. Now I see that every flower needs the good and bad to bloom; it must stand strong, its face toward the sun, absorbing the rays it needs to stay alive when darkness falls.

I loved interior designing. First, you have to learn about the people, understand them before creating their home or work space. Everyone's needs are unique; one client's vision of perfection can be another's idea of catastrophe. I would spend hours listening to clients' needs, their ideas about what their abodes should look like. Retreating to the privacy of my own space, I would go through color schemes, matching one with another, careful not to stray too far from the boundaries they left unspoken.

The real joy was in the shopping. Bringing an array of pieces together, fitting them to make a whole set. From one place, I would buy a modern piece of art, and from another an antique lamp, using colors and the other pieces to connect the two. Every time, without fail, I made it work. My clients were astounded with the results, gushing that they never would have thought to do the same. My response was always the same: "It's hard to believe until you try."

Now I am the empty house, and I'm trying to put together all the pieces—the memories and experiences of my life—to make me whole. How do you connect the tragedy with the joy, the heartbreak with the serenity? Who am I when I can't even remember the night that defined my life? How do you characterize a person if they are unde-fined, a façade still waiting to be exposed? Maybe when one door shuts, another one doesn't really open. Maybe, instead, it's just a sign that you are locked in forever.

Reaching out, I prick my finger on the thorn, watching the blood drip out, slowly, then each drop faster than the last. Laying my head on my knees, I wrap my arms around my legs, listening to the water, the only sound that makes sense.

SONYA

Mom and I don't talk about Trisha's revelation. That she knew what he had done and continued to live with him makes me furious. I don't understand, but I fear if I demand an explanation it will fall short, and I will finally have the excuse to hate her. I wonder if I haven't been searching for one forever.

Trisha continues to stay with us, sleeping in my bed with me as if we are once again children. She barely comes out of the bedroom, preferring the security of the blankets and the bed to returning to real life. Mom brings her food in the room, leaving the plate on the table next to where she is sleeping. It is the only way Mom knows how to offer comfort—feed away the sadness.

Mom and I limit our conversations to Trisha's well-being. She asks me how Trisha slept; when I return home from work, I ask her how Trisha's day went. We play this back and forth for an entire week, neither demanding any further answers from the other. I know when Trisha finally showers—there's a wet towel neatly hung in the bathroom. When I check the room hoping to find my sister awake, she is curled yet again under the covers. I try to talk to her, but she simply shakes her head no. Not yet, she seems to say. Not yet.

I return to the hospital, finding the place I have used as an excuse to remain in the area has become a haven. I work with the patients, spending hours teaching them how I escape my world so they can escape theirs. When I find them getting lost in the beauty they can create, I see through their eyes how photography became my flight, and once again I am thankful that my vocation found me.

I have successfully avoided seeing David since our last encounter. I don't work the long hours I used to, choosing instead to leave at my designated time so there's little chance of us running into each other in the halls during the evening hours. Once I am out of the hospital, I drive around the city, using my camera as a guide. The other day I arrived at an outdoor wedding. Keeping my distance, I shot over a hundred pictures of guests and the happy couple. I suddenly found odd comfort in the gathering. Afterward, I gifted the couple the memory card containing their pictures, telling them I was just an amateur photographer.

Today, I drive to San Jose and walk the streets, appreciating the diversity of people who inhabit the city. I photograph faces and interactions, capturing moments so that they can last a lifetime. Returning to what I love helps me forget what happened between David and me, and what I almost did in the bar.

My phone rings in the middle of the shoot. "This is Sonya," I answer automatically.

It's a nurse asking if I'm nearby. A patient has come in, a teenager with a neurological condition. Would I be able to spend some time with him this evening? I glance at my watch. Normally I would have still been in the hospital, available. "I'll be there in fifteen," I promise, ready to hang up.

"Oh, Sonya?" the nurse says, "Dr. Ford asked me to let you know he's the attending." There's a question in her voice, curiosity as to why David would feel that was important enough to mention.

What I don't confide in her is that David is giving me a way out. An opportunity to say no so I don't have to see him. I don't take it, not analyzing the reason why. "Thanks. Let him know I'll call him as soon as I finish with the patient."

*   *   *

"I've been playing soccer since I was a kid. You know those kid leagues where everyone gets a medal for participating?" Will is fifteen. He's staring at the camera in his lap. He's had three grand mal seizures in the last two days. "I'm the captain of my team."

"You must be really good," I say, feeling his pain from my seat next to the bed.

"Yeah, I am, actually." He glances out the window. "It's all I do. My dad had dreams of me becoming the next Beckham. Until the seizures started."

"When was the first one?" I ask, unsure. I feel like a surgeon who never trained in the field but has a patient opening up in front of me, waiting for me to heal him.

"A week ago. I hit a header," he glances at me, clearly assuming I don't know what that means. "I tried to score a goal with my head."

"Right." I offer him a weak smile.

"A few minutes later, I was down on the ground, seizing." He turns away again, his hand absently playing with the camera. "In front of everyone. My girlfriend, my friends, my dad," he says quietly. "He's scared I'll never be able to play again." He shakes his head, finally picking up the camera. "So, what's this for?"

"A type of therapy," I answer, reaching over to open the camera's lens. "There are studies that show different types of therapy, including photography, can be part of the healing process. What do you think?"

"What am I supposed to take pictures of?" he asks, looking around. "The room?"

"If you want. Or we could walk around the halls, see if there's anything interesting." I see his hesitation, his lack of interest. "Dr. Ford thought it might help you."

"I thought that's what this was for," he says, pointing to the wrap around his head with electrical probes attached, meant to study his brainwaves through the night. He hands me back the camera.

"This is meant to help in a different way," I say, holding the camera like a lifeline. "Want to try? It might make you feel better. Maybe get you back to playing sooner rather than later," I tease, trying to find common ground with him.

He shakes his head slightly, no. "Want to know the truth?" he asks. Before I can answer he says, "I hate soccer."

* * *

David is not on the main floors. I ask the nurse to page him, waiting while she does. "He said he could meet you here or in his office." She waits, with David on the other side of the phone line waiting for my response.

"Tell him I'll be there in five." I drop the camera in a safe spot behind the desk. I fight the anxiety that seeps through me, ordering myself to get it together. I take the empty elevator to his floor and walk quickly down the hall to his office. From a distance, I can see his door ajar, awaiting my arrival.

He's behind his desk, reviewing a file. When he hears me, he glances up. In the second before he shutters his emotions, I see want and need in his eyes. My breath catches and I look away, staring through the window at the darkness that has fallen outside.

"He wasn't interested in taking pictures," I say. "He took a photography class in high school. Wasn't his favorite."

"I see." He stands, coming around to the other side of the desk. "Thank you for trying."

"What's his prognosis?" I can't help myself.

"We're not sure yet." He rubs his hand across his face. "A neurologist is scheduled to see him first thing in the morning." He leans his weight against the desk. "We'll have more information then." He shakes his head, as if fearing he will fail the young man. "He's hurting. Confused. I was hoping taking some pictures might cheer him up."

I yearn to reach out, to offer comfort when I have none to give. What could I possibly offer another human being? "He doesn't want to play soccer," I reveal. David looks up in shock.

"He told you that?"

I nod. "He plays it for his dad."

David shakes his head, puzzled. "It was all his father could focus on when they brought Will in. He must have asked me at least five times whether his son will be able to play soccer again."

"Sometimes parents are the last ones to know what their child wants," I murmur, not considering my words before saying them.

"Is that what happened with you?" he asks, his hands clenched around the edge of the desk. "Your dad didn't know what you wanted?"

I want to walk—no, I want to run. To hide, to be safe. But Trisha's revelation has left me rawer than I was, empty in a way I couldn't imagine. When your life is a dark hole, you believe everything passes through without having an effect or making an impression. The fact that my sister's heartache makes me want to lie down and weep forces me to realize I am not as hollow as I believed. Maybe my father hasn't stolen everything.

Everyone must reach a point in their life when they stop running. When it is easier to stand still than to keep being chased, even if the person chasing you is only in your head. When a fire burns, it rages fast and furious, devouring everything in its wake. But when the job is done, when all that is left is smoke and ashes, you wonder what has become of the fury that propelled the flames to destroy everything they touched.

I assumed I would never stop running, never stop being one step ahead of the demons that are in constant pursuit. I accepted that I would do that for a lifetime, and I was sure that if I ever stopped I would be devoured by the memories, be haunted by those still living. But now, standing before David, it has become harder to run than ever before.

"He didn't care," I admit, tired of my escape. Our status quo has created so much loss, I wonder what it would be like to do it differently. To try, to trust. "He . . ." I struggle for the words, search in vain for a way to describe what he did to me, to my family. "He beat us," I finally say—the truth, the words harder than I thought. "All the time." I wait for the pity, the disgust, all the things that come with someone knowing you are damaged. The acceptance that the scars that cover your body and soul have shriveled you to nothing but a fragment of what you once were.

"No." His voice is broken, shocked. He shows pity but no disgust. I look up, sure I have missed it, but his eyes are filled with warmth. "I'm so sorry." He comes toward me, but I take a step back. He watches me, not missing a beat. "There was no one who was able to stop him?"

"No one wanted to," I whisper, confiding in him. "In the eyes of our community, he was perfect. In the eyes of my mother, he was right." I have revealed too much to this stranger. Given too much of myself away.

"Sonya," he starts, but I have to stop him. I can't accept what he is offering. It is too much for someone like me, someone who is beneath him, beneath everyone, I am sure.

"I'm just like him," I blurt out. It is the belief that I couldn't even admit to Trisha. When she told me her fear, I kept silent about my own. *But it is time to tell him*, a voice urges me. Once he is aware of the truth, sees past the illusion to the reality, he will run from me. I won't have to hide anymore.

"I don't understand," he says, stopping.

"I'm dark, evil like him." I turn away, wrapping my arms around myself. The room has gone cold, quiet. My breath comes in gasps as I struggle to even it out. "I read stories, watch movies of women," I pause, scared. What has not begun between us will be over forever once I tell him. The hope of more will become impossible. The burden of my secret has always been heavy before, but with David, the weight of it has become too much to bear. Only in revealing the truth can we be free of one another.

I imagine all his diplomas crashing down around us, his crystal accolades shattering, an earthquake tearing the room into two to give me an escape. But only silence echoes off the white walls. The only sound is him waiting for me to speak. "Of women being hurt." I laugh to fill the silence. "It's the only way I can find release."

Images of the men I have slept with swarm before me, each one oblivious to what was happening in my head. "When I am making love," I pause, my eyes shutting with shame, "the only way I can have an orgasm is by imagining a woman being broken."

I will not cry. Not now. He has to see the malevolence, all the shades of black that I am. "It's my definition of love." My chest is heaving with dry sobs. "But if a man ever dared to touch me that way, if a man ever actually raised a hand to me, I know I would kill him where he stood."

I don't remember the first time my father hit me. They say you form your first memory when you are four. If that's the case, then I imagine he started hitting me long before my brain knew to make an imprint. The recollection I do have is when I was barely six. Like a stream searching for a river to belong to, I was sure if I became beautiful like Trisha, I too would become favored, loved by the father who barely gave me any attention. I sneaked on one of my mother's saris and wrapped it around myself as best I could. I powdered my face with talcum and used her red lipstick to highlight my mouth. A quick perusal in the mirror told me what my young brain needed—I had succeeded in becoming a swan.

I found him in the living room. "Look, Daddy," I announced, twirling in all my glory. The sari proved too much for me to navigate; I tripped and fell onto him, sending his chai flying. He hit me over the head and then threw me across the room, the sari coming undone and floating over me like a sheet over a corpse. I lay there silent, in disbelief that I hadn't succeeded when I was so sure I would.

"So, you see," I start, watching David watch me. It is time to say good-bye. "There is nothing for you to get to know. Nothing for you to miss. I'm not good enough, and I never will be."

MARIN

The memory of her father's words came to Marin while she was sleeping. "It is all a game," he had said. Marin hadn't understood until now how important those words were. How critical the lesson was. The game wasn't over; it hadn't even begun. The last play she had lost. Gia and Raj had made their move, and they stood as the victors. But Marin would not lose her daughter, not now, not ever. She sat in her office, contemplating the next step with more thought than she had ever given to any of her business dealings. The answer came to her just as she feared there might not be one. It was simple, really, but she realized most things were. It was emotions that made things difficult. As long as you kept those in check, everything else would fall into place.

"Raj?" Marin says, knocking softly on his office door. He glances up, his face shuttered from revealing too much. He has been working more from home, wanting to be near Gia in case she needs anything. "Do you have a minute?"

"Sure." He motions her in but stays in his seat behind his desk. "What's going on?"

"I wanted to talk about us." Marin begins, not breaking eye contact.

"I was under the impression there wasn't an us."

He is not going to make it easy on her, but that is fine. She has fought larger battles and won. "Things have been difficult; we have gone through a lot with Gia." Marin pauses, trying to find the right words. "We've been married a long time. I'm not ready to give up on that yet."

Raj falls silent, watching her carefully. Marin sees the distrust but also the hurt, and she is surprised at the emotion. "What do you propose?"

"We try again. Go slow, but with the intention that our family remains intact."

Raj finally stands, coming around to face her. After so many years of marriage, of having and raising a daughter together, they stand as strangers. "Why?"

"What do you mean?" Marin demands.

"Why now?" Raj asks. He shakes his head, knowing her better than she thought. "You didn't like Gia's decision, so now you rethink the strategy, right? Is this really what it comes down to?"

Marin contemplates denying his accusation, screaming at him for thinking she is capable of such callousness. But he has caught her off guard, his assessment too accurate to negate. "I can't lose her, Raj," Marin finally says, after a long pause during which they both seem to stand on a cliff that is crumbling. "She's all I have."

"You had me," he says so quietly that Marin would have missed his words if the room weren't deadly still. She doesn't respond to him, doesn't give his declaration its due. He appears to wait for something, but when seconds tick by and only silence continues to fill the room, he sighs. "What do you propose?"

"We keep living in the house, together." They can return to the way they were, three souls coexisting under the same roof. "We help get her through this."

"What about school?" They are negotiating now, a divorce settlement without the legalities. "That's not something I will budge on."

The control Marin was so sure she had starts to slip away again. Her instinct is to lash out, demand to know why Raj can't see what the school means for Gia's future. But the battle lines have been drawn, and Marin is on the wrong side of them. "Can we table the final decision for later?" Marin asks.

"I've contacted some private tutors," Raj says, surprising Marin. "She can finish the school year out at home. I've also scheduled tours of the local schools. That way, Gia can have some options if she decides she wants to return to a school setting."

"Her résumé may suffer with the homeschooling." Marin tries to get him to understand. She can start to feel her dreams of Harvard or Yale slipping away. "She won't have access to the types of activities she has now."

"I'm not particularly concerned about her college right now. The priority is keeping her alive, and her wanting to stay that way."

Marin wants to argue, but his face is set. Any argument will fall on deaf ears and may impede the delicate negotiations they are in. "Fine. Let's agree to take it day by day. When she's stabilized, let's revisit the situation."

TRISHA

I have lost count of how much time has passed since I learned the truth. Days blend into night. The only way I know the difference is when Sonya goes to sleep and awakens. She keeps a tight schedule, something else that is different from the girl I knew. As a child, she used to be the last one to wake up, as if facing life were too much to bear. At night, she was the last one to sleep, fearing what the night could bring. I used to mock her for such thoughts, believing it a sign of immaturity. Now I wonder if she wasn't on to something, if she knew the true danger Papa represented, while I lived in my own world.

I try to put as many pieces together as possible. None of them fit with the image of the father I loved, the man I adored beyond reason. Last night, I had a dream that we were dancing on an empty dance floor. A father-daughter dance at my wedding. But soon the floor changed from white to red. When I looked down, my red sari—the traditional garb for a wedding—had changed to a white wedding gown, and the front was soaked with blood. I screamed, but he kept dancing, insisting everything was fine. I awoke with a start, sweat lining my body. Sonya stirred at my movement but continued to sleep.

I glanced around, noticing a chair shoved up against the door, locking us in. Or locking everyone else out, I realize. How long has Sonya needed to do that? How many other ways has she needed to protect herself from nameless fears? Shame fills me, knowing my sister has been suffering in indescribable ways while I lived in comfort. But it was all a sham, a smoke screen I created to hide what had happened to me.

I have never really lived, never fully allowed myself happiness. There's so much about myself I have never understood. I love pickles but hate cucumbers. Pictures of nature fascinate me, but I can't stand camping. Give me fresh tomatoes any day to munch on, but tomato sauce on pizza makes me gag. I love children, but the thought of having one scares the hell out of me. I have never bothered to dissect the reasons I am the way I am—just accepted myself with an openness others lack. But as thoughts of the assault start to filter through along with images of a baby, I begin to wonder how far the pain of my father's act reaches. Curling into a fetal position, my hand cradling my stomach, I feel myself falling into another fitful sleep.

* * *

Mama brings me an early dinner of one my favorite meals—*pani puri*. Puffed balls of fried wheat are popped open at the top and filled with potatoes, lentils, mint chutney, and onions. Topping it off is yogurt and sweet brown chutney. It is one of the few indulgences I could never resist, eating fifteen to twenty puris in one sitting. She sets the plate down in the normal place—by my bed—and strokes a hand across my hair. Assuming I'm asleep, she starts to walk out when I call her name.

"You're awake," she says, sounding surprised.

"Yeah." I sit up in bed, avoiding looking into the mirror that hangs nearby. "I have been for a few hours."

She says nothing, coming to sit by me instead. I scoot over, making room. She fits easily alongside me, her body smaller than I remember.

Her hand next to mine, I see the wrinkles and the frailty I have always glanced over before. "I have been worried, Beti," she murmurs.

"I know." I lay my head back against the headboard, feeling the knots in my hair. I ventured into the shower once or twice but found even that to be too exhausting. "I'm just . . ." I try to find the words, but instead a tear falls silently down. I wipe it away quickly only to have another follow suit. "It's just hard."

"Do you remember?" she asks.

"Just flashes, here and there." I am thankful it's not more but ashamed for being so. "I see myself walking down the hall afterward. Trying to find someone. But I don't remember the actual act, what he did to me." I rub my head, hoping to jog my memory. "But that doesn't mean it didn't happen. Somewhere in my mind there's a memory of it." I yearn to pull it out, like a rabbit from a hat, and make it disappear forever. "Part of me always knew the truth. I just couldn't see it." My voice cracks, terror lining every word. "What if I don't get better? What if this"—I motion to myself and around me—"is all I am?"

"Did I ever tell you the old Hindu parable of the rope and the snake?" Mama asks, facing forward, not responding directly to my plea.

"No," I say, unsure where she is leading. Mama rarely read stories to us as children. At first she said it was because she wasn't fluent in English and didn't want to impede our learning with her interpretation, but years later she admitted to me she had stopped believing in fairy tales; she just couldn't remember when. "I don't think you did."

She pulls her knees up to her chest, almost like a child, and begins to recite the parable from memory. "There was once a man who worked a very long day. He had a hard life, this man. Worked from morning until night in the fields of India without a rest or break to eat. The sun would beat down on his head and, without a hat to shelter him, sweat would pour onto his forehead and down his neck. With little water to drink, it was fortunate he did not collapse from heat exhaustion.

"This man was not a happy man," Mama continued. "He had no family or anyone to call his own."

"No children?" I demand, lost in her story.

"No." She pauses, allowing the information to sink in. "He walked home every day after work filled with despair. His life was worthless, he was sure. One day, his normal route was blocked by a mudslide. The monsoons had just come through, making the road impassable. He hesitated to take an alternate route, for it was said that path was filled with all forms of evil. From bandits to dark magic, the tall tales were plenty. But accepting his providence and whatever may follow, he took it, prepared to face the danger he was sure was coming."

"Stupid decision," I say, common sense demanding to be heard.

"Trisha," Mama warns. "The story?"

"Go on." I settle back.

"He could barely see. The moon was hiding behind dark clouds, and there were no streetlights. But he continued on, growing prouder of his bravery with each step. Soon he started to feel like a new man, capable of anything. Until he accidentally kicked a large rock. A sound stopped him where he stood. He came face-to-face with a snake. Now this wasn't just an ordinary snake. It was the king of cobras, and it had been disturbed by this man."

She pauses while I take a sip of water.

"Their face-off validated all this man's fears—that his life was worthless, that he was meant to die a horrible death, that only bad could come to him. All of it, right there in the eyes of this snake," she continues. "As the snake lunged toward him, its teeth bared, the man did what any normal man would do. He ran. So fast that he almost got away. But the man kept his head turned back, watching for the snake as he ran, sure it would keep up with him. Because he did that, he missed the boulder sitting in his way. Hitting his head, he bled to death within minutes."

"What happened to the snake?" I demand, now captivated by the story.

"The villagers found the man in the morning. A few feet away, they found a coiled rope someone had dropped. There was no snake."

"Mama," I say, confused. Before I can continue, she takes my hand.

"Beti," Mama says, her eyes meeting mine. "What he did to you can never be undone. But don't let it color your life. Don't let his actions or his way of living become your truth." She gets out of the bed and cradles my face in her hands. "You are your truth. You have always been and will always be your own woman. And I couldn't be more proud of the woman you are." Slowly bending down, she puts her weathered lips on my cheek and offers me a simple kiss.

"Mama," I say, stopping her as she starts to leave. "Would you have told me? If I hadn't come to you, would you have come to me?"

She hesitates, myriad emotions dancing across her face. "I didn't want to. I wanted to bury it as I believed you had. I wanted you to keep being happy," she admits.

"That wasn't your decision to make," I say, angry that she had assumed it was.

"Maybe not," she admits, her struggle clear. "But given what he had done and how it might affect you, it was the only decision I thought to make."

"Did you know?" I demand, needing to lash out. She is an easy target, and I am relentless. "Did you have any idea when it happened?"

She drops her head, clasping her hands together. Slowly she shakes her head. "I knew he was capable of causing great heartache, but what he did to you . . ." She shudders. Raising her head, she meets my gaze. "You have to believe me—I had no idea. If I had . . ." she stops, unable to finish the sentence, both of us left to wonder what she would have done. A man who held all the power—what were we supposed to fight him with?

I believe her. Maybe there were clues, but both of us had been desperate to ignore them. At some level, a moth has to know the flame will engulf it and try to avoid it. "After you learned the truth, were you going . . ." I falter, pausing before I ask the next question, fearing her answer. "Were you going to stay with him?"

"No," she says, her answer sure, without any hesitation. "But he would have made it difficult for me to leave."

"Then I guess it's a good thing he's dying," I say.

"Yes," she agrees. "It is a good thing."

MARIN

It is Gia's sixteenth birthday, a momentous occasion for every teenager. Marin decided to throw her a party, inviting all her former friends from the school. Gia has taken Raj up on his offer to leave school for a while. During the week, Raj brings Gia to a therapist and waits outside while she reveals her secrets to a stranger. Marin never offers to drive or go along. She does not stop them, but she certainly doesn't support Gia's going, even though she herself suggested it. That was just for leverage in her negotiations with Raj, and she was angry at him for insisting Gia needed outside intervention. Marin still believes they would have been able to handle it within their small circle. Having done that in her childhood, there is no reason to do it differently now.

After their discussion in the office, she and Raj talked no further about separating or about Raj and Gia leaving the home. Everyone seemed to understand that such a step couldn't be undone, and besides, no one had the capacity to deal with such an event. They were all emotionally drained, with nothing left in the well to draw from. Instead, they each escaped to their separate rooms, using the main parts of the house to coexist in.

Except for Gia's therapy appointments, she spends the majority of her days in her room, accompanied by either loud music or complete silence. Sometimes Marin stands outside the door, waiting for permission to enter, to talk to Gia. It never comes, so Marin never enters.

Gia insisted she didn't want a party, even begged her parents to cancel it. But Marin forged ahead, getting caught up in the arrangements. The planning took up most of her time, leaving little room for her to think about much else. Feeling an inexplicable shame about her visit to her father's hospital room and the tears she shed, she buried the memory under work and the party.

What was initially supposed to be ten to fifteen girls ended up being over a hundred and twenty guests, adults and girls both. Marin hired a party planner and had tents set up in the backyard. She reviewed the menu and changed it three times before settling on casual fare. She was sure to include some of Gia's favorites, along with a variety of other items. A live DJ and entertainment finalized the plans.

"You don't think it's a bit much?" Raj asks now, during one of their rare conversations.

"It's her sixteenth," Marin replies. "She only has one of those."

"Right." Raj sips his iced tea, watching the tents going up in the backyard as workers file in and out of their home. "She hasn't been down all morning."

"Getting ready, likely," Marin decides, keeping an eye out for the caterer. "She'll be down soon enough." She starts to leave, but Raj stops her.

"What are you hoping to accomplish with this large a gathering?" Raj asks quietly.

"That our daughter will know how much we love her," Marin answers tersely, taking her leave to check on the setup. As everything falls into place, the guests start to arrive. First Ranee and Sonya. Trisha is nowhere to be seen. Marin hasn't encountered her since they exchanged words at Trisha's house. With all that happened since, Marin hasn't had the time to think about it. Now she wonders what she missed in the ensuing time.

Leaving the place settings to the planner, Marin approaches her family. "Thanks for coming," she murmurs. "Where is Trisha?" She directs her question to both Sonya and Ranee.

In India as children, Marin and Trisha were close. Trisha was the little sister Marin cared for when Ranee was busy or off running errands. Their house was filled with Dalits cleaning and cooking meals for mere pennies a day. But the Dalits weren't allowed to touch infants for fear of marking them with their inferiority. As a result, Marin was often called on to babysit her younger sister.

Marin would feed Trisha the smashed-up vegetables the Dalits prepared, and then swing her in a cotton hammock while she read her storybooks to lull her to sleep. On the flight to America, Trisha spent almost the whole time on Marin's lap, as her older sister stared out the window at the clouds below, wondering if the ones over America would be different from the ones over India.

Once they landed and Brent couldn't find a job, things started to change. His interest in Marin's education became obsessive, while his attitude toward Trisha was one of love and concern. By treating his two daughters differently, he created the fault line that existed to this day. It was the only explanation for their relationship. Without realizing it, Marin began to hate the little sister she had loved so much. To envy her the affection she received, so unlike the hatred directed toward Marin. Her father placed no demands on Trisha to be anything except who she was, while Marin had to mold herself to whatever Brent deemed worthy.

Trisha's natural beauty earned her even more accolades, making her the star in everyone's eyes. Marin and Trisha were the pride of the family, community members crowed. Marin's smarts and Trisha's beauty made Ranee and Brent fortunate indeed. Members of the samaj never bothered to mention Sonya, who stood to the side, her heavy tummy hanging over the tight hand-me-down pants she was forced to wear. With neither brains nor looks, she was tossed to the side as unnecessary.

"She's not here," Sonya answers now, while Ranee looks away, biting her lip.

"Why?" Marin was confident that, of all the guests, Trisha would most appreciate the work that Marin had done to ensure a successful party. Having thrown so many herself, she could relate to the time and energy spent on it. "It's not because of what happened? At the house?"

"No," Sonya is quick to assure her. Marin glances at Ranee, who remains silent. "She's going through a hard time right now."

"Because of Eric," Marin assumes, angry that Trisha wouldn't show up. To Marin, she is breaking a sacrilegious rule, one created in childhood that demands no matter what hardship any of them are enduring, they still have to put on a happy face. If for no other reason than to convince the world to continue believing that they are fine.

"No, not because of Eric." Sonya and Ranee share a glance, a silent message clearly passing between the two. "She's barely eating. Sleeps all day," Sonya finally says. She runs her hand down the length of her sundress, as if she's uncomfortable with the attire. Now that Marin thinks about it, she has never seen her sister in anything other than jeans and T-shirts. A way to hide herself from the world. "She could use both her sisters right now."

"What happened?" Marin asks, glancing around to gauge the number of guests that have arrived. She wants to keep talking to Sonya, to understand what her sister is dealing with. "Don't speak to me in puzzles, please. Is it about not having children?"

"No," Sonya says, a ghost of a smile haunting. "If it were only so easy." Lowering her voice, she glances around as if to make sure no one can overhear. "It's her story to tell," Sonya says. "But she was hurt, very badly."

"By whom?" Marin demands, unsure what had happened that could cause Sonya to be so serious.

"Dad," Sonya says, shocking Marin. It is the last person whose name she expected to hear.

"I don't understand." Marin can't imagine a scenario where he could hurt Trisha. "What are you talking about?"

"Ask her. I know you have a lot on your plate, but one day, when you have some time, ask her." Sonya reaches out, takes Marin's hand. "What happened between the two of you at the house, she didn't mean it."

"I know." Marin did; deep in her heart she understood. It was rare for one of them to lash out. They were so used to keeping their thoughts and feelings in check. When one of them did explode, there was a reason. A volcano that had stayed silent for too long had to erupt, spewing lava, a trembling the only clue of what was coming.

When they were young, Marin would catch Sonya staring at other children crying and throwing tantrums. She would watch as parents consoled them rather than punishing them for daring to share their emotions. As a family, they were never allowed to display anything except obedience. Any emotion they had was always second to Brent's.

"Why are you defending her?" Marin asks quietly, curious. "It wasn't your fight."

"Because it is. We're all in the same battle, always have been." Sonya stares down at the grass before facing Marin. "I don't know if I ever knew that. I just hope it's not too late."

Marin starts to mingle with the arriving guests, her concern for Trisha slipping to the back of her mind. She busies herself with welcoming people to her home, ensuring the waitstaff offers everyone a drink and an appetizer to munch on. Belatedly, she realizes Gia hasn't made an appearance. Searching through the crowd, she looks for her but comes up empty. There aren't any signs of Raj either.

Quickly making her way into the house and up the stairs, she throws open Gia's door to find Raj and Gia on the bed. Gia is still in her pajamas and Raj is quietly speaking to her.

"What are you doing?" Marin exclaims, keeping her voice down so no one else will hear. "The house is filled with people for your party, and you're sitting in your room?"

"I never asked for the party," Gia says quietly, glancing at Raj for support. "I'm not ready to face all these people." Her lower lip quivers, revealing her helplessness.

"Yes, you are," Marin says, refusing to coddle her. "This is your opportunity to show everyone you are fine, that you will be back on your feet in no time."

"That's what matters to you?" Gia asks in obvious disbelief. "What people think?"

"Did you think you could live your life in here?" Marin asks. She comes to stand next to the bed, reaches out to caress Gia's hair. "It doesn't work that way, Beti," Marin explains. "Whether you like it or not, you have to live in a society. How that society perceives you will determine your place in life." Marin begins to rifle through Gia's closet, searching for clothes. Finding a suitable sundress, she pulls it out and offers it to Gia. "You look beautiful in this one." She offers Gia a smile. "Come, Beti, everyone you love is downstairs waiting."

"No," Gia corrects, "not everyone." She fidgets in her bed. "Not Adam."

Marin starts to correct her, but Raj interrupts, stopping her before she does more damage. "Marin," he says warily, his voice sounding strained. "It's her birthday. Let's table this, shall we?" He takes the dress out of Marin's hand. "Gia, you are sixteen now. More than capable of picking your own clothes, am I right?" Softening his voice, he prods, "Get ready and come down, Beti. Your mom is right, everyone is waiting for you."

* * *

319

In every culture, there is a coming of age. Marin has attended a number of bat and bar mitzvahs of colleagues' children. At thirteen, they are assumed adults, and the welcoming ceremony is an elaborate party after years of learning Hebrew and Jewish transcript. From then on, they are deemed responsible for their own actions in the eyes of the community and the religion. Marin has heard of debutante parties in the American South, where a mature girl is introduced as a woman to eligible bachelors. In the southern region of India, a small subset threw parties when their daughters began having their periods. An intimate gathering of close friends to celebrate the transition from girlhood to womanhood.

No matter what the age, reason, or belief system, a coming-of-age party was meant for the individual who had passed the milestone and also for the parents who must now see their child in a different light. The child was no longer a baby to be held or guided, but instead his or her own person on the verge of adulthood. After the celebration, they would make their own decisions, have their own emotions, and seek guidance only when they deemed it necessary.

Growing up, Marin had seen her friends experience the events that transitioned them from child to adult. She envied them their bridges, their confidence in walking across them and over the threshold to the other side. She instinctively knew that only one event would free her from the chains her father had shackled her with—her marriage. No other moment or natural event would cause him to see her as the woman she was, allow her to be her own person. She was his until the night of her marriage, when she became someone else's. Only then would he release her, but by then, it was too late. She was already his creation, and nothing would free her from that.

But Marin would give her daughter what she didn't have—a celebration for her coming of age. A few hours where everything would be good, a party filled with joy and laughter as Gia embarked on a new stage in her life.

Gia enters the party dressed in a pair of capris and a T-shirt. It's not the attire Marin prefers, but she's happy her daughter has showed up. The band plays music while guests mingle with one another. Marin makes a point to speak with each of the attendees, keeping an eye on Gia from a distance. She seems fine, even taking time to talk to some of her friends from school. Marin can imagine they are asking her what is going on and when and if she's returning to school.

The guests talk for hours. The party is a success, just as Marin had hoped. From a distance, Marin sees Gia's joy in being around her friends. It's exactly what Marin had anticipated, why she had gone to such great lengths to organize it. They bring out the cake, and Gia blows out her sixteen candles.

"Make a wish, Beti," Marin says, wondering what Gia is hoping for when she shuts her eyes and does as her mother asked.

Night falls and the California bugs begin to bite. Guests start to take their leave, each one thanking both Raj and Marin for a lovely evening. Ranee and Sonya stay, helping the crew to clean up. When only a handful of people remain, just as Marin is saying good-bye to them, a hush falls over the group.

"Don't make a scene, Marin," Raj cautions, walking toward her.

"What are you talking about?" Marin demands, still in the dark. Only when Ranee and Sonya join them does Marin see what is going on.

"I assume that's Adam?" Sonya murmurs, pointing to Gia, who is embracing him.

"What the hell is he doing here?" Ignoring Raj, Marin makes her way to Gia. Raj follows, close on her heels. Upon reaching Adam, Marin pulls Gia away. "You have some nerve," she bites out. "There's a restraining order against you." She holds tightly to Gia's arm, even as her daughter struggles to be let loose. "I look forward to seeing you locked away."

"I invited him," Gia says, finally succeeding in freeing herself. She takes her place between Marin and Adam, a wall of defense. "It's my birthday party. I can have over whomever I want."

"Call the police," Marin orders Raj, her gaze locked with Gia's. "Gia, you have no idea what you are doing."

"I just came to wish Gia happy birthday," Adam says, holding his hands up in surrender. "I'm not trying to cause trouble."

"I don't want to hear a word from you," Marin barks at Adam. She notices Raj hasn't called. Turning to Sonya, she holds out her hand. "You have your phone?"

"Marin"—Sonya cautions, glancing between Gia and Adam— "don't."

It is not the answer she expected. One of them has to be on her side. Feeling everything slipping away, she finally begs, her desperation clear. "Sonya, give me your phone right now."

Everyone disappears while images of the past crowd around her. Locked in a closet for an A-minus, hits that never stopped coming, prayers that were never answered. Sweat lines her palms while her heartbeat speeds up—the telltale signs of a panic attack. Her tongue starts to thicken, making words almost impossible. She has no one else to turn to, no one willing to support her in the battle she is losing. She waits, wondering if she is truly all alone, when Sonya silently lays the phone in her palm. Gutted, Marin stares at her younger sister, who with a simple nod assures Marin she is standing by her side.

"Look, I'm leaving," Adam murmurs, taking two steps back. "No harm done."

"Don't go," Gia pleads. She turns toward Marin. "Mom, please understand."

"Understand what, Gia?" Marin says, finding her voice. "Your behavior is self-destructive. I can't allow it."

"It's not your choice!" Gia yells. Without Gia noticing, Ranee has joined them. Slipping her arm around Gia's waist, she effectively moves her away from Adam and closer to her family.

"Why did you call him?" Marin repeats, devastated. The last few guests have taken their leave, offering Marin and her family the privacy they deserve. Marin barely registers their exits, her entire focus on her daughter. "Why did you invite him here?"

"Because I love him," Gia admits, her stance seeming to beg her mother to accept this. "You still love Dada, even after what he did to you. Why is this any different?"

*　*　*

The house is empty, the bustle of the party long past. Raj took Gia out after Adam left, insisting to Marin he needed time alone with his daughter and saying they would be back later. Now numb, Marin watches with detachment as Ranee brings three cups of chai to the table. Needing something to do, she starts to make a list of the guests who witnessed the interaction. She will call them tomorrow, apologize for the scene. Having to do so is salt on a wound, knowing everyone's life is perfect while hers, in shambles, is on display for the world to see.

"Drink this," Ranee encourages, scooting her chair closer to Marin's. "When I was young, and there was a problem in the family or village, we would all gather at someone's home and have cup after cup of chai. After enough hours, the problem that seemed insurmountable was suddenly solved."

"The children drank chai?" Sonya demands. "Filled with caffeine?"

"Of course," Ranee answers, smiling. "In India, chai is one of the main food groups." Ranee pushes the cup closer to Marin. "Take a sip, Marin. Things will seem clearer."

"Chai's not solving any problems," Marin returns. Her hand trembling, she pushes the steaming cup away. She checks her phone for a message from Raj. Nothing. She slams it back down, the tremor of her hand the only clue to how scared she is. "I don't want to keep you," she murmurs, her shame having no limitations. "I appreciate you staying but we're fine." She begins to pace, glancing out the window repeatedly. Almost to herself, in a daze, she admits, "I can't imagine where they went."

"Is there someplace Gia likes to go?" Sonya asks gently, trying to ease her sister's concern.

"No." Marin picks up the phone and calls Raj again, but it goes straight to voice mail. She follows up with another text. Only silence in response. "Where are they?" she cries. Her hands shaking, she accidentally drops the phone, watching in horror as it bounces on the marble floor. Rushing toward it, she checks to make sure it's not broken. Like a compass without a magnet, she is lost, only she hadn't realized how much until now. "It still works," she says aloud, reassuring herself. A frenetic energy driving her, she glances around. "I have to clean up."

"It's all done," Ranee says gently. "The waitstaff took care of it."

"Right." Marin begins to pace, oblivious to Sonya and Ranee watching her with worry. "Where are they?" Glancing at her watch, she calculates the amount of time they've been gone. Only minutes have passed since her last call. "Let me try Raj again."

"Hey," Sonya says, slowly pulling the phone out of her hands. "What Gia said outside, about you still loving Dad?" She pauses, giving Marin a chance to talk. When she stays silent, Sonya asks, "You've never told her?"

"Told her what?" Marin demands, pushing because Sonya is the only one in front of her.

"That you're scared," Ranee says quietly. When Marin turns toward her, Ranee starts speaking slowly, every word difficult. "That you don't trust her."

"Trust her with what?" Marin asks.

"The truth."

Marin's face falls, grief washing over her. She tries to hide it, keep even this last secret hidden, but everything has become too much. With no turn left to take, she collapses into a chair, tears coursing down her cheeks. "What do I do?" she pleads.

"Offer her your trust—the thing I never gave you," Ranee answers quietly. She starts to play with the gold bangles that line her wrists, three on each hand. She seems to hesitate, struggling. She swallows twice, biting her lip. Finally she begins to speak, her words halting, unsure. "When the three of you were young, I took all the gold I had received in my marriage dowry and melted it down to have six gold bangles made, two for each of you. But you were young, so I wore them, saving them for when you were old enough to take care of them." She slowly slips each one off, setting them in the middle of the table. "You see, the gold was the only thing in this world that was mine. Everything in our life was bought with your father's money. But the gold from my dowry, that was mine, given to me by your grandparents."

Ranee reaches for Marin's hand, holding it tightly. "But I have yet to give you them. I didn't trust what you would do with them if I did." Ranee lowers her head. "Maybe you would throw them in a drawer. Maybe you would laugh at the value I gave them. Maybe you would reject me because it is all I have to give to you."

"I don't understand," Marin murmurs.

Ranee's face fills with grief. "Forgive me, my daughter. I was too weak to stand up for you. To tell you that I loved you. To stand in front of him when he hit you. All I had was these," she says pointing to the gold bangles, "and even this I was too afraid to give. I see now it wasn't the three of you I didn't trust; it was me."

"Mummy," Marin whispers. Closing her eyes, she allows Ranee's words to break through. The armor that has protected Marin from herself and the world slowly starts to fall away, leaving her vulnerable and open. "What do I give her? What do I say?" She grips Ranee's hand tightly, begging for an answer. "How do I get my daughter back?"

"You tell her the truth. You let her in." Ranee pushes the bangles toward both of them, handing Marin hers first. She watches as Sonya and Marin slip them on, leaving two on the table. "You give her all you have, the truth that is both good and bad, and then trust it is enough."

* * *

Gia and Raj arrive home late that night. Marin sat on the sofa in the den, waiting in the dark for them. Raj finally texted Marin to let her know they were fine, but that was it. No further information. Marin had seen her mom and sister out, both of them offering hugs. For the first time in a long time, Marin had returned their embraces, thankful they were in her life.

When Marin was four months pregnant with Gia, she had been offered a promotion. It required a move back to California, near her childhood home. For Marin, the move, like everything else in her life, came after careful consideration to arrive at the most pragmatic choice. She never went on emotion, trusting logic more. Rationality worked with facts and figures, each decision based on a careful analysis of the pros and cons. It was how she had survived her childhood. Every time her father hit her, she assessed the circumstances, tried to evaluate what led to the beating. She promised herself it would not happen again. Next time she would be sure to get the A-plus instead of just the A. She would control every aspect of her life so she would never again be vulnerable to attack. Her plan had worked. Her life was mapped out to perfection. Until Gia grew up and became her own person.

Gia fell in line for so long that Marin became used to it, assumed life would go on as she planned. But now nothing is working. She is losing her daughter, if she hasn't already lost her completely.

Marin twists the bangle on her hand. She examines the diamonds set throughout the thin gold, making the bracelet sparkle. She had admired the bangles on her mother's wrist, but never imagined they were meant for her and her sisters.

It is hard for her to admit Ranee was right to have feared Marin's reaction. Before, Marin would have thanked Ranee for the gift and then placed the bangles in a drawer, worn them occasionally. Not understanding the sentiment behind the bequest, she would have treated them like everything else in her life—something to use only when it served her purpose. Now she understands her mother's directive—appreciates what she has given because the gift symbolizes all she has to offer.

The sound of the garage opening causes Marin to sit up straight. She wipes her sweaty palms on her pants, never having been so nervous in her life. She starts to pull her hair back and then chides herself for it. Gia is her daughter, she reminds herself. She will accept whatever explanation Marin offers. Just like she has accepted Ranee's explanation.

"Raj, Gia." Marin meets them in the hallway, facing her judge and jury. "Where were you?" she demands. When she sees their wariness, she kicks herself for defaulting to the same behavior. Cautioning herself to take it slow, she whispers, "I'm sorry." She takes a step toward Gia, who automatically steps back. "Are you okay, Beti?"

"I'm fine," Gia murmurs, moving toward Raj.

"I can't imagine you are," Marin says, seeing their surprise at her words. "This wasn't the best birthday."

"No," Gia answers, avoiding looking directly at Marin.

"That was my fault." The words, which once would have been impossible for Marin to say, now feel right. They make sense. "The party, it wasn't the best idea."

"Marin, I think Gia is tired. She wants to go to bed," Raj interrupts, fatigued. "Let's just call it a night."

"Actually, I was hoping to talk to you for a few minutes, Gia?" Marin shrugs. "I haven't given you your birthday gift yet."

"I don't need anything, Mom," Gia answers. "Dad's right. I'm pretty tired."

"A quick story," Marin returns. "While you're getting ready for bed." Marin takes a breath, saying a word she had never before thought to. "Please."

"No, Mom," Gia says. "Maybe another night."

TRISHA

I finally find my way back to some semblance of living. I borrowed Sonya's clothes while living at Mama's. Mama seemed to enjoy the company, having two of her daughters under her roof again. The house felt different without Papa in it; it was quieter, calmer. Though I was never the recipient of his rage and violent anger, I knew it existed and lived under the cloud of darkness he perpetrated. I felt the fear of my loved ones. Watching them walking and breathing freely within the same walls where they once moved in fear was a revelation. It was as if they were different women but with the same bodies and features.

After Mama and I spoke, I decided to return to what still feels like my house. Once inside, I glance around at the home I had spent so many hours perfecting, feeling like a stranger in it. Shaking off my malaise, I check my phone, the bracelets Mama gave me slipping up my arm. There are no messages from Eric demanding the house be cleared. He must be as hesitant to return to the home as I once was reluctant to leave it. When I walk around, only silence welcomes me, but I am quickly reminded of what is mine, what has always been mine. My home, my decorations, my life. All of it waiting for me to claim.

I run my hands over the boxes still stacked—I was so sure when I packed them. I stood in righteous indignation of Eric's anger and felt his betrayal was greater than mine. Now it feels like a window has been opened—one whose glass was opaque, impossible to see through. I have built my marriage on lies, and Eric and I both suffered for them. I owe him an apology, an explanation for my actions. I know I don't deserve an audience with him, but I have to ask.

I cringe at the thought of saying aloud what happened to me. Sonya and I have lain awake for hours talking about it. She has given me a shoulder to cry on, offered me a safe place to speak without worry about judgment or condemnation. When I told her that I still loved Papa, even as I reviled him, she nodded in understanding. When I told her I still loved Eric, she said she would be surprised if I didn't.

"He's a good man," she said. "And he loves you." She got a faraway look. "You're very lucky you found him."

I didn't tell her what I fear—that I have lost Eric's love forever. That what I had is in the past, no matter how much I still wish for it, it is gone. "Have you ever been in love?" She has never mentioned anyone to me, never given any indication she has given her heart to another.

"I don't know what love is," she answered. "But you do. You're very lucky."

As I stand now in my empty home, I don't feel so lucky. I grimace, my life so different from what I have always imagined. Grabbing the stack of mail that was stuffed into the mailbox, I start to sort through the junk mail and the bills that continue to come in. A large manila envelope addressed to me grabs my attention. When I read the return address, I start to feel my own heart beating. It's from Eric's lawyers.

I tear open the seal slowly and pull out the thin sheaf of papers. In clear and distinct language it lays out the divorce agreement between Eric and me. As I demanded, there is no alimony, no division of property. Everything we came into the marriage with we still own. Everything else is Eric's. All that is required to make it official is our signatures. Mine first, and then I send it back to the lawyer for Eric's. The attorney will be kind enough to do the rest. Dropping the papers onto the envelope they came in, I walk away, unable to sign.

* * *

Mama asked us all to meet at the hospital. She didn't give us a reason, just scheduled a time and told each of us it was critical. I was hesitant at first, unwilling to see Papa. I haven't seen him since I learned the truth, since I learned what he did to me, against me. But I can't hide. If I do, then he has won. There is a part of me he has taken; if I run, I allow him to keep the power, to keep me in the place he put me.

He is still as he has been since he arrived here—no emotion, no capacity to speak. Where before I would have smoothed out his sheet, run my hands through his hair to straighten it, now I keep my distance. I stare at him from afar, seeing a stranger in a face that is as familiar as my own.

"Why, Papa?" I whisper. "How could you do such a thing to me?"

If he were awake, if he were able to communicate, I wonder how he would respond. What rationalization could he create for his actions? Maybe he would apologize to me, beg for forgiveness that I can't give. Salvation is not his to demand, not from me, now or ever.

"I loved you unconditionally," I tell him, though he already knows. All this time I have spoken to him on every visit, hoping my words of love and hope would wake him, bring him back. Now I need him to hear my anguish, feel the pain he has caused. It is all that is between us—questions with no answers. "I was so grateful to you."

The admission gives me pause. I had never seen it that way before; instead, I assumed that his love for me was deserved, that I was deemed worthy, while the rest didn't measure up. But it was not so, my own mind deceiving me. It was gratitude; I convinced myself I owed him for loving me. No child should ever feel such a thing. A family should be connected by love and appreciation for what every person brings into the relationship. A unity of hearts and souls, where fear has no place.

"You are lost. You always have been. And you tried so hard . . ." I pause. Biting my lip, I stare out the window, over the bedsheet that covers him. "To make sure we lost ourselves. But it didn't happen, Papa. Somehow, some way I am going to survive," I say with a certainty I don't yet feel.

RANEE

It is time to say good-bye.

In Hinduism, no event, no matter how small, can occur without consulting an astrology source to gauge whether it is a good time. Before an engagement, parents consult with a priest to determine if the two people who are to be married have good energy, based on their birth times and dates, that can be matched for a fulfilling life. Marriage plans are made and broken based on the results. A child's time of birth can lead a family to rejoice or despair. A child born during a dark period is sure to lead to hard times for the mother, whereas a lucky time will bring great fortune and happiness to the family.

Celebrations, rituals, travel are all decided based on the time that is most propitious. If an occasion occurs during a dark time, then pujas are held where the gurus, around a fire and statues of the gods, chant mantras and prayers that will help ward off all potential evil.

Ranee, like every other believer, checked her astrological calendar religiously, never daring to hold an event unless the stars were aligned to guarantee happiness. It was that way with the generation before her and every generation prior to that. It was the way it was done, as natural as breathing.

This time, though, Ranee did not check the calendar. Nor did she meet with a guru who would tell her the most auspicious time for the event to take place. She couldn't foresee finding the right moment to unplug Brent's life support, to cut off all oxygen to him so he could leave this world, freeing Ranee and her daughters at last. Instead, haste was the conductor, the one who determined when it would happen.

But as much as Ranee wants it done already, she accepts it is no longer her decision alone. All three of her daughters are finally together, with her, and she will not disrespect them by failing to give them the voice they have earned. They lived through him—it is up to them when he should die. There is no calendar to consult, no time that proves better than another. No stars have aligned to protect her three girls; fate has failed to intervene. Their combined voice is now more powerful than the universe's, their strength earned from having survived. They will do this now because it is past time for them to say good-bye.

When Ranee arrives at the room, she assumes she will be first, since she's come earlier than the time she designated. She is surprised when she sees Trisha standing by the window, her back to where Brent lies on the bed.

"Beti," Ranee exclaims, going over to wrap her arm around her daughter's waist. "You're here early." When Trisha returned to her own house, it left Ranee's quieter, emptier than she thought possible. Odd, she never missed Brent's presence, but Trisha's departure left the home barren, even though Sonya was still there.

"I needed to see him," Trisha admits, turning fully into her mother's arms. "To ask him why."

"What did he say?" Ranee asks, unsure. Somehow, they would have to find their way, and, maybe, by holding one another's hands along the charred trail, each of them would find their own path to healing.

"He didn't answer." Trisha sobs the obvious. "But you know what?" She pulls away, facing Ranee, "I don't think, even if he were awake, he would have cared enough to."

"I don't think he had a reason," Ranee says, holding her daughter as closely as she can. "But it doesn't matter." Each of them has fallen behind, but they will wait for one another. They will never abandon the others, never stop holding out their hand to help. "When I was a child, I used to watch flocks of birds as they traveled across the sky, leaving their home for another. Without fail, one or two would always fall back."

"What happened?" Trisha asks.

"They always found their way." Ranee glances at Brent's body before turning back to her daughter. "You're going to be fine," Ranee promises. "We all are going to be fine." It is the first time she has ever given her word. For the first time in her life, Ranee is sure she can keep it.

Marin and Gia arrive soon after. Ranee had specifically asked for Gia to join them. No matter how desperately they tried to keep the secret, Gia has become part of their conspiracy. Having suffered from the fallout of their existence, she deserves a voice in the inheritance she has never asked for. Ranee immediately moves toward Gia, taking her grandchild into her arms. "How are you, Beti?" she asks, stroking the young girl's hair in affection and love.

"I'm good, Mumji," Gia answers, glancing at Marin.

"I'm sorry I missed your party," Trisha says, coming over to join the hug. "I thought I could take you shopping? Let you choose your own birthday gifts? I'm not sure I know what a sixteen-year-old needs." She is teasing, some of her old self filtering through the dark clouds.

"That would be great," Gia says, sounding shy.

"Then it's a date."

"Are you all right?" Marin asks as Trisha moves closer to them. "Sonya said you were hurting."

"I'm getting there," Trisha offers, smiling. "Thank you."

"Maybe we could spend some time together soon? Talk?" Marin asks.

"I would like that," Trisha answers, giving her sister's hand a squeeze.

"Good." Marin turns toward Ranee, her voice gentler, kinder than before. "Why did you call us here? Is there news on his condition?"

"No," Ranee begins, just as David enters. "Ah, here is the gentleman I was waiting for. Dr. Ford."

"Good to see everyone," David says, offering them a smile.

"Thank you for meeting with us." Ranee glances around. "Sonya is not here yet. I wonder if we could wait just a few minutes? She said she would be here."

There are nods and murmurs of agreement.

"Where is Raj?" Ranee asks Marin.

"He's waiting downstairs." Marin glances at Gia, who is staring at the floor. Ranee understands immediately—Raj drove them to the hospital to be with his daughter. "Since you only asked me and Gia to the meeting, he wanted to give us privacy."

Ranee nods. "That was kind of him."

Just as the room falls silent, Sonya bursts in, harried. "Sorry I'm late," she murmurs, her gaze encompassing the room. When her eyes fall on David, she visibly tenses. Ranee turns toward the doctor, who has locked eyes with her youngest. Startled, Ranee turns back toward Sonya who, in seconds, has shuttered her outward emotions, as if refusing to reveal any more. "It looks like everyone is here."

"Yes," Ranee murmurs, tucking away this new revelation for later. "I asked everyone to meet here so we can move forward with your father's situation."

"I don't understand," Sonya says, speaking for everyone. "Has there been a change?" She automatically turns toward David before seeming to catch herself.

"I want to remove the life support," Ranee answers. "Let him go."

The room falls silent, each of her daughters obviously lost in her own thoughts, her own memories. Ranee watches them carefully, the three women she bore and raised. How many mistakes she has made, how many wrong turns, her only excuse being she didn't know which way was the right one. This would not rectify that, would not make the past disappear, but it might give them a chance to begin again.

"Why now, Mumji?" asks Gia, the first one to break the silence.

"So we can heal, Beti. Together," Ranee answers, trying not to reveal too much in front of the doctor. "What do you think?" She knows Gia loved her Dada. He gave her what he failed to offer anyone else—unconditional love.

"Yes," Marin answers before Gia can. "If it's a decision to be made, then I say yes." Her voice is strong, sure.

"Yes," Trisha murmurs, her answer barely audible. "If there's any part of him that can hear us, he has to know it's time."

Sonya slips her hand into Trisha's. "I agree." Ranee doesn't ask on which point; it doesn't matter. She has given her vote—they are unanimous.

"Doctor, please tell us what is the next step."

Before David can answer, explain how to take away the life of someone who had taken so much, Gia speaks up. "I vote no," she calls out, willing everyone to hear her. "I don't want him to die."

"Gia," Marin starts, but her daughter refuses to listen.

"He's my grandfather. He's a good man. I love him so much," she cries. "Why is everyone so ready to do this? He could still come out of it. We could have him back, and then everything will be fine again."

* * *

Ranee sits next to Brent, staring at his stillness. Marin took Gia home, her outburst leaving the decision in limbo. Trisha gave Ranee a hug, telling her she would speak to her later. Sonya simply left, David watching her the whole time.

"It's hard for families to make this kind of decision," explains David, the only one left. "If there's anything I can do . . ." he begins, but Ranee interrupts him, facing him across the expanse of the bed.

"You care for my daughter," Ranee says, so sure of the statement she doesn't need to ask. "And she for you."

"No," David says, clearly hesitating to answer the question. "She wants nothing to do with me."

"That's not what I saw in her eyes." Ranee pauses, trying to find her way through unfamiliar territory. She rarely discusses her daughters' love lives with them or anyone else. Deep within her, she feared hearing their stories, learning how their childhood affected them in adulthood. "I apologize if I am speaking out of turn, but I know what I saw. My daughter is in love with you, I am sure." She thinks about her relationship with Brent, what defined them. "That is different from love for someone familiar—something I have learned in my advanced years. Love is sometimes demanded, expected when you have blood relations. But to be in love with another, to care for them more than for yourself—that is powerful. And you, you are concerned, worried for her?"

"Yes," David answers, quietly. He glances out the window. Taking the opportunity to study his profile, Ranee sees whom her daughter has fallen in love with, his strength, his character. Everything Brent is not, could never be.

"Then why the hurt, the distance?" Ranee demands, confused.

"That's something that you should ask her," David says quietly, turning back toward her. His voice holds respect, both for Ranee and Sonya. "I don't want to presume to speak for her."

"I understand." Ranee falls quiet, watching the rise and fall of Brent's chest as the machine pumps oxygen into him. "The vote today must have surprised you," Ranee says at last. "A family so quick to release the man who raised them, provided for them. To let him go with just one word, an agreement." She reaches again for the mangal-sutra that had a permanent place around her neck for years. Only when she touches bare skin does she remember again having removed it. "Is it always so simple for a family?"

"No," David says truthfully. "But Sonya told me what he did." He pauses, staring at Brent. "How he hurt all of you. I can't imagine what that must have been like."

Ranee lowers her head, hiding her shock. Each of them has hidden the secret for so long, gone to extreme lengths to keep anyone from learning it, and yet Sonya, in a few short months of knowing this man, has revealed to him the one thing she has been running from her entire life.

"It destroyed her," Ranee shares, understanding dawning. Sonya was refusing to love this man, refusing to accept what he was offering her. Ranee could now acknowledge her part in that, recognize her inaction had caused her daughter to react this way. With that knowledge came acceptance, an understanding of what she has to do. Her words will change each one of their paths irretrievably. "But I helped," Ranee admits, confiding in this stranger as her daughter had already done. "I made her believe she wasn't wanted, she wasn't loved."

"I don't think . . ." David starts, but Ranee holds up a hand to silence him.

"My daughter must know the truth. She can never be free of him until she does," Ranee says. "She will never be able to acknowledge or trust her love for you until then."

"Why don't you tell her this?" David asks.

"Because I haven't earned the right," Ranee admits. "She was the one I left behind, the one I couldn't be a mother to." She notices his tie—a mix of superheroes. "Are you a parent, David?"

"Yes. I have a daughter."

"You would do anything for her," Ranee says, confidently.

"Of course. Like any parent." David sounds self-effacing.

"No, not any parent. Not me." Ranee shifts in the chair, her body hurting past its age. "Sonya believed I didn't want her, that she was an accident. I told her I wanted to have her aborted; she was right."

Ranee waits for David to process the admission, to accept what she is saying before continuing. "But not for the reasons she believes. I didn't want her because I couldn't protect her. I knew what he would do, and I couldn't stop him. But my failure was not loving her as she deserved, not saying the words she needed to hear. That was my fault, not his," Ranee admits, turning her gaze on Brent. "So I lost her because she didn't know I loved her."

"Why don't you tell her then? Why me?"

Ranee thinks back to the day of the graduation. She knew what was happening, knew Brent would never let Sonya be happy with her decision. Sonya had to be free, so Ranee said the only thing that would release her—the truth, knowing it would push her daughter away.

"Because I already told her the truth," Ranee says. "She won't believe another truth now. Would you?"

David watches her, his emotions guarded. He finally shakes his head, admitting his confusion. "Telling me all of this—I don't know what to say," David says, clearly struggling.

Ranee nods in understanding. "It may very well be too late for my daughter and me, but it is not late for her to accept the love waiting for her. I can imagine there is no greater joy than to offer someone love, knowing it is returned completely." Ranee offers a sad smile, knowing that will never happen for her, but grateful that her daughter can have it, willing to pay the cost. "But a mother cannot give birth to a child and not lose a piece of herself. The child takes a part of the parent with them, holding it as their own. Whether it be their heart or soul, they are now connected for always."

"She never knew how you felt?" David asks.

"No. I let my daughter go." Ranee shakes her head. "But then I got tired of missing her. Of yearning for her as only a mother can for a child born from her womb. They are a part of you and when they leave, they take that piece with them, leaving you half of your whole." Sweat lines her palms and pools in her bra—she fears what she is about to do, but knows there is no choice. "I had to make a choice—either my husband or my daughter."

She glances at Brent, shocked that after all the steps taken, this would be the one that decided everything. That the man Sonya loved was the final piece of Ranee's life. He would hold the fate of her future in his hands, but it was worth it for Sonya to finally be free. Ranee says the words slowly, forcing David to strain to hear. "I knew she would never come back as long as Brent was alive."

"Ranee," David says, comprehension dawning on his face. He holds up a hand to silence her. "I don't think you should say any more."

"No, I think it is finally time for me to say the truth." Ranee stands up to put as much distance as she can between the man with whom she spent most of her life and the person she is now. "Brent had started to lose his eyesight. The only thing that helped him was his prescription eye drops." Ranee rummages in her purse, finding what she is looking for. "It was important he take three drops every day, if only to help him see our loss. It is truly a miracle drug. It helps you to see when you fear you are blind. With it he used over-the-counter drops, to help with the redness."

Ranee sets the Visine bottle down on the table next to the bed, only inches away from Brent. "But it is a drug with many uses, I learned. Something so simple used the wrong way can kill." Ranee swallows the breath she is holding. Her fingers play with the bottle, remembering the drops she put in his chai every day.

The night of Sonya's birthday, when Brent said Ranee and Sonya were alike, he meant it as an insult, but Ranee wanted it to be true. She wanted to have the strength Sonya exhibited—to take control and refuse Brent the permission to continue destroying.

Looking up, she sees the shock on David's face. She feels a moment of shame, of remorse for having revealed the truth to the man Sonya loves, but as with so much of their life, their choices are limited. For the daughter who refused to let anyone in, David may be the only person she will love. Ranee had tried to tell Sonya she loved her but accepted it was too late. Sonya didn't trust her enough to believe. But she trusted David, and maybe, if the news came from him, she would finally accept the truth that she was loved.

"But tell Sonya this. It is important she knows. You see, my daughter believes everything I do, I do for Trisha. This I did for Sonya. Because I love her. Because I missed her and wanted her to come back to a safe home."

Ranee turns away, accepting what she has done and the consequences that will follow. She knows David will have to report her, that the world will soon know her crime. She has left one prison only to be headed for another. But it is the only way she knows how to free Sonya. The only gift she has to give to the daughter she has previously given nothing.

"And one more thing," Ranee says before leaving. "Make sure my daughter understands it was before I learned the truth of what Brent did to Trisha, not after. It was long before."

SONYA

I left the hospital room as soon as possible. I want the decision done, the life support turned off. I will never be sure if I am ready for him to die, but after hearing Marin's and Trisha's unequivocal yeses, I knew it was past time. But with Gia's refusal, we are back to limbo. Waiting indefinitely for something other than what we have now.

"How's Will?" I ask the attending nurse. "Any updates?"

"Discharged last night," she says. "Diagnosed with epilepsy. Sent him home with meds to take if the seizures continue."

"What type?" I ask. I know there are all types of epilepsy, some that can last a lifetime, others intermittent.

"Benign rolandic," she says. "He should grow out of it by eighteen." She pauses to answer a patient's call before continuing. "Late onset is a good sign. He'll only have a few years to deal with it."

"What about the soccer?" I ask.

Swiveling her chair toward me, she says, "As they were leaving I overheard him tell his father he didn't want to play anymore. His dad hugged him, said all that mattered was that he get better."

I watch her leave to attend to a patient. Will and his family had no choice with the epilepsy, but how they handled it was their decision. I think about my own reaction to the events that shaped my life. How many times have I hurt myself, by my actions, my running, because it was the only way I knew how to handle the situation.

What if there was another way to right the wrongs? What if happiness was the trajectory, and not sadness? I see David coming down the hallway, his face looking tight with worry. He sees me just as I start to turn away; our gazes lock. With a simple nod, we acknowledge one another and then both, as if in agreement, turn away, accepting what cannot be. I dismiss my thoughts, accepting the choices I have no option but to make.

MARIN

They are silent on the drive home, everyone still processing the scene in the hospital. Marin sits quietly next to Raj while he drives, a rare departure from her giving him directions at every turn. She yearns to speak to Gia, to ask her about her decision, her vote, but no words feel like the right ones. From the side-view mirror she sees Gia's earplugs in, imagines music is blasting through them. Stealing a glance at Raj, she sees his face set, his concentration on the road.

They have come a long way from the day they circled the fire seven times to bind them together in marriage. The wedding took place in a church hall her parents rented for the occasion. A makeshift gazebo was built inside, where the Brahmin conducting the ceremony could sit and recite the vows in front of the five hundred members of the Indian community who had come to bear witness. If pushed, Marin can only remember a dozen or so names of the attendees—most of the guests were her parents' friends, not hers.

"Thank you for today," Marin says, startling Raj. "I know you had work." It is the only thing she can say to convey her appreciation.

"I did it for Gia," Raj explains quietly, glancing at their daughter in the backseat. "I wanted to be there for her."

"Right." Marin turns back toward the window, watching the trees fly by on the ride home. On the day they married, Marin assumed it was forever, because the culture dictated it be so. She didn't factor in love or care for the other person; it was a marriage of equals, brought together to raise a family and offer support through the years. Brilliant, when Marin thought about it. Businesses could learn from the practice.

Two people whose résumés, backgrounds, and accomplishments had to match before even being allowed to meet. After, even more pieces were required to fit. Looks had to match. A dark-skinned individual couldn't dream of landing a light-skinned partner. A heavy person could only hope for someone equal or heavier to be matched with. Each factor considered with excruciating detail before the match was blessed by both families. But love was never an element mentioned or discussed. It was assumed, because when everything else fits, love should follow.

But it didn't. Marin can accept that now. She never fell in love with Raj. Never needed him like you should someone you love. Never thought of him above herself or considered his needs more important than hers. She did exactly what was expected of her when the marriage was decided—she merged with him to create a perfect union. A home and life filled with all the luxuries hard work could offer. A daughter molded to perfection, her every step ahead of others. But love's absence took its toll. Without it to bind, the connection proved too fragile, too susceptible to breakage. They each stood separate, only familiarity and comfort keeping them in the same place.

Gia's cry to save her grandfather was instinctive, born from a place where love was the inspiration. She faced all of them without fear, saying whatever was necessary to give him another day, another chance to come back to them. She couldn't lose him, she said. Because she loves him. Marin wanted to scream at her daughter that her grandfather is incapable of love, that he has shown her a version of himself that doesn't really exist.

A master magician, Brent created a fantasy for Gia to believe in, a trick of the mind to serve his own purpose. Another means for him to feel needed, to feel special. But Gia wasn't privy to any evidence that would reveal his hand, and that was Marin's fault. Desperate to create an illusion, for her own sake and for Gia's, she hid the truth from her only child. And if Ranee was right, that was because Marin didn't trust that Gia would love her for who she was, past the chimera she had created. Marin didn't love her true self enough to believe someone else could love her too.

*   *   *

"Gia?" Marin knocks on the door gently, opening it a crack to peek in. "Can I talk to you for a minute, Beti?"

"About school?" Gia asks warily.

"No, nothing to do with school, I promise." Marin enters completely, shutting the door behind her. She swallows her nervousness, tries to rein in her fear. "There's something I want to tell you, that I should have told you a long time ago."

"Sure." Gia's confusion is clear, but she doesn't say anything. "I was just going to change real quick."

Marin watches silently as Gia throws her top and capris onto the floor before pulling out an oversize T-shirt from her dresser drawer. There are no scars marring her body anymore. Instead, it is smooth, the skin clear and free of the black and blue that decorated it not long ago. Raj retired to the guest room after giving Gia a quick peck on the head and sending a warning glance to Marin. She acknowledged it with a nod, more afraid of Gia's reaction to her than of any damage she could do to her daughter.

Gia steps into her adjoining bathroom, brushing her teeth with just a few strokes. Marin bites her tongue, choosing wisely not to say anything. She takes a seat on the bed, waiting for Gia to finish up and join her. Exiting the bathroom, Gia walks around to the other side and climbs under the covers, fluffing her pillows, and leaning against them. "What did you want to talk about?"

"A story I wanted to tell you." Marin takes a deep breath, praying for courage. "I've never told you about my childhood. About who I am."

"Why?" Gia asks. The innocence that once emanated from her is lost.

"I don't know," Marin lies, still hiding. She berates herself silently, yearning for a hand to guide. But she has to take these steps on her own and allow everything to fall where it may. "I didn't want to move to America," Marin starts, admitting it aloud. "We used to live in a small house, barely two rooms, in India. Most of my friends still cooked their food over coals, but we were fortunate enough to have a stove. That was it for luxuries, though."

"That's crazy," Gia murmurs, listening attentively. "How could you stand it?"

"It was home," Marin explains. "All I knew, and I loved it. Dada was so good to me when we lived in India. He used to play with me, bought me toys." When the visas came, he showed her pictures of America from books. From their small village it looked like paradise. A place all their dreams would come true. "He loved me." Marin can still remember the feeling of being his girl. With no sons in the home, Brent gave all of his attention to her. Once upon a time, Marin considered herself fortunate for that.

"You make it sound past tense."

"When we moved to America, that's what it became." Marin shifts closer to Gia on the bed, bringing her sock-clad feet onto the covers. "How did you know what he did to me? Who told you that?"

"He did," Gia replies. She tenses, playing with the covers on the bed. "I don't remember how old I was, but I was young. Maybe nine, ten years old. He asked me what I wanted to be when I grew up. I told him I wanted to be you."

Marin catches her breath, unable to remember a time when her daughter exalted her so much. How much more had she missed, she wondered. "I never knew that."

"Yeah, well, it wasn't exactly cool to tell your mom you wanted to be like her."

"And I can't imagine I made it easy." Marin never wanted to be like Ranee. She refused to be weak when she needed to be strong. Brent was the easy choice to mimic. "What did he say when you told him?"

"That you were you because of him." Gia stares at the wall. The silence in the room is deafening. "He said you weren't very smart or disciplined. That he used to hit you to make you learn. He said he did it because he loved you."

Marin's head falls back as she tries desperately to swallow the cry that comes instinctually. How could any father convince himself of that and then dare to pass the message on to his only grandchild? "The first time he hit me was on the first birthday I celebrated in America," Marin divulges, hearing Gia's intake of breath. "I dropped the ice-cream cone he bought me."

"Mom," Gia starts, looking pained.

"Then, when I spelled the word 'whole' as h-o-l-e on a spelling test and received a ninety-eight percent."

Marin had been in school for two months. The teacher had put a smiley face and sticker on the paper, so proud of her new student for having mastered the unknown English words. Marin had shown the test first to Ranee, who had hugged her daughter and told her how proud she was. Then she waited anxiously for her father to arrive home. When he did, she ran to him like she used to in India upon his arrival, waiting to be picked up and thrown into the air with joy. But those days were long past, never to be seen again.

"He slapped me twice and told me if I didn't get one hundred percent next time he would disown me."

"Mom." There are tears in Gia's eyes. The barrier between them starts to crumble, each piece falling slowly away. "Why would he do such a thing?" Gia asks.

"I don't know," Marin finally admits. "He never told me." Marin says the words she has never been able to accept before. "He didn't love me. He may have before, in India, but somewhere along the way he stopped."

"How do you stop loving your own child?"

Marin thought about the last few months, how she and Gia ended up on separate sides of the same story. Throughout the hell, not once did she stop loving her daughter. It was impossible. "You don't," Marin answers. "You may not agree on everything, but you don't stop loving them. My father is the example of what a parent should never be. Any lesson I took from him on how to raise you . . ." Marin stops, taking Gia's hand in her own. She grasps for the right words, ashamed of her actions. "He hit me every opportunity he had. It didn't matter if I got great grades or was first in my class. Nothing was good enough. He hit me because he could. I wasn't able stop him," Marin chokes back a sob. "That's why I did what I did with Adam."

"Because you could stop him," Gia says with understanding.

"Because I couldn't let you be hurt the way I was hurt. I wasn't able to fight for myself, but I would do anything to fight for you," Marin answers. "Because I knew the damage the violence and abuse had done and couldn't bear to allow that to happen to you. When you were born, I felt like everything that had happened to me was worth it if it meant getting you."

"Mom," Gia whispers, tears rolling down. "Why didn't you ever tell me about your past? About what had happened to you?"

"Because I was afraid you wouldn't love me," Marin, her voice catching on her words, is finally able to admit the truth to both of them. "If you knew I had been broken, maybe you wouldn't love me with flaws." Marin realizes something she never has before. "Now I know it wasn't about me. It never was. He beat me because he was broken." Marin pauses. "But I was so afraid of losing your love."

"You're my mom," Gia answers, laughing between her tears. "I love you no matter what."

"I hope so," Marin answers, her eyes shining. "Because there's a lot I can live without, but not . . ." Marin can't finish the sentence, the words lost. She holds her arms out for Gia, who crawls into them. They hold one another, both quiet. "Why did you let him hit you?" Marin finally asks. "Why do you love him so much?"

"Because I didn't have to be perfect with him," Gia says after some thought. "Because I didn't have to always be in control."

"The way I wanted you to be," Marin accepts.

"I think so."

"And when he hit you?" Marin finally asks the question that has tortured her since she learned the truth. "How did you feel?"

"It's weird, but numb when he hit me and alive after." Gia lays her head on her knees. "He told me he needed me, just the way I was. I was the only thing that kept him happy. The only one he trusted." Gia looks up, staring at her mother. "Afterward he always cried, told me how sorry he was." Gia shakes her head. "But I don't think he was."

Marin wonders how much heartbreak one lifetime can contain. Hearing her daughter admit the truth, accepting her own culpability in the situation, is overwhelming. "I wanted you to have the perfect life," Marin explains quietly, finally understanding how all the pieces came together. "I believed being in complete control would make that happen."

"I miss him. When I see him, I feel safe," Gia explains.

"I know." Marin thinks about her visit to the hospital, her need for her father's love even after everything he did to her. Her rationalization of his behavior when he had no excuses. All of it because she was sure she needed his love more than he needed her. Because she was sure no one could love her, not even herself. "Can I help you?" Marin dares to ask. "On your terms?"

"I'm scared," Gia replies, curling up. "I don't understand why I feel like I do. Why I need him."

"I don't either," Marin admits. "But what if we make a deal to take it one step at a time?"

Marin thinks about the steps she needs to take, her own recovery. It may take her a lifetime, and she may not ever fully heal, but she needs to go on the journey, if for no other reason than to hold out her hand to her daughter and help her along the way. To model the right behavior. "I won't push you or criticize. I'll just be right here, beside you, always." Marin bites her lip, her eyes filling with tears. "And I'll love you, now and forever, no matter what." And maybe, somehow, she thinks, she'll even learn to love herself.

"What about you and Dad?" Gia asks, looking like a young child instead of someone on the brink of womanhood. "What are you going to do?"

"Help you, together." For now it is all Marin can offer. But it's enough. Their priority is being there for Gia. Marin finally understands the only way is standing side by side with Raj, creating a wall against any harm that can befall their daughter. In time, things will fall into place. No matter what, Marin will always be grateful to him for giving her the greatest joy of her life—their daughter. "And every single day, tell you how much we need you, and that we will do whatever it takes to help you."

"OK," Gia says, holding Marin tightly. Together, they watch through the window as the sun disappears behind the horizon, and the moon rises to take its place in the sky, offering light and guidance to those searching for their way.

TRISHA

I arrive at Eric's in the evening and know he's home when I see his car parked outside. He sent me his address after he left, in case I needed anything. I needed him to come home, but I didn't say that, never went to him to make the request.

He answers on the first ring. Shocked to see me, he stares before seeming to remember his manners and inviting me in. A frozen pizza sits on the counter, cut in half, an open bottle of beer next to it. He's dressed in torn jeans and a battered T-shirt, an outfit I have seen him in hundreds of times before. I rub my sweaty palms on my thighs, nervous and afraid.

I took almost two hours to get dressed this afternoon. First, I slipped on a dress, then decided it was too much. Afterward, I tried a pair of jeans and a button-down shirt. That didn't work either. I finally settled on a skirt and summer shirt, feeling parts of my femininity return with the outfit. Thinking of Papa, I hesitate to show skin, feel shame in doing so. I started to ask myself if I led him on, encouraged him. Memories washed over me; I obsessed about how much affection I showered him with, how I loved him blindly. I stopped myself. I'd done enough research to understand all of my emotions were normal.

Including fearing I was the instigator instead of the victim. I told myself, over and over, that I was never at fault; in time I hope I can believe that.

"Trisha," Eric says, showing a level of calm I don't feel. "I'm surprised to see you here."

"I hope it's not a bad time?" Maybe he has someone here, I realize. Glancing around quickly, I look for telltale signs of a woman's belongings. A purse or lipstick on a glass. The only thing I see is a sofa, a chair, and a desk. Stacks of papers hug the sofa, and his computer bag lies on top of the desk, with his laptop open and booted. "I should have called first."

"It's fine," he says. "I just wasn't expecting you." He is clearly uncomfortable, unsure.

Married for so many years, yet we are strangers trying to find our way. Hating the feeling, I surge forward, not stopping to consider my words. "I wanted to give you an answer to your question."

"Question?"

"Why I didn't want a child," I blurt out. I had rehearsed a number of scenarios in my head, different ways I would introduce the topic, the level of detail I would go into. I had every word I would say down, but the only part I couldn't script was his reaction. No matter how many times I tried, I always came up blank.

"You asked me that a number of times, and I didn't have an answer for you. Now I do."

"Trisha," he says, warily. "It doesn't matter anymore. It's over."

"I know," I say, remembering the envelope with divorce papers inside. "But I just learned the answer recently, and I thought you should know." I lower my voice. "You deserve to know."

Sighing, he motions me toward the sofa. I sit down, pushing some of his work papers to the side. He takes the chair across from me. I cross one leg over the other and then decide they are better flat on the floor. My palms on the leather couch, I raise my eyes to meet his.

Where I once saw unconditional love and acceptance, I now see distrust and suspicion.

"I started having these memories," I forge ahead. "They didn't make sense to me. A young girl walking down a hall, screaming silently for help." I swallow, trying to get the words past my closed throat. "The more we talked about a child, the faster the images came. This girl had been hurt, terribly."

"You never mentioned anything."

"I thought it was about someone else. Not me," I try to explain. "But the girl was walking in my childhood house."

"Who would it be about?" he demands, exuding impatience.

I take a deep breath, steady myself, and search for courage. I kept so many secrets from this man, from myself, that I don't know quite how or where to begin. He loved a woman I had created for the world to see, not the one who lay deep within me. He might hate the woman I am, the scars I bear, the wound that was open for so long I became oblivious to it and yet—yet it dictated every day of my life. "Papa wasn't the man you knew. I was his favorite." I stand up, start to pace in his small apartment, hoping it will make this easier. "But Sonya, Marin, and Mama weren't. He beat them, constantly."

"Trisha," Eric says, his voice sounding torn. I can't look at him, not yet. Not when I have barely touched the surface of the truth. "Why didn't you ever tell me?"

"I was ashamed. I changed what happened to fit my version of reality. Convinced myself it wasn't as bad as it was, maybe. I don't know," I say. "But he never hit me." I want to laugh now at my stupidity. My desperate need to believe anything other than what really happened. "So even as they hated him, even as Sonya ran to escape the memories, I stood by his side, loving him, needing him. Believing in him."

"He was a good father to you," Eric says quietly, watching me. "I saw that in all your interactions."

"He loved me," I acknowledge, trying to make sense of Papa's definition of the word. "During our childhood, he would get angry. He used to bring home liquor when he wanted to scare everyone. It was always a threat, a scare tactic that he might lose even more control if he drank. But the bottle always remained unopened."

"I never saw Brent take a sip of liquor. I assumed that's why you didn't drink," Eric says.

"That's what I thought too," I murmur, sure I was the good daughter for following his example. I finally face Eric, needing to see his reaction when I tell him the truth. "The night of Marin's wedding"—I pause, gathering courage—"I was fifteen. Papa did drink the bottle he brought home," I whisper. "Mama was asleep, tired after the festivities. I was now the oldest child at home." I can feel the tears start to gather but I wipe them away, needing my strength to admit the truth. "I was sleeping in my bed . . ." I stop, exhale. "Sonya was asleep in her room."

"Trisha?" I can hear his pain, sure he is already imagining the worst.

"I didn't remember," I say, still unable to say the words. "I escaped to Sonya's room afterward and told her, but the next morning all of it was gone. Like it had never happened," I cry, wishing that was the truth.

"He raped you?" Eric's throat rips out the words.

"Yes," I whisper, seeing his shock and despair.

"Jesus." He rubs his hands over his face.

"But these images wouldn't let up. Just fragments of memory, never revealing the face. I was sure it was Sonya I was seeing. The night you came over to the house, the last time we saw one another." I run my hands down my skirt, feeling exposed. "I remembered most of it. I had a breakdown at my mother's house; the memories flooded me and Mama told me . . ."

"She knew?" I can hear the fury in his voice, the confusion.

"Papa admitted it to her before he fell into a coma." With the revelation out, I feel a burden lift off of my shoulders. "I never understood why I feared having a child. Now I do." He becomes still, staring at me. "I was sure that no matter how much I loved my child, like Papa loved me, I would end up hurting them. I just didn't know why I believed that." My head drops, so many things now clear. "Regardless, I couldn't do that, ever." I reach for my purse, ready to leave. I glance at him, sure it will be the last time I see him. "I never meant to lie to you. I never meant to hurt you. I'm so sorry I did."

"Trisha," he calls out, just as I reach the door. I turn, prepared to say good-bye. "Are you seeing someone for this? A therapist? Someone who can help you?"

I nod. "I'm planning to. I'll look for someone who deals specifically with childhood rape." I shrug. "All of it has been a bit overwhelming."

"I imagine that's an understatement," he says kindly.

"Yes." I try for a smile, finding it easier than I believed. "Thank you for listening to me." I laugh self-consciously. "Thank you for our life together. You meant everything . . ." I pause, holding back the sob that threatens. "I'll sign the papers, send them back immediately."

"Trisha," he repeats, this time closer than before. Standing right in front of me, he asks, "I wonder if I could attend a few sessions with you? To try and understand what you're going through?"

"Eric?" I am blown away, never expecting such an offer. "Why would you want to do that?"

"Because we were husband and wife, but I don't know if we were ever friends," he says simply. "Maybe now is the time."

As a child, I was fascinated by falling stars. I would watch for them in the night sky, sure that each one meant a child somewhere had his or her wish granted. I always made the same wish every time I saw one— that I would live happily ever after. It was how every story I read ended, making the whole book a prologue and the happily ever after the real story. I was sure my life would have a storybook ending, though yet unwritten. Growing up, those childhood dreams segued to reality and the realization that not every ending is fair or happy. That often people get hurt, and there's no real reason for it. No silver lining in the event. But I kept my hope alive, if only to hold on to that part of childhood where everything felt possible.

"Yes," I answer him.

I imagine another falling star, but this time I don't make a wish. Instead I smile, understanding that even though not every story ends with a happy ending or begins with tragedy, along the way there are moments of both. And those moments don't define you or even break you—they are simply parts of the whole.

I have a lifetime to try to understand what my father did to me and, in contrast, the love he surrounded me with. I may never find a reason or know why I chose to forget his actions. But what I do know, and what I will never forget, is that I still have me and the right to make my own choices. That is what I will hold on to, that and the people whom I love.

I vow to find myself, to learn who I am, never again to be the daughter my father needed or the wife I convinced myself I should be. For as long as the journey takes, I will walk alone, fearless, discovering the woman that I can be. I never meant to hurt Eric, never believed I was betraying him more than I was saving me. With his words, I know how fortunate I am. Maybe, if we are lucky, one day Eric and I will rediscover our love and find a path to healing; but I promise to never forget the past as I redefine my future.

SONYA

I am home alone. Trisha is back at her house and Mom is at the temple, praying. She told me not to wait up, that she would be late. She gave me no reason why and I did not ask for one, both of us most comfortable respecting the invisible boundaries we have erected. Needing something to do, I start a fire in the living room, warming my hands against the roaring flames.

The sound of the doorbell shatters the silence. I start, not expecting anyone. Mom's friends used to visit, only staying for a short while—to either drop off food or pay their respects for our father's condition. Now those visits have started to spread farther apart, with fewer people bothering to stop by. It's as if they have accepted what we refuse to—that life goes on.

"Who is it?" I ask, squinting my eye through the peephole. When I see David's face staring back, I unlock the door and open it fully. "What are you doing here?"

When I filled out the requisite application forms for the position, David noticed my home address and we talked about the neighborhood. He knew it well, had friends who had bought a house down the street to raise their children in.

"I wanted to speak with you if you have a minute." He looks wary, and his face seems drawn with concern.

I consider closing the door, stopping this before it begins. But I can't. Seeing him here, in the home that used to be my prison, helps me in a way I didn't know I needed. "Come in." I lead him into the den, where the fire is now roaring, sending sparks flying.

"Is your mother home?" he asks, glancing around.

"No," I admit, "she's out for the evening." I absorb his features, having missed what is not mine. "Are you here to talk about the other day? The decision to stop support for my father?"

"No," he says, uncharacteristically quiet. "That's your family's business, your decision."

"Then why?" I ask, worried. "Has something happened to him?" When he shakes his head no, refusing to break my gaze, I plead, "Then what?"

"After your family left your father's room the other day, your mom and I started talking," he says slowly, as if gauging each word. "She asked me how I felt about you."

"David," I say, feeling the familiar fear start to creep up my spine. "Please."

"Without me saying a word, she knew the answer. But I told her there was no chance for us. That you couldn't be with me."

"I can't," I whisper, wanting to more than anything I've wanted in my life. But fear is a terrible thing. It paralyzes you with the expectation of the worst happening, never allowing room for something better, something that gives rather than takes away.

"She said she knew why," he says, shocking me into silence. "She said it was because you never knew she loved you, that she wanted you. Needed you."

"No," I insist, the words thundering in my ear. Every cell in my body rejected the notion, refused it an audience. I knew the truth, deep in my heart, and nothing would convince me otherwise. "You have no idea what you are talking about."

"She said she knew she failed you," he continues, refusing me a reprieve. "That's why she let you go, to save you."

I collapse into the sofa, envying the logs as they disintegrate into ashes. It is a funny thing when you have believed the worst about yourself your entire life. No matter what anyone says, you are the strongest voice of opposition, insisting to anyone who will listen that they are wrong, that you really are worthless.

"But she was tired of missing you, needing you." He takes out a piece of paper and hands it to me.

I read through it, trying to understand. It's a blood test, with one blood count. The name on the top is my father's. I look up at David, "What is tetrahydrozoline?"

"Your mother's gift to you," he answers. "The test proved what your mother told me. She slowly poisoned him with tetrahydrozoline, the main ingredient in Visine." He starts to recite facts, his stance that of a professional. "Over time it can cause difficulty breathing, nausea, headaches. For those with weakened immune systems, such as from diabetes—a coma."

My stomach seizes and I drop the sheet, watching as it flutters to the floor. It finds its place at my feet, like a dog resting by its owner, prepared to do its bidding. "She tried to kill him?" I whisper, the answer already spoken. "Why?"

There were so many reasons to want him dead. Each of us had our own, even Trisha. But not one of us dared to take the necessary step to end his life, ever imagined doing so. Of all of us, Mom was the one who had the most to lose. She remembered him when he was kind, when he knew how to love. Those memories would have served as a buffer between her and any desire to seek freedom.

"To bring you home," David says. "Because she loves you."

It is too much, a dam waiting a lifetime to burst. I start to shake, unable to accept the lengths to which my mother went. I stare numbly at the ground, the colors of the rug starting to mix together, swirling like a whirlpool. "Who else knows?" I demand, fearing for her future.

"No one," David says, causing me to jerk my head up and stare at him. "I ran the test privately and deleted the results from the computer."

"Why?" I demand. Finding my footing, I come to stand before him.

"I took a vow to save human lives, no matter who it is." He holds me without touching me, his words refusing to give me any room. "But if your father wasn't lying in a coma already, knowing what he did to you, how he hurt you, I can't promise I wouldn't want to put him there myself." He cups my cheek in his palm, his warmth seeping into every part of my body and soul. "Those results are yours to do with whatever you want. I can't begin to claim I understand what you went through as a child."

I visited a village where every crime was punished under the rule of an eye for an eye, the sentence handed down accordingly. If you stole something, the hand with which you stole could be cut off. An act of adultery could lead to a public stoning or being forcibly assaulted by other members of the village. A death could only be made right by the death of the assailant. A draconian ruling system that left no room for excuse or explanation, sentences handed down without the benefit of a jury to weigh fault or circumstance.

But I cannot stand as judge and jury against my own mother. I will not allow her to face the consequences of the only act left available to her. No matter her reason, I had the benefit of escape when she was forced to stay behind. I have never viewed it from that perspective before, never seen past my pain to envision hers. Now, knowing her act of desperation, I am ashamed to know I never bothered.

I slowly pick up the results, the bracelets my mother gave me slipping down my arm. I scan the page one last time before making my way toward the fireplace. Without David's permission, I release the sheet into the fire, watching the edge of the paper catch the flame before being engulfed. In seconds there is nothing but ashes. Turning toward David, I expect to see disappointment, sure a man whose life has been lived under the ray of perfection cannot understand the complexities of our heartbreak. But he only nods, accepting my decision without judgment, with an understanding I have not earned.

"You didn't try to stop me," I say, amazed.

"You thought I would?" he asks, shaking his head in bewilderment. "That's not how love works."

I am silenced by his declaration, by his trust. But never having allowed myself the luxury of the emotion, I am unaware how to respond. I look away, searching, though I know deep within me the answer is standing right in front of me.

"When my ex-wife asked me for a divorce," he begins, watching me, "she said it was because her illusion of me had been shattered. I wasn't perfect like she thought, the ending wasn't what she imagined." Stuffing his hands into his pockets, he stares at the fire that is slowly dying. "So I made myself a promise. Next time I fall in love, I will make sure to get all the bad stuff out of the way first. From both sides, that way there's no surprises."

"There are always surprises," I say, thinking of my sisters' lives, the struggles they are facing. "Nothing is ever guaranteed."

"Maybe," he agrees. "But the core of the person, what makes them who they are, that never changes."

"Then how can you love me?" I ask, the question slipping out before I can censor it. I want to take it back as soon as the words are out, ashamed for revealing too much.

"How could I not?" he asks, turning toward me. "You believe you're damaged." He nods, accepting what is. "And because of that you've decided you're not allowed happiness, or love. I have to respect your decision." He pauses, his yearning palpable. Leaning down, he kisses me softly on the cheek. "But just for the record? You're the most amazing woman I know. It's not in spite of your childhood, it's because of it." Holding my gaze, he says quietly, "Not everyone can survive what you did and come out the other side with your strength. I love you for who you are, the good and the bad."

Releasing me, he starts to walk away, the first time he is the one leaving. I watch him, convinced it is the right thing. But for the first time it does not feel acceptable. I don't want him to go. I want to stop the hurt, to heal the wounds that have been ripped open for as long as I can remember.

One day I will ask my mom about why she did it. How could she have taken such a risk to free me only to chance being imprisoned herself? But I don't know when that time will come—when I will be able to accept what she has offered me. Even after a wound heals, the skin has to rebuild, and even then the scar will always remain.

But until I can hold on to her love as my right, I will offer her what I can—my gratitude and my hope that one day, we will clasp our hands together and the only thing between us will be the knowledge that today is not defined by yesterday and tomorrow is truly another day.

Energy doesn't stand still; it moves, shifts with time. I think maybe we are meant to do the same, to see the world not as we fear it is but as we hope for it to be—kinder, gentler, each lesson not meant to destroy but to enable. To learn that we are not stagnant, but rather move with those around us, each one of us melting into the other, becoming one though our bodies separate us. Our hurts and our joys are meant to be shared, the burden easier when another holds your hand.

"David," I call out. Making my way toward him, I reach out, wanting to touch, to hold. "If we were going to . . ." I pause, unsure of the words to describe what we are about to embark on. "To be together, what would be your faults that I should know about?"

His smile fills the room, offers hope when I was sure there was none. "I snore. Really loud. Like a truck rumbling through the room," he says, holding up his hand to count them down. "Horrible at directions. Can't tell left from right or north from south. Which is why I was kicked out of the surgical program, by the way," he admits. "They were scared I would do more damage to the patient than help. Worst part—I won't ask for help." He holds up another finger, "Third? I'll burn down a kitchen if I dare to step in one. It's a real problem. The fire department has my address on "Frequently Visited" in their GPS." He starts on the fourth when I grab his hand.

"OK," I say, laughing.

He wraps his hand around mine as we stand there, our fingers clasped together as if in prayer.

"OK."

And somehow, for the first time, I know it will be.

EPILOGUE

RANEE

They arrive in India when it is still daylight. Ranee looks around at her native country, understanding what she never could before—that home is not a place or a lifestyle, but the state of your heart and all the people who take their place in it. Brent said that their arrival in America made him what he was, but it was just an excuse. The evil was always lurking, latent, and he allowed it to become his default. He used whatever rationalization he needed to absolve himself—but like a true tyrant, it mattered little to him whom he hurt or how. But now he can never hurt them again. She knows they are not completely free and may never be, but they stand together, each one of them trying to fill the emptiness in the others, offering one another support, knowing they will never stand alone again.

Taking the three-wheeled rickshaw to the Ganges, Ranee balances the urn with Brent's ashes in her lap. Gia and Marin sit in the back, while Ranee sits next to Sonya and Trisha on the front bench seat, each daughter wearing her bracelets. They are silent as the motorized vehicle zips them through the villages and toward the town. Ranee watches the scenery go by, remembering all the years past. So many dreams lost, years already lived. But life isn't over—nor is it just beginning. It is a continuation, all the memories coming together to create a life.

On arrival, they make their way slowly toward the flowing water. Hundreds of devotees bathe themselves in the river, steadfast in their belief that it is holy water spewed from the head of Lord Shiva. The women stand shoulder to shoulder on the shore, Gia and Ranee in the middle. Ranee silently offers her granddaughter the urn, watching as she opens the top. They kneel down as Gia slowly tips it, allowing all the ashes to fly free, float into the water, and disappear from sight. When there is nothing left, she drops the urn at their feet and they clasp hands. Each of them watches silently as nothing remains but the clear water sworn to wash away the sins of all who touch it.

Ranee turns toward each one of her daughters and her granddaughter. They stare back at her, quiet, as a bell from the nearby temple tolls loudly and clearly, signaling to anyone listening that they are being watched over, protected. With a silent nod, she leads them away from the water and back toward the rickshaw to take them home, where they belong, together.

ACKNOWLEDGMENTS

Kiran, Sienna, and Akash, a thousand times I would walk the steps of my past knowing they led to you. You are the light I dreamt of, the joy I prayed for. Every day I am awed by you and forever grateful for you. I love you. Hema, my best friend, when I reached for the stars, you held me up. Thank you for your strength, honesty, grace, and love. Keith, your love is my foundation and your support my strength. Thank you for believing in me and for always being there. Hina, thank you for being there when I've needed you. Your strength is an inspiration and your sense of purpose an example. Mom, thank you for being strong enough for all of us and for showing us the real meaning of love. Prashant, we were friends but fate made us family. Thanks for being a great brother. Meghan and Serena, you are the miracles who have made our family complete. I love you as if you were mine. G. M., Jasumama, Rekhamami, and L. B., thank you for your unconditional love and support. I miss you. Sarahlou, you are the voice of assurance in the darkest of times. Thanks for your guidance and friendship, but I will still never vacation with you (LOL). Ms. Johnson and Donna, you opened your hearts and lives to me. Thank you for being the example that set the standard.

Benee, you encouraged me, pushed me, and believed in me. You are the greatest mentor any writer could wish for. Your friendship, generosity, and kindness are gifts I can never repay. Victoria, thank you for believing in my work. Your support and enthusiasm for this book meant so much to me. Danielle, I'm so excited to be working with you and your team. The adventure is just beginning, and I very much look forward to it.

To all the victims of abuse, believe in yourselves, keep dreaming, and always reach for the stars.

ABOUT THE AUTHOR

Photo © 2014 Hema B. Ravani

Sejal Badani is a former attorney. She currently lives on the West Coast with her family and their two dogs.